THE
PLANETSIDER

G J OGDEN

ACKNOWLEDGMENTS

Thanks to Sarah for patiently editing and proof-reading this book and helping to make it the best it could be.

And thanks to you for reading it.

CHAPTER 1

Maria Salus tightened her hold on the control yoke as another bolt of energy hammered the hull of the ship. Her fingers were white from the pressure of gripping the stick and her muscles burned from the effort of holding the vessel's course. But the planet's atmosphere was looming large in the window now and she knew that a change in their entry angle could kill them.

From behind her, Chris Kurren reached out and grabbed the co-pilot's chair to steady himself against the impact. He scanned the controls and watched as warning lights flashed on and off, beaming spots of red light onto his angular, rough-shaven face. Text in red, yellow and green flicked across the panels and Kurren studied it, finding the information he needed. "Thirty seconds!" he shouted, adjusting the controls of the console in front of him. "The heat shields are holding, but the aft armour plating is buckling; if we sustain another direct hit we're finished!"

Another red light came on in Maria's main console, bathing

her face in a red glow. She checked the scanner display on the dashboard and analysed the readings from the two fighters in pursuit. A warning light flashed on and off rapidly, accompanied by a shrill alarm. "Hold on!" she shouted.

Kurren barely had time to react before she jerked the control yoke sharply left then right. The ship's thrusters responded, forcing the ship to zig-zag violently. Thin strips of energy flashed past the cockpit glass, causing Maria to involuntarily duck, before she centred the controls again and cut back towards the planet's atmosphere. The manoeuvre was completed with masterful precision, ensuring the ship remained perfectly on course towards the planet's surface.

"Nice move, Sal. A little more warning next time, though?" Kurren said sternly. Maria didn't look back to check, but she knew he was smiling.

"I thought you liked surprises," she replied, also smiling. Another alarm sounded, focusing both of them once again on the matter at hand.

Kurren sat in the co-pilot's chair, read his console and then adjusted several more controls. Energy hummed through conduits all around them, adjusting the power distribution to compensate for the damage they had sustained. The multi-coloured text continued to flood onto Kurren's screen as the ship continued on towards the blue planet. "Twenty seconds!" he shouted to Maria, "Prepare to enter the atmosphere!" The ship was rocked again by another blast from the pursuing fighters. A console exploded behind Kurren, spitting fire over his flight suit, followed by another to his left, which showered the side of his face with white hot splinters of debris, like needles. Kurren screamed and pressed his hand to his cheek.

"Kurren, are you okay?" Maria shouted, but her voice was drowned out by another explosion that rammed into the starboard side of the small craft. Kurren, already disorientated from the previous blast, lost his balance and fell backwards, landing heavily on the cold metal plating of the ship's floor. Maria called out again. No answer. More lights flickered on the dashboard – all red – and Maria quickly scanned them, trying to force back her panic and remain composed. The fire from the control panel was spreading now, feeding on the oxygen in the cabin. With Kurren's comfortingly soft voice gone, Maria was suddenly very afraid. It was a different fear to any she had felt previously, worse even than the stomach-churning anxiety she experienced after accepting the mission and learning of the dangers involved. At least then Kurren had been there to share her anxiety; now she was alone, and this realisation was terrifying.

Another alarm sounded and Maria responded instinctively, punching three buttons and sending the ship forward into the atmosphere. All around her she saw fire, but still she felt cold.

Ten seconds until atmospheric entry would be completed.

Another volley of energy struck the ship, slamming into the forward section next to her command chair. The yoke flew out of her hands and slammed into her thigh, crushing muscle to bone. She screamed in pain, but though she felt the cry rush from her lungs, she heard nothing over the ferocious noise engulfing the cabin as it pierced the atmosphere. The ship penetrated further into the fire and more alarms sounded, continuing to drown out her screams. She grabbed the control yoke again, pushing it away with all her strength, forcing the ship to resume its course. She pressed her hand to her leg as the pain moved up her thigh and into her stomach, making her vomit. Tears streamed down her face, but she held the yoke tightly. More spears of light flashed past the cockpit glass, this time further away.

"You'll have to do better than that!" shouted Maria, as the shards of energy missed the ship.

The fire inside was spreading too, over the legs of Kurren as he lay unconscious on the floor. Blood oozed from the fracture in his skull and pooled on the plating under his head.

Five seconds and they would be through.

The pain had subsided and the lights and sounds in the ship were beginning to sound dull and distant. Maria could feel her grip loosening as she reached out to the square panel in front of the yoke and punched the last button in the sequence. A buzzing sound filled the cabin but Maria did not hear it. The control yoke fell through her limp fingers and she slumped forward on the chair's safety harness, barely conscious. Moments later the shuddering stopped and the cabin was flooded with a brilliant clean light, more intense than had been seen by her or her people for generations. But Maria was aware only of the darkness behind her eyes, and then nothing.

CHAPTER 2

Ethan watched as another bright light smeared a fiery streak across the night sky. He was lying on his back, under his favourite tree, on a hilltop next to the walled settlement that was his home, and home to around two hundred others. Strictly speaking, he was not supposed to be outside the settlement's walls after dark, but there hadn't been a Roamer attack for weeks, and Ethan would be on the front line if there was one anyway. The governors knew this too, which was why no one reprimanded him about his frequent excursions outside.

There had been an unusually large number of lights that night, Ethan thought. Their strange, eerie quality had fascinated him since he was a child of perhaps no more than five or six years old. But now they were much more than a mere curiosity to him. As a boy he had been taught about the many theories concerning the lights – what they might be, how they are formed and so on – none of which had any basis in fact, of course. Most were old wives' tales and elaborate fantasies created by philosophers from the twenty-seven known settlements that had discovered each other, generally by accident, long after The Fall.

The first scholar philosopher that Ethan had known, a blusterous and completely bald man named Mr Boucher (who was more a spiritual leader, Ethan had discovered as he got older), liked to talk about how the lights were really angels that watched over everyone, and guided the people to a better future. For many years Ethan had believed this; he even used to spend hours watching and talking to the 'angels' in the sky. But when a large band of Roamers came to attack the settlement, resulting in the death of his mother and father, there were no angels to protect them. They didn't hear his cries for help, or come to his aid. They left Ethan and his sister, Katie, to be burned alive in their house. They did not save his mother and father, who lay unconscious on the burning floor, while Ethan and Katie were pulled, barely alive, from the furnace. And they did nothing while he sat on the cold, wet earth outside, hearing their screams as the flames took them from him.

It wasn't just his parents that had been abandoned; Ethan saw that the angels had failed to watch over a great many more people in the settlement that night. Despite this, when the flames had been extinguished, the houses rebuilt, and the walls fortified again, the scholars still continued to talk of angels, and the children still believed it, including Katie. But Ethan did not; for him, a light streaking across the sky was no longer an angel, but a question seeking an answer. And Ethan had so many questions as he grew older, not only about the lights, but also about the world around him – the creeping insanity of the Roamers, the horror of The Maddening, the reason for the devastation of the cities, the ruins which littered the landscape in all directions, and the terrifying, fragile scarcity of living people; the scarcity of life itself. What had happened to leave the planet in this state?

A gust of cold wind swept over the hill and Ethan pulled his coat tighter around his chest as it whistled passed him and rustled the branches of the naked old tree standing over him. In the distance, he could hear the faint ringing of wind chimes that hung outside his sister's house inside the settlement walls, and it made him think of her, and her son. He sat up and shivered.

"I don't suppose you could turn the temperature up a bit could you?" he said, looking skyward.

A sliver of light appeared low on the horizon, then vanished. "Thanks a bunch," he commented wistfully. He thought about Erik's famous apple wine and wished he'd brought a flask to drink and warm his insides. Erik was the man who had pulled him and his sister from their burning house, and had become a sort of uncle to them over the years. But since he didn't have a flask he decided it was probably a good time to head back to the settlement, where he had a plentiful supply of wine, as well as a comfortable bed.

He was about to push himself up from the floor when he heard a sound from behind him like a twig snapping, coming from down the hill. Ethan froze motionless and listened. The wind carried the sounds of rustling leaves and branches but there was something else moving. No wild animal had been seen near the settlement for months, and if any had escaped from the farms he would have been called upon by the governors to 'rescue' it long ago. He reached down inside his dense woollen coat and removed a long knife from its scabbard. The sound was getting closer and Ethan recognised it as footsteps, slow and careful. Someone was sneaking up on him. *A Roamer* he thought, and tightened his grip on the knife's cold bone handle.

Slowly, he backed himself up against the tree and got into a sitting position, still holding the knife inside his coat so that it didn't reflect any light from the moon and alert whoever was approaching. He waited as the footsteps got closer. They were now on the top of the hill close to the oak, still creeping carefully. Then the footsteps stopped. Ethan listened. The wind gusted again and rustled the branches of the tree, but through the noise Ethan heard the man approach. He pulled the knife out of his coat, span around the tree and knocked the man to the ground. The figure fell in a heap and Ethan pounced on top of him, knife poised to strike.

"Argh! Argh! Argh Argh! Get off me! Argh, Argh! Filthy Roamer! Argh! Help! Argh!"

Ethan breathed a deep sigh of relief, quickly returned the knife to its scabbard inside his coat and clamped his hand over his young nephew's mouth. "Be quiet, you little saphead, I almost gutted you!" he said, perched over him.

Elijah, still trying desperately to scream and shout despite being very effectively muffled by Ethan's hand, looked up at him and suddenly relaxed. Ethan took his hand off Elijah's mouth, examined the slimy mess that his frantic bawling had left behind, and then casually wiped it on the front of Elijah's tunic.

"Ewww, that's disgusting!" Elijah complained.

"It came out of your mouth!" Ethan pointed out, smirking at him. "Now, do you mind telling me what you are doing creeping up on me like that? No, wait. Let's start with why you're outside the settlement walls, you know it's forbidden."

"You're outside, though..." Elijah said, meekly.

Ethan raised an eyebrow. Elijah was as sharp as the knife he had concealed inside his coat. And he shared Ethan's curious nature, something his mother blamed entirely on his adventurous and exciting uncle. "Never mind that," said Ethan. "I'm not the one who almost got impaled. If your mother knew you were outside the walls, especially with me, that would probably change!" Ethan paused to check Elijah's expression. He looked back sheepishly. "I'm assuming she doesn't know you're gone?"

"Of course not," said Elijah, defiantly. "I'm not that stupid, Ethan."

"Well, at least that's something," said Ethan. "So how did you get out, anyway? The Rangers should have stopped you long before you even got near the outer wall. I certainly wouldn't have let a shifty character like you skulk about."

Elijah smiled "I got out the same way you did. I watched you to see where you went."

Ethan laughed. "You're more cunning than you look," he said. "You must get that from me!" Then he took a more serious tone, because being outside at night was a genuinely serious matter. "Still, that doesn't explain why you've risked a grizzly death at the hands of the Roamers, or me for that matter, by venturing outside at night."

"I came to see you," Elijah replied, as if it were obvious, which Ethan supposed it was, after he thought about it. "You're always telling me about how you like to watch the lights at night, and how one day you'd show me the best spot to see them. I'm guessing this is it, right?"

Ethan frowned, got up, and pulled Elijah to his feet. "I suppose I did say that," he replied, annoyed that Elijah seemed to be getting the better of him. "But I wasn't planning on doing it until you were a bit older, certainly older than ten, anyway. It's not safe out here, like I keep telling you."

"I know, Ethan. I'm sorry," said Elijah. "But Mr Boucher told us stories about the lights today and, well, it just made me think of you. So I followed you." Elijah looked around the hill and at the huge tree above them. "This is the place, right?" he asked again.

"Yes, this is the place," Ethan replied. He looked around, contemplating the surroundings. "My father used to bring me here, when I was younger than you. From here you can see the light curve around the sky. See, where that peak and the river line up?" Ethan pointed far into the distance at a mountain peak with a river flowing in jagged lines towards them.

Elijah followed Ethan's hand movements, and then scanned the sky above in the arc he had indicated. Straight away he saw several flashes, some bright and directly overhead, and some dimmer and further away above the mountain peak. "What are they?" he asked.

"No idea..." Ethan replied, wistfully. He glanced back down at Elijah, who was still staring skyward, and placed a hand on his shoulder. "Did you know Mr Boucher used to tell me the same stories? He must be about a hundred now." Elijah didn't respond. "I suppose he told you that the lights are really angels that watch over us, didn't he?" said Ethan.

Elijah's face lit up suddenly, and he looked at Ethan. "Yes, he did! He told us how the angels watch over the twenty-seven settlements to make sure everyone is okay, and to make sure that the Maddening stays away. We're lucky that they watch over us, aren't we?" he asked, his face beaming.

Ethan felt angry and turned away, trying to hide his bleak expression from Elijah.

"Isn't that what he taught you at school?" asked a concerned-sounding Elijah.

"Yes. Yes it is," replied Ethan, half-heartedly, still facing away. He sat down next to the old oak and gestured for Elijah to sit down too, which he did, looking slightly puzzled. Ethan fiddled with the buttons on his coat and was silent for a while. Elijah sat patiently, looking at him, waiting for Ethan to impart some great wisdom. The wind, seemingly bored of toying with the branches of the tree, was now playing with Elijah's untidy brown hair; wafting it in loose tufts across his young face, a face so full of wonder and youth and adventure. Ethan had looked that way once, he supposed. Suddenly he was afraid of robbing his nephew of that innocence. Elijah didn't need that burden, not yet. He turned away again.

"What is it Ethan?" Elijah asked, breaking the silence.

"Nothing," said Ethan, gently. "I was just thinking how much you look like your grandfather, that's all," he lied. Strangely, now that he'd said it, Ethan realised that Elijah did actually look a bit like his father, and he wondered why he hadn't noticed before. Ethan had only vague and often fleeting memories of his father and mother now. They had died when he was only nine years old; a year younger than Elijah was now.

He thought back to his childhood and remembered how the story of the angels had comforted him. He longed to feel that security again; to feel that the world made sense, despite its apparent hopelessness. But in all the years since his parents had been killed, Ethan had felt no comfort, just anger, loneliness, and even despair. In his early teens, he'd even considered suicide. It wasn't uncommon. It didn't help that he had few friends. Outside of his family – Katie and Elijah – there was only really Summer that he truly considered a friend and really cared for. Others found him closed off and self-centred. He didn't really enjoy socialising, and preferred being either alone or with his family. To most people, he was as cold as the barren landscape around them. If it weren't for his sister, and certainly for her son, he would have left the settlement long ago, to go who knows where? In many ways, he resented the fact that they tied him down to the settlement. Often, when he was sitting on this hill outside the walls, he would consider just leaving, and heading to the city, or some other ruin, and hunting for clues about the past; something to put his life into perspective and make sense of it all. But he could never quite bring himself to do it. He had made it about a mile one night, but turned back. Elijah wasn't like him. He was gregarious and open, and almost too trusting. Ethan had no right to rob Elijah of his blissful ignorance, no matter what his own personal feelings were.

"Mum says that all the time," Elijah chirped in.

"What?" said Ethan, surprised.

"That I look like Granddad," Elijah said.

"Oh, yes," Ethan remembered. "It's not a good thing really, you know – he was a hideously ugly man."

Elijah chuckled and huddled up closer to Ethan as another flash of light streaked overhead. Both of them watched it in silence. "Where do they come from?" Elijah asked, after the light had burned away into nothing.

"Nobody knows," said Ethan. "I think that's part of the fascination with them; that they can't be explained."

This puzzled Elijah, and Ethan decided against trying to explain any further. Besides, he didn't really know exactly what he meant himself, so there was no way he could explain it to anyone else, especially not a wonderstruck ten-year-old.

"I can tell you where the name came from, if you'd like?" Ethan said, trying to answer the question in some small measure at least. Elijah nodded and looked at him, expectantly.

Ethan thought for a moment, trying to remember the story as it had been told to him, years ago. "It's a word that was used by the Firsts. Do you know anything about them?" he asked.

"A little," said Elijah. "Weren't they the ones that started the first settlements? After The Fall, I mean?"

Ethan was slightly surprised that Elijah had heard of The Fall; they were apparently more liberal with the information they gave to youngsters these days. Ethan was several years older than Elijah before he heard the story of The Fall – the name given to the event that destroyed the towns and cities that now lay in ruin, and turned most of the landscape into the barren and near-lifeless wasteland it was today. No-one knew how many died, as there were no records. Whatever civilisation preceded the rag-tag collection of settlements that existed now did not record their history, or anything else, on a physical material. At least not that anyone had found, and truthfully, few had any desire to look. But certainly the sheer size and complexity of the huge cities that now lay wasted across the land suggested that a huge number must have perished. Most of what was known today had been passed down from the survivors of that event – The Firsts. It was a period of great turmoil though, and little of their knowledge was recorded either, simply because of panic or because there was nothing to record it with. As a result, practically nothing was known of the people that came before.

This was not helped by the fact that most of these early survivors died soon after The Fall. That was not in itself surprising, but what was unique about the deaths was the age of those dying. Almost everyone over the age of around seventeen or eighteen died over a period of several years, though some lasted for longer. Some died from injuries or illness, and many from suicide, but the majority succumbed to a previously unknown sickness, which later was to become known as The Maddening.

Ah, 'The Maddening'. What a quaint name for a thing so insidious and terrible. As if the near total annihilation of the planet wasn't enough, then came along a disease that threatened to kill off those lucky enough – or unlucky, depending on how you viewed it – to survive.

The Maddening only affected adults, mostly leaving those under the age of around eighteen untouched. There was no obvious transmission method or carrier, and this was part of its terror – not knowing how to avoid it. If you were of a certain age, death was a looming certainty.

The first cases of The Maddening began around a year after The Fall, or so the stories told, but it took many more years for people to really understand its nature. This was because, at least at first, those affected seemed largely normal. But then, like the creep of rot through wood, the disease would start to chip away at a person's soul. The first sign was a steady erosion of basic human empathy, followed by emotions, such as love, compassion, happiness and anger. Those in this stage of The Maddening would simply take what they wanted, and only communicate or co-operate if it was in their interest. They also stopped caring about the pain and suffering of others, and used often brutal violence as a cold, blunt instrument to get what they wanted.

Understandably, such people were soon banished from whatever settlement or travelling group they were part of, and so they set out alone, aimlessly wandering, scavenging for what they could find to survive. And remarkably they could survive on very little, eating and drinking things that would make normal people sick. Although their emotions were gone, their intelligence and ability to function remained, and so sometimes they would cluster together into groups to attack and raid caravans or even settlements, killing indiscriminately. But there was no camaraderie, no celebration of 'victory' and certainly no helping their fallen companions. If there was no mutual gain, there was no co-operation. If successful, they would simply fight amongst themselves for the spoils, then they would disband again, heading off alone into the wilderness, or into the cities. Constantly moving. That is how they got their name – 'Roamers'.

At first, people just thought they had gone mad, that the pressures of living were too much, and that their brains had simply 'switched off' or reverted to a more primitive state, so they didn't have to feel or care anymore. But this wasn't the case. If it had been, somehow it would have been more bearable; something that people could at least relate to and understand, but this was simply the first stage of The Maddening. It could take years, or sometimes only weeks, but the result was always the same. They would start to physically change; sunken, dark eyes and a face that looked somehow longer, with sucked in cheeks and an elongated jaw. Their hair would thin out and turn a dirty grey to match their mottled, oily grey skin. But it was the eyes that were most horrifying; dark, feral eyes with nothing behind them, as if the person's soul had been consumed, and all that was left was a dark bile, filling up their insides. Ethan had known someone who had witnessed such a creature chewing the putrid remains of some long dead animal. The creature had glared up at the onlooker with its dead, black eyes and just kept chewing. The man had vomited and then ran, and has never set foot outside the settlement since.

Other stories had told of the maddened creatures sheltering in the same place for days, maybe even weeks, barely moving. And like a spider waiting in its lair, they would spring upon people without warning should they stray, unwittingly, too close. Ethan knew of five Rangers in the last two years who had been killed in this way, straying too far into the cities, looking for tools to bring back to the settlement. It was why the cities were off limits.

Another reason that the cities were off limits was because it had been observed that The Maddening progressed more quickly in or near to the built up areas, or other areas of particularly heavy destruction. This was why the few adolescent clusters of civilisation that had succeeded in becoming established settlements were all high up in the mountains, or in remote areas, distant from, and always more elevated than the ruined metropolises.

Ethan cut off his daydreaming when he noticed Elijah still looking at him, now with a rather more impatient look of expectation. It took him a moment to reset his train of thought to Elijah's original question.

"That's right," he continued, consciously trying to sound more upbeat, "the Firsts were survivors of the civilisation that existed before The Fall, and so pretty much all we know of that period comes from them." Elijah continued to look at him, wanting more. "Sadly, it's not very much, though," Ethan continued, seeing that Elijah was not yet satisfied. "Most of them died shortly after The Fall, so all we really have are the stories and memories of the younger survivors, which have been passed on from one generation to the next."

Ethan decided not to elaborate further. The Maddening was not a subject he wanted to get in to, and so before Elijah could manage to ask the inevitable 'why?' question, Ethan pressed on.

"Incredible to think of it, really," he lamented. "Imagine being in your teenage years and suddenly your childhood just ends. Just like that. One moment, you're a kid, having fun, and the next you're a leader, literally with the survival of the species resting on your shoulders. It's astonishing we made it at all."

"And these survivors, they taught us about the angels?" Elijah asked, focusing back in on the subject he was most interested in, and encouraged by Ethan's apparent candour.

"Yes, or so the story goes," Ethan continued, hazily, his mind wandering. "The full name is actually 'guardian angel', which is why some call them Guardians instead. You may have heard some people use that name?" Elijah nodded, enthusiastically. "The story goes that each survivor of The Fall had his or her own guardian angel," Ethan continued, "and that this angel, or guardian, is the reason they survived and didn't succumb to The Maddening," Ethan pointed up into the night sky. "The angels watched over them and protected them," he said, tracing a line from star to star with the tip of his finger. "It's what made them special, what led them to survive. A reward for their 'faith', apparently, although faith in what, no-one really knows."

Elijah was completely enthralled, and Ethan began to worry that he might be saying too much.

"Go on…" Elijah prodded. Ethan sighed; there was no point stopping now.

"Anyway," said Ethan, "these stories got told down the generations, by people like Bald Boucher…" Elijah giggled, and Ethan realised his slip. "Don't tell your mum you heard that name from me!" he gasped, waving a finger at him. Elijah giggled again and nodded. Ethan smiled and went on, "Anyway, it was the responsibility of these scholar philosophers to tell the stories to a new generation…"

Elijah looked excited, and cut in. "…and so when our ancestors looked up into the sky and saw these flashes of light, they decided to call them angels?" he said. "The same angels that had watched over the Firsts, and now watch over us?"

"Yes," said Ethan. "You catch on quick. Too quick," he sighed. Elijah smiled. "It makes us special, Elijah, do you see? Which is why you…" he poked Elijah mischievously on the chest as he said this, "…have been learning about them too. So you can understand how important you are; how important we all are. There are not many of us left."

Elijah lay back again, looking up at the stars. "I understand, Uncle," he said, contentedly.

"It's actually one of the very few things we know about the Firsts," said Ethan. "It's one of the few things that still connects us to them."

Elijah smiled the sort of broad, gleaming smile that Ethan

usually only saw on the morning of his birthday, or on a 'biscuit' day, which was when Elijah's mother allowed him first pick of her speciality amber biscuits from the bakery she ran in the settlement. And then, suddenly, the smile fell away and was replaced with a frown. "But why, if the angels watched over the Firsts making sure they survived The Fall, did so many of them then die?" he wondered.

Ethan smiled at him. *Razor sharp, this kid, just like his mother*, he thought. But still blessed with the naivety and gullibility of childhood. Ethan was corrupted by the harsh reality of fact and reason. At some point this would corrupt Elijah too, but now was not the time, as he had decided earlier. So he resigned himself to telling a lie; a white lie perhaps, but still a lie. He told the story that the bald old goat, Boucher, would later regurgitate as fact. "They stopped believing in them," he said, trying to sound genuine, "and so the angels stopped protecting them and went away."

"And that's when people started to disappear or turn into Roamers?" Elijah asked, looking slightly concerned. Ethan nodded. "But if I believe, they'll stay and protect me?" Elijah continued.

Ethan was finding it more difficult than he had expected to repeat a lie designed to give hope in the face of hopelessness. He suddenly felt sick, but he forced a smile and nodded.

Elijah's face lit up, joyful. "Wow, so I've got my very own guardian watching over me?"

"Yes..." Ethan said, still forcing the smile, still sick to the stomach. They both lay there for a time, just looking up, Elijah looking contented, and Ethan guiltily glum.

"Thanks for telling me, Uncle," said Elijah, breaking the silence. "And thanks for not telling mum that I sneaked out too!"

"Hey, who said I wasn't going to tell your mum?" Ethan

joked. "Besides, I won't need to unless you get your backside back inside quickly, before she, or grumpy old Administrator Talia, realise you've gone."

"Aww, do I have to?" Elijah complained. "I really like it up here. It doesn't smell bad, like it does in the settlement."

"It smells a lot worse since you arrived," Ethan joked. "Now get back, before I find a group of Roamers and auction you off as a slave boy. Or worse... dinner."

"Okay, okay, if I have to!" Elijah laughed. He knew Ethan was joking about the Roamers, but even the mere thought of being captured by a Roamer suddenly made Elijah feel extremely anxious about being outside the settlement walls. "Are you coming too?" he asked, looking around nervously.

"No, not just yet," said Ethan. "But I'll watch you from up here to make sure you get inside. So don't go making any detours."

"I won't, I promise," said Elijah. And then he sat up, leaned over and kissed Ethan on the temple. "Thanks, Uncle," he said, and with that he scuttled off back down the hill.

Ethan watched as he reached the wall of the settlement and sneaked though the small gap behind the sprawling fruit bush, with its heart-shaped leaves and sweet, fragrant blossoms that had just begun to burst forth in the past few days. He was slightly worried about leaving the gap open, but the bush concealed it well enough, and he was sure it would be fine until he got back and replaced the stones he had removed earlier to get out.

Ethan rested against the tree and gazed out over the land surrounding the settlement. Elijah had been too consumed with looking at the flashes in the sky to notice what the world outside the walls really looked like; barren and desolate for the most part, save for a few pockets of life. Their settlement, high on a hill with a dense woodland, sprawling out behind, was one such pocket. It was called Forest Gate because of its proximity to this woodland area, although calling it a forest was perhaps a little generous. The woodland was the reason for the settlement's existence in the first place. Not particularly for its wood, although that was used of course, but for its other resources, such as nuts and mushrooms and natural oils, which were harvested by the settlers and traded with other settlements. Forest Gate's nearest neighbour was a farming settlement about two days travel to the east. It was slightly larger, containing 403 settlers, at the last count (counts were done monthly), not including the animals, which were precious beyond belief. Ethan laughed at the thought of taking Elijah to see it someday, or more specifically, to smell it. Perhaps then he wouldn't complain so much about the smell inside Forest Gate, which was positively fragrant in comparison.

The settlements traded with each other, but mostly there was no competition, no commerce in a traditional sense. There were so few left that the discovery of any new pocket of population was treated as an event worthy of great celebration. Everyone shared what they had, for the greater good of all, simply because if they didn't, they risked dying out completely.

Outside these settlements there was very little alive, besides the Roamers. Roamers that had yet to fully succumb to The Maddening congregated near the ancient derelict cities. There were still some structures intact, many of which were considerably more hospitable than the average settlement hut, but no sane person would dare live there. This was partly because people were afraid of what the cities represented – a relic of a past that clearly didn't end well – but it was primarily because of The Maddening, and the belief that being near them would bring on or accelerate the disease.

It was The Maddening that scared Ethan more than

anything. More than loneliness and far more than Roamers. True, it was becoming increasingly rare, certainly among the young, but the prospect still terrified him. This was because, unlike most people, Ethan had seen first-hand someone in the end-stage of The Maddening. It had been during a simple escort task, taking supplies to a nearby settlement to trade. They had encountered one of the creatures at the mouth of an old tunnel exit, presumably linked to the city. It watched them with hollow black eyes, before eventually skulking away back into the tunnel. It was a lucky escape, but the sight of it still haunted him. Fear of The Maddening kept people inside and away from the cities and it also helped to keep order, not that there was ever much dissent. After all, nobody wanted to risk exile.

Some natural life did exist outside of the farms, of course. There were still birds (though not many), and pockets of wild animals too. Insects, annoyingly, seemed to thrive, but at least this meant that bees were still around to make honey and to pollinate the hardy crops that most settlements cultivated to a greater or lesser extent, depending on their other local resources. Because animals were so rare and so precious for food and materials, the settlement would send out regular three-person scouting parties to search for and capture them for the farms. They could be gone for days, camping out in the wilds. These dangerous sorties were volunteer-only, and Ethan was a regular. He liked the peace and quiet, and the fact he could pick and choose who he spent time with, which usually meant roping in Summer to go along. He even managed to find a few sheep on one outing, an achievement that had gained him significant notoriety. It was why the administrators overlooked his frequent transgressions outside the walls at night; that and the fact he was one of the more skilled fighters.

Ethan obviously understood the need to capture and breed

animals, but he also wished they could be left to run free. The few living creatures that remained in the wild were the only things that made the world feel alive. Ethan looked out towards the city – clearly visible, despite the considerable distance, thanks to a clear, cloudless sky – and it was obvious it had not always been this way. The city was huge, sprawling, and despite lying in ruin, there were still signs of its former greatness. Some structures still towered skyward by a hundred metres or more, before ending abruptly in a jagged stump. They looked like trees, snapped in half by a force beyond even nature's immense power.

As a boy, no older than Elijah, Ethan had not been the first to ask the questions – why? how? when? – just as his nephew had been doing earlier that night, and he was not the first to be warned not to ask such questions. It had always surprised and even baffled Ethan that no-one wanted to know. The view was that this civilisation, no matter how advanced it was, had failed catastrophically, and it was best forgotten. The descendants of those who survived were a new people, a civilisation detached from these ancestors. We had our stories which linked us to the past, but that was as far as it went.

As he had become older, and more influential, Ethan had managed to learn more. There was evidence that the ancestors possessed the ability to travel great distances, perhaps even to the stars, but most dismissed this as nonsense. Still, Ethan had been to the cities, and seen the machines – some of which remained intact, if decayed with age – and it fuelled his wonder that perhaps there were survivors from this time, and perhaps one day they would return. But, theories and guessing aside, the reality was that there was little hard evidence of anything. The earliest accounts were simply based on heresay and half-remembered stories that had been passed on from one to another. Any reliable record of history began an unknown number of years after The Fall, when settlements had been established and life had become ordered enough to allow for leaders to start chronicling their days. These records told of a time of fear and uncertainty; almost chaos. As The Maddening took hold and the adults starting dying, many of the other survivors simply died of starvation or exposure. It chilled Ethan to his core to think of children, younger even than Elijah, left alone to fend for themselves in the aftermath. They must have known fear like no human before them, or since. But, incredibly, some survived, enough to build a future. In the ashes, new leaders rose. Young men and women – boys and girls really – who managed to make it away from the cities, and their Maddened elders – some of whom were their family members, even parents – and lay the foundations of the settlements that exist today. Successive generations had enhanced these settlements and built new ones, eventually linking up with other settlers to form the network of twenty-seven that were known to exist today.

But for Ethan it was still a hollow existence. The settlements ably provided for people's survival, but to merely survive was not enough. Ethan thought of Elijah and tried to imagine the kind of life he would have as he grew up. In a few years he would begin to learn more about life outside the settlement and he would see how little of it there was left, and how little there was for him to experience. Then, having learned all this, he would be told that he couldn't know the reason why; that it was best left forgotten. Perhaps Elijah wouldn't care, like everyone else Ethan knew. But Ethan believed differently. He believed that to understand who you are, and to know where you are going, you must first know where you came from, and why.

He picked up a stone from underneath the tree and hurled it down the hill. It hammered into the rocks at the bottom and a sharp crack rang out into the still night air. As the sound died away, a flash of light appeared in the distance, hanging low near the horizon. "Ah, my guardian angel, come to watch over me," he said out loud. Sarcasm always sounded better to Ethan when spoken out loud, rather than in his head.

He watched as the light snaked across the sky and wondered for a moment if Elijah was watching it too. The light grew brighter and seemed to be getting larger, which was unusual. Ethan sat up. Suddenly a thrill ran through his body, giving him tingles. "You're a bright one..." he said out loud again, and then felt silly for talking to himself. The light continued to grow brighter. Ethan pushed himself up, and scrambled out from under the tree canopy. The thrill he had initially felt began to be replaced by the cold chill of fear. No light lingered for this long, or this brightly, he realised. Something was wrong.

A mighty roar filled the air, like the sound of a thousand pounding waterfalls, crashing onto the rocks with him at the centre. The light cut across the sky directly above him. Instinctively he ducked and covered his ears, shutting his eyes tightly too. As the noise started to pass into the distance, he opened his eyes again and watched as an object, trailed by fierce red flames, slammed into the open ground on the edge of the visible horizon, close to the city. The sound of the impact reached him moments later and caused him to jolt backwards. A huge cloud of dust arose from the impact site.

Ethan stood motionless on the hill and just watched, for how long he didn't know. Then he heard the cries from the settlement, and saw torches being lit along the walls, and inside, surrounding the main square. He realised that soon he would be missed, and raced off down the hill towards the opening behind the bush with the heart-shaped leaves, craning his neck all the while, trying to catch more glimpses of the dust cloud in the distance. He reached the wall, pushed past the branches and squeezed back through the small opening he had made, quickly replacing the stones behind him. People were already moving about inside and talking nervously. Ethan slipped past them unnoticed and ran – his heart pounding in his chest – for the guardhouse, feeling both exhilarated and terrified in equal measure.

CHAPTER 3

Maria opened her eyes. Smoke was all around her and she coughed violently. Her head felt like it had been used as a training bag by an entire squadron of rookie pilots, and her vision was blurry, as if she was underwater. She tried to find her bearings. She was still in the command chair. All around her she could hear the fizz of damaged circuitry and the crackle of fire. But somehow she was alive. Coughing again, she looked at the console in front of her and squinted to focus. It was smashed – useless – as were most of the controls around her. She checked her command chair and found that the auxiliary panel was still working. Words and numbers streamed across the booklet-sized screen, showing damage reports, weapons status, navigation data and a host of other things that no longer mattered. Her head was beginning to clear and she was able to make some sense of the information. The braking thrusters had activated, at least enough to slow their descent to a survivable velocity. But she didn't need a sensor to tell her that; it was obvious, really, seeing as she was still in one piece and not a red, pulpy stain on the inside of the cockpit glass. The navigation readout was only partially complete, but it still managed to tell her the one piece of information she needed to know – *Distance to objective = 0.0m.*

"Not your best landing, Sal," she said out loud, although her voice came out as more of a guttural croak. She reached down and unfastened the harness that kept her strapped into the command chair and stood up. An intense stabbing pain immediately shot through her thigh and groin taking her completely by surprise. She collapsed heavily on the floor, letting out a pathetic sounding yelp. *The damn control yoke...* she remembered. *This is the last thing I need!*

She stayed down, waiting for the pain to subside, and called out, "Kurren! Kurren! Are you okay?" Then she remembered that Kurren had fallen during the attack, and for a split-second she panicked. Maria twisted herself around and looked towards the back of the cabin to see if she could see him through the smoke. Her vision was still foggy, but she could just about make out a figure, lying motionless on his back. The fire was creeping up on him but it had not yet become out of control, so there was still time, if he was alive.

She called out to him again, "Kurren, can you hear me? It's Sal, we made it! We're planetside!" There was no response.

Maria's training kicked in and adrenalin started to rush through her veins. She reached underneath the co-pilot's console and dislodged the emergency medpack stored there. She then pushed herself towards Kurren with her good leg, using the medpack in one hand to guide her while keeping the other hand pressed firmly on her thigh, as this seemed to ease the pain. She slid up next to him and systematically checked the area for any potential dangers; only the encroaching fire was a visible threat. She lifted her hand off her thigh and winced as the pain rushed back in. Fighting back tears she shook Kurren's shoulders, shouting his name again and again.

"Kurren! Chris! It's Sal, can you hear me?" Kurren lay unconscious, but Maria saw that his chest was rising and falling slowly and this made her feel a little calmer. She reached over and grabbed his right hand by the wrist, pulled it across towards her and pushed up his sleeve to reveal his personal vital signs monitor, or PVSM. This displayed basic information, such as heart rate, blood pressure and toxicity levels, all of which looked stable. She let go of Kurren's hand, which fell limply to the floor, and checked him for any obvious sign of injury. There was some minor burning to the left side of his face, probably from the electrical fire, and there was some matted blood in his hair at the back of his head, no doubt from the fall, but it didn't look serious. As she worked, she could see the fire was getting closer.

Maria laughed. "You had me worried for a while there, old man," she said, opening the medpack and rifling through its contents, "but you're going to be all right. In fact, once I've pumped you full of this stuff, you're going to feel pretty fantastic. Until it wears off of course, and then you'll feel like I do right now."

She took an injector from the medpack, inserted a small blue capsule in the bottom of it and then held it firmly against Kurren's neck. She squeezed the trigger gently and the capsule instantly liquefied and shot into Kurren's neck, accompanied by a slight hissing sound. Reaching back into the medpack, she picked out another capsule, this time in a very light yellow colour, and repeated the procedure on herself. "One for you and one for me," she joked, as the injector hissed and the capsule emptied into her neck. She put the device back in the medpack and took out a bandage. "Well, make that two for me," she said, and then wrapped the bandage tightly around her thigh, putting as much pressure on it as possible. "Now, I need to get us both out of here." She pushed herself up and winced again as the pain shot through her thigh; the painkiller had yet to take effect. But there was no time to worry about that, the fire was creeping closer and they had to get out.

She struggled over to a storage compartment on the other side of the cabin, away from the fire, opened the door and pulled out a rectangular metal plate – about a metre by a half metre in size – and an emergency fire extinguisher. She rested the metal plate on the floor underneath the compartment and turned to aim the fire extinguisher at the source of the fire, near the auxiliary power distributor at the rear of the cabin. A clear gel shot from the extinguisher's nozzle and coated the wall of the cabin, immediately extinguishing the flames. She repeated the procedure, tackling the most dangerous fires first, finally aiming down to where the flames were beginning to lick at Kurren's feet. She actually covered him with the gel up to his ankles to make sure. *He won't be pleased about that,* she thought, *those are his best boots.*

With the fires put out, the cabin started to clear of smoke and she proceeded to inspect the rest of the damage. It was bad. Most of the consoles were smashed and only the main screen on the engineering console was still working, although it was currently showing only static. Maria's adrenaline rush was subsiding, the painkiller was kicking in, and for the first time since they'd crashed, she started to think about what had just happened, and how lucky there were to both be alive. It sent a chill down her spine.

Maria took a moment to compose herself, then picked up the metal plate from the floor and knelt down next to Kurren. She carefully slid the plate under his back and then pressed a switch on the edge closest to her, causing the lower lip of the plate to extend underneath Kurren's legs to just below the knees. Then she pulled out two black straps from the sides and ran one across his upper thighs and the other over his chest, clicking them into place on the opposite side of the plate. The plate emitted a low hum and rose about five centimetres off the deck. It remained hovering there with Kurren strapped to the top. Maria double-checked the straps to make sure they were secure, got up and moved to the main hatchway next to the engineering console. A small screen at head height flicked on and started to display some information: atmospheric composition, temperature, humidity and toxicity levels. All levels showed green, apart from toxicity, which was in the mid portion of the Yellow quadrant. Still within tolerances, though, Maria accepted. The temperature was probably the most remarkable of all the figures, though; it was registering as half the average ambient temperature of the moon base. The base was kept at a steady twenty-five degrees, and even though this only ever fluctuated by a couple of degrees either way due to sporadic and occasional power variances, Maria could usually detect the change, especially when it went colder – she hated the cold. She wondered for a moment what it would feel like outside and decided there was only one way to find out. She threw the emergency release lever on the door and stepped back.

The door pushed away slightly from the cabin wall and air hissed through the gaps around the seal membranes as the pressure equalized. It then swiftly retracted up and over the outer shell of the craft. As the hatch disappeared, a blast of cold air washed over Maria, literally taking her breath away. She had not been remotely prepared for it and she could do nothing but stand and stare, trying to process this new sensation. Not just the temperature, but the sensation of wind on her skin, of feeling and even hearing wind for the first time. It was like being jolted awake by a pulse of electricity. The moonlight was also like nothing she had seen before. The lighting in the base was constant, and while their relative position to the sun did alter the light level in some areas, especially the domed sectors, the photo-reactive coverings always moderated the brightness, so that it varied only very slightly. The only place where light varied naturally was in the observation lounge, which is where Maria went to relax. And while the sunlight on the observation deck was beautiful, the light on the planet was entirely different, almost ethereal. It felt alien to her, and incredibly powerful. The wind licked her face again and she felt invigorated. The sensation of pain was a distant memory as she stood looking out on the planet for the first time. Her heart was pounding so hard in her chest that she thought it might explode.

Another gust of wind broke her trance-like state, nearly knocking her off her feet and forcing her to adjust her balance. Then a shiver ran through her, not from adrenalin, but from cold. *I'm going to have to get used to this*, she thought. She stepped back inside and gathered her survival pack, placing Kurren's over his legs, and then stepped down the walkway, leaving Kurren hovering on the stretcher inside.

Her first steps onto solid ground were cautious. It felt strange, soft. She crouched down and pressed her hand into the loose dark soil that had been churned up by the ship's violent landing. The wind hit her again and without the shelter of the cabin Maria felt its full force. She lost her footing on the uneven ground and fell backwards, landing rather inelegantly on her backside. To her surprise this made her laugh out loud.

"Not the most graceful way to set foot planetside for the first time in almost a generation!" she laughed. "Archer would be most displeased..." She looked at Kurren as if expecting a reaction. He lay still, the grav plating humming gently beneath him. "You're no fun today, old man," she mused.

She got herself up and onto her knees, and then a little

gingerly, pushed her hand into the loose soil again, letting it fall through her fingers with a sort of quiet exultation, as if it were a million tiny, precious jewels. Then she looked up at the sky and everything else paled to insignificance. Of all these new sensations, this was the most powerful. She had felt soil before (or a manufactured version of it), but she had never seen a sky before. Tears began to stream down Maria's face as she watched the wisps of cloud move slowly across the moonlit expanse above her. She had dreamed of seeing the sky all her life; a real sky, not a picture or holo. It was everything she'd hoped for and so much more.

A crack of electricity from somewhere on the hull of the craft snapped her back to reality; or at least the reality of her situation, which had not altered and was far from ideal. She stood up and walked around the craft, still getting used to the buffeting of the wind. The hull was pocked with dark scorch marks, about as wide as a fist. They had clearly taken quite a beating from GPS fighters as they had made their run into the atmosphere. As Maria circled around the ship, inspecting it, she spotted two larger blast marks on the hull just to the side of where Kurren's engineering console was. One had actually penetrated through the hull plating, but luckily not anywhere near a key system. The same could not be said of the aft quarter, which had taken most of the damage. The main engines were badly damaged and it was these that were producing angry, electrical sparks.

Maria hurried back inside the cabin as quickly as she could and sat back down in her command chair. She tried the main console in front of her but it still would not turn on, so she switched on the auxiliary console on her chair and selected 'damage control'. Pages of information zipped across the screen listing the extensive number of damaged systems, until she came to main propulsion and stopped. A red border appeared around the screen as Maria read the words. She slumped into the chair, threw her head back and sighed.

She pushed herself out of the chair and knelt beside Kurren, checking his PVSM again. He was still stable, although his blood pressure and heart rate had dropped slightly, probably due to the drugs. She took out another capsule from the medpack, which was lying beside the hovering plate, pressed it into the injector and administered it to Kurren. She waited for a few moments and then leaned close to his ear. "Kurren, it's Sal, can you hear me?" she said. No response. She waited a moment and tried again, and this time Kurren stirred. He opened his eyes, turned his head towards Maria and then grimaced.

"Sal? What happened? Where am I?" he said weakly, still groggy from the combination of head injury and powerful medications. He groaned. "I feel like I've got the mother of all hangovers..." He tried to lift his arms but the straps resisted him. "What the...? Sal, why am I strapped into this thing?" he said, and then panic took hold. "Am I okay?" Maria could hear the fear in his voice. "Sal, I am hurt?"

"You're fine, old man," Maria said, unclipping the straps so that Kurren could lift his arms. The plate dropped gently to the deck and Kurren sat up gingerly. He then anxiously touched the back of his head. "You hit your head pretty hard during the attack," said Maria, "so I strapped you in here. I had planned to keep you unconscious for a while longer to let the meds work, and just wheel you out, but things have changed."

Kurren looked around, quickly surveying the damage to the ship. "We made it then?"

"Just about," said Maria. Kurren tried to stand, but dropped back, grimacing from the pain. He felt queasy from the concoction of drugs that were circulating around his system. Maria put a hand on his shoulder. "Take it easy, you've had a rough ride," she said.

Kurren nodded and attempted a smile, then shivered. "It's damn cold in here," he said, "did they shoot out the heating controls too?"

Maria smiled. "Why, do you want me to get you a blanket?" she teased, happy to see the old Kurren coming back to life.

"Yes, please, nurse," said Kurren, "and any chance of a bed bath?"

Maria laughed out loud and Kurren joined in, but soon regretted it as pain spasmed through his chest, making him cough. It tasted bitter, like burnt plastic. After he had recovered, he spat a globule of black phlegm on the silver decking.

"Lovely," said Maria.

"I made it for you," said Kurren smiling. "So, what's the plan, Captain?"

Maria's face tensed up. "We're in pretty bad shape," she said, flatly. "We came down on automatic, just as planned, but the main drive is shot and the core is unstable." Kurren looked over at the rear of the ship and saw the sparks arcing from the engineering consoles. "There's nothing we can do to stop it," said Maria, "so the plan is to salvage what we can and get the hell away from here before it blows."

"How long?" asked Kurren. He had stopped smiling.

"No way to tell exactly," said Maria, "but not long. We need to get moving; can you stand?"

Kurren looked down at his feet and saw that they were covered in gel. "You owe me a new pair of boots," he said with fake seriousness.

"Perhaps you would have preferred your feet to be on fire?" Maria replied, sarcastically. "Now, can you stand?"

Kurren took a deep breath and let it out slowly. "Only one way to find out..." he said. Slowly he pushed himself up with

Maria standing beside him for support – the little she could manage with her own injuries to account for. "Damn Sal, can you stop wobbling, this is hard enough as it is," said Kurren, half teasing, half serious. Then he saw the bandage around her leg, and concern took over. "Hey, Sal, are you okay?"

"It's alright, nothing is broken," Maria replied as both of them finally got to their feet.

"Well, I guess we both got lucky then," Kurren said, stretching his limbs. He felt much better now that he was on his feet again. "I sure hope all this is worth it."

"I hope so too," said Maria, "but however it turns out, it's going to be an intense experience."

"What makes you say that?" said Kurren.

"Step outside," Maria said, calmly, trying not to spoil the surprise. Kurren looked at her and then looked at the open hatchway; he hadn't even noticed it was open until now. He looked back at Maria. "Go on, I can handle getting the supplies," she said, comfortingly.

Kurren moved slowly to the hatchway and stepped outside, steadying himself on the door arch as he went. He stood on the soft earth just beyond the opening – in the same place Maria had stood earlier – and turned around and around, again and again, looking in every possible direction at the scene before him, chuckling to himself like a child. Maria heard him and went to the opening to watch. The smile on his face alone was almost worth the journey, whether their mission was a success or failure. It was the same look he'd had when he saw his newborn baby, she remembered. Maria had been there with him and his wife, Naomi, as they'd both just returned from an assignment, and Kurren didn't even know he was a father until he walked in to the maternity ward and saw his son resting quietly in his wife's arms. After Naomi and the baby had been killed following an attack two weeks later, Maria thought she would never see that look on his face again. Whatever else there was in store for them during the time they spent planetside, she was glad of this. Kurren came back inside and looked at Maria. He tried to speak, but no words came out – there was no way to describe it.

"I know," said Maria, smiling back. "Come on, there will be plenty of time to talk about it later. Right now we've got to move." They both set about cramming as much as they could into two emergency supply packs; food, extra clothes, tools and utensils, and as much medication as they could salvage.

After they had finished, Maria headed for the hatchway, but Kurren reached over and grabbed her arm to stop her. "Wait, there's one thing we've forgotten," he said. Maria looked at him, puzzled. She had everything she could imagine them needing already. Kurren moved over to another, smaller locker, near the hatchway. He took out two handguns from the rack inside, then two webbing belts, filled with ammo clips, and offered one set to Maria. "We don't know what to expect," he said to Maria. "We might need these."

Maria hesitated. She disliked carrying a weapon, but understood the necessity. She nodded and took them. They both clipped on the webbing belts and slid the weapons into their holsters. Then they slung the bags over their shoulders and left the craft.

"Our first priority should be shelter," Kurren said, bracing himself against the cold wind. "Then we can worry about what we came here to do."

"And how we do it without a ship," Maria added. As she spoke, a plume of blue-grey vapour hissed out of the rear of the craft and dissipated into the atmosphere.

"Emergency venting," Kurren said, matter-of-factly. "We need to hurry. This thing is a ticking bomb; it could blow in twenty minutes or twenty hours, but I definitely don't want to be around when it does."

They moved as fast as they could to the top of the gorge that the ship had carved out in the ground, and looked around.

"There!" said Maria, pointing to a derelict house up a hill, surrounded by a smattering of trees. It was about a kilometre away. "That will do nicely for shelter. It looks like a lovely little summer house."

"Yeah, and what if someone already lives there?" Kurren wondered, unamused.

Maria thought for a moment and shrugged. "Then I suppose we say hello."

CHAPTER 4

Ethan wasted no time in volunteering for the scouting party, a request that came as no surprise to anyone. He had already packed his gear and changed into travelling clothes by the time the other two members of the party had arrived in the Ranger hut. One of these was Rex Dorman, more commonly known amongst the Rangers as 'The Door Man', as he had authority over who came and went through the settlement gates. It was a bad joke, but one that had stuck. He was a good head shorter than Ethan, with a lean build, but he was also far stronger than he looked. Dorman was in his early forties, which made him one of the oldest Rangers in the settlement. He was fair-minded and Ethan respected him, but he didn't personally know him that well and, like most people, Ethan didn't consider him a friend.

Also in the party was Summer Rain, so-called because she happened to have been born on the day of a sudden and unexpected rainstorm during a blazing hot summer in the settlement, twenty years ago. In fact, 'rainstorm' was something of an understatement, hence why that day was infamous to those old enough to remember it. Her mother had been a traveller and part of a small caravan that went from settlement to settlement, trading what they had for what they needed at the time. Ethan found it strange that some people chose to live this way, rather than reside in the relative safety of a settlement. Dorman had told him that he'd once met an old man, who had spent his life travelling alone like a hermit, quite unconcerned at the prospect of Roamers lurking around the next corner. The caravans were rare, though, and in Ethan's twenty-one years as a resident of Forest Gate, he recalled perhaps only three or four travelling caravans visiting the settlement. They were formed of individuals or couples who had, for all sorts of different reasons, decided to join together and either search out territory for new settlements, or simply travel from place to place, because they didn't like being stuck behind walls. But, despite being strangers, such caravans were always welcomed whenever they appeared, and no-one was ever prevented from choosing to leave and join a caravan if they so wished, even if their departure would leave a skill shortage. The guarding of the gates was simply precautionary, for the protection of everyone inside. But if anyone wanted to leave, for whatever reason, they were free to do so. This notion of freedom was extremely important and was common throughout all twenty-seven settlements – it was a principle that had come from the Firsts. The Firsts chose to leave all vestiges of the past behind and start again, and as such the freedom to choose your own path and your own destiny was of the utmost importance.

Unfortunately, The Maddening ate away a person's principles and values, and it was Roamers that had attacked the caravan that Summer's mother travelled with. A Ranger party from Forest Gate, out scouting for food and animals, had stopped the attack and fought off the Roamers, but by that point most of the travellers were injured beyond the skill of any healer. Summer's mother, heavily pregnant at the time, was one of the few who made it back to Forest Gate, but she never regained consciousness and died two days later as the storm raged overhead and rain fell as heavy as hail stones. Summer was cut from her mother's lifeless body soon after, and – incredibly – survived. In fact, she didn't just survive, she thrived. It was as if the storm had somehow relinquished some of its power and given her life. Summer grew up to be the superior of anyone in Forest Gate when it came to hunting and tracking, and was probably the settlement's best archer. And she was a skilled fighter; even better than Ethan, though he would never admit it.

It was decided that Summer would live with Ethan and his older sister Katie, on account of their similar ages; Ethan being born only eight months previously, during a particularly bleak and hard winter. Summer was basically another sister to them, especially to Katie, and they formed a close bond over the years. This bond had only grown stronger in recent times, especially after Elijah's father disappeared one night when Elijah was still a baby. No-one knew where he went or why, or what happened to him, but Ethan believed the pressure of being responsible for a new life was simply too great for him, and he ran. This was how it was for many people; living dangerously on the edge, always close to breaking. It was likely the reason why there were so few children in all of the twenty-seven settlements. Why bring new life into such a desolate existence? Katie was different, however; she was an optimist, and powerful, positive force in the settlement, the best evidence for which was Elijah himself.

Elijah also adored Summer, and as he had gotten older, it was clear he had become totally smitten by her. Elijah wasn't the only one, because Summer was beautiful. She had deep auburn hair, usually worn in a short ponytail, an athletic body as a consequence of her training, and bright hazel-green eyes. When Ethan and Summer were teenagers, all the boys lusted after her and would badger Ethan to put in a good word, introduce them, and generally suss out what Summer thought about them. But she wasn't really interested in being chased or wooed; she was more interested in competing with the boys at whatever game they were playing... and beating them.

Ethan hadn't been oblivious to her charms either, but this was a source of much internal conflict. Ethan had grown up with Summer, and although they were not related, and Katie did her best to encourage them, he was deeply ashamed whenever he caught himself staring at her like the other boys. They had kissed one evening when Summer was seventeen and Ethan had just turned eighteen. Given their aptitude for physical activities, both had been selected to join the relatively elite ranks of the Rangers. This was as a secondary duty, because the primary responsibility of all the settlers was to provide for the essentials, such as food, shelter and clean water. Summer had instigated the kiss, quite to Ethan's surprise, but despite his initial shock he didn't pull away. Summer had then dragged him into one of the grain stores, and they kissed again. It had progressed to some rather inept fumbling before they were disturbed by the storekeeper dropping a measuring pan inside the storehouse. They had then looked sheepishly at each other for a time, neither knowing what to do next. The interruption was long enough for Ethan to feel shame and guilt stab at his insides, and he felt that he had somehow done wrong. He fled, leaving Summer behind, confused and, as he would later discover, deeply hurt. For weeks afterwards things were awkward between them; Ethan trying his best to avoid being alone with her and even speaking to her for a while.

About two months later, Summer stopped Ethan in the middle of the settlement square and demanded he talk to her and explain what she'd done wrong. It was quite a scene, and the talk of Forest Gate for several weeks. Ethan grew tired of the raised eyebrows, knowing smirks, and occasional ironic pats on the back, followed by a 'telling wink' from the older Rangers who were training him. But soon it was forgotten for some other more salacious piece of gossip and things returned to normal. Ethan and Summer became friends again, and even managed to joke about it, but there was still tension between them, even now.

"She loves you. You do know that?" Katie would often tell Ethan, especially when he spent any time with Summer, which was often because of their training.

"Don't be ridiculous, Katie, she's like a sister to me," Ethan would reply, or words to that effect, trying as much to convince himself as to convince Katie. But Ethan knew she was right. The attraction was undeniable, and he still felt it too, though he had become skilled at hiding it.

"She's not your sister, Ethan, I am," Katie would continue, undeterred by Ethan's attempt to bury the subject. Ethan had also become skilled at hiding his feelings from Katie, but unlike most people, Katie could see through his unruffled calm. "Don't be so hard on yourself, or her," she would push on. "You deserve a chance to be happy, and so does Summer. This place doesn't give us many chances. Life throws us 'lucky' survivors more bad luck than good, so take your good luck when it comes."

But Ethan would just make excuses and find a way to leave or change the subject. Talking about it, contemplating it, gave Ethan a sick, nervous feeling in his stomach. Many times he'd considered just ignoring his gut, and telling Summer how he felt, but he could never manage it; something always held him back.

Ethan was rudely awakened from his daydreaming by a firm punch to the top of his arm. "Ow!" he protested. It actually had hurt. Summer never pulled her punches, even when playing.

"Hello? Anyone in there?" Summer said, sarcastically. "We're ready, I say again." Ethan looked up to see Summer and Dorman both looking at him quizzically.

"Are you with us, Ranger?" said Dorman stoically. Dorman always called him 'Ranger', never Ethan. It was his way of keeping things professional between them, and assert his authority as the older and more responsible Ranger. "When I say with us, I mean coming with us on this fool's errand that will probably get us all killed," Dorman went on, enjoying himself now. "Or is your daydream more important? Care to share?"

Ethan looked back at Summer. She was standing with her arms crossed and a broad smirk across her face, evidently enjoying herself. Ethan threw a rock at her, and it hit her boot. "Hey!" she said, still smirking.

"I'm ready," Ethan said, turning back to Dorman.

"No-one was ever more ready for a fool's errand," said Summer, beaming now. "You're the biggest fool I know."

"Knock it off you two," said Dorman, in his best assertive voice. "Grab your gear. We'll head out now and aim to make it to the hilltop clearing by nightfall and make camp there." Then Dorman marched off, looking purposeful. Ethan followed, punching Summer's arm as he went past her, which knocked her slightly off balance. He laughed and smiled at her.

"Hey!" she said again, though this time unable to contain her laughter.

The clearing that Dorman had referred to was about two-thirds of the way towards the city, and about an hour's travel from where they estimated the impact site to be. If they trekked at a fast pace, only stopping for two or three brief breaks, they could reach the clearing by dusk. It would be a tough slog for sure, but nothing they weren't used to.

The gates were opened at Dorman's request. As Ethan approached, he saw that a crowd had gathered, looking on anxiously. Then he saw his sister Katie rushing towards him with Elijah not far behind.

"Ethan, wait!" shouted Katie, rather embarrassingly. Suddenly Ethan felt like a child about to receive a public telling-off. Mercifully, Katie seemed mindful of the public setting and waited until she was close enough to speak at a normal, discrete volume. But she was clearly agitated. Elijah stood at her side, smiling at Summer. "Ethan, let someone else go this time," said Katie in a hushed but urgent-sounding tone. "There are others who can take your place; I don't want you on this one."

Ethan reached out and held her shoulders, trying to offer some reassurance. "Sis, don't worry," he said confidently. "I've been out a hundred times, this is no different."

Katie pulled back. She did not want to be mollified. "You know very well this is different," she scolded, in a very motherly way. Elijah's attention was now focused on Ethan and Katie. He had recognised his mother's 'telling-off' voice and had sidled away slightly, his eyes flicking between the two like a snake's tongue tasting the air. "You always volunteer for the most dangerous expeditions," Katie continued, looking and sounding fierce, "and you never consider how it makes me or Elijah feel when you disappear, sometimes for weeks on end." Elijah's eyes flicked back to Ethan. "But this..." Katie was struggling to contain her anger now, "this... light falling from the sky. This is dangerous, Ethan. Let someone else go."

Ethan tried to fight back. "We don't know it's dangerous,"

he said, "we're just going to have a look."

Katie ignored him. "Think of Elijah," she said. Using Elijah to make him guilty was always her last resort. "You're like a father to him, think of how he'd miss you if you got yourself..." she hesitated and glanced over at her son, whose eyes had now flicked back to her, "...if you got hurt," she corrected.

"Hey, don't bring me into this!" Elijah piped up, feeling brave. That was a mistake. Katie gave him a look that could turn milk sour.

"You're in enough trouble as it is!" she scolded. "Sneaking off outside the wall at night!" Ethan shifted uncomfortably; he knew what was coming next. "And you!" she pointed at Ethan when she said this, her voice no longer discreetly muted. "You should know better, letting him hang around outside the walls. You're reckless. You don't care about us!" Then she started to cry. She pressed her hands to her face trying to hide it, from Ethan and the gaggle of onlookers.

Ethan put his arms around her and held her tightly. She had succeeded in making him feel guilty. He *was* being selfish by wanting to go, but despite this he was no less determined to do so, and that made him feel worse. "Katie, don't worry," he said, "and I'm sorry about Elijah, that won't happen again." He looked over at Elijah and winked. Elijah smiled. "I'm not reckless Katie, I'll be safe, I promise," he continued. "But this is something I have to do. I love you, both of you. You're all I have, after all."

Katie pushed back and looked into his eyes. "Then why go?" she pleaded, trying to understand. "You're all we have too."

"Because I have to know," Ethan said calmly. "This life, this rotting planet we inherited, this is not our fault. Something happened, and I want to know what. And this falling light, it could help me understand. It could help us all understand."

Katie composed herself and stepped back, away from Ethan's hold. "There are no answers out there, Ethan," she said, "only more questions. Whatever you find, it won't change anything. We have to live as best we can, and work for something better; a better life for our children, Ethan," she gestured imploringly towards her son. "For Elijah's children," and then grabbed Ethan's jacket. "For *your* children, Ethan."

Ethan took hold of Katie's hands and gently removed her hold on him. "How can we have a future if we don't understand and learn from our past?" he said. He glanced over to Summer and Dorman. They were waiting by the gate, patiently, but expectantly. "Look, I have to go, but I promise I'll be back," said Ethan. "I promise, Katie. I love you both." And with that he let go of Katie's hands and walked towards the gate to join Summer and Dorman. After a few quick paces, he glanced back at Elijah and gave him a 'thumbs-up' gesture and a smile. Elijah smiled and returned the signal. Katie walked up behind Elijah and put her hands on his shoulders. There was a deep sadness in her eyes that he hadn't seen for a long time, not since Elijah's father had left and perhaps not even since their parents had been killed. Ethan felt another intense stab of guilt, but pushed it deep inside him. Then he looked away and picked up the pace.

"Everything okay?" Dorman asked as Ethan drew level with them.

"Everything is fine, let's go," said Ethan, not stopping. Summer and Dorman followed him out and the gate was closed behind them. The party set off without another word between them, towards the clearing, low on the horizon. Ethan was out in front, and setting a furious pace.

CHAPTER 5

It took Maria and Kurren just under two hours to reach the house, far longer than either had expected. The meds had worked to repair their injuries, but after the excitement and adrenaline had worn off, weariness had set in so that each step felt that it required double the effort. It didn't help that the gravity on the planet was six percent higher than on the moon base. The climb up the hill to the house was particularly exhausting, and when they reached the ramshackle building, which was larger than it looked from a distance, they were just about done in. But they knew they still had to be on their guard.

Out of breath, Kurren said quietly, "better leave the gear and draw your weapon. Let's make sure no-one is at home first."

Maria nodded, dropped her pack, and drew her sidearm. Swiftly, professionally, she loaded a magazine and chambered a round; she may have disliked weapons, but she was still proficient with them. Without speaking again, Kurren signalled that he would take the side door, while Maria entered at the front. They moved quietly towards the house, using the trees as cover, until they reached the building. It was near derelict, with smashed windows and a section of broken wall, but the roof was still intact and it was more-or-less water-tight. Maria carefully looked through the window and saw furniture, broken plates, and other items that she couldn't make out littering the floor. She couldn't tell how recently any of it had been disturbed. She saw Kurren opening the side door, and took her cue to move inside, keeping to the walls and covering Kurren with her weapon. They moved swiftly, checking from room to room on the lower floor, finding no signs of current or recent lodgers. Then came a sound from upstairs, something moving. Perhaps a bird, Maria thought, though they hadn't seen any of those, a fact that hadn't occurred to her until that point.

"You hear that?" whispered Kurren.

Maria nodded, and indicated in the direction of the stairs with the barrel of her pistol. Kurren took the lead, and Maria followed, covering his back. They climbed each step with the care and precision of a hunting cat, careful not to make a sound. Then, just over half-way up, Maria stepped and the stair creaked. They both froze, not in terror because their training kicked in to control fear, but in anticipation. Daring not to move any further, and barely twitching a muscle between them, they waited and listened. The sound came again, this time more distinct. Something was definitely moving. Their position was tactically poor and they both knew it. Kurren indicated for Maria to move back down the stairwell, and she did so as carefully as possible, her heart now thumping in her chest. Kurren followed, his weapon raised and pointing at the landing at the top of the stairs. Five steps from the bottom, Kurren stumbled and his foot smashed through a rotten panel. Without warning, a shape darted out from the top of the stairs and hurtled towards them. Kurren pulled his foot loose and tried to dodge, but he was too late; the shape hurtled past, crashing into his side and knocking him hard against the banister, before itself then falling heavily to the foot of the staircase. Maria was faster; she was already at the bottom and had trained her weapon on the attacker.

"Stop or I shoot!" she shouted.

But the figure did not stop. It got up and charged Maria. She could see it clearly now, and despite her training, she was afraid. It looked essentially human, but also not. Its face was elongated, as if it had been stretched, and set deep into this mottled, grey face were deep, black eyes that shone like pools of ink. Two sharp sounds rang out cleanly in the night air as Maria released rounds into the attacker's chest. It fell heavily to its knees, but other than the dull thuds of flesh on wood, it made no sound. Then it stood again and fixed its inky black eyes onto Maria. Dark red blood oozed from its chest, but it did not appear to be in pain.

Maria backed away. "What the hell are you?" she demanded, but the creature did not reply, it just stood, staring at her. Then it charged again, and Maria reacted instantly, firing twice more, the second round into its skull. It fell forward, heavily, its head breaking apart as it smashed into the floor. Maria almost vomited, and turned away.

Kurren arrived at the bottom of the stairs moments later, clutching his right arm. There was blood soaking into his clothing. "It it dead?" he asked, breathlessly, but surprisingly calmly.

"I think so..." said Maria, looking at the blood. Kurren flipped the body onto its back with his boot and covered it with his pistol, just to be sure. The figure lay still, its eyes still open, still as inky black as when it was alive, if it were ever really alive. Maria noticed that Kurren's left forearm was bleeding. "You're hurt, let me take a look," she said.

"Not now," said Kurren, calmly. "We need to make sure there are no others."

"I think if there were, we'd know about it by now," said Maria. "What is it? It doesn't look... human," she added, unable to hide her disgust.

"That's what they call one of the Maddened," said Kurren. "It was in the briefing."

Maria's face scrunched up even more tightly. "That's what happens?"

"Yeah," said Kurren flatly. "So we need to step up, and get this done before our meds run out."

"Roger that," said Maria, in hearty agreement.

Kurren crouched to inspect the creature more closely. It was wearing dark rags, mottled with dirt and substances that Kurren didn't even want to identify. At one time, it looked like they would have been fairly normal-looking clothes, but judging by the wear and the grime, that was clearly many years ago. Its face was contorted and also filthy with grime; its teeth misshapen, broken and black; its skin grey. But it was the eyes that unsettled him the most. Black, cold, set back into its oddly-shaped skull. Despite his experience and training, they made him afraid. "Do you think there is anyone left down here, Sal?" Kurren said after a few moments. "I mean anyone that's not like this?"

Maria sighed. "I hope so, or this has all been for nothing."

She checked her PVSM. "Toxicity is a little higher here, but still okay. We have four hours before needing another hit of meds, though you're going to need a broad-spectrum anti-con once I've patched that up."

Kurren looked at his arm. "Great..." he said. "Those things always make me feel like shit."

"Better than feeling like him," Maria replied, and Kurren couldn't argue with that. "Between the ship exploding and my four rounds into our friend here, I'd say that if there are any normal people still planetside, they will be well aware of us by now. Or at least they'll have seen something strange going on, and be on their way to check it out."

"Agreed," Kurren said. "But I don't see any choice other than to stay here tonight and get some rest. We're both running on fumes."

Maria took a closer look at Kurren's arm. It looked angry. "Come on, let's get our gear and get this taken care of. You take first watch. The upstairs should at least give us a vantage point and some warning if any more of these things come by."

Kurren nodded. Then he looked down at the distorted mass of flesh on the floor. "What do we do with our friend here?"

Maria holstered her weapon and then stood with her hands on her hips, thinking. "Normally, I'd say burn it," she suggested, "but that would definitely come under the category of drawing attention to ourselves." Then, looking around, she spotted a door that looked like it could lead down into a basement. "Let's just sling it down there, so it's at least out of the way."

"Yeah, and then bolt the door and move something heavy in front of it, to be sure," said Kurren, nodding in agreement.

"To be sure of what?" asked Maria, confused.

"To be sure the damn thing doesn't get back up in the middle of the night and decide it wants to go a second round!" said Kurren.

Maria visibly recoiled as she considered this. "Dammit, Kurren, I hadn't even thought of that. How the hell am I going to sleep now?"

Kurren smiled. "Well, then I suggest you take first watch instead."

CHAPTER 6

Thanks to the clear, calm weather, Ethan, Summer and Dorman had made good time. They had reached the location to camp overnight on schedule, and had had an uneventful night. They had started out again early in the morning, and now they could see some smoke rising just over the horizon, so they knew they were close. Dorman suggested a quick rest-stop, so they would be fresh when they eventually encountered whatever it was they were about to encounter.

"Remind me again why I agreed to this?" Summer panted as they sat resting in a small cutting in the hillside.

"You'll do anything to spend more time with Ethan, admit it," Dorman teased, and Summer scowled back at him.

"I'd do anything to get out of washing duty," Summer retorted, spikily. "And besides, we already spend plenty of time together in sparring practise, usually with me kicking his butt. I can give you a personal demonstration, if you like?" Dorman laughed, satisfied that he'd got a rise out of her.

"Hey, I am still here you know?" Ethan cut in, trying to

break up the banter, which was making him feel unconformable.

Summer looked over at him and smiled, but Ethan was busy rifling through his backpack. It was difficult to tell since his cheeks were already flushed from the exertion of trekking across country at such a fast pace, but Summer was sure he was blushing.

Ethan began breaking out some supplies, throwing a linen-wrapped packet of dense bread towards Summer, which she caught without looking at him. He then looked at Dorman, who was smirking back at him with that 'knowing' look he remembered the Rangers giving him during the brief time that Summer and Ethan's flirtations were top of the gossip list. He threw a packet at Dorman too, a little more fiercely, forcing him to react quickly to catch it before it smacked into his nose. It did the job of wiping the smirk off his face. "Eat quickly people," Ethan said, unwrapping his own piece of bread, "we haven't got far to go now."

"Let's just hope that whatever it is over there lives up to your expectations," said Dorman, seriously.

"He's expecting to find a friendly group of 'Angels' aren't you Ethan?" Summer teased. "Ooh, hello there Ethan, glad you could visit and learn the meaning of life!"

"Shut up, Summer," Ethan shot back, clearly agitated.

Dorman quietly regarded them both, took a bite of bread, and then shook his head. "Honestly, you two are this pathetic world's worst kept secret," he said blithely. "Just get on with it and allow yourself a bit of happiness. Because whatever is over that hill, I promise you, it won't be as good as what you're denying yourselves."

Now Ethan was clearly blushing, but Summer was used to this sort of macho jostling.

"How would you know Dorman?" Summer said, feigning

seriousness. "The most meaningful relationship you've ever had is with your right hand." Dorman and Ethan burst out laughing, Dorman spitting his bread out uncontrollably.

"Hang on, I thought it was his left hand?" spluttered Ethan, grateful that the attention was now focused on Dorman, rather than himself, and they all burst out laughing again. He chanced a look at Summer, hoping she wasn't looking back. She wasn't. Summer was at her most beautiful when laughing and smiling, just like she was now. Maybe Dorman was right, he thought, maybe there was more to their relationship than mere friendship. But he valued that friendship too much to risk losing it.

An explosion in the distance made them all stop, and stand up in readiness, hands reaching for weapons. It wasn't a big explosion, but it was clear it came from the direction of the crash site, because there was now a lot more smoke.

"Come on, let's get over there before there's nothing left to see," said Dorman. "I'll be damned if I've come all this way, and put up with your pathetic company, for nothing."

They packed up quickly and set off at a jog in the direction of the black plume that was rising into the sky.

CHAPTER 7

The explosion woke Maria with a start. It was Kurren's watch, and as her vision cleared, she could see him standing cautiously by the window. "What was that?" asked Maria.

Kurren didn't look back at her. "Probably the ship's power core rupturing. The explosion wasn't significant enough for it to be a fuel-cell leak; at least I don't think so. I'm not sure how far we travelled from the crash site."

"Landing site..." Maria corrected.

Kurren looked back and smiled. "Sorry."

Maria got to her feet. She didn't feel especially rested. "How long was I asleep?" she asked, groggily.

"Just a few hours, I'm afraid," Kurren replied. "It's getting light, though, so we should get moving. I've scanned the horizon, and it looks like the toxicity level reduces significantly over to the North, about thirty klicks or so. And then it seems to rise up into the hills. There's a flat area just before some heavy woodland; it's elevated, near shelter, and the toxicity levels there seem low. It's probably our best bet for a settlement in this area. Assuming there is anyone left."

Maria checked her PVSM. It was showing her toxicity level was about to enter the red zone. She reached into her arm pocket and took out two yellow-tipped injectors, throwing one to Kurren, who caught it. "Dose up, old man," she said as she pressed the injector into her neck.

"Oh great, more drugs," said Kurren, injecting himself before casually discarding the device onto the floor.

Maria got up and walked over to Kurren. Without asking, she pulled up his jacket sleeve to inspect the wound from the previous night. The treatment had worked, stemming any bleeding and accelerating healing. There was no sign of infection.

Kurren noticed the look of concentration on Maria's face and asked, with genuine concern, "Everything okay?"

"Well, the wound has healed nicely, but there's a problem," Maria replied, gravely.

"What problem?" said Kurren, sounding concerned.

"You're still a jerk," said Maria, before letting out a chuckle.

"Damn it, Sal, you had me worried!" said Kurren pulling down the sleeve of his jacket crossly.

Maria slapped him on his good arm. "Don't worry, you're fine," she said. "So long as we keep up the meds, we should both be off this rock without any negative effects," she added, more seriously. Kurren didn't respond, but he knew exactly what negative effects Maria was referring to.

They both started to gather their gear and headed cautiously down the stairs, and then quickly scouted the perimeter, weapons drawn, making sure there were no more unwanted guests. When they were satisfied they were alone, they met at the rear of the house, overlooking the city in the near distance.

"First order of business should be to secure our ride back," said Maria. "If we can't get back, there's no point trying to bag our prize."

"Agreed."

Maria checked her PVSM and flipped up a panel to reveal the data display. "According to the survey of the area the best place to find a ship is the underground space port, north of the city. Due to my exceptional piloting skills..." Kurren snorted, Maria smiled at him and continued, "...as I was saying, due to my steely piloting skills, we've actually landed..."

"Crashed," Kurren said, trying to disguise the word as a cough.

"...*landed*..." Maria stressed, "about ten miles away from the port. We've already covered some of the distance there, so if we get a move on, we should be able to find an entry-point in a few hours. Once we've tagged a ride out of here, we can perhaps also find a city transit car or utility, and if we're lucky, we can grab the prize and be out of here by tomorrow."

Kurren looked at her, eyes wide and eyebrows raised. "Are you sure you've been taking the right meds?" he said. "Because it sounds like you've had an overdose of wishful thinking."

Maria gave him a friendly punch on the arm. "Gotta stay positive, fly boy!" she said. "Besides, I'm already sick of your ugly mug. So let's get this done as soon as we can."

"Yes boss," said Kurren. And they set off towards the outskirts of the city.

CHAPTER 8

Ethan, Summer and Dorman approached the smoking object with their weapons drawn. Summer hung back with her hunting bow held low, and arrow nocked, while Ethan and Dorman held short wooden batons, about a metre long; the preferred weapon of the Ranger.

This was their first close-up view of the object, and it was now obvious to all of them that it originated from before The Fall. It was metallic, about ten body-lengths long and half that in width, and just tall enough for an average-sized human to stand up in. Smoke was billowing from the side furthest from them, jutting straight up into the clear, windless sky, and there were some ominous-sounding hisses and crackles coming from it, like logs burning in a fire. On the outer surface closest to them was an open door or hatch that led inside.

Summer regarded the object with suspicion. "Has this thing really just crashed or has it always been here, and just, I don't know, exploded?"

Ethan glanced back at her. "Why do you ask that?" he said

with genuine surprise.

"I mean, look at it. It looks sort of... old. I mean beat up," Summer said, unsure what she really meant.

Ethan stopped advancing, cautious not to get too close. "It's from before The Fall," he said, casually.

"Don't jump to conclusions," said Dorman. "But, I agree it does look similar to some of the things we've seen in the cities."

"We saw it come down from the sky," said Ethan, "so we can be pretty sure it hasn't always been here."

"We should go, this doesn't feel right," said Summer, nervously. She was on edge, continually looking around, arrow partly drawn back.

"Take it easy, Summer," said Dorman. "Let's just do what we came here to do, and head back." Dorman was closest to the object. He edged closer to the open hatch, but not close enough to see inside. "There's blood on the door frame here," he said gravely. "Someone was inside when it crashed."

"That's enough!" said Summer, fiercely. "We've found what we came for, now let's go back."

Ethan dropped back alongside Summer. She looked scared, and Summer wasn't one to scare easily.

"Hey, it's okay," Ethan said, trying to calm her down. "But we're here now, let's find out what we can."

"Ethan, this isn't a game," said Summer, relaxing her bow. "If there were people on that thing, they're not here now; they could be watching us. We don't know why they're here. We need to be careful."

"I understand, but I want to know why they're here," Ethan replied. "Don't you?"

Summer shook her head vigorously, "No!" she said firmly.

"Then why did you come out here?" said Ethan, feeling frustrated.

"I came to be with you, you idiot. Don't you know that by

now?" Summer retorted. "And besides, Katie asked me to watch out for you, make sure you didn't do anything stupid. I didn't expect we'd find anything. Not like this, anyway."

Ethan looked away. "I didn't... realise," he said, embarrassed.

"Of course you did!" said Summer. "We're not kids any more, Ethan, so let's not play games."

Ethan looked back at her. She looked more angry now than scared. "Okay, I know," he admitted. "But this is hardly the time for a heart-to-heart."

Summer scoffed. "I'm not sure there's room in that shrivelled thing for anything more than you and your personal crusade."

"That's not fair!" said Ethan. Summer's remark had hurt.

Summer tilted her head back, her eyes closed. "I'm sorry," she said. "I'm just worried that this thing here will cloud your judgement, make you reckless."

"It won't," said Ethan, confidently. "But, you're right, Summer. This is what I've been searching for." He turned and pointed at the crashed object. "Look at it," he said. "Finally, we could get some answers. Whoever arrived on that thing... maybe they can tell us what happened. Help us understand."

"Help *you* understand," Summer corrected him. "The rest of us are perfectly happy not knowing."

"Then why send us out here?" Ethan argued. "Why bother if no-one cares?"

Summer shook her head. "We're not out here for answers, Ethan," she said in a mocking tone, as if it was obvious and Ethan was stupid for asking. "We're here to find out if it's a threat. That's what we do, Ethan. We protect our people. Or have you forgotten that?"

Ethan rubbed his forehead and temples. He hated arguing with Summer, and hated that he could never turn her to his point of view. He really wanted her to understand and to have the same drive to know more. It was a rift, and perhaps one of the reasons why their relationship had never developed further.

Summer reached out and grabbed Ethan's jacket. "Maybe some things are best forgotten, Ethan," she said sombrely. "Maybe we should live for now, and be thankful that we escaped whatever it was that did... that," she nodded in the direction of the derelict city in the distance.

Ethan looked over at the city and then back at Summer. He'd never heard her talk this way, and he'd never had the courage to open up to her like this himself. But how could he make her understand that he couldn't live for now until he understood why this had all happened? It gnawed at his subconscious every hour of every day. He was about to speak, to try to explain this, when Dorman interrupted. He was standing just outside the open door hatch of the object, some distance from Ethan and Summer, so that he needed to shout.

"Hey, can you two save whatever it is you're talking about for later?"

They both turned to look at him, just as the side of his face exploded into a mess of blood and bone. Dorman fell, motionless in a crumple on the ground, twitching chaotically. A figure casually stood over Dorman's body, looking down at it impassively. It had been inside the object – stupidly, no-one had checked inside, and Ethan had been too pre-occupied with Summer to think about it, until now.

The figure, dressed in tattered, soiled clothing, now splattered with the bright red blood from Dorman's broken skull, wore a vacant look on its face. A human-looking face. It wasn't yet fully maddened, Ethan realised. The Roamer remained standing over Dorman, staring blankly at the twitching body at its feet, before it slowly looked up and saw Ethan and Summer; both frozen in shock.

Summer reacted first. She pushed away from Ethan, and in a flash drew back the string of her bow and fired the arrow deep into the Roamer's chest. It stumbled back, and fell to one knee. It looked at the arrow and reaching up with a blackened, disfigured hand, grabbed the shaft and pulled. There was no cry of pain, even as dark red blood oozed from the wound. It tried in vain for several seconds to remove the arrow, grunting inhumanly, but it was sunk too deeply into its corrupted flesh. Eventually, it fell to its side, still holding the arrow shaft with one hand, and fell still.

Summer expertly nocked another arrow and they both stood there, waiting, watching, hearts pounding so hard that Ethan could hear the blood pumping in his ears. He quickly surveyed their surroundings again, looking for any signs of movement, any indication that there could be more. The Maddened moved alone, Ethan knew this, but Roamers sometimes travelled in groups, even ones this far gone. There could be more. Neither spoke for what seemed like an eternity. Then, slowly, another figure – a man – appeared from inside the object, followed by two others, one male and one female. They also had not yet become fully maddened, but they were long past the stage of being recognisably human. All three looked at the lifeless body on the ground and then up towards Summer and Ethan. Then without a word or gesture between them, the Roamers charged straight at them.

Ethan was a good runner; one of the best. Tall, strong and agile, he was swift and able to outrun any Ranger in the settlement, something he did every year whenever a new Ranger graduated and fancied challenging his status. But as the Maddening progressed, it not only changed a person's mind, but their body too. They stopped feeling pain, and could perform feats of exertion that would seriously injure a normal person; their brains simply did not tell them when to stop.

Three years ago, Ethan had seen a Roamer tear open a section of the settlement's perimeter wall with its bare hands, pulling out stone and wood as if they were weeds. The effort was so great that it actually tore an arm from its socket. And then, just as suddenly and violently as it had begun its assault, the pressure on its heart and lungs become too severe, and it collapsed, dead. But the damage to the fence was done, and more Roamers had gotten inside the wall; four settlers were killed before they were stopped. Ethan had fought them that day, as on others days, and he had learned the hard way not to underestimate them. They would not retreat, would not surrender and would not negotiate. They simply wanted what the settlers had, and would stop at nothing to get it.

Ethan heard the tell-tale 'swoosh' of an arrow being loosed, and he watched as it sank into the eye socket of the female. It fell flatly forward, driving the arrow through its brain and out the back of its skull. But even Summer couldn't draw fast enough to take out the next one before it reached them, and so there was no choice left but to fight.

Ethan had already begun moving before the second Roamer had taken the arrow to its head, his weapon clenched tightly in his grip, muscles pumped with adrenaline. Summer threw down her bow and reached for a knife but Ethan knew she wouldn't get it in time. He charged into both Roamers, using his staff to ram them off course. It worked, and both were knocked off balance, stumbling and falling roughly to the ground. Ethan too was down, and he knew he had to regain his footing quickly to stand any chance of surviving the attack. His own physical prowess came to the fore now, as he rose swiftly and swung at the nearest Roamer, striking a glancing blow to its side. The second was on its feet almost as quickly and launched at Summer, who deflected it frantically with her knife, but the attack was enough to send her falling backwards.

Ethan saw Summer fall and switched his footing to take on her attacker, dealing a powerful blow to the creature's face, smashing its nose and cheek bone with a nauseating crunch. Then Ethan was hit on the back. Somehow the other Roamer had managed to recover quickly enough to land an attack. Ethan fell, trying to block out the pain, and rolled over to face his attacker, just in time to evade a second blow. The Roamer lashed out again and this time instinct took over, and he kicked out its legs. It dropped solidly to the floor, and Ethan followed up quickly, crushing its throat. He scrambled to his feet barely in time to see the other Roamer advancing again, its face a bloodied mess, with Summer's knife in its hand. Ethan saw the glinting metal and backed away, panic rising in his gut. The knife rose high and was about to drive forward when Summer appeared and hooked the creature's arm with her bow. Ethan had no idea where she had come from, but he was grateful for the opening it gave him. His staff did the rest, and a moment later the Roamer was back down in the dirt, this time for good.

They both stood there for a few seconds, struggling for breath, arms and legs buzzing with adrenalin and raw energy.

"Thanks…" Ethan managed breathlessly, still watching the bodies to make sure they were dead. Summer nodded, similarly breathless, muscles still tense and alert. She was still coiled and ready to strike. Ethan stepped closer and placed a hand on her shoulder; a simple gesture of reassurance to diffuse the tension. "It's okay, we got them," he said, calmly.

Summer threw her arms around him and Ethan winced as she squeezed the area of his back that had taken the brunt of the Roamer's assault, but he didn't complain. He dropped the staff and embraced her with similar intensity. This was as close as either of them had come to death, and they both knew it. All he wanted right now was to feel Summer, to know she was still breathing, warm and alive.

They remained this way for several seconds, but as the true realization of what had just happened sank in, Ethan began to feel guilt and shame. He held on to Summer as if letting her go might mean that she could blow away with the wind, and stared out towards the derelict city on the horizon. He'd always been so sure of himself, of his ability, confident in the knowledge that he'd never been badly hurt during any of his previous confrontations. It had made him feel invincible, infallible, though others might call it cocky. Now he better understood his sister's anguish. He understood this as he held Summer close to his chest and felt sick at the thought that she could be lying broken in the dirt, beside these diseased creatures. Her instead of Dorman. *Oh no... Dorman*, he thought.

It was as if Summer had heard him, because at almost the same time, she said, weakly into Ethan's ear, "What shall we do about Dorman?"

Ethan pulled away slightly, but did not let Summer go. He noticed her eyes were wet. Not quite crying, but close. He'd never seen her like this.

He finally let go of her, though it was hard to do so, and looked at the scene before them. Three dead Roamers and a dead Ranger. He shook his head. "We should burn the bodies," he said, coldly. "We take Dorman's gear, and we burn them all together."

"Ethan..." said Summer, sounding unsure, almost shocked at the suggestion.

"It's what he'd tell us to do," said Ethan. "It's what he'd do if it was us. He's just a shell now, what does it matter?"

Summer rested her forehead against Ethan's chest and exhaled. She stayed there for a few seconds, and then rested her hands around his waist. Despite the situation, Ethan felt a slight thrill, and instantly rebuked himself for feeling it. It was like he was a kid again, fooling around in the yard.

Summer raised her head and met his eyes. "Okay," she said with quiet determination. "Let's get it done." She moved away from Ethan and they stood side-by-side, the cool wind calmly blowing across them, oblivious to the violence that had taken place only moments earlier.

"And then what?" said Ethan, realising he had lost his firmness of purpose, and no longer knew what to do. He thought that he would probably do whatever Summer asked, no matter what it was.

She looked at him, her expression plain, her composure regained. "Then we find whoever came here in this thing," she said severely, "we find out why they came, and we shake some answers from them. We do it for Dorman, agreed?"

Ethan looked into her eyes and his doubt disappeared. "Agreed," he said.

CHAPTER 9

The door was buried behind a jungle of weeds and plants the like of which Maria Salus and Chris Kurren had never seen before. Their base on the moon was home to a very limited variety of plant life and it was all very neatly kept, even inside the huge arboretum.

It had taken them just over two hours to reach the spaceport on the outskirts of the city, and their journey had been uneventful, to their great relief. Even so, they were very cautious while pulling back the undergrowth covering the service door that led inside the spaceport. After ten minutes of solid de-weeding, the door was exposed enough to gain access to the main control panel.

"You're up," said Maria, slapping her palms together to shake off the dirt.

Kurren approached the door and snapped open the hatch to the service panel. The screen was blank, but the ports inside looked clear, despite some tarnishing of the metal components. He took out an override jacker from his belt and hooked it up to his PVSM with a short cable, then to the port in the control panel with a second cable. The display screen on the control panel flickered into life, and diagnostic text scrolled down the screen.

"It looks okay," Kurren said, squinting to read the fast-scrolling text dancing across the panel's screen. "The air inside is pretty stale, but not toxic. It looks like the internal air conditioner failed long ago, but the emergency vents opened."

"That means some of those things could have gotten inside," Maria commented, gravely.

Kurren looked over at her, wearing an unusually serious expression. "Possibly, yes," he agreed matter-of-factly, before returning his eyes to the panel. "The generators still appear functional, but they have no fuel," Kurren continued.

"Ironic," Maria quipped.

"The fuel cell backups are intact," Kurren went on, "and remarkably it looks like some still have a bit of juice in. Probably enough for what we need." He stepped back and drew his sidearm. "Ready?"

Maria also drew her sidearm, and then nodded. Kurren tapped a square on the panel and the door hissed open. They were both hit with a blast of cool, stale-tasting air. Without speaking, they switched on the flashlight attachments on their weapons. Kurren went in first, Maria behind, and they advanced down the corridor, carrying out a well-rehearsed dance of advance and cover, advance and cover, ensuring that if anything did surprise them, at least one of them would be in a position to fire. About a hundred metres in to the underground facility, they reached another service doorway. Kurren again attached the override jacker and indicated to Maria that he was ready to open the door. Maria raised her weapon and stood behind the door, poised. She nodded to Kurren, without taking her eyes off the door, and Kurren pressed the button. The doors hissed open, as before, and Maria advanced inside, quickly checking the corners, before moving to cover. Kurren entered and swiftly moved to cover on the opposite side to Maria. The manoeuvre was slick and professional, and went exactly according to their training.

They were now in the main circular viewing gallery, which overlooked the central deck area, from which passengers would transfer into the eight launch bays that led off from the concourse like the spokes of a wheel. It was dark, but there was some light filtering through the open emergency vents in the roof, and it was enough to see by, if somewhat dimly. The roof itself was closed, and roots dangled down from it like entrails. What light there was from above created shadows that danced and flickered along the walls and decking. Both of them switched off their flashlights and stood quietly surveying the landing platform.

"This place looks in bad shape," Maria whispered over to Kurren. "Do you really think we'll find a ship here that can get us back into orbit?"

Kurren walked carefully around the circular viewing gallery, straining his eyes to survey as much of the deck as possible. A port like this, with only eight launch pods, was fairly exclusive, and would typically be used by private contractors and the very wealthy. As such, Kurren had surmised it to be the best place to find a suitable orbit-capable vessel that could have survived these long years. The larger, public spaceports were easy to survey from the base, and intel had suggested these had all been destroyed or very heavily damaged, making this small port their best bet. Kurren's reasoning was that the port authorities would have been unlikely, or simply unable, to requisition a Private UEC shuttle for use in any attempted evacuation, simply because they would not have had security authorisation to access it. As he studied the deck, he saw that six of the eight security doors leading to the launch pods were open, so he knew there was a chance.

Maria half watched Kurren and half watched the shadows flickering around the walls, each one making her gut churn with the fear that it could be one of those things. Wind howled through gaps in the roof and water dripped from the dangling root ends, like blood oozing from an open wound. The place gave Maria the chills, and she was not one to be squeamish. It was why she had been chosen, alongside Kurren, whose bluster was equalled only by his ability to deal calmly with a crisis.

"Well, this is a cheery place," said Kurren, sarcastically, after a couple of minutes had passed, and it became clear they were safe, at least for the moment.

"It reminds me of your quarters," Maria shot back instantly with a crooked smile.

Kurren laughed and shook his head gently. "If only your flying was as sharp as your tongue." Then he stopped and straightened up, military training kicking back in. "There," he said, pointing towards the far corner of the deck. "Outside door seven, there's a UEC emblem on that flight case."

Maria squinted, looking over to where Kurren had indicated. "Are you sure? I can't see it."

"Great, a short-sighted pilot, no wonder we crashed."

"*Landed!*"

"Whatever..." teased Kurren, smiling.

Maria scowled and pushed past him, making sure to stand on his foot, and headed towards the emergency stairwell that lead down to the deck.

"Ow! Hey, where are you going?" said Kurren.

"To get a closer look," Maria replied.

"Hold up, Sal," warned Kurren, sternly. "Take it slow; there could be more of those things in here." He joined Maria and raised his weapon, aiming towards the foot of the stairwell that lead down to the main deck. They both went down together, side-by-side.

"To be honest," said Maria, still smarting from Kurren's earlier comments, "after several days of your stimulating conversation, one of the mindless savages might make for better company."

Kurren snorted. "Good luck with that, even these things couldn't handle your levels of crazy."

Maria laughed and looked back at Kurren warmly. It was at that moment, as Maria faced away from the corridor at the bottom of the stairs, that it came through an open doorway, arm raised, a jagged splinter of metal in its hand.

"Down!" Kurren shouted, and Maria Salus, without hesitation, dropped to the floor, reacting instantly to the command. She was showered with debris and dust as the metal shard swung over her, cutting ugly chunks out of the wall next to where her head had been only seconds ago. Two shots rang out and the figure was hit in the chest and neck. It careered backwards, dropping the weapon onto the hard floor with a clinical, metallic chime, even more piercing than the sound of the gunshots.

Maria recovered and jumped to her feet, weapon at her side. She backed up next to Kurren, and between them they swept the angles, and checked the doorway. Inside, the room was now empty save for some old containers. Neither spoke. They stood, perfectly still, Maria desperately trying to calm her breathing. Then a sound, scuffing on the ground, perhaps something being moved, perhaps something shuffling closer.

"Footsteps?" Maria whispered to Kurren. Her heart was racing, and adrenalin was making her legs shake.

Kurren listened. The sound came again, clearer, closer, and more frequent. "Footsteps," he confirmed.

Maria looked at him, panic starting to swell inside her. But

Kurren was calm and unshaken. His reputation for coolness under pressure was well-earned, and seeing his strength helped Maria to regain her own.

"We're exposed out here," said Kurren, looking around. "We need to get to hangar pod seven, and seal the door behind us. The pods are self-contained, nothing could get in."

Maria nodded, the plan seemed sound. Her heart was pounding, and her hands shaking despite the effort of all of her will to stop them. "But, what if they are already in there?" said Maria, trying to work out all the angles.

"One way or another, we have to fight," said Kurren, stoically. "This is our best shot, Sal." The sounds were getting louder, and more distinct. Kurren looked around, and saw a corridor off to the right. "There!" he said. "That passage will lead onto the deck near to seven." He ran past Maria, slapping her on the shoulder as he passed. "Go!" he shouted.

The slap shook Maria into action, and she took a deep breath and ran after him. The footsteps were getting close now. Lots of footsteps; fast, disorganised, frantic. Kurren reached the end of the passage first and was confronted by a door. Without pause, he shot out the lock and then kicked it open. Seamlessly, he moved through, checking the area beyond. He could see door seven now, tantalisingly close. Maria caught up with him, and swung around to cover their rear. Kurren checked ahead.

"Clear! Let's move, move, move!" he shouted.

Maria went first this time, running as fast as she could. She could hear the heavy clump of Kurren's boots just behind her as they approached hangar door seven. "Cover me!" shouted Kurren, as they reached the door. He flipped open the access panel, and got to work.

Maria moved up behind some crates, stacked a few metres in front of the door, and dropped to one knee, weapon raised.

She flicked the barrel of the weapon from corner to corner, doorway to doorway, watching, waiting. And then she saw them. Fifteen, twenty, maybe more. She couldn't be sure, as she couldn't quite make them out clearly, but they looked different to the thing they had encountered in the house a couple of days earlier. More human, but still not human. Their clothes were tattered and filthy, and some were clearly badly maimed from the way they moved, yet despite their handicaps they came forward at a horrifying pace.

Maria aimed and fired repeatedly, focusing on the ones closest to her, and those moving the fastest. Several dropped to the floor, but there were simply too many. "Hurry!" she shouted.

Behind her, she heard the door start to wind open. When it was wide enough for them to get through, Kurren unplugged his security jacker, slipped underneath and quickly attached it to the panel on the reverse side.

"Maria, get in here!" he shouted through the opening, but Maria did not hear it over the crack of gunfire. She fired again and again, watching body after body fall, but still they came. No more than ten metres now. Kurren ducked down under the door opening. "Maria, get in here now!" came the shout again, at the top of his lungs.

This time Maria heard it, but still she squeezed the trigger. But now, instead of the crack of a round being fired, she heard a click. Empty. Pushing off hard against the crates she was using for cover to gain some initial momentum, Maria turned and ran for the door, ducking underneath at a frantic pace that was fuelled by both adrenalin and fear, but several meters inside the hangar she lost her balance and collided heavily with something solid and metallic.

As soon as Kurren saw Maria clear the threshold, he hit the button and the door began to close. It moved painfully slowly.

"Come on!" Kurren shouted.

He dropped to a prone position and shot rapidly at the horde of advancing creatures, hitting several in the legs, but it was not enough. The door reverberated with the sound of bodies slamming into it at full running speed. Kurren could hear bone crunching, such was the ferocity. He scrambled away, watching as hands appeared under the lip, trying to pull the door open, but it would have taken a hundred of them to even slow it down. Eventually the door closed, thudding powerfully into the locks, and Kurren lay back, exhausted, heart racing and breathless.

Maria tried to stand, but dizziness overcame her. There was a searing pain in her head and she clasped a hand over it, trying to squeeze away the agony. Her eyes began to darken. She heard banging, the sound of flesh hitting metal, a pounding almost as savage as the pain in her head. She fell, and the noises became more distant. Her vision blurred, then came darkness, then nothing at all.

CHAPTER 10

Maria Salus awoke with a start. Her vision was blurry and her head pounded. Groggy and disorientated, it took her several more seconds to realise she was lying down, but when she tried to sit upright, pain shot through her right arm and she collapsed on to her back again.

"Easy, Sal," came a familiar, reassuring voice. "You hit your head pretty hard and your upper arm was cut up. Nothing serious, but it's going to hurt like hell until I can get some meds into you." As he said this, he pressed an injector into Maria's neck and squeezed the trigger.

"Just returning the favour, you know?" said Kurren, before casually discarding the injector. It rattled across the metal floor and came to rest against the wall.

"Should you be making so much noise?" asked Maria weakly, remembering the reason why they were in this predicament.

"I haven't heard anything for a few hours."

"So I take it that we're still alive then?"

Kurren stood up and patted the dust off his legs. "Just about, that was a seriously close one though," he said, honestly.

Maria's vision had cleared enough that she could see the room and Kurren fairly clearly now. "Wait, you said you hadn't heard anything for a few hours," she said. "How long was I out?"

"You've been out cold for a good twelve hours, I'd say," said Kurren, "though some of that was probably due to the initial hit of meds I gave you. Those crazy bastards tried for two hours solid to get in here, bashing at the door with fists, rocks, bars and hell knows what else. Then it sounded as though they just started fighting amongst themselves, and a short while later it went quiet." He removed a pistol from the waistband of his trousers and held it up to Maria with the grip facing towards her. "Here, you'll be needing this again."

Maria looked at the weapon and recognised it as her sidearm. Kurren had flipped the safety back on, even though the clip and chamber were empty. Despite his outward bravado, Kurren was always cautious and professional. She took the weapon and placed it back in her holster. "Hopefully not," she said with sincerity.

Maria looked around the room. In the centre of the hangar, which was a circle around fifteen metres in diameter, was a small transport vessel with UEC markings. "Is that what I think it is?" she asked.

Kurren traced her gaze to the ship and said, "Yep, you were clever enough to discover that earlier on. With your head!"

Maria laughed. "Well, I always was the brains of this operation."

"You almost left your brains all over it," Kurren replied candidly. "Luckily, you have a hard head to match your stubborn nature."

Maria rose to her feet, steadying herself against the wall with her good, left arm. "Does it work?" she asked. "I assume you've taken a look at it?"

Kurren walked over to the side hatch, flipped a panel and hit a button. The side hatch door hissed and slid open, the lower section extending forward to form a ramp into the compartment. "It's a bit dusty inside," he said, wafting the dust away from his face, "but as far as I can tell, it's in working order."

"Finally, some luck!" said Maria, feeling more confident.

"And it's fuelled too," Kurren added. "It looks like some UEC execs were down here when it happened. Luckily, these UEC private transports were pretty well made, so the reactor shielding has prevented any radiation leakage and kept the ore inert and stable."

Maria wandered over and leaned on the ship, peering inside. "Lucky for us those poor UEC suits didn't make it here in time," she said.

Kurren looked over at her and then reached into his pocket and held out a folded plastic wallet. "What's this?" said Maria, taking the wallet and opening it. Inside was an ID card and transport pass.

Kurren looked down at his feet. "That's one of your suits," he said, in a low voice. "Shaun David Fields. Hotshot UEC lawyer, thirty-two years old. Trade negotiator."

"You knew of him?" Maria said, reading the details.

"Nope, never heard of him," Kurren answered. "Probably an arsehole, looking at the self-satisfied smirk in his ID photo. It just makes you think, you know?"

Maria handed the wallet back to Kurren. He took it, but Maria held on for a short while, causing Kurren to look up into her eyes. "It's just another suit, Chris," she said coldly. "Just one of billions, dead long before you were even born. Don't get sentimental on me now, I need you. You're supposed to be the grounded one, remember?"

Maria let go of the wallet and Kurren took it. He looked at it briefly and then tossed it to the floor, where it landed, next to the discarded injector. It was open on the photo of Shaun David Fields, his smug eyes staring timelessly into the room. Kurren reflected on the fact that this man's loss – his death – was their gain. Considering the epic scale of the event and the unimaginable numbers involved, it was easy to forget about individual lives. Maria was right, this 'suit', as she had called him, was just one among billions who had died, or worse, become like the creatures they had faced earlier. When the numbers get so big that you can't even picture in your mind the scale of the loss, it becomes impossible to relate to. One million here... ten million there... fifty million in this city alone. It was easy to distance oneself from the reality of what had happened, easy to disconnect. But this one person; this was easy to understand, easy to feel. How strangely the human mind worked, Kurren thought. If people could feel the loss of millions as keenly as the loss of one, maybe this all wouldn't have happened in the first place.

"Yes, Boss," he said softly to Maria.

The silence was broken by a noise from outside, perhaps a door being opened. Soft footsteps, different to before; more careful, more considered. Kurren and Maria looked each other in the eyes, and there was instant understanding between then. Both drew their weapons and reloaded, as quietly as possible. Kurren moved silently to the far side of the hangar, and stood beside the door. Maria moved cautiously into the shuttle, resting on the hatchway, using it to steady her aim, which was still impaired given her drugged-up condition and bruised arm. Just holding the weapon upright was difficult and painful, but she bore it with gritty determination.

Muffled voices were heard outside, and more footsteps,

then it was silent for a time. Shortly afterwards came the sound of a panel flipping upwards outside.

Shit! thought Maria. *They are going to open the door!* Maria considered that whoever was on the other side must be in a much earlier stage of the disease. More self-aware. She disabled the safety on her weapon and aimed at the hangar door, close to where she had heard the sound. Through the cockpit glass, she could see Kurren. He had shifted position, probably with the same idea. Whatever came through that door would be dead in seconds.

The door mechanism engaged and the motor whirred, lifting the dense slab of metal upwards. Maria tensed, her finger on the trigger, squeezing softly so that just a fraction more pressure would fire the round. The door opened fully and the mechanism locked, still nothing appeared. Maria exhaled, fought back the pain, breathed in and held her breath to steady her aim. A shadow of someone standing to the side of the door spread into the room. It must be daylight outside. It was a huge tactical error, because now both Maria and Kurren knew exactly where they were. Maria aimed fractionally to the left of the door. Her sidearm was powerful enough to breach the wall and, if her aim was accurate, hit whatever was standing outside. She was about to fire, but then a voice caused her to pause.

"Hello? Is anyone in here?" It was a male voice that sounded... normal. Confused, Maria lifted her finger off the trigger, but maintained her aim. Again the voice. "Hello?"

And then Kurren spoke. Loud, clear, confident. "Walk into the centre of the doorway with your arms raised," he commanded. "Make no sudden movements or we will kill you."

Silence. No movement from inside or outside the hangar.

Kurren repeated his command. "Last chance. Walk into the

centre of the doorway now!"

Then the shadow moved, and a figure walked out and stood, arms raised, in the centre of the door arch. It was followed by a second figure with hands also raised, but only about half-way.

"We're no threat," the male voice from the doorway said, calmly. And then he moved into the light. Maria studied him. He was quite young from what she could tell, and tall with an athletic build. His hair was dark, rough and cut short. Good looking, she thought.

The second figure stepped forward now. It was a woman, also athletic, strong and determined-looking, with fiery red hair and intense but pretty eyes.

The male spoke. "We tracked you here from a crashed object," he said. "Something that fell from the sky, back outside the city limits. Was that you? Who are you?"

Kurren moved out from his position, weapon still raised towards them. Maria remained inside the transport, but shifted her position so that she was more clearly visible to the two people standing in front of Kurren. "That was us," Kurren said. "What are you? Are you... like them?" Kurren gestured to the dead bodies still littered outside on the deck.

"If we were like them, you wouldn't be talking to us now," the male voice said. "It's not safe here. We must leave."

"Leave to go where?" Maria replied curtly. Her interjection caused the female to fix her gaze on her. She looked Maria over, obviously sizing her up. Maria felt uncomfortable and threatened. The figures both stepped forward again, now more fully into the light of the hangar. Kurren stepped back, still aiming his weapon.

"No so fast, stay where you are!" he demanded.

The male replied again. "My name is Ethan," he said. "We are no threat to you," he reiterated, this time more firmly. He really was handsome, Maria thought, distractedly, and then chastised herself for letting her mind wander, blaming the drugs for her lapses of concentration. "We are from a settlement, about two days travel away," Ethan continued. "We saw something crash from the sky. We came to find out what it was, and it led us here, to you. We must go; the Roamers will be back soon."

Kurren lowered his weapon. "Roamers? Do you mean... those things?"

"Yes," Ethan replied calmly. "I see you've met some already. We've already lost one member of our party getting here. The longer we wait, the more we risk they will return."

Kurren thought for a moment and then said, "What's your name again?"

"I'm Ethan, and this is my companion and friend, Summer." Summer just glared, but not at Kurren, she was still fixated on Maria.

Kurren holstered his weapon and stepped closer, signalling a gesture of trust. "We came here looking for you, or people like you," said Kurren. "We need your help."

Ethan stepped closer, eager to hear more. Kurren flinched but stayed composed. Ethan sensed that the man was still a little edgy and held back from advancing any further. "Came from where?" Ethan asked eagerly, failing to contain his obvious curiosity. "From the sky?"

"Yes. Sort of..." said Kurren, not really knowing how to explain. And, concerned that their situation was very precarious, he didn't want to get into it now. "Look, we'll tell you everything you want to know, but, as you said, this may not be the best place to do it."

Ethan went to speak again, but Summer stepped between them and exerted control. "Save the questions for later," she said, assertively, directing the comment to no-one in particular, though Ethan felt it was aimed at him. "Grab whatever gear you have and follow us, we'll take you back to our settlement."

Summer stepped in towards Kurren with such intensity that he thought she was about to hit him, and it took a significant amount of self control to stop from raising his guard. He was glad that he didn't though, as he didn't want to appear threatened by this girl, no matter how formidable she appeared.

"You look like you might be useful in a fight," Summer said, gesturing casually towards Kurren, "so you pick up the rear. I'm guessing whatever that is in your side pocket there is a weapon, so be ready to use it." Summer turned away, but then hesitated, and turned back. "Ready to use it on Roamers, I mean, not us." It wasn't said or meant as a joke. Kurren felt a chill go down his spine. He was impressed with Summer's intensity and control, and her awareness. She was clearly no-one to be trifled with. "Hey, you over there hiding in that... thing," Summer shouted. She was referring to Maria in the transport ship. "Are you coming too, or are you just going to sit in there?"

Maria bristled. She did not like this woman's tone. "I'm not hiding," said Maria, through gritted teeth. "And yes, I'm coming." She stepped out from the shuttle and winced in pain. Circumstances had distracted her from her injuries, but the pain was a sharp reminder. She grabbed the door panel of the shuttle to steady herself.

Ethan looked at Maria. Her hair was a dirty blonde, or perhaps just blonde but dirty (it was hard for Ethan to determine, either way) and tied back tightly into a short ponytail at the rear. She had intense blue eyes, and a soft skin colour that reminded him of the pale honey biscuits his sister baked. She was striking, and Ethan found himself staring, something that did not go unnoticed by Summer.

"Are you coming?" Summer repeated, this time more curtly.

Maria's scowl deepened. She had taken an instant dislike to this woman, a feeling that was clearly mutual. She took a few steps away from the ship but felt suddenly dizzy. Her vision blurred again and the room began to spin.

"Maria!" she heard a voice shout. It sounded like Kurren, but she wasn't sure. Everything went into slow motion. She could feel herself falling. Her body hit the ground, but her head struck something soft. She tried to focus her eyes, tried to stay conscious, but searing pain blinded her. Through the fog she could make out a face set against the stark strip lights in the ceiling. A kind, reassuring face. It was the man she had just met and, she realized, he was holding her head. The man was speaking, but the words made no sense. She watched his lips move until she could no longer focus on them. She felt herself moving, being carried perhaps. And then the room faded again as she passed into unconsciousness.

CHAPTER 11

Maria Salus opened her eyes and squinted. The room was dimly lit, quiet and warm, but still the light hurt her eyes and caused a throbbing sensation in her temples. After a few moments, the pain subsided enough to get a better look at her surroundings. She noticed that the ceiling above her now appeared to be made from wood, and as she moved her hands to rub her aching head, she discovered she was in a bed. Wherever this was, it wasn't the hangar in the spaceport. She tried to push herself upright.

"Hey, take it easy," said a vaguely familiar voice from behind her, "you've had a rough night." Then she felt hands on her back and shoulder, helping her to sit up. She looked behind her to see the man from the spaceport. He had been sitting in a chair to the side of the bed.

"There you go," he said, comfortingly. "How do you feel now?"

Maria felt awkward and oddly anxious. Waking up in a strange house in someone else's bed was not how she had imagined meeting the natives. She slowly moved her head and neck and felt the bruises on her leg and side. She still felt pretty rough, but for some reason didn't want to show any weakness to this stranger. Then she realized he still had his hands on her back, and she tensed up.

"I feel great," she said curtly. "Now, do you mind getting your damn hands off me?" Ethan instantly stepped back, surprised by the woman's abruptness, but he also felt embarrassed. Maria sensed his discomfort and pressed her advantage. "Where the hell am I?" she asked, looking straight at him, "And where's Kurren?"

The man looked awkward and a little red-faced, but he was not scared. He was handsome, Maria thought, and she felt instantly ridiculous for thinking this. Now it was her turn to feel embarrassed, and she looked away.

Ethan crossed his arms in an attempt to look less awkward and more assertive. He tried to sound commanding and impressive, but actually came across as a little petulant. "If by 'Kurren' you mean your companion," Ethan said, testily, "he's fine. He's over in the hall talking to the settlement administrator, and a couple of other administrators from nearby settlements." Then he added, with a slight sneer, "I suppose they are trying to figure out what to do with you." Ethan hadn't intended to be so passive-aggressive. He wanted to be friendly and normal, but for some reason he found himself trying to impress her, and this made him feel a little foolish.

Maria raised her eyebrows at the veiled threat. *So he has a bit of fight in him*, she thought. Aloud, she said "Well, that sounds important. Let's get over there." She flung back the covers and swung her legs over the side of the bed. It was at that moment she realized she wasn't wearing any trousers, and in fact was simply in her underwear. Ethan's mouth fell open.

He couldn't help but look. After all, there was a mysterious, beautiful, semi-naked woman in his bed. It was like a dream, literally. He attempted to compose himself, and tried to explain and apologise in the same sentence, and ended up just spouting gibberish. He also wanted to make it absolutely clear that he hadn't been the one to personally undress her, but nothing came out as intended, and in the end he just stood there looking stupefied, with his mouth gaping.

"Where the hell are my clothes?!" Maria yelled, scrambling to pull the sheet back over her bare legs. Her face had flushed a hot red.

Ethan scrambled over to a nearby desk and clumsily gathered up Maria's clothes. "Sorry, sorry!" he stammered, returning back to the bed with a fresh bundle of clothes from the Ranger's stores. He was trying to look away, painfully conscious of the awkwardness of the situation, but this only served to impede his efforts, and he unhelpfully dangled the bundle of clothes just out her reach. Maria stretched forward, trying to grab them, while also trying to keep the sheet tight over her chest, but she only succeeded in sliding off the bed onto her knees, dropping the bed sheet and again exposing her semi-naked body. She let out a gasp.

There was an awkward pause that felt like an eternity. Ethan decided to drop the clothes and try to recover the bed sheet to again shield the woman's modesty. Maria, unfortunately, concluded also that recovering the bed sheet was the best course of action, and as they both reached frantically for the sheet, they inevitably collided, Maria head-butting Ethan solidly in the midriff. There was a muffled grunt and he dropped to the floor like a felled tree. Maria became tangled in the sheet, lost her balance and made a last, desperate, and ultimately futile attempt to avoid Ethan as she fell. The sheet slid under Ethan, and Maria landed heavily on top of him, her breasts squashed up against his face.

And then Kurren walked in.

"Oh! Oh! Oh, damn, oh sorry!" he jabbered, looking at them and then looking away, and then looking at them again, and then away, trying to figure out what to do.

Ethan grappled with Maria, trying to free himself. "I was just helping her to get dressed!" he blurted out, finally succeeding in rolling Maria unceremoniously into a heap on one side. She landed with a thump, becoming entangled in the sheet and the clothes, which had been scattered on the floor.

Kurren, now regaining some of his characteristic composure, naturally found the situation hilarious. "You Planetsiders sure work fast!" he said to Ethan, finding it impossible to stifle a chuckle.

From beneath the sheet and pile of clothes, they both heard a fabric-muffled cry of, "Shoot him!"

"What?" Ethan exclaimed.

Kurren laughed out loud. "Now, Sal, I know you've not always had the best taste in guys, but don't you think that's a little drastic!?"

"Get out!" was the only reply, though it was more of a shriek.

Ethan scrambled to his feet and vanished through the door and into the dusk. Kurren had never seen a man move so fast and, laughing hard, blurted out: "I hope he was worth it, Sal!"

Maria emerged from the pile of clothing. She held the mass of fabric to her chest, which succeeded in partly covering her modesty, albeit rather crudely. She looked half woman, half laundry heap. She was breathing heavily, her blood laced with adrenaline, her face red. When she spoke, Kurren was actually quite scared. "Chris Kurren, you have exactly five seconds to leave this room, or the next thing you'll see, is my fist in your face."

Kurren knew when he was beat. He backed off, hands held up towards the wooden ceiling. "Okay, Sal, okay... I'll see you outside." He began edging back through the doorway, still holding up his hands as if Maria was about to shoot him. But just before the door shut fully behind him, he stopped and called out, "I'll tell your boyfriend that you said he was wonderful..."

As the door closed, Kurren, grinning broadly, heard her scream.

CHAPTER 12

Maria Salus was escorted out into the main settlement square by two men who had knocked on the door of the house about fifteen minutes after Kurren had left. It had taken Maria a solid ten minutes to fully calm down after getting dressed, which she had done at breakneck speed as soon as Kurren had vacated the room. The men had simply asked that Maria follow them to the settlement hall, where she would be reunited with Kurren and the settlement's Chief Administrator. Maria hadn't seen any reason to refuse the request, and was in no mood to ask any questions, as she was still feeling sheepish about the escapade earlier on.

Her flight suit was missing from the room where she had woken up, so she had dressed in the clothing left out for her, which was similar to that worn by the two Planetsiders she had met, and the two men escorting her. She hadn't noticed at the time, for obvious reasons, but Kurren had also been dressed in similar clothing. Using a heavy, thick woven fabric, the garments were well made and warm, and they fitted surprisingly well. She guessed they had been hand-made for a woman of similar build, and she wondered idly whether they had belonged to the red-haired woman who had raised her hackles back in the hangar.

They approached a large wooden structure, which Maria assumed to be the meeting hall. It was quite rudimentary in design, and Maria estimated it was perhaps twenty metres wide and twice that again in depth. The roof structure comprised two sloping sections on each side, forming a sort of rough semi-circle, about five metres high at its peak. Despite its simplicity, it was elegant and quite attractive.

As she approached it, Maria was conscious that she was being watched closely by some of the settlers. The attention made her feel anxious, as if she was still in her underwear, and she checked herself reflexively to make sure she was not. The two men escorting her looked at each other, puzzled, as she did so.

As Maria neared the entrance to the hall she spotted a small crowd at the left-hand side, and some of them had noticed her too. They were standing around a tree, around ten metres tall, with spidery branches that arced off it like wizened old fingers. There were few leaves, and it did not look in the best of health, though that could be said for much of flora on the planet. The branches were adorned with decorations of hand-made ornaments and what looked like a drawing or sketch of a man's face. She was acutely aware of each pair of eyes regarding her with curiosity and, Maria thought instinctively, a fair amount of suspicion too. It felt almost hostile.

She made it to the hall and her two escorts peeled off and stood at each side of the archway like guards. Inside she could see Kurren. He was talking with a man and two women, who Maria estimated to be in their mid-to-late fifties. To the side of them were Ethan and Summer. She felt her stomach twist in knots upon seeing Ethan, and made a concerted effort to not look directly at him. This was a lot harder to achieve than she expected it to be. "Get a grip, Sal," she said to herself, angrily.

"Maria!" Kurren shouted, waving her over. She duly obliged and walked up beside him, taking care to position herself to Kurren's left side, furthest away from the cause of her discomfort. "Maria Salus, meet Talia, the Administrator of this settlement," Kurren said, brightly. He gestured to a thin woman, around a metre and a half tall, with greying hair, a thoughtful face, and a stoic expression that gave very little away. A politician's face, she recognised.

The woman nodded at Maria, respectfully, and then said warmly, "You are welcome here, Maria Salus." Then she turned and with an open hand gestured in turn to the woman and man to her left. "This is Administrator Freya and Administrator Hector," she said. "They are responsible members of the two closest settlements. They have travelled a long way to be here."

"Why?" asked Maria. She was aware that she sounded defensive, which had not been her intention.

Administrator Talia seemed taken aback at her directness, and her expression tightened further. "Your arrival here is quite an event, Maria," said Talia. "Naturally, your presence is a matter of great interest."

Maria recognised the politician's response; the manner in which one can respond to a question without really answering it. "Of course," she said, smiling genially; she could play this game too.

Talia regarded her for a moment and then spoke again. "You were injured and unconscious when you arrived," she said. "Your companion here arrived with you, and our two Rangers, in a transport device from the city."

Maria looked at Kurren. "You found a working transport?"

Kurren shrugged and look smug. "What can I tell you, I'm just that good!" he replied.

Talia's eyes flicked to Kurren briefly and then returned to Maria. Her expression didn't change. The atmosphere felt frosty, and was not helped by Kurren's attempt at levity.

"We are aware of such vehicles of course," Talia continued, "but no one has ever actually seen one in use. So you can imagine that your arrival made quite an impression."

"I apologise for my companion's lack of subtlety," said Maria, playing politician. "We did not mean to startle you."

"Perhaps we should continue this in the chamber, where we can all sit down," said Talia, directing an open hand further into the wooden structure. "We have food and drink too," Talia continued. "It's probably not what you are used to, but hopefully to your liking. So, if you'll follow me, please..." Administrator Talia then turned and started to walk towards the centre of the building. The other administrators followed, wordlessly, while Ethan and Summer waited a short distance away.

Maria leaned in closer to Kurren so they could not be overheard. "What's going on here, old man?" she hissed. "What did I miss while I was out?"

Kurren could see Maria was flustered, despite the politician's front. He took her forearm and gave it a reassuring squeeze. Ethan saw this and found himself glowering at Kurren. Summer noticed and nudged him with her shoulder, giving him a glower of her own.

"Easy, Sal," Kurren said to Maria. "They've been perfectly reasonable so far, considering the entrance we made, though I certainly get the impression that they've been keeping us well out of public view." Maria relaxed a little, welcoming the reassurance, although the news that the settlers had tried to keep their arrival low-key nagged at the back of her mind.

Kurren continued. "You've been out for a day, perhaps a little more. I put you under with the last of the sedation meds to give your body a chance to repair," Kurren took a small box out of his trouser pocket. "Speaking of meds, this is the last of them," he said as he pressed the small box into Maria's hand. She swiftly pocketed it. "I had to argue pretty hard to get them back," Kurren added. "I said we needed them to adjust to the air down here or something like that, but I'd still keep them out of sight." Maria nodded and then Kurren added: "the holo-emitter is in there too, I managed to smuggle that out of my gear before they took it."

"Thanks," said Maria. "That should make what comes next a bit easier. How are we for other meds, by the way?"

Kurren shrugged, "There's enough full doses for another week, maybe," he replied. "Should be enough for us to complete our mission and get off this rock."

"Here's hoping..." Maria said, wistfully. Then she thought of something Kurren had said earlier. "Hey, you said you had to argue to get these things back?"

"Yeah," Kurren replied. "Some older guy confiscated our gear. Another 'Ranger' I think; that's what they call the guards or police or soldiers, or whatever these guys are. Same as the two who found us. You know, the cute red head..."

Maria scowled and interrupted, "Cute?"

Kurren smiled. "Sure, she's cute!" he said. "But so are you. At least, I know someone who thinks so."

"Cut that out!" said Maria, voice raised, finger pointing at Kurren like a gun. This attracted some attention, so she quickly dropped her hand back down to her side, and tried to act nonchalantly. Kurren fought back the urge to dig at her some more.

"Anyway, the redhead is called Summer." Kurren continued, with Maria still scowling at him. "But she's the coldest damn summer I've ever heard of. And the guy with the hots for you..."

"He's called Ethan, I know," Maria interrupted, her voice stern. "Don't push it..." Kurren backed down, trying to look apologetic.

"Anyway, as I was saying, they took our gear," Kurren went on, more serious now. "And that includes our weapons and PVSMs. However, these injector packs have a basic toxicity tester built in, so we can do what we need to do without the main units in our suits."

Maria nodded, and then regretted it as pain shot through her head again. She closed her eyes and rubbed her temples. "Am I... okay?" Maria said, genuinely concerned.

Kurren put a hand on her shoulder. "You'll be fine, Sal, don't worry," he said. "You had a pretty bad concussion, a compound fracture and some bruising. The meds took care of most of it, but you still needed rest. Hence why you woke up in lover boy's bed," Maria jabbed Kurren in the ribs. "Ouch, okay, sorry!" he said, fighting back another chuckle. "Actually, it was Ethan who suggested you stay in his house," Kurren added. "He pretty much insisted, actually. His sister, Katie I think, was the one who undressed you and put you to bed, but the guy sat with you all night. He barely left your side; I think he's kinda smitten with you."

Maria looked down, "That was his house?" she asked sheepishly.

Kurren smiled, but chose not to provoke her any further. Instead, he changed the subject. "While you were out cold, these two other council members arrived," he said, looking over to where Talia and the other two administrators were waiting. "They've been talking in private quite a bit, but to be honest, I haven't felt unwelcome here." Kurren stopped and span on his heels, looking around the hall. "I'm pretty blown away by it all, in truth, "he said. "I half expected them to be savages."

Maria looked up again, grateful that Kurren had stopped teasing her. "Our ground surveys showed evidence of settlements like this on this continent," she said, "so we already knew they had established some simple form of civilisation."

"I know," Kurren shrugged. "Still, I guess I'm just relieved – or maybe impressed – that the people down here are, you know, just normal people."

Maria appreciated the point. She hadn't been sure of what to expect from the people on the planet, and despite knowing from the surveys that there were settlements, she was surprised at how organised, and orderly, they were. "Did you find out any more about what they know?" she asked Kurren. "You know, about us and what happened?"

"I talked to both of them quite a bit on the journey back," Kurren nodded towards the two Rangers, who were still watching them from a distance, mistrustfully. "I kept it loose, tried not to make it too obvious that I was probing."

"Find out anything useful?"

"Bits and pieces," Kurren said, shrugging. "The girl, Summer, kept shutting me down hard, saying it was forbidden to discuss the events before The Fall."

"The Fall?"

"That's the term they use for the refinery event," Kurren explained, "but, although the girl was frosty, it turns out the guy is actually pretty into the subject. It seems to be of genuine importance to him, and he gave up some information just in casual conversation, before the girl stopped him."

"It's forbidden to discuss what happened?" Maria asked, surprised.

"Yeah, seems so," said Kurren. "I'm not sure why, but I'm guessing the stone lady over there will tell us soon enough. The weird thing is, bar this guy, Ethan, I don't think anyone gives a damn. I really don't think they want to know. It will make our job harder."

Maria nodded again. "I'll keep it in mind, and adjust our story," she said. "Hopefully, they are not too closed-off on the subject; I'd hate to have to Plan B this thing."

"I hear you, Sal," said Kurren, solemnly.

Maria looked around. The two Rangers, Ethan and Summer, were starting to look impatient. Maria was about to suggest they move further into the room, but then she became aware of what sounded like singing or chanting coming from outside. "What's with the gathering out there?" she asked, remembering the group of people by the old tree.

Kurren stiffened up slightly, both in body and tone of voice, which is something he always did when he was about to talk about something serious. It was like he flipped a switch in his brain, which suppressed the more roguish side of his personality. "It's a sort of wake," he said. "Apparently, there were originally three of these Rangers who set off to investigate the crash site. One of them, an older, more senior guy called Dorman, was attacked and killed by a Roamer near the ship. The people outside are mourning his death."

Maria exhaled slowly. "That could complicate things. There will be resentment."

"Perhaps," Kurren replied. "I haven't sensed any animosity towards us, just a general air of uneasiness at us being here. But the reception from Administrator Frosty over there..." he cocked his head in the direction of Talia again, "...is beginning to make me wonder."

There was an audible and very obviously-faked cough, and they looked over to see Summer standing, hands on hips, looking at them with widened eyes. She didn't need to say, 'What are you waiting for?' because it was written plainly on her face. Ethan, on the other hand, was looking down at his feet, absent-mindedly scuffing one boot on the wooden floor. The attempted nonchalance was so evident that Maria almost laughed out loud.

"Well, I guess we should get in there," Maria said loudly, while looking Summer dead in the eye. If looks could kill, Maria expected she would now be dead.

Kurren took the cue, and they both headed off towards the chamber, followed closely by Ethan and Summer.

CHAPTER 13

They were seated at a large square table made of a dark-coloured hardwood. Around the table were eight chairs. Talia sat at the head, with the other two administrators either side. Kurren and Maria sat next to each other on the left-hand side of the table, with Ethan and Summer opposite them. They had been speaking for around five minutes, with Talia doing most of the talking. The conversation had started well enough, with pleasantries and formalities, but soon there were awkward silences, during which time the administrators looked apprehensively at each other.

Maria and Kurren began to suspect that this meeting was not reactionary, not an ad-hoc response to an unexpected situation, but part of a plan or contingency. It was simply too organised, too calm. It suggested preparation. But Maria wondered how these settlement leaders could be prepared for the arrival of visitors from off-world if they knew nothing of the events that led to The Fall?

The sense that the administrators knew more than they

were letting on was seemingly shared by Summer and Ethan, who had both worn anxious frowns from the moment they sat down. They were, in fact, surprised to be sitting down at all, having expecting to be asked to leave; they had even attempted to do so, but Administrator Talia had told them to stay. They both now sat at the table, arms folded, looking confused and slightly worried.

It was Administrator Talia that broke the awkward silence. "Well, I think it is perhaps time we moved onto the subject at hand," she said.

Maria recognised the politician again. They had exchanged platitudes, but throughout it all, Maria had sensed no warmth from the older woman, very little curiosity, and also no surprise. It was the latter that bothered Maria. Talia was not surprised by their sudden appearance, and had reacted more as if they were estranged family members, finally returning home, for reasons as yet unknown. It was suspicion that Maria felt most strongly from Talia. Simmering just beneath the surface, there was also fear.

"Clearly, from the way you were dressed and the rather unconventional manner of your arrival, you are not from one of the neighbouring settlements," Talia continued, "So, Maria, tell us, where are you from?"

Neither Maria nor Kurren quite expected her to ask the question so directly, and both were caught a little off-guard. They looked at each other and then Kurren nodded toward Maria, and sat back slightly. They had, of course, discussed and planned how to handle this situation during the mission preparation, and it was agreed that Maria would be the one to explain the story. Despite Kurren's cutting sense of humour, he had a very direct and unsubtle manner when it came to more serious conversations and negotiations. The virtual switch in his brain would flip again, and he would talk as if giving a military briefing. Both felt that this formal delivery lacked the human touch needed to tell their story. Kurren had also suggested, in a blatantly sexist way as Maria had complained at the time, that it might 'sound better coming from a woman'. Kurren insisted he simply meant that women were more empathetic and sensitive, though Maria knew full-well that what he really meant was that Maria could use her 'womanly charms' to win them around, and she had chastised him for this at the time. In what turned out to be an equally sexist assumption on their part, neither had expected to be talking to a female leader.

Maria cleared her throat and tried to remember the content of the briefing she had prepared for this occasion. This was more difficult than she had imagined due, in no small measure, to her still being slightly concussed.

"Thank you, Administrator Talia," she began formally, trying to set a serious tone. "You are, of course, correct, we are not from any of the settlements on this planet." Maria noticed that Ethan had leaned in and was giving off the expectant wonder of a father about to witness the birth of his first-born child. He was holding his breath; it felt like he was about to explode. Talia and the administrators, on the other hand sat in quiet anticipation. Summer had her arms folded and looked angry. Maria tried to ignore her, and returned to her briefing. "We are part of what was known as the Universal Energy Corporation, an organisation that existed on this planet, before the events that led to its near annihilation. We came here, at great risk, from our base – our home – on the moon orbiting this planet."

"The moon?" said Talia, unsure of whether she had heard correctly.

"You're from the moon?" Ethan added, unable to contain his astonishment, but the stern look that followed from Talia encouraged Ethan to fade into the background again.

"Yes," said Maria, half looking at Talia and half at Ethan, noticing his far more positive and interested reaction. "Well, yes and no," Maria corrected herself. "It's hard to explain. Our ancestors were from the planet, the same as yours, but ours were trapped in space, on a city on the moon, while your ancestors were here, Planetside." Talia's eyes widened. "I know this must sound crazy to you," said Maria, realising that saying she was from the moon, out loud, sounded a bit ludicrous even to herself, "but, please give me some time to explain." Maria looked around the table at the different expressions; a mix of shock, confusion and fear, all except for the Ranger, Ethan, and Talia. Talia did not look shocked, but she did now appear more anxious than earlier, and this gave Maria an unsettled feeling. Eventually, Talia asked that Maria continue.

"We understand that you know little of the events that led to the catastrophe that left this planet, and its population, in ruin," said Maria. "We even know that this is a subject you actively avoid, as is the topic of what existed before 'The Fall', as you call it." At this, Talia raised an eyebrow and glanced, very briefly, over towards Ethan. But Ethan was transfixed and unaware of Talia's silent accusation.

Maria took out the small injector pack that Kurren had given her earlier and placed it on the table. The Planetsiders all eyed it with suspicion, especially Talia. "This device will project some images," Maria continued. "The images will describe what happened far better than I can in words alone. You no doubt won't have seen anything like this technology before, but it is harmless, so please don't be afraid." She pressed a button on the device and a panel slid open, revealing an emitter array. Moments later, the device hummed into life and began to display a three-dimensional, holographic image of a planet with the UEC logo hovering above it.

This time Talia was visibly startled. Her eyes flicked from the images over to Maria and back. The other administrators started to chatter to each other nervously. Ethan was wide-eyed with wonder, but Summer had slid back in her chair and appeared deeply uncomfortable with the object and the images it was displaying.

Maria continued, hoping that the novelty of the emitter would soon wear off. "The reason we are here concerns both The Fall and what happened before it," she said, talking louder to be heard over the chatter. The administrators fell silent. "Put simply, we need your help," she said once quiet had resumed, "because our people are in grave danger."

The atmosphere was tense and electric. She glanced back to Kurren, who had kept silent, as was the plan, but she could tell from his eyes that he was concerned. The meeting was already balanced on a knife's edge, and Maria had much more to tell them. She wasn't sure if they could handle it, or even want to listen. But she had no choice, she had to try. She tapped the emitter panel and the picture switched from the UEC logo to an image of a planet, hovering above the table like an apparition, steadily rotating.

"The moon base was owned by an organisation called the Universal Engineering Corporation – the UEC. Prior to The Fall, the UEC was responsible for mining and refining orrum, a precious mineral found only on the moon, that was capable of generating huge amounts of energy." Maria tapped the emitter again, and it zoomed in to the planet to show a great city as if viewed from high in the sky. All eyes were on the image, all except Talia's. She continued to look at Maria.

"Prior to The Fall this planet was home to billions of people," said Maria, choosing not to look directly back at Talia, but instead at the images in front of her. "The population was spread across the entirety of the planet, concentrated in megacities. Much like the city where we found you," Maria added, gesturing over towards Ethan and Summer.

"Where we found you, you mean?" Summer interjected bitterly, staring intensely at Maria. "You would still be out there, rotting in the remains of your precious city had it not..."

Talia cut her off, sharply, but without raising her voice any more than was necessary. "That's enough, Ranger," the older woman said, fixing her with an equally sharp stare. Summer backed off, but looked furious. "Let us hear what Maria has to say," Talia added, looking back at Maria. But despite the interjection on her behalf, Maria was not comforted. She could feel her pulse starting to quicken. The room was turning against her.

"Everything depended on orrum," Maria continued, trying to not let the strain show in her voice, "and the mining, refining, transportation and use of orrum to generate power for the cities and its inhabitants was the cornerstone of civilisation on this world."

As Maria spoke, the holo-emitter showed images of the moon and of the substance – orrum – which, to Ethan's eyes, looked much like any other large lump of rock. Maria continued to present a potted history of the planet, the holo-emitter following her words, showing images pertinent to the content, as if it were listening to her voice and reacting independently to help tell the story.

"To ensure that the supply and use of orrum was secure, the controlling alliances agreed that an independent body should act as protector, ensuring non-interference. This organisation was GPS, or Global Power Security, and it was resourced with people from all allied continents, with the sole mission to police and protect orrum production." The emitter now displayed the emblem of GPS, which was a circle, representing the planet, with a clenched fist in the centre, palm facing out towards the viewer. As Maria continued, the images switched again, following her words automatically.

"GPS protected the UEC from criminal elements, rogue factions and states, and from itself," continued Maria, "and they provided oversight for the UEC's own internal security service. Collectively, GPS enforcers numbered more than any civilian police force, and also any army," Maria paused, letting what she had said sink in, and then added, "and it was here that things began to fall apart." Maria took a sip of water. She noticed that Summer was staring down into the folds of her arms, and rapidly bobbing her leg up and down, like it was attached to an electric current and unable to remain steady. Ethan was looking directly at Maria, hanging off her every word, but his expression had become noticeably more solemn as the briefing had progressed.

"I take it that relations with GPS took a turn for the worse?" asked Talia, to Maria's surprise. This was perhaps an obvious assumption, but her composed delivery and evident lack of surprise made Maria wonder if she was actually telling the older woman something she didn't already know.

"Yes," Maria said, trying to emulate Talia's composure. "GPS made a play to control orrum completely; to own the Global supply and distribution of energy and to control energy security for the entire population. It would have made them the unchallenged Global superpower. They would have had command over every continent, every government, every individual. But they failed."

"War," Ethan said quietly.

Maria, half-hearing him, looked over and was surprised to see that Ethan was head down, staring at the table, his earlier brightness and enthusiasm diminished. "I'm sorry?" she said, awkwardly.

Ethan raised his head and met Maria's eyes. "You're saying

all of this was the result of a war."

Maria could now see a sadness in the young Ranger's eyes that she had not seen before. In others, perhaps, but not in Ethan. "Yes," she replied, sombrely, "the last war. At least, the last to take place on the planet." The holo-emitter switched to a new view, and began to re-enact key moments from the conflict, in time with Maria's narration. "The UEC had a comparatively small, but well-trained security force," said Maria. "They were a last line of defence, in the unlikely event that GPS was overpowered. We had trained for small-scale terror attacks, we had trained for counter-insurgency, and for counter-espionage. But we never expected to be defending ourselves against our own protectors."

Retelling the history, Maria also felt a sense of sadness wash over her, but she pushed it down, determined not to lose focus. She had yet to explain why they were here and, in retrospect, wished she hadn't begun the briefing by discussing the conflict at all. When planning the mission it was thought that recounting the history of the conflict would provide necessary context, and also help to engender trust through openness and honesty. But it was now clear that this was a mistake. Instead of building trust she was stoking their fears and creating a rift between them, but there was no going back now. She continued, quickening the pace of her speech. The holo-emitter responded in kind, speeding up to stay synchronised.

"The attack was unexpected, co-ordinated, and on a massive scale," said Maria, watching the emitter display the events as she told them. "UEC installations all over the planet, such as the space port where..." Maria paused briefly, remembering Summer's earlier reaction, and adjusted her words, "...where your Rangers discovered us," she said carefully, "were all overrun. Orrum shipments were seized. GPS had succeeded in all but one area; if they were to achieve their goal they had to take the primary UEC mining control base on the moon. They assaulted, but the UEC forces pushed them back. The moon base was a veritable fortress and well protected, but had one major weakness. In order to transport the vast quantities of orrum around the planet, the UEC, over a period of decades, had built an orbital refinery and distribution network. It was an incredible feat of engineering, encasing the entire planet, like a net."

The holo-emitter switched to a display of the planet, rotating slowly, and everyone watched as a monumental web of metal and machinery gradually built up around the sphere. Underneath was a number, steadily increasing as the contraption evolved and expanded. Ethan considered that this might be time, perhaps years. If so, the refinery was a long time in the making. Maria indicated to sections of the display, and the emitter obliged by zooming in.

"The Refinery had distribution nodes located above every major capital and city on the surface," she said, highlighting some of the megacities, "but, ultimately, it was linked to the moon base at one key location, like an artery leading to the heart. This artery was the most sophisticated element of the refinery, as it had to detach and re-attach to the refinery in perfect synchronisation with the relative motion of the moon and planet. When connected, it opened a conduit that led directly into the moon base, allowing for vast quantities of orrum to be fed into the refinery from the mines on the moon. But it was also an unrestricted path into the base, and a passage GPS needed to control. Unfortunately, the attack went catastrophically wrong."

The holo-emitter zoomed in to the moon base to show a number of objects, similar to the shuttle they had found crashed near the city, swarming around the refinery's metal skeleton, plus a single and much larger vessel, waiting further away. Maria reached into the display and seemed to physically manipulate it. "GPS calculated that they could attack the primary valve and detonate a small amount of orrum," said Maria, pointing to where the refinery's vast umbilical conduit adjoined to the moon base. "Orrum is highly explosive and unstable in raw form, so in order to breach the primary valve and create an opening directly in to the moon base, GPS intended to detonate the orrum travelling in that section of the conduit. But they miscalculated." Maria gestured to the emitter and it showed the vessels firing weapons of some kind at the base of the conduit, followed by a flash as the conduit exploded. The light from the emitter shone so brightly that the observers had to squint and shield their eyes.

Maria continued, even more urgently. "Instead of breaking a hole in the valve, they caused a chain reaction in the conduit," she said. "The initial blast destroyed the attacking ships, and the shock wave pushed this larger support vessel into a higher orbit, taking some damage, but nothing critical." Maria highlighted and zoomed in to the larger vessel they had seen on the display earlier. Ethan, Summer and the Administrators watched the holo display showing the vessel spiralling away into space, partially on fire, the flames dancing around it like ethereal, glowing liquid. "The explosions cascaded along the conduit," Maria continued, and the emitter switched back to the base and the metal umbilical stretching from it, with explosions rippling along it. "The cascade eventually hit the first refining node, which contained refined orrum in additiona to the raw orrum flowing through the conduits. Together the explosive force was amplified more than a thousand times."

The holo display showed the explosion. Even this small recreation lit up the room, causing everyone to again squint against the brightness. In the glow, Maria saw Ethan's face.

Gone was his eager excitement of earlier, replaced now by shock, but still in his eyes she could see the wonder. Maria supposed that he was getting what he desired, though perhaps they were not the answers he'd hoped for. The light diminished and the holo paused, waiting for her next words. Her throat was dry. She moistened her lips and continued; conscious that the room had been silent, save her own voice, for several minutes.

"The explosion caused a cascade reaction," Maria went on. "It ignited the orrum in the conduits, which in turn led to other nodes, like touch paper. As each node exploded it spread the fire to an ever-widening web of conduits. It quickly grew out of control." The holo zoomed out, and showed the progression of the cascade. As each node detonated, it lit the 'touchpaper' trail to other nodes, expanding exponentially around the planet with each explosion. A chain reaction like that could have only one end. Everyone watching could see it, and even though Maria and Kurren had witnessed this re-creation a hundred times, its impact on them had never diminished.

"There were disaster plans for isolated events, of course," Maria continued, "but these assume the UEC and GPS would collaborate to have an emergency response to combat any fire spread. But no contingency plan had accounted for the UEC and GPS being at war with one another." The emitter pulled back to show the cascade of explosions rippling around the planet. "In only a few hours the fire had spread through the entire refinery. Every node, above every population centre on the planet, detonated with a force beyond imagination. The refinery was completely destroyed, with terrible consequences..." she faltered as the holo display switched again, zooming in to an individual node as it exploded. The viewers looked on as fiery debris erupted in all directions, spreading and overlapping the expulsions from adjacent nodes and eventually shrouding the atmosphere in a tormented blanket of burning metal and rock.

Maria forced a dry, painful, swallow and continued. "The fragments of the refinery fell into the atmosphere," she said, watching the emitter replay the events as she told them. "The larger pieces penetrated the atmosphere and bombarded the surface, destroying every major population centre." The holo emitter moved on to display images of burning hulks of metal and rock slamming into cities and towns on the surface, and exploding with a ferocity that made the Planetsiders in the room gasp, even Talia. Summer clasped a hand over her mouth, while Ethan nervously clenched his hands. Neither could tear their eyes away from the images. "The smaller fragments burned up in the atmosphere, polluting it and causing toxic rains that fell for years afterwards," Maria finished, solemnly. "The effect was a near-total annihilation of the planet's population."

There was a moment's pause, as the holo display reached the end of its depiction, and gently turned off, with a soothing hum and slow dimming of its light. The grace with which the emitter ended its story was so at odds with the violence of the images it had displayed that it only added to the intensity of the event.

Eventually, Talia spoke, her eyes burning with intensity. "But we survived," she said, looking at Maria. "We are here!"

"Yes," Maria said, her voice trembling slightly. "Some of the suburban areas escaped the heaviest bombardments, and more remote areas and populations were less severely hit," she hesitated, "but there is more..."

"Killing everyone on the surface not enough for you, was it?" The interjection was from Summer. She had been silent for long enough.

Maria looked over the table and saw the flame-haired warrior staring at her with dagger-like eyes. Maria chose not to respond directly, and instead continued to direct herself to Talia, albeit a little more hesitantly than before. "A side effect of the detonations on the surface was a spread of toxic dust. The chemical composition of this contaminant had disastrous effects on our biology, mutating genes and causing irrecoverable neurological damage. It would begin relatively benignly, but as the damage progressed over time, the affected would begin to lose all sense of self and all emotional empathy, turning into a base, almost primal being, yet one that still possesses the knowledge and core abilities they had prior to being affected."

Ethan had no idea what the words, 'biology', 'genes', and 'neurological' meant, but he knew precisely what Maria was referring to. "The Maddening," he said, sombrely. Ethan had come into this room expecting knowledge to set his mind free and help him put his life into perspective, but nothing he had learned had made him feel any easier, and more in control. If anything, he felt foolish for being so naive.

Maria looked at Ethan. He had the look of a man who had been told an awful secret and instantly regretted knowing it. Maria could tell that Ethan was in turmoil. "The Maddening, as you call it, is not really a disease," said Maria, "it is worse. Those who survive long enough eventually change. They become something else; something... inhuman."

"So why are we not affected?" asked Talia. It sounded like a challenge.

Maria shifted in her seat. She was not used to the bare wooden furniture and was starting to feel numb. "You are second-generation descendants of people who survived," she said. "Your grandparents and great grandparent were not affected because of a very rare natural immunity, which you have inherited."

"Oh, aren't we so special and lucky?" It was Summer again, the bitterness clear in her voice.

Talia looked over at Summer and held a hand up. Summer bit her tongue, but her eyes remained fierce and locked onto Maria. "So that explains us, Maria," said Talia, a little frostily, "but, forgive me, we did not ask for or desire a history lesson, and you have still not explained why you are here."

Maria nodded. "No, I understand, but the background is important as to why we're here, and we also wanted to show that we're not your enemy."

"That remains to be seen," snapped Summer. "Just get to the point." This time Talia failed to reprimand her. Clearly, she mirrored her feelings, and was also beginning to become frustrated. The girl was starting to grate on Maria now, but she pushed her anger aside. Now was not the time.

"We're here because of your immunity to the toxic effects of orrum radiation poisoning," said Maria, unable to fully mask her own irritation. "We do not possess the same resistance."

"Why do you need to?" said Talia, confused. "You don't live here."

"No, I appreciate that, but it wasn't only the planet that was affected by the collapse of the refinery." Maria replied, feeling now that the meeting was a mistake. Perhaps Plan B should have been their first choice, after all. "The moon was also bombarded with debris, albeit to a far lesser degree," she continued. "Many died, but the structure of the base, and the lack of atmosphere, meant that contamination was largely averted. But not prevented entirely. We had to fight to survive, just like you."

Summer spat out a laugh. "You're nothing like us!" she cried, enraged. "You're the cause of all this. Whether directly or indirectly, it doesn't matter. You're the reason why there are so few of us, fighting to survive, living in fear every day from Roamers and The Maddened. It's all because of you!"

Maria tried to reason. "We didn't cause this; we were victims, like you. We were attacked!"

Summer stood up angrily, throwing the chair out from behind her. It crashed against the wall and broke. "Victims!?" Summer yelled. She hammered her fists on the table and leaned in, glaring at Maria. "Dorman was a victim," she added, coldly. "Go and tell his family how we should feel sorry for you. Go on, they're just outside."

"Please, this isn't helping," said Maria.

"Go outside and tell them!" Summer screamed.

Since Maria's presentation had ended, Ethan had been quiet, lost in his own thoughts. Much of the last few minutes had washed over him, registering more on a subconscious level. War had always been a theory, of course, amongst the few who ever talked about The Fall, but to Ethan it seemed impossible. What war could possibly have led to such destruction, and for what purpose? Surely, one side would want something to 'win', so there would have been no reason to lay waste to everything. And since all that remained after The Fall was a desperate few survivors, Ethan never believed in the war hypothesis. To him, the only logical explanation was some sort of natural disaster – on a catastrophic scale, to be sure – but not engineered or contrived by human minds. And, as one of the few who had seen the great machines in the cities, he had always held out a faint hope that some had escaped the devastation, and fled to faraway, safe lands, or even to the stars, and would one day return and help rebuild their world.

Maria had shattered these fantasies in less time than it took Ethan to cook a meal. War had been the cause; their ancestors had been at fault. And though some did survive, out in the darkness above them, they were not saviours. They had come here looking for their help. Boiled down to the basic facts, it was almost an insult, and Ethan could see why Summer was angered.

Ethan simply felt like a naive fool. He had encouraged the search for these people, and persuaded the administrators to hear them out, confident in his own mind that they were on the verge of some universal truth, something that would give them hope for a better future, maybe give them direction. But, here they sat, the cold truth laid bare. And the truth was that two strangers had come, asking for help, and the administrators wanted no part of it. The story of The Fall was like a cautionary tale – a fairy story – taught to children to make them fear the past, so they would look to the future, free from its corrupt influence. These two strangers were a living reminder of that time, an embodiment of everything the settlers were taught to fear. But Ethan was not afraid, and he would not abandon the visitors. Perhaps it was guilt over Dorman's death in pursuit of his own, selfish obsessions, or stubborn pride, or just a need for something good to come from this, but Ethan would not let them be pushed away.

He looked up at Summer, her clenched fists still pressed into the table, unable to contain the anger that was now spilling out of her in the direction of Maria Salus, as if this woman alone was responsible for the billions that had died. For the death of her own mother. As if by pushing her away, by hurting her, it would somehow make up for everything that had happened. Ethan resolved there and then not to allow it. He would stand up for the strangers, even if no-one else would. It was his responsibility. And, perhaps, somewhere along the way, they would help him find the meaning he still desperately needed. He had to believe that was possible, because he had to believe in something.

Ethan stood up and turned to face Summer, his back to Maria. He tried to inch her away from the table, to cut them off from each other, so that Summer would focus on him, and not her anger. He reached out and held Summer's shoulders, and looked into her eyes. "Hey, Summer, back off," he said calmly, assertively. "These people weren't even born when The Fall happened. They came looking for our help."

Summer looked back at Ethan with an expression that was a mixture of surprise and disgust. She firmly pushed Ethan away and took three paces backwards, leaving a clear gap between them. Her fists remained clenched at her sides, but her dagger-like stare had returned to Maria. She did not want to meet Ethan's eyes, because she knew he would douse the rage she felt, and she still wanted to feel it. She wanted to direct all her anger at this woman. Ethan would calm her, and Summer knew it. He had that power.

"I don't want to help them," Summer said bitterly, still looking at Maria. "I don't want them here at all." Then she dared to look at Ethan, her resolve set. "All of this, it means nothing," she said, shaking her head. "What does it matter how it happened? The planet is still dead."

"They didn't kill it, Summer," said Ethan, trying to reason.

"It makes no difference," said Summer, not understanding why Ethan had jumped to the defence of these strangers. Her anger was now directed at him. "They are not like us," she continued. "We owe them nothing! Let them solve their own problems, like we've had to."

Ethan tried again to move closer but Summer recoiled. He held a hand out towards her, hating that she was distancing herself from him, but hating more that he empathised with what she was saying, but was choosing to set himself against her. "Pushing them away won't change anything either," pleaded Ethan. "Okay, I admit it, this is not the answer I'd hoped for. And maybe I was wrong to bring them here, to convince you to go looking for them with me. But it's done, and I will not turn my back on these people now."

Summer recoiled. "But you'd turn your back on us? On me?" she said, aghast. "How many more have to die for your quest, Ethan? When will you accept that there are no answers? There is just this life. It's just us. We have to stick together."

"We survived by helping each other," said Ethan, upset that Summer had used Dorman's death against him. She knew Ethan well enough to predict the guilt and shame he would be feeling over the Ranger's death, and by bringing it up, publicly, she meant to hurt him. "You're just angry," Ethan continued, feeling the anger swelling within himself. "I know you; you wouldn't abandon someone in need. That's not who you are." He was pushing now; he wanted to force her to see his point of view by challenging her own sense of pride and honour. But Summer was in no mood to be manipulated.

"I know who I am, Ethan," she said, defiantly, "and I know you, better than you know yourself. I'm telling you now, none of this... this childlike pursuit to find your angels – it won't bring them back." Now it was Ethan who recoiled. His stomach twisted into knots and he felt sick. "Your parents are dead," Summer continued, callously. "It was senseless, and that's just the way it is. No flash of light across the sky will make it any different. No mystical truth. It's time you dealt with it!"

Ethan dropped his head and stared aimlessly at the ground, words escaping him. Summer did know him well; better even than Katie. Ethan had confided in her, as one of the few people – perhaps even the only person – that he trusted and connected with. And now she was using it against him. But worse than this, she was right. "Summer, I..." Ethan tried to speak, but faltered.

Summer knew she had struck him hard by bring up his parents' death, and instantly regretted what she had said. Guilt stabbed inside her, but she was still too angry, too proud, to take it back. She hated that Ethan could not be happy in the settlement, with this life, with her. She wanted to hurt him, to make him see her pain and anger. It would be easier than telling him what was really in her heart. Part of her wanted to say sorry, to run over and hold him, to tell him she loved him, and that he should live in the now, with her, and stop looking to the stars. She wanted to be the light that fills the void a meaningless death leaves behind. She wanted to heal him, but she could not. So instead, she would hurt him.

"'I'? 'I', Ethan? Forget about yourself for one moment!" Summer would not let him speak, would not let him get to her. There was no way back now, she had committed. "What about Elijah? Elijah needs you! Does he matter less than these strangers? What about your sister, should she lose someone else she loves because of your obsession? You should be ashamed of yourself!"

"Summer, please!" Ethan implored. But she would not be placated, not this time.

"No, I've had enough of this!" she spat. "I've had it with not being enough, so go! You're more like them than us anyway," and she pushed past him and ran out of the room before Ethan could have a chance to stop her, to make her relent.

"Summer, wait!" Ethan called after her, but she was gone. He ran after her, desperate for her to understand, to tell him he was right. That he should help them, and she would help them too. More than anything he wanted her support. But this time he was truly on his own.

CHAPTER 14

There was a long and uncomfortable silence. Summer's resistance had long been clear, but the outburst was unexpected, at least to Maria who was feeling numb and anxious. She was not quite sure what sort of reaction she'd expected, but certainly nothing so vehement and hostile. Maria looked at Kurren, and there were even cracks showing in his armour, with sweat beading on his brow. The other two administrators were talking to each other in hushed voices, while Talia simply watched the two visitors, with implacable, eerie coolness. Finally, Maria decided to speak.

"Should... should you go after them?"

"No, I think it is best to let them go," said Talia, calmly.

Maria opened her mouth to speak again, but nothing came out. They had prepared contingencies should there be resistance towards them. Different arguments they could make, and different ways to convince them. But this situation was like nothing they had planned for. Talia looked almost smug. Had she planned this? Had she allowed this meeting knowing how it would self-destruct and leave no choice but to turn them away?

"We have not been entirely honest with you," Talia said, cutting the silence again.

"Oh?" Kurren said, defensively. "And how is that?" It was the first time he had spoken since they had all sat down. Now, realising that their plan had failed, and sensing a darkening mood, he would be a silent partner no more.

Talia regarded Kurren for a while, taking her measure of him. He held her gaze, not blinking once. "It is true that we know little of what happened before The Fall, Mr Kurren," said Talia. "But you are mistaken if you think that we know nothing. Furthermore, you are not the first remnants of the pre-Fall civilisation to visit here." Maria was surprised by Talia's sudden honestly, and it showed on her face. Talia appeared more relaxed and forthright now the Rangers had left. "It was many years ago, more than a generation ago in fact. And their story was different to yours, as they had not intended to come here. They had crashed, like you. Shot down, as it happens." Kurren flinched at the mention of this. "They too spoke of a conflict," Talia continued, "although the detail of that meeting is lost, the outcome is well-remembered, at least amongst the administrators."

"The outcome?" said Kurren.

Talia sat back in her chair slightly and folded her arms. "Unfortunately, they did not... integrate very well," she said.

"Integrate?" Maria repeated, confused.

Talia looked at her and her lip curled slightly, betraying some emotion for the first time. It appeared to be a sore point. "Yes, integrate, Miss Salus," she said curtly. The switch to 'Miss Salus' was telling, Maria thought. The tone of the conversation had certainly turned. Talia continued. "You have already seen the effect that talk of The Fall and what came before has on people. It divides us, Miss Salus. We, here on this planet, are the survivors of your fallen civilisation. We have battled hardships you cannot comprehend to survive and leave that time behind. And we want no further part of it."

Kurren now also folded his arms. "It seems that at least one of you does," he said.

Talia's eyes flicked over to meet his. "Ethan is a romantic," she said. "There are very few of those left in this world. The hard life we lead tends to drain the idealism from people, and leaves us only with essential truths."

Maria felt the hair prickle on the back of her neck. It matched the spiky atmosphere around the table. She said calmly, "And what is the truth, Administrator Talia?"

Now Talia's expression betrayed her feelings. She was angry, and it was starting to bubble to the surface, despite her attempts to mask it. "The truth, Miss Salus, is that you represent a world that no longer exists, and that your very presence here serves to create disharmony and division."

Now it was Kurren's turn to betray some anger. "You set this up, didn't you?" he said. "You knew that the girl, Summer, would explode, and you knew it would create a rift between her and the kid? You're setting them against us, hoping he'll side with her."

"You set them against each other when you arrived," replied Talia.

"Don't you even want to know why we're here?" asked Maria.

"I don't care why you're here!" Talia retorted, bitterness clear in her voice and expression for the first time. Whatever she was holding beneath the surface was close to flowing over. Talia appeared to recognise this and drew back, taking a deep breath and exhaling it slowly, before adding, "All that matters is what happens now."

Maria understood the meaning. "You mean, whether we 'integrate' or cause more trouble," she said, pointedly.

Talia did not respond directly to the question, but Maria could see the truth in her eyes. "You are free to remain in this Settlement," Talia continued, "providing you play a role here like everyone else. This is what the previous visitors we mentioned failed to do, and why they volunteered to go their own way."

Maria wondered what became of them, and just how voluntarily they had left. Given the bleakness of the landscape, and the danger from Roamers, she imaged they did not last long. In fact, without meds, they probably succumbed to the Maddening themselves and became of one the creatures they had fought and killed. Not a fate she wished to share.

Talia was still speaking, "... and on the clear understanding that you do not discuss where you are from, or what you know of The Fall with anyone in the settlement."

"And if we don't comply with your conditions?" Maria was careful to keep the tone of the question neutral, so as not to betray any rebellious intent.

There was a brief silence as Talia also considered her reply. "Then we will provide you with supplies and equipment, and you may follow the path of your predecessors and leave."

Maria nodded, the reality of the situation now clear to her and, judging from the look on Kurren's face, to him too. Not so voluntary, after all, she thought. Kurren looked over at Maria and there was an unspoken understanding. The contingency plan would be required, it seemed.

"Can we have some time to think about it?" Maria asked.

This appeared to surprise Talia, who said "of course you can, Maria." The familiar, subtle smile was back again, along with the intentional switch back to first names. "You may remain in the settlement, under the charge of the Rangers until you reach your decision," said Talia. And then she added, almost warmly, "We could certainly use people of your abilities around here." Another brief pause followed and then she added delicately, "To avoid any further... excitement... I would require that you remain out of sight until you decide."

"We understand, of course," said Maria, and then she made the first play of their contingency plan. "Perhaps we can stay with the Ranger, Ethan? He's already aware of us, and maybe we can help to smooth things over with him. He seemed pretty upset, and that's our doing."

Talia was clearly suspicious of this request, but she didn't want to expose the visitors to any more of the settlement's inhabitants than was necessary at this point. "Very well," she said. "But Summer will also accompany you."

Maria's expression remained calm, though inside she was cursing. She knew the addition of the firebrand Ranger, Summer, would make their task harder. "Of course," she said, mirroring Talia's half smile.

Talia rose, and her silent companions rose with her. Maria had almost forgotten they were even in the room. "Very well then, Miss Salus, Mr Kurren," Talia said as she waved a hand to the two Rangers who had initially escorted them to the hall, and were now standing at the back of the room. They walked over. "The Rangers will escort you back to Ethan's house," she added, looking directly at Maria. "We will talk to Summer and explain the situation. We'll have them both meet you there, with some food and hot water."

Maria bowed her head respectfully, "Thank you, Administrator Talia." She rose and turned to face the Rangers, who were stony-faced and unwelcoming. A soldier is a soldier, no matter where they are from, she thought. Kurren rose also, thanked Administrator Talia for her time, and turned to stand beside Maria. Then, with escort in tow, they began walking back to the house where Maria had awoken earlier.

Quietly, so that no-one else could hear, Kurren whispered, "The guy is our best chance. He may even want to come."

"I don't know," Maria replied in hushed tones. "Before this I would have agreed, but he looked shaken. The girl laid into him hard."

Kurren contemplated this for moment, and then said, with some hesitation, "You... you can help make him want to come with us, if you know what I mean? You know he's sweet on you."

Maria felt the knot inside her stomach return. She wanted to punch Kurren in the eye, and were it not for their current location, she would have done.

CHAPTER 15

Maria and Kurren had been in the Ranger's house for only a few minutes when Ethan's young nephew, Elijah, walked in. Ethan had not been there when they arrived, so while the other Rangers stood guard outside, Maria and Kurren had quietly discussed their tactics, checked their toxicity levels – which were creeping steadily towards the amber, but still fine – and taken another dose of meds.

"Hey, Ethan, are you in here?" Elijah shouted as he bustled in through a back door that neither Maria nor Kurren had spotted, since it was obscured with a curtain. The surprise entry startled them and made them jerk around to face the young boy. Equally, the shock of seeing two complete strangers in his uncle's house drew Elijah up short. But he was not afraid. "Who are you?" he asked, filling the void with his inquisitive, confident voice. And then before either of them could answer: "Hey, you're the ones from the crash, right? The people my uncle found?"

Maria looked at Kurren, hoping for him to take the lead –

she wasn't used to children – but he just shrugged, unhelpfully. Maria rolled her eyes and looked back at the boy. "That's right," she said, in a friendly tone, "so, Ethan is your uncle?"

"Uh-huh," the boy replied, "I'm Elijah. Uncle Ethan told me a little bit about you already, before my mum said he should stop." Kurren chuckled and Maria dug him in the side. "He said there was an older guy, a soldier I think," Elijah then pointed at Kurren, "I guess that must be you," Kurren didn't have time to confirm the boy's assumption before he added, "and a blonde-haired pretty lady." Maria blushed. Kurren laughed out loud. Maria dug him in the ribs again. Blissfully unaware of the embarrassment he had just caused, Elijah continued talking. "So, why are you here? Are you from space? Ethan said you might be from space!" the boy blurted out with barely a breath between sentences. Maria had no time to even consider a response, before Elijah, unable to contain his excitement at meeting these mysterious travellers, asked a further question. "Are you angels?"

Maria was totally lost for words, and looked at Kurren, imploringly, for help. Kurren smiled at her, and then stepped out a little closer towards the boy. "No, we're not angels," he said, and then held out his hand towards him. "Commander Christopher Kurren, space soldier, at your service," he said in his best military voice, but with a wry smile. Elijah didn't really know what to do so he stuck out his hand too. Kurren took it and shook it vigorously, making Elijah jolt up and down. "Pleased to meet you, soldier, welcome to the space corp!" Kurren said enthusiastically as Elijah bobbed up and down, giggling.

Taking her cue from Kurren, Maria walked over and back-slapped Kurren. "At ease, Commander," she said, mimicking Kurren's faux military voice. "I'm Maria... I mean, Space Pilot Captain Maria Salus, or Sal to my fellow pilots," she said nodding her head towards Elijah, and then saluting. Elijah let go of Kurren's hand and returned the salute, clumsily, a huge grin on his face. Maria lowered the salute and smiled. Then she asked, "Hey, what did you mean just then, when you said, 'are you angels'?"

"Oh, it's what we call the flashes of light in the sky," said Elijah, pointing up towards the ceiling of the house. "You can see them at night. Ethan told me they are angels that watch over us to keep us safe from Roamers and The Maddening. We've all got one, us survivors that is. Hey, I wonder if you've seen them?" Maria opened her mouth in an attempt to answer, but no words came out. As it happened, it didn't matter, because Elijah just carried on talking, ignoring his own question. "Mr Boucher, he's the scholar here, says it's the only bit of history that's worth knowing. Uncle Ethan doesn't agree and calls Mr Boucher an 'ignorant old bastard', whatever that means." Kurren laughed and Maria rolled her eyes at him again. "Ethan likes to watch them at night," Elijah went on, "the lights I mean. And so do I, when he lets me anyway."

Kurren and Maria felt out-of-breath just listening to him. As he was talking, Elijah walked over to the kitchenette, opened a cupboard and took out a wooden box. Inside were some biscuits. Elijah took one and held it in his mouth, and then held out the box towards them, inviting them to take one too. Maria took two and handed one to Kurren.

"Thank you, Elijah," said Maria.

The boy said something, but it was just a muffled jumble of sounds because the biscuit was still held between his teeth. Maria took a bite of the amber-coloured biscuit and was pleasantly surprised to find it was sweet and delicious. "My mum makes them, she's the baker," Elijah said proudly, having removed the biscuit from his mouth. He then walked over to the table and sat down, remarkably at ease, considering he'd only met them moments ago.

"She's great at her job, these are delicious," Kurren said with his mouth half-full.

"So what are you doing here?" Elijah asked again. "Ethan said he wasn't allowed to tell me, and mum says I should mind my own business. So it must be important!"

His smile was infectious. Maria laughed and sat down at the table next to Elijah, nibbling a corner of the biscuit. Elijah was looking at her expectantly. "If your uncle and mother said you shouldn't know then we should respect their wishes," Maria said, and Elijah's face fell.

"But you look like a man who can handle super important, secret information," Kurren said.

"I am! I am!" Elijah replied, unable to contain his excitement.

"Okay then, soldier," Kurren continued. "We're here for your help. Our home base, on the moon, way up there in space, is in trouble, and we think your uncle might be able to help us save it, and everyone living up there."

"Kurren..." Maria said severely, giving her companion a dirty look.

Elijah didn't know what to process first, the fact they were from space, or that there was a base on the moon, or that somehow Ethan was the key to saving it from whatever grizzly fate it was destined for. "Ethan will help you!" he said excitedly. "He's a Ranger, that's what they do. Oh please let him!"

"Please let him what?" a voice came from the direction of the doorway. Startled, Kurren, Maria and Elijah all turned to see the figure of Summer standing just inside the room, hands on hips, her face scornful and wary. Elijah was about to say, 'help the space soldiers to save their moon base,' but Kurren was quicker to react and spoke before he had a chance to drop them in it.

"The young man here wants me to show him the vehicle we arrived in," Kurren lied. "But I said the settlement administrators wouldn't allow it."

Elijah closed his mouth, remembering what Kurren had said about the information being 'super secret', and felt both sheepish for nearly revealing the secret, and slightly guilty at now being complicit in a lie to his Aunt Summer.

"That right, Elijah?" Summer said looking at the boy, clearly still highly distrustful of Kurren.

Elijah committed to the lie, partly because he was afraid of being told off by Summer – or worse, his mum if Summer told her – but largely because now he really did want to see the vehicle that Kurren had just referred to. "Oh yeah, that was it," said Elijah, casually. "Can I, Aunt Summer, please?"

Out of sight of Summer, Kurren winked at Elijah, and this made him feel slightly better, but still a little uneasy. Maria couldn't help pick up on the fact that Elijah had called her, 'Aunt Summer'. "So, are you and Ethan siblings?" Maria said to Summer, mostly to change the subject, but she was also genuinely interested in the answer. "It's just that he called you Aunt Summer".

Summer appeared to be annoyed at the question. "No, we're just..." and she faltered for a moment, searching for the right word, or at least for the word she wanted to use with these strangers, "...just friends," she said, cautiously. "We grew up together, not that it's any of your concern."

"Summer and Ethan grew up together with mum, after mum and Ethan's parents died in a fire a long time ago," revealed Elijah.

"Elijah!" Summer snapped.

"What, Aunt Summer? It's true isn't it?" Elijah said, unsure as to why Summer was so cross and angry, which was very unlike her, at least with him.

Summer took her hands off her hips and attempted to soften her tone. "Yes, it's true, Elijah, but it's also personal," she said, "and we don't know these people. You shouldn't trust them."

"They seem nice to me," he replied, honestly.

Maria stood up, "I'm sorry; we didn't mean to cause any trouble."

"You've already caused plenty," Summer said, managing to keep her seething rage under control, for the sake of Elijah. She did not want to alarm him. "Elijah, run home now and fetch your uncle, he's over at your house."

"Okay!" Elijah replied, chirpily, and he got down off the chair and ran out.

"Take care, soldier!" Kurren called as Elijah passed him, tossing a casual salute in his direction.

"Yes, Commander!" the boy replied, a wide smile on his face. He turned his head towards Kurren and returned a lazy salute, and seconds later he was out of the door.

When he was gone, the air in the room seemed to thicken and become suffocating. Summer bristled. She jabbed a finger aggressively towards Maria. "Stay away from him, do you understand me?" she demanded.

"Calm down, he walked in while we were here," Maria replied, disliking her tone even less now. "What would you have wanted us to do, throw him out?" Maria had grown tired of Summer's relentless hostility and now, away from the Administrators (and the need to show restraint), she was close to her limit of patience.

Summer strutted over to Maria and stood tall, muscles tensed, barely half a metre away.

"Woah, hey, take it easy now you two!" said Kurren, holding both hands up, palms facing outwards, as if he was trying to placate an angry dog that was about to pounce. But neither woman was listening.

Summer jabbed her finger into Maria's sternum. "I expect you to do what I tell you to do, got it?"

Maria snapped and slapped the hand away. It was like springing a trap. Summer swung first, but Maria blocked the punch and pushed away, giving herself room to strike. But Summer was fast, and came at her again, breaking through Maria's guard enough to land a blow to her side. Maria shifted position and swung back with a forearm, which Summer ducked, but she failed to anticipate Maria's follow-up, which struck her to the side of the head, knocking her off balance.

Maria's fighting style was new to Summer, who had not anticipated her ability, but she wouldn't make that mistake twice. Maria advanced, trying to follow up her advantage, but Summer moved aside and landed a swift kick to her side. Maria backed off, clasping a hand to her ribs, bracing them against the pain. Summer's guard was still raised, her expression composed and serious. This was no spar. Summer was determined and Maria could see that she meant to do her real harm. She switched up a gear, and raised her guard in response. Both ignored Kurren's repeated calls for them to stop.

Maria moved first, stepping in with a jab and then landing a right cross. Summer felt blood trickle from her mouth, but stayed focused and blocked the next attack, countering with a fast left hand, which stunned Maria. Summer moved in, grabbed Maria's arm and then swung her using all her weight into the cabin wall. The whole building seemed to shake. Maria winced, and took another punch, before she could recover. Summer had the advantage now and tried to grab Maria, looking to choke her, but Maria slipped in a skilful knee to the kidneys, followed by an elbow that sent Summer reeling backwards, colliding with the table in the centre of the room, knocking the cups and the box of amber biscuits onto the floor. The biscuits rolled away into the far corners of the room, like frightened mice scurrying from a predatory cat.

Summer looked winded, but also furious and feral. On the table there was a knife. Summer took it without hesitation, rage surging inside her like a volcano about to erupt. She was not used to being tested in a fight, and the fact that her equal was this woman, this trouble-causer who had somehow wheedled her way into Ethan's mind, made the taste of blood in her mouth all the more bitter.

Maria saw the knife in Summer's hand and her face fell. A brawl was one thing, but adding a knife into the equation escalated this into a fight for survival. She looked desperately around the room for something she could use to defend against this weapon, but there was nothing. Summer's eyes burned and adrenaline pumped through her veins. She stepped forward, knife angled with deadly intent and was about to lunge at Maria when a voice resonated through the room with a power equal to their fury. It was not Kurren, who was still looking on, helplessly, but Ethan.

"Stop!" he shouted again. Both women remained in fighting positions, guards raised, but both looked over at him. The blade in Summer's hand glinted ominously. "What the hell are you doing?" he demanded to know, with a mixture of anger and exasperation. There was no immediate response as Ethan moved into the room and stood between them, facing Summer directly and focusing all his attention on her. She glowered back at him, angry that he had stepped in to defend this stranger again.

"Get out of my way, Ethan," she growled.

"Summer, put the knife down," Ethan insisted.

She didn't move. "You take her side and we're done," she said, now even more furious at Ethan than at the other woman.

"What are you talking about?" said Ethan, stepping closer. Summer recoiled. "Give me the knife."

Summer tried to run past him, but he caught her hand and, expertly, disarmed her. The blade flew across the room and then clanked and scraped across the stone floor. The violent noise seemed to wrestle Summer from her frenzy. She looked at him, still clearly filled with bile, but no longer with murderous intent.

"This is not the way," Ethan said.

Summer ignored his words, and shook his hand loose from hers. "She was talking to Elijah, Ethan," Summer said, as if it was a crime. "Who knows what lies they've been feeding him. I don't trust them, especially her," she looked over towards Maria, who had lowered her guard, and had a hand again clasped to her bruised side.

"Elijah was here?" Ethan asked.

"He came in while we were waiting for you," said Maria between laboured breaths. Ethan turned his head slightly to see her, but not so much that he could not also still see Summer in his peripheral vision. "We were just talking," Maria continued. The interruption was tactical. It was both an attempt to diffuse the situation and also prevent Summer from telling her version of events first and setting Ethan against them.

Summer again tried to advance on Maria, but Ethan caught her and pushed her back. "You're lying!" she raged, before trying to rush Maria for a second time. Ethan caught her again, but this time he held her tightly.

"Summer, I think you should go," Ethan said, his voice firm.

Summer looked wounded and stared, imploringly, into Ethan's eyes. "Ethan, there's something they are not telling us," she pleaded. "Why do you keep defending them? We're a team, me and you; we always have been. What's gotten into you?"

"I'm still on your team, Summer," Ethan said, hurt by the accusation. "And I understand, I do." He loosened his grip on her a little so it was less of a restraint and more of a reassuring embrace. Summer softened into it, her muscles relaxing slightly, and Ethan felt confident that she was now not likely to try to charge off and kill Maria. "Let me handle this, okay?" Ethan said holding her. "Go get some rest, and some food, maybe. Katie will sort you something."

Summer shook her head. "You're too close to this, Ethan," she pushed away a little and looked into his eyes. "You want to believe them, but its blinding you to what really matters."

She meant Ethan's family, but really she was thinking of herself. She hated how Ethan had latched onto this pair, and especially to the woman.

"Summer, I don't know what I believe anymore," said Ethan, and the truth of this statement surprised even himself, "but I do know you're tired and angry, and that's a bad combination for you."

Summer took a deep breath, and rubbed her aching jaw. Ethan's admission of doubt was at least some comfort to her. Maybe she wasn't losing him. Maybe the stranger's revelations about The Fall had not given him the answers he'd hoped for or wanted. Maybe the truth was not worth him giving everything up. It gave her enough confidence to feel safer leaving him, at least for a short time.

"Okay, I'll go for now," said Summer, "but they are not staying together. This one..." she pointed at Kurren, who up until this point had been very happy to sit on the sidelines and stay out of the drama. He looked worried at being drawn into the proceedings, and awkwardly pointed at himself, as if Summer could possibly have meant someone else. "He comes with me back to the Ranger hut," Summer insisted. "He can sleep there. I don't want them together."

"Okay, Summer, that's a good plan," said Ethan, eager to grab any opportunity to diffuse the situation and get Summer away from Maria, before they decided it was better to attempt killing each other again. "You take him with you and I'll stay here with Maria." Maria watched on, anxiously; her muscles still tight and aching from the strain. She couldn't help notice that Ethan used her name, 'Maria', but referred to Kurren simply as, 'him'.

Summer closed her eyes and held them shut for a second. *Damn*, she thought. She had instantly regretted her suggestion, because although it seemed sensible to separate the two visitors, she had also inadvertently engineered a situation where Ethan and Maria would be alone together. She opened her eyes and looked at Ethan with a solemnity that he had not seen in her before. "Be careful around her, Ethan. She is not what she seems, I can feel it." Ethan frowned, unsure why she was so hostile to Maria in particular, but he nodded in acknowledgement, even if he hadn't really understood her meaning. Summer then backed away, glancing briefly at Maria, her eyes conveying her feelings in no uncertain terms – she was her enemy and there was unfinished business. Then she turned her attention to Kurren. "Come with me, now," she ordered.

"Yes, ma'am," Kurren replied, his tone still belying some of his customary candour, but not enough to come across as sarcastic or insincere. Without hesitation, he set off towards the door, with Summer following closely. "I'll see you tomorrow, Sal," Kurren said in a matter-of-fact manner just before passing the threshold. It seemed unnecessary to say anything, but Maria knew what he meant by this, and why he was being so atypically compliant. The opportunity for Ethan and Maria to be alone was part of a plan they were trying to engineer. Luckily, circumstances had created the opportunity for them, naturally, without any plotting or scheming that could unravel and cause suspicion.

Summer followed Kurren out of the house. But before she left, she paused and turned back towards Ethan. "Remember what I said," her tone was firm, serious. "She is not one of us." And then she left, not giving him an opportunity to reply.

When they were alone, Ethan and Maria stood in the room, trying to avoid looking at one another. Maria suddenly realised that she would have preferred a fight to the death with Summer, over being alone with Ethan. At least then she would have had some level of control.

It was Ethan that finally plucked up the courage to speak. "I'm sorry about Summer," he said, softly, looking into her eyes. "She is only worried about me. We live on a knife's edge here as it is, and change makes people anxious and scared, you know?" The use of the phrase 'knife's edge' was perhaps not the most tactful, and Maria caught sight of the blade that Summer had intended to use on her nestling in the corner of the room.

"Don't worry about it, it's understandable," she replied, forcing herself to look him in the eyes. She felt the knotted sensation in her gut again, although couldn't be sure if it was because of Ethan, or because of the various punches that Summer had landed. "She's just protecting her own, which includes your nephew." Bringing Elijah back into the conversation was deliberate. Now that it was clear that the settlement's leaders were not going to cooperate, their only option was to gain Ethan's trust and friendship, and make him want to defy the leaders and help them anyway. Maria knew what she had to do, but it didn't sit well with her knowing that she was intentionally trying to manipulate him.

Ethan smiled. "Yeah, he's an interesting one for sure. Curious, like his uncle. It drives his mother mad."

Maria laughed and smiled back. It was a genuine reaction;

Maria liked this young Ranger, and though she had denied it to Kurren, there was an attraction on her side too. Kurren hadn't believed her – he knew Maria too well – and had cautioned her to keep her mind clear, and to use Ethan's feelings to their advantage. Maria hated how he could be so callous, but he was also right. Maria was aware of how Ethan looked at her; how he was looking at her right now as she laughed. Kurren was right, Ethan was undeniably attracted to her, and Maria knew these feeling could be manipulated. And although she hated herself for it, there was a mission to be completed, and so it had to be done.

Now that Maria had relaxed and dropped her guard, she was suddenly aware of her stinging jaw and aching stomach muscles. Summer had certainly not held back. She rubbed her face. "Your friend sure knows how to hit," she said, almost with admiration.

Ethan stepped close to Maria and, without invitation, held her face in his hand, and inspected her bruised jaw. Maria didn't know what to do. She was uncomfortable with being scrutinized, but at the same time the feeling of Ethan's hand on her face was thrilling. She tried to fight back the feeling. *Mind on the mission, Sal, mind on the mission...*

"It doesn't look bad," said Ethan, in a matter-of-fact way. "She normally knocks out a tooth or two, so you've either got a really hard jaw, or you're a pretty decent fighter yourself." His tone was jovial, friendly. He gently let go of Maria's face and stood there, smiling at her, his hands on his hips.

"It doesn't feel like I got off lightly," said Maria, mindlessly stroking the area of her face that Ethan had just held. "If you hadn't come in when you did, I think she would have gutted me like a fish with that knife over there."

Ethan glanced over and spotted the knife, glinting ominously by the wall. "No, I don't think that's likely," he said, his mouth curled into a slight smirk. He left a pause, inviting Maria to ask why.

"Why?" she obliged, still smiling.

"She wouldn't know how; all the fish died decades ago," said Ethan, grinning. "Squirrel, though. We have loads of those still." They both laughed, and smiled at each other. The tension between them had ebbed away and she was starting to feel comfortable being alone with him. She really did like him. *Damn, Kurren, you smug bastard, why do you always have to be right?* she thought.

"Are you hungry?" asked Ethan, remembering that he was meant to be playing host. "I mean for something other than my sister's biscuits."

Maria thought that if Kurren were here now he would have grinned and twisted this innocent offer into some sort of sexual innuendo. "Sure," she replied. Ethan walked over to the table and invited Maria to sit down. She accepted the offer and hobbled over to the chair, wincing as she discovered several more aches and pains from the fight. Ethan then moved over to the wood-burning stove in the far corner of the room, which was also acting as a heating source for the small house. Out of a cupboard, he took out some boxes of ingredients, and some utensils. He talked while doing this, his back to Maria.

"We don't have an enormously varied menu, I'm afraid," said Ethan. "But we've a good stock of hens, and wild mushrooms grow in and around the settlement in pretty plentiful supply at this time of year. We have some sheep too, and they keep us stocked up with butter and milk." He cracked some eggs into a bowl and started mixing them, then cut some mushrooms and threw them into a flat pan, which he had placed on the stove with some of the butter he had just mentioned. The mushrooms were starting to sizzle; Maria had never smelled anything like it before. Her mouth was watering.

She'd forgotten how hungry she was. Ethan threw in the whisked eggs, and adjusted the position of the pan on the stove, varying the heat.

"That smells incredible!" Maria said, closing her eyes to intensify the experience.

"Wait till you taste it," said Ethan, glancing over his shoulder at her. "This is a speciality of mine. It's all in my secret blend of herbs." Ethan took a pinch of herb mixture out of a small pot and sprinkled it into the pan.

"We don't have animals on the moon base," Maria said, "all of our proteins are manufactured. Though we do grow vegetables, partly because that's good for the air supply, and for making the base look less sterile." She knew she was taking a risk by bringing up the moon base, but she had not actually planned it as a way to steer the conversation in any particular direction. She just felt like talking about her life.

Ethan was silent for a few moments, working the pan to shape the mixture as it set, and then expertly turning it out onto a wooden platter. He brought it over along with a couple of forks and placed it on the table in front of Maria. He stood on the other side, leaning casually on the wooden surface, watching her. "After you," he said, handing her a fork.

Maria tried the food. It was delicious, and packed with a richness of flavour that she was not used to, especially after several days of ration packs. Nothing like this existed on the base. Their engineered proteins certainly didn't taste bad, but this was a revelation. "This is incredible!" she mumbled, her mouth full of food.

Ethan laughed, and cut off a piece for himself. He tried it and, with an exaggerated, thoughtful look on his face, contemplated the food in his mouth, and then agreed that it was indeed a culinary masterpiece. This made Maria laugh and almost choke at the same time.

"Not just a pretty face then," Maria teased. "Ethan, brave Ranger and flamboyant cook."

Ethan bowed elaborately with a flourish, accepting the compliment. Maria's laugh again came, naturally, easily. She sat there looking at Ethan and toying with the food on her plate, knocking pieces from side to side and taking occasional bites, in between smiling at him.

"Does nobody cook for you back home?" Ethan asked. Maria's eyes widened slightly. Was he trying to ask if she was in a relationship or single, she wondered? Should she tell him she was single, or keep him guessing? She reprimanded herself for again acting like a love-struck teenager. *Get a grip, Sal!* she told herself. She was glad that Kurren was not here to witness this; it would give him ammunition to use against her for years to come.

"We don't really cook, our food comes pre-prepared, in individual portions," she said, and then realised how boring this answer was. *He must think you're scintillating, Sal,* she told herself.

"So, what do you eat up there, on your moon base?" Ethan said, continuing to probe about Maria's home. "From the mildly ecstatic look on your face while eating that, I'm guessing you don't have eggs."

The question caught Maria off guard, partly because she was trying to work out what her 'ecstatic face' looked like, and if this was a compliment or not. But also because she was surprised how easy it was to get Ethan talking again about their base, despite what had happened in the meeting hall earlier.

"Are you okay if I talk about it?" she asked, making sure she was on safe ground. "I mean, I know I sort of brought it up earlier, but I don't want you getting into any trouble." Maria meant this genuinely. She didn't want Ethan getting into any trouble. But then she realised how foolish this was, considering that it was her mission to get him talking. She felt a twinge of guilt again; she did not like this duplicity, and the more time she spent with Ethan, the more uncomfortable the thought of deceiving him became.

"I think it's okay," he said and laughed. "I don't think knowing what food you eat is really the sort of seditious knowledge that Talia is trying to protect me against."

"You might not say that once you know what – or who – we eat," Maria replied. This time it was her turn to curl her lips into a mischievous smirk.

Ethan raised an eyebrow. "Is that why your people are in danger?" he asked with mock surprise. "Because you're eating each other?"

Maria laughed again – another easy, comfortable laugh. She noticed she was twirling her hair, and stopped abruptly, and obviously. This didn't go unnoticed by Ethan, and Maria screamed internally again. The funny thing was that this encounter had felt more like a date than any actual date she had been on in years, perhaps ever. She didn't find it easy opening up to people, which was a consequence of the often secretive nature of her work. But this felt good. Until she remembered what she was supposed to be doing here. She swallowed hard, and tried to focus on the task, fighting the urge to just carry on enjoying her time with the charismatic young Ranger.

"You are more comfortable talking about moon bases and all the other forbidden topics than the others around here," Maria said, trying to lead them on to the subject of why Maria was here. This double-dealing robbed her of the giddy, elated feeling she had had moments earlier, when they were just chatting freely as two people, getting along while sharing a meal.

Ethan looked at her for a moment, considering his response. He was surprised to find that, for the first time in as long as he could remember, he didn't actually want to talk about The Fall or anything related to it. He was too caught up in the here and now, and Maria's question had brought a sobering reality back to their interaction. "I used to believe it was important to learn about our past," he said, choosing his words carefully, "but after today, I'm not so sure." Speaking these words out loud, he surprised even himself.

Maria understood now how much the briefing, and Summer's outburst towards him, had rattled him. But she believed that deep down he still wanted to know more. She decided to gamble a little and push him. "Ethan, you do know that we can't stay here, and become part of your community?" Maria said with a dispassionate coldness that was the opposite of her earlier flirtatiousness. She saw in Ethan's face a slight narrowing of the eyes and tightening of his jawline that betrayed either discomfort or irritation. Maria pushed some more. "If you can't help us we will have to leave," she went on. "You heard our story, but missed the end. Don't you want to know why we need your help?"

Ethan held up a hand, "Maria, please, we're not supposed to talk about it..."

"Sal," Maria said, cutting across him.

"I'm sorry?" Ethan said, confused and distracted.

"Call me Sal, Ethan. Only people who don't know me, or don't like me, call me Maria."

Ethan was thrown off guard a little. "Okay, Sal... Well..." he stumbled over his words.

"Look, you're true to your people, I understand that," Maria continued, not allowing Ethan to voice further objections. "But I came here, risking my life, to help my people. You're not the only ones who have suffered. We've also lost so much..."

Ethan stood up, flustered. "Look, Maria... I mean Sal. We

can't discuss this. I don't want to discuss it. I'm going to leave and come back later." He turned and tried to escape through the door.

Maria got to her feet, worried that if Ethan left she would not have the opportunity to be alone with him again. She panicked and, remembering what Elijah had told her earlier about Ethan's family, tried a riskier strategy. It was her best shot to reach him. "Haven't you ever lost someone, Ethan?" Her voice was cold. Ethan stopped. "Tell me you wouldn't do whatever it takes to help the ones you love. If it meant saving your sister. Saving Elijah. Saving your parents, Ethan? Tell me you wouldn't risk everything, including your own life, the same as I have."

Ethan felt anger building inside him. What right did she have to talk to him about loss? She knew nothing of the loss and suffering that people had endured on the planet over generations. And all caused, he now knew, by a petty and pointless war for power. He turned to face her, and Maria could see he was angry. "You don't get to talk to me about loss," he said bitterly. "Everyone here has lost someone. And every day there is the threat we'll lose more. Every day here is a fight for survival. Can you say the same, up there on your base?"

"Ethan, I'm sorry, I didn't mean to..." Maria tried to apologise. She had pushed too hard, and she was losing him. More than that, she had hurt him, and that made her deeply uncomfortable.

"And you're right," Ethan continued over Maria's attempts to apologise, "I do want to know why. Why so many died, why we survived. And then why, after all of that, The Maddening came to corrupt so many of those who escaped the initial horrors into something... inhuman. I *do* need to know why."

"I didn't mean to upset you, Ethan, I was just trying to help you understand," Maria said, trying to close the gap between them, but Ethan still looked too defensive, too angry. She stopped a few paces short, and he turned away.

"I was excited when I saw the crash," Ethan said, calmer now, but still facing away from Maria. "I thought maybe this was it, finally some answers. I left my sister and Elijah here, without my protection, and I found you. I really did hope you'd be able to help me understand. But now I regret knowing what you told me. It just makes it all the more pointless."

It was starting to make sense to Maria now. The disappointment that Ethan must have felt when hearing the story of The Fall, and it not matching up to his expectations. All Maria had done was deliver a bitter reality, instead of the idealised fantasy that Ethan wanted to hear. The fantasy that somehow it had all been an accident, and that there was a way to make sense of everything, and to move forward, leaving the darkness behind. What a disappointment she must be to him. She stood there looking at him, wanting to help him, to ease his pain. But how could she help him when she was responsible for destroying what little hope he had left?

"We have always been taught that we were special, did you know that?" Ethan said, turning again to look at Maria. "That the ones who survived were protected by guardians in the sky who watched over us, making sure we were safe, as long as we believed in them. But I stopped believing when my mother and father burned to death in a fire, leaving me and my sister alone. My parents believed in these 'angels'. So did I, until they let my mother burn."

"Ethan, I'm so sorry, I..." Maria tried to interrupt, but Ethan wasn't finished.

"Not a week goes by that I don't wake up, sweating, feeling like my heart is going to explode in my chest, reliving that day," said Ethan, his voice wavering. "Seeing the smoke and the flames. Hearing my sister sobbing beside me. And looking up and asking, why? Why did you not protect them? I stopped believing then, but I never stopped wanting to understand why." He took a deep breath and exhaled, then walked over to the window. The shutters were still open and he peered through, looking up at the sky.

Maria watched him, conflicted. Part of her wanted to go to him, to tell him she was sorry and to forget about everything she'd said. But the other part knew that she couldn't do that, the mission depended on it.

"And then you appear from the sky, and I wonder if there could still be some truth to those stories," continued Ethan. "And you know the really great part?" Maria shook her head, though Ethan could not see it. "The best part is that you're not guardians or angels, but the ones who actually caused all this suffering in the first place!" Ethan laughed bitterly and turned to face Maria again. "And the real gut punch is that you come asking for our help, lecturing me on loss." Ethan was angry and upset and it was all focused on Maria. "Tell me, Maria Salus, what can you possibly know of loss and suffering compared to what we've endured?"

The words stung Maria. She felt sorry for Ethan's loss, and upset that she had raked these feelings to the surface, but she was not responsible for the death of his parents, and it irked her that Ethan would assume his pain to be greater, without even knowing what she'd been through herself. "I really am sorry, Ethan," she said, her own anger acting as an anchor that centred her emotions, and allowed her to regain her composure and dispassionate, military temperament. "I can see how much of a disappointment I must be to you." Ethan realised he'd gone too far. He wanted to tell her that she wasn't a disappointment, and how much he liked her, but it didn't seem like the right time. Maria looked wounded, and she lashed out like a wounded animal with her words. "But I didn't kill your parents," she went on, feeling the need to defend herself, "and you have no right to assume your loss is greater than mine; you know nothing about me."

Ethan shook his head. He was not interested in a debate over whose loss was greater, not after everything that had happened. He was angry that she couldn't see how much of his world she had torn down. He was angry that she would now try to trade her loss against his. "Well I know one thing," he said, bitterly. "I know Talia was right. Nothing good can come of this. You should go, go back to your moon base and leave us alone." He turned again and headed for the door, determined this time to leave.

Maria was still reeling from their exchange, and she wanted to hit back, but she knew this would push him away. And despite the way she felt, she couldn't let that happen. There was no more time for subtlety or nuance, it was now or never.

"If you walk away then I'll die, Ethan."

The words electrified the air as if lightning had struck the room. Ethan stopped a pace short of the doorway. He stayed there, in the shadows, letting the words sink in. "What do you mean?" he said, his voice betraying obvious concern.

"Without your help, we'll all die," Maria repeated, her voice now a little shaky with nervous energy. This was a risky play. She had put all her cards on the table. "You want to talk about loss, Ethan? There are only a few hundred of us left, and soon we'll all be gone."

"Are you...?" Ethan began, struggling to ask the question for fear of the response. "I mean... how soon?"

"Soon," replied Maria, as calmly as she could manage, but the stress was taking its toll, and she could feel her emotion rising to the surface again. "Something terrible is about to happen. Without your help, it will kill everyone." Ethan stood there silently with his back still to Maria. His anger had gone, replaced by shock. He thought about Maria, dying, and a sickening feeling filled his stomach. "We need someone who is immune to orrum poisoning," said Maria. "It's the only way we can survive, Ethan. I came here because I need you. We all need you." There was a long silence. Maria had given everything she had. Now she waited.

"Are you... can you still... survive?" said Ethan. The words came out weakly; it was a struggle to ask.

"Those born here on the planet have a natural immunity that we lack," said Maria. "Our medical specialists can use this to protect us against what's coming."

He turned, slowly, and looked at her. "That doesn't answer my question."

"It means there's a chance, Ethan," said Maria, and Ethan let out a heavy sigh of relief. "But the work will take time," she continued, "and it's more than just your blood we need. We also need your help to recover a device that's essential to synthesising the serum we need."

"I don't understand..." Ethan began, but Maria spoke over him.

"I can help you understand. If you help me, and trust me, I'll explain everything." She walked over to him and took his hands. Ethan tried to withdraw, but she refused to let go. "We are alike in many ways, Ethan," said Maria, softly. "We're both victims of a war. We're both lost and isolated, and afraid. I *am* afraid, Ethan. I don't want my people to die, and I don't want to die here, on this planet, exiled and alone. Why won't you help me?"

Ethan suddenly felt a stabbing guilt. He had believed his pain was unique and special, and hadn't thought it possible that Maria's suffering could in any way match his own. But he was wrong. And, more than that, he realised that her pain actually mattered to him. He did not want her to die. He barely knew this woman, but he felt a powerful connection to her. He liked her being around, and he liked himself when they were together. If he turned his back on her then she would be exiled, and Ethan knew, as did the council of administrators, that being put outside the protection of a settlement was tantamount to a death sentence. The best she could hope for would be to survive merely long enough to succumb to The Maddening. He knew now that he'd never forgive himself if he allowed that to happen.

Maria watched him intensely, trying to figure out what was going on inside his head, why his demeanour had changed. Then Ethan squeezed Maria's hand gently, a sign of acceptance and reassurance. "I'm sorry for what I said, Sal," he said, dropping his guard completely. "This has been harder than I imagined, but that doesn't excuse my words."

Holding Ethan's hand had been a tool to help Maria break through to Ethan, but she was painfully conscious of how much she enjoyed the feel of his hand around hers, and the gentle pressure he had added. She let go and looked away. Without physical contact, or eye contact, she hoped she could detach her emotions again, but it wasn't working. Maria was always at her best when there was conflict. She understood conflict, and was able to use it to keep herself focused. She was not used to opening up to people, and it had left her vulnerable. Now, without the conflict between Ethan and herself to use as an anchor, she found herself succumbing to her own emotions, which were washing over her like a strong tide.

"You asked me what I know about loss," she said, quietly. Ethan waited, concerned that in his anger and self-righteousness, he had not considered that Maria also may have actually lost someone she loved. "I had a family too." Her voice was unsteady and Ethan felt the stab of guilt. She *had* a family, past-tense.

Talking about her life had always been hard for Maria, even to those she was closest too. Even to Kurren. She chose instead to bury her feelings and keep them locked away, but she wanted Ethan to understand. She wanted him to know that she had suffered too. Not because of the mission, but because she wanted him to know that she wasn't just a soldier following orders, that this was personal for her too. "The war I told you about never ended, not for us," she went on, trying to stay composed. She walked over to the window where Ethan had been standing earlier, and stared out, as he had done. "GPS lost the war for the planet, but they have never stopped fighting."

"They're still up there too?" said Ethan. "But... what are they fighting for, the refinery was destroyed?" Maria glanced at him. He was still partly in the shadows, but a streak of light from the window caught his face, and she could see he looked concerned, even sad.

"When the refinery was destroyed and the scale of the devastation had become clear, both sides struggled to process what had happened," said Maria. "In the end, we gave way to fear and anger, each side blaming the other, each demanding the other surrender and submit themselves for judgement."

"But they caused it," said Ethan, struggling to comprehend. "How could they blame you?"

Maria shook her head. "It doesn't matter anymore," she said, with an air of fatalism. "All that matters is they never stopped blaming us, or hating us, and have passed on this hate to the next generation, and it will continue until one of us is destroyed. I know this much; they will never stop fighting, not until we're all dead. Not until they've won."

Ethan stepped out from the shadows fully now and stood

beside Maria, barely a body's width apart, his back to the window. "Perhaps our lives are not so different, after all," he said.

Maria looked up at sky, which had been growing darker as they had been talking. A faint streak of light fell across the horizon, barely visible. Maria watched it fade out of view, and remembered what Ethan had told her about the night his parent's died. "My mother and father were killed in an attack when I was sixteen years old," she said.

Ethan shut his eyes tightly. He had been an arrogant fool.

"I hated GPS before, for the sleepless nights and nightmares they had caused me as a child," Maria continued. "Can you imagine, Ethan, being woken up in the middle of the night, the room vibrating as energy bolts shook what few toys I owned onto the floor? And then being grabbed – still half asleep – by my father and rushed to the safe room. Each time, not knowing if this would finally be the night when GPS broke through and killed us?"

Ethan understood about nightmares and sleepless nights. It didn't seem to make a difference if it was energy bolts or the cries of terror from inside a burning house, the effect was the same. "I can't imagine how that was," he admitted, "but I've known fear like it, and I'm sorry you had to go through what you did."

Maria did not hear him. She was reliving the screams, the panic. The sound of the blasts hammering into the the shields around the base. The sirens from the emergency crews being dispatched to plug holes and tend to the wounded. The agonised shouts of families caught under the rubble. The sight of people being sucked out into the cold vacuum of space. The memories fuelled her anger. "Then one night it happened to us," she said. Her voice had hardened. "Our quarters were hit. I tried to pull her free – my father was already dead – but I couldn't... I couldn't get her out, I wasn't strong enough. They dragged me, screaming, away from her. I held onto her hand for as long as I could, but they pulled me away. And as the shields failed, I saw her vanish into space."

Maria turned away from the window and locked her eyes on Ethan's. "She was still alive at the time," she said, her voice still hard and cold. "I used to wonder what she thought in those last moments, and if she blamed me for leaving her."

As Maria had gotten older she avoided thinking about that day, because the pain made her cold and hollow. The guilt had never left her, and the anger was always there, locked away, but still a part of her. She hated how it made her feel. "Do you know what it feels like to die in the emptiness of space, Planetsider?" she asked, bitterly.

"No," said Ethan flatly. He recognised the pain and anger in her voice, and understood that no words could offer any comfort. Trying to put out the fire in her eyes was a pointless as trying to extinguish the flame that burned inside him.

"I joined the resistance fighters the very next day," Maria continued. "And *every* day since, I have fought those bastards. But now they may actually win."

Ethan ran his hand though his hair and massaged the back of his neck. There was so much to take in. So much more to her story than he had realised. "You say they may win," he said, piecing together different parts of what Maria had said. "Are they behind whatever is threatening to kill you?"

"Yes."

"But they can be stopped?"

"Not without your help, Planetsider," Maria replied. "And you won't help us."

She turned away from him again and faced the window once more, her eyes tightly closed, fighting hard to keep her strained emotions intact, her mind filled with images she had battled for so long to forget.

Maria felt Ethan's hands on her shoulders and despite all her rage, some of which was directed at the young Ranger, she did not pull away. Maria did not know what to do. She was paralysed with a mixture of fury and intense sadness, but the hands closing around her shoulder muscles were somehow squeezing the tension from her, like water being pressed from a sponge.

Then she felt him turning her around, to face him. And she let him. She opened her eyes, but looked down at his chest, fearing what would happen if she met his gaze. Then he pulled her close and Maria felt her face resting on his chest. She could feel his heart beating, powerful and fast. Then his arms were around her back and, slowly, confidently, a hand pressed softly around the base of her neck. Her whole body tingled and she was sure she was trembling. She did not want this sensation to end. All her feelings of anger and bitterness were melting away. She stayed there in his arms, listening to his heart beat, feeling the warmth of his body redden her cheek.

Ethan relaxed his hold and Maria looked up into his eyes. There was a damp patch on Ethan's shoulder and Maria realised she was crying. But she was no longer sad or angry. In fact, at this moment she had never felt more alive. Ethan gently wiped away a tear from Maria's cheek and she let her face fall into his hand. Ethan looked deep into her hazel eyes.

"Tell me what you want me to do."

CHAPTER 16

Commander Chris Kurren was woken abruptly by the sound of a bell being rung and people shouting outside the Ranger hut, where he had been put under house arrest by the headstrong female Ranger, Summer. He had no idea how long he'd been asleep for, but he could see through the slatted windows that it had started to get dark. He got out of his bunk and put on his boots. The door swung open and Summer stood in the threshold, wearing her utilitarian Ranger clothing, holding a staff. A bow was slung over her left shoulder and Kurren could see the feathered tails of arrows poking up from the quiver behind her right shoulder.

"Get up! Roamers are attacking the settlement," she said firmly, but without any panic in her voice.

"Roamers?...Attacking where, how...?" Kurren began, but Summer cut across him.

"I take it that you know how to fight?" she asked.

Kurren shrugged and said, "Sure, but with what, you've taken my weapons."

Summer threw the staff at him, which he didn't anticipate and so caught clumsily. He felt a little embarrassed. "I don't trust you with *your* weapons," Summer continued. "I barely trust you with that. But we need every capable fighter, and since your life is on the line here too, I'd suggest you fight well."

Kurren began to speak, but Summer had already left. After their last encounter with Roamers, he didn't much like the prospect of what lay in store should the fight not go well, so he quickly pulled on the coat that he had been given upon arriving, and followed Summer outside. In the courtyard, lanterns had been lit on the watch platforms along the crude stone walls that surrounded the settlement. The settlement was certainly no fortress, with rough-cut stone bonded together by some form of mud-like cement, and wooden platforms built at intervals, providing enough room for two or three people per platform to get an elevated view of the surroundings. The main gate was the most elaborate construction and looked solid enough. It was hinged at each wall with material salvaged from the city, perhaps originally the gate hinges of a scrapyard or large warehouse, and was operated by two Rangers per side. It, like the walls, stood around three to four metres tall, and certainly couldn't be breached by a mob of Roamers wielding crude, hand-held weapons. Based on what he'd seen so far, Kurren assumed that the Roamers were capable of nothing more sophisticated than that.

He looked around, assessing the tactical situation. People were scurrying into their homes and barricading doors. A body of Rangers were concentrated around the front gate, ten in total, by Kurren's count. Summer was around twenty metres to the left, on a watch platform. He ran over and climbed the stone steps to stand alongside her.

"What are you doing here, space man? Go help the others."

Kurren gazed out over the wall, trying to see what Summer was looking at. The bright lanterns nearby made it hard to focus too far out into the distance, and all he could see was an abandoned old barn, perhaps two-hundred metres distant, near a cluster of ancient-looking and most likely dead trees. To the right, he could see the shapes of figures moving outside the wall. A small group were running up to and then hurling burning objects at the Rangers and at the wall and gate, and then scurrying away. The Rangers had already picked off two or three with arrows, but the sorties had still succeeded in setting a section of the wall on fire. A few people were running to a well to fetch water.

"I thought that these Roamers were savages," said Kurren, concerned that he had underestimated the Roamers' capabilities. "How is it that they are throwing firebombs at the walls?"

Summer glowered at him for a second, and then looked towards the barn again. "The Maddening has different stages," she replied, not trying to hide the annoyance in her voice. "In the early stages, you lose empathy and compassion, but can still function with the skills and knowledge you had before. For a time, at least."

Kurren shivered, but not from the cold wind. "So, it's like they don't have a conscience?"

"Yes," Summer replied. "In that respect, they're a lot like your ancestors." Kurren let this slide. He had seen the darker side of this woman, and didn't want to see it again; at least, not focused on him. "We don't often see groups like this," Summer continued. "My guess is that they were a travelling caravan that passed too close to one of the KCs, where the sickness appears more concentrated."

Kurren thought for a moment and then said, "KCs, what are they?"

Summer shot him a look that could shatter stone. "This is not the time for a cosy little chat, space man," she spat. "Now go away and fight before I shoot you myself."

Kurren was growing tired of the girl's attitude and it showed in his response. "Look lady, if you want me to fight I need to know my enemy," he said, trying to remain calm. "Now cut the attitude and give me something that could help."

Summer felt anger swell in her stomach, but she also knew that Kurren was right, and so grudgingly she relented. "Keep Clear Areas, If you must know," she answered. "KCs for short. They are just big scorched areas of nothing, but you find them in the worst damaged parts of the cities too."

"Thank you," said Kurren, sincerely. He was trying to form a bond, but this girl was even more stubborn than Maria.

"Another gift from your little war," Summer added spitefully. Kurren rolled his eyes, but let this slide too. He considered what Summer had told him. It made sense that some elements of the refinery that made it though the atmosphere without burning up would create areas of particularly intense toxicity. Satisfied with the explanation he fell silent and resumed his survey of the landscape.

One group of five Roamers had clustered together further from the wall. Some had objects in their hands, possibly weapons, though he couldn't make out what from this distance. They certainly seemed reasonably organised, not like the more savage Roamers that they had encountered in the space port. He shook his head. He'd rather go quickly than end up like them, slowly degrading until they eventually changed into something vile and obscene.

"There seem to be enough of you manning the gate," said Kurren, "and I don't think hurling rocks and petty fire-bombs is going to cause much of a threat, so I'll stick around here, if you don't mind." He knew she would mind. His attempt at levity went unnoticed, or at least unappreciated, by Summer.

"I don't need your help," she said curtly, still looking out over the wall into surrounding darkness.

"So what are you up here for?" Kurren replied, ignoring her continued slights.

"It's none of your concern, and I told you I don't..." She stopped abruptly. Two figures emerged from inside the barn and started to run towards the settlement wall, between where Summer and Kurren stood and the gate. They both had bulging bags slung over their shoulders and were holding something in their hands, but Kurren couldn't identify what. The objects glinted and were clearly metallic, and looked like cylinders of some kind. He felt his senses heighten. Something was not right.

"What's in the barn?" Kurren asked with no trace of his usual chirpiness. His military instincts had kicked in.

"Nothing," Summer said, unconvincingly, and then she tried to move away from him, along the wall's walkway in the direction of the gate, but Kurren caught her by the arm. Summer glowered at him, murderously. "Let go. Now!" she demanded, and Kurren could see her hand close around the handle of a dagger in her belt pouch. Kurren let go of her arm, but he wasn't going to give up.

"Stop screwing me around!" he said, agitated. "Whatever else you think I am, above all else I'm a soldier. So if you really want my help, tell me what's in that old building."

Summer stood there momentarily, weighing up the pros and cons of telling Kurren whatever it was she was hiding from him. The Roamers from the barn continued at speed towards the gate. "The barn is where we hid your... vehicle, or whatever it is," she said, finally. "The thing that you arrived in from the city. And it's where your weapons are stored too," she added, reluctantly.

Kurren look shocked. "Why the hell did you leave our weapons out there, for anyone to find?" he asked, genuinely baffled.

"No Roamer would know what they were or how to use them," Summer replied, angry at having her decision questioned by this outsider. "And I couldn't risk you finding them inside the settlement and using them against us."

Kurren looked back towards the running figures. They were now perhaps only forty or fifty seconds from reaching the wall, and so were easier to make out. He felt his heart rate climb. "We've got to stop them!" he said, urgently.

"What have they got?" said Summer, squinting hard at the figures, trying to spot the danger.

"Fuel cells," said Kurren. "They are fuel cells from the transport."

"But they can't know what they are," said Summer. "What are they, anyway? Are they dangerous?"

"If you don't know what they are then chances are they won't," said Kurren, thinking on his feet. "They're heavy, so maybe they want to use them to smash chunks out of the wall, who knows?"

"But?" said Summer, sensing there was more.

Kurren looked at her with a cold seriousness that gave Summer chills. "If they rupture, the explosion will be big enough to punch a hole in your wall," he told her.

"Damn it!" Summer cursed, and then without another word she started to sprint along the wall towards them, unhooking the bow from over her shoulder as she ran.

Kurren was about to follow when he heard a familiar voice.

"Kurren, what's going on?" It was Maria. Kurren looked down and saw Maria standing at the foot of the steps with Ethan.

"Roamer attack," he shouted down to them. "Look, Sal,

they've got..."

"How many?" said Ethan urgently, cutting Kurren off mid-sentence.

"I don't know, maybe forty or fifty. They're pretty organised..." Kurren replied, but before he could add any details Ethan had set off running in the direction of the gate. Maria looked as if she was about to follow when Kurren shouted down to her to wait. She stopped and looked up at him, puzzled. Kurren came half-way down the steps to be closer so he didn't need to shout. "Sal, the Roamers found our transport," he said. "These idiot Rangers hid it in a building about two-hundred metres outside the wall. They've taken a couple of fuel cells."

Maria understood instantly. "If they rupture they could blow these walls sky high."

"I know," said Kurren. "The red-haired pain-in-the-ass has gone charging off after them already."

"I've got to warn Ethan!" Maria said urgently. She started running, but again Kurren called for her to wait.

"Sal, forget him!" he called, frustrated that Maria's first reaction was to run to Ethan and not help him. "We know where the transport is, let's make use of this distraction and get the hell out of here, before they change their minds and burn us as heretics or whatever."

"Kurren, no, we need to get him!" Maria protested.

"Sal, I know you like this kid, but he's with them and we need to look out for ourselves," said Kurren. "Leave him and let's get the hell off this forsaken rock!"

Maria ran back and climbed the bottom few stone stairs so that she was only a few metres from Kurren, still perched on the platform. "He's with us, Kurren," she said, enthusiastically. "He's going to come back with us."

That stopped Kurren in his tracks. "What?" he said.

"I'll explain later, but he's going to help us," said Maria. "We need to get him, and preferably before he gets blown to pieces."

Kurren nodded and then smiled as an idea came to him. "Okay, Sal, go get your boyfriend, I have a plan." Maria felt like charging up the stairs and punching him in his smug face, when an explosion rocked the settlement causing both to instinctively duck and cover their heads. A section of the wall between them and the gate had erupted and sent flaming debris raining down into the settlement, igniting the roofs of some nearby buildings. "Damn it!" Kurren said, and then he looked at Maria. "Go on, go get lover boy and be ready."

"Be ready for what?" Maria asked crossly. The quip about Ethan had irritated her.

"For me to arrive with some wheels and roll us all on out of here," he said with a grin, and with that, he disappeared over the top of the wall.

Maria understood. She took a deep breath, steeling herself for a fight, and ran in the direction of the explosion. Within moments she was standing beside a group of four Rangers, who had come down from the watchtower next to the gate and were waiting, staffs raised, ready to take on anything that came through the breach. A group of settlers had started to form a fire-fighting chain, passing along buckets of water from the well to other settlers who were dousing the flames on the houses that had caught fire. Maria spotted Ethan just ahead of the group and ran alongside him.

"I'm here to help," she said to Ethan's back, slightly out of breath from the run. Ethan turned around, surprised to see her.

"No, Sal, I don't want you to get hurt."

"Look, Ethan, I'm probably a better fighter than everyone here," said Maria, without ego, "and it looks like you need the help. So just give me a weapon, okay?" Ethan meant what he said about not wanting Maria to get hurt, but he'd also seen her fight, so he tossed her his staff. Maria caught it and said, "And do me a favour?"

"What's that?"

"Don't die!"

A shout from on the wall brought their senses into sharp focus. "They're coming through," said Ethan calmly. A Ranger passed Ethan and handed him another staff. "Ready?" he asked.

"After you," replied Maria.

Five Roamers came charging through the burning opening in the wall, two of them catching fire as they did so, yet the flames appeared not to bother them. The front line fought them back, but one Roamer broke through. Maria advanced faster than the others and slammed the end of her staff into its face, smashing the nose into its skull. It fell, limp and lifeless, to the floor.

More came, again catching fire, but continuing on, as if the flames were nothing more than splatters of mud. Maria could smell the burning flesh and she struggled not to gag. The front line of Rangers again fought them back, maintaining an arc around the opening in the wall, trying to prevent any from breaching the inner settlement area. Then a Roamer hurled itself at one of the defenders, wrapping its arms around him and setting him alight. The Ranger screamed as the flames torched the skin on his face and neck, causing panic amongst the nearby fighters as they both tried to help the injured Ranger and tear the Roamer away. The gap in the arc allowed another burning Roamer through, and this one ran straight at Maria. She waited, patiently, then dodged and swept its legs from under it, knocking it flat. Spinning around, she pummelled the end of the heavy wooden staff into its chest and heard the crack of bone as its sternum collapsed. She drew the staff back and looked around. Ethan was several metres away, near the main cluster of fighters, and holding strong. Then she looked beyond him towards the breach and saw Summer on the wall, loosing arrows at some of the Roamers that were advancing through. Maria watched as Summer drew another arrow and nocked it, but then the Ranger hesitated and lowered her bow swiftly, a dread look on her face.

"Move away! Move, now!" she heard Summer shout to fighters inside the walls, but they did not hear her. Maria ran a little closer, trying to understand the reason for Summer's frantic warning. "Move clear!" she heard Summer shouting again. She was trying to get a shot, her bow was waving from side to side, up and down, string at full tension, but Summer did not shoot. Maria moved again trying to get a better view, and then she spotted it – a Roamer, prone in the centre of the melee, unseen by the Rangers. Its right leg was smashed and contorted, and the other was on fire. It was dragging itself forward, one hand clawing at the dirt, while in the other it held a metal cylinder. A fuel cell. Maria wasted no time, she turned back to Ethan.

"Ethan, fall back, fall back now!" she shouted urgently.

Ethan heard Maria's cry and then saw the creature on the ground. He turned and sprinted away from it, legs and lungs burning with pain, crying out for others to follow him. Seconds later the fuel cell exploded. Bodies were flung out in all directions, Roamer and Ranger alike. The shockwave sent Maria hurtling backwards through the air. She landed awkwardly, but without much pain. Something broke her fall. Dazed, winded, ears ringing and unable to hear she called out to Ethan, desperately. She could not even hear her own voice. She looked around, desperate to find Ethan, and then she saw him. He was face down, blown perhaps ten metres into the settlement by the force of the explosion. He was not moving.

Maria tried to get up, but dizziness overcame her and she could not stand. Then her nausea was intensified by fear. Through the smoke she could see more figures appearing. The remaining Roamers were coming in and now there was no-one to stop them. She fought to stand and with an intense force of effort managed to get herself upright. Again she called out to Ethan, but again the cries barely registered in her own ears, sounding muffled and distorted. Ethan was still lying prone, blood visible from his ears.

Maria looked around for a weapon, but could find nothing. A Roamer advanced toward her and soon she was faced with its cold, indifferent eyes. She scrambled away from it, but it was no use, she could not muster the strength to escape. She closed her eyes and waited. Her mind was filled with thoughts of her mother. Through the eyes of her younger self, she watched as her mother's hand was snatched away from hers and then, powerless to do anything to help, looked on as she floated, helplessly into the cold darkness of space. She had never forgotten the look on her face. The look of someone knowing they were about to die and lose everyone they ever loved.

"I'm sorry," said Maria, tears wetting her face. "I'm sorry I couldn't make it up to you."

She had always wondered how it would feel to die. She was going to find out now. Then her thoughts turned to Ethan – the Planetsider she had convinced to help her, and maybe even to love her. Did Ethan love her? she wondered, and in that instant she realised that she actually wanted him to. Did that mean she loved him too? She would never find out, because soon this too would be snatched away from her, forever.

She opened her eyes and looked upon the face of the Roamer standing over her. Its eyes showed no evidence of hatred or malice. Its heart pulsated with no desires. In all the ways that mattered, it was dead already. The Roamer held in its grimy, flame-blistered hand a crude wooden club. It raised the weapon above its head, all the time looking at her, coldly and with disquieting indifference. Everything appeared to Maria to be happening in slow motion. She refused to close her eyes; if she was to die, she would stare death in the face and spite it. The weapon began to fall and she waited for the pain to strike, but the end did not come. Instead, the creature spasmed and its face contorted, not so much in pain as in confusion and bewilderment. It fell to its knees and then crumpled over backwards in a lifeless heap.

Maria's eyes focused on a figure behind it. It was screaming at her, but she could barely make out the words. It shouted again. "Sal! Are you okay?" Chris Kurren stood in front of her, smoke oozing from the barrel of a rifle. He swung around again and Maria saw the muzzle flash as he fired. The sound was still muffled, but her hearing was returning. "Sal! Get up, we've got to go, now!" Kurren shouted, the words barely registering. He was pulling her to her feet. She put an arm around his shoulder and her head started to clear. Again the muzzle flash of the rifle and this time she heard the shots ring out. In front of them two more Roamers fell to the ground. "I have the transport. Where's the kid?" he shouted.

Maria groggily gestured over towards where she had last seen Ethan, lying prostrate on the ground. He was still there, but she didn't know if he was alive or dead. Maria felt panic overwhelm her. *Please don't let him be dead*, she thought. She implored Kurren to get him, to save him. But all that came out was an incoherent babble. Kurren dragged Maria to the transport and put her inside, closing the door. He aimed and shot another Roamer, then ran around to the driver's side of the transport and opened the door. More Roamers were coming in through the opening. He considered getting in and just leaving. Screw these bastards he thought. He only wanted to save Sal. But the mission needed Ethan too, and besides, Sal would never forgive him if he left the kid. She wouldn't leave without him. "Damn it!" he cried out in frustration, realising he had to go back. He slammed the door of the transport and ran towards Ethan. From the hip, he fired two more bursts, hitting three Roamers and stopping them in their tracks. He reached Ethan and, slinging the rifle over his shoulder, hoisted him onto his back. "What the hell are you made of? You weigh a ton," he said out loud, straining under the added weight. Ethan just groaned. Kurren battled his way back to the transport as quickly as possible and then unceremoniously dumped Ethan into the back compartment. He groaned again. "You're welcome, kid," said Kurren, and then darted back to the driver's side door. Standing in front of it was Summer – bow raised, arrow nocked and pointing directly at his heart.

"Put down that weapon or I'll kill you!" she demanded, venom seething from every pore. Kurren held up his hands, a conciliatory gesture that Summer had seen him give before, and she trusted it even less this time.

"Look, lady, I'm doing want you wanted," he said. "I'm getting out of your hair. So how about you lower the bow and let me get the hell out of here?"

Summer did not flinch. "You can go, but you're not taking Ethan," she said. "You think I'm stupid? I saw you put him in the back, don't deny it!" She pulled back harder on the string, adding even more tension. Her fingers, calloused and bloody from the arrows she had shot previously, throbbed with pain.

"Okay..." Kurren said, his hand still raised. He could see that Summer was on the edge and would respond at the slightest provocation. "I was just trying to save him. Okay?..." Kurren said again, trying to soothe her. He slowly took the rifle from his back, dropped it and then backed away.

Summer's eyes narrowed. "I don't believe you, space man," she said bitterly. "Give me one reason why I shouldn't kill you now?"

Kurren didn't have a chance to answer as the driver's side door swung open and smashed into Summer's face, knocking her flat on her back. The arrow sprang from the bow and screamed past Kurren's face so close that he could feel the rush of air as it shot past his ear. Maria leaned out of the side of the cabin.

"That felt good," she said, looking at Summer's body, lying in the mud.

"Are you crazy? She damn near shot my head off!" Kurren exclaimed, recovering the rifle from the ground.

"You're welcome," replied Maria, coolly and with an air of satisfaction. "Now get in." Maria slid back to the passenger side and Kurren went to get in.

"Wait." It was a weak voice from the rear of the transport. "You can't leave her like that," Ethan croaked.

"Kid, we don't have time for this," said Kurren.

"If you... leave her... I stay," Ethan said, struggling to form the words.

More Roamers were coming in through the opening, but now were being met by a re-grouped Ranger force. Kurren knew that once the Rangers had tackled the remaining Roamers, they would turn their attentions to him and the transport. There was no time to spare. He swore under his breath and went over to where Summer lay, still out cold. He hoisted her up, grateful for the fact that she weighed considerably less than Ethan did, and slung her in the back with him. He was careful to remove her arrows, and her knife.

"Buckle up..." he said to Ethan, before sliding back into the driver's seat.

In front of them the Rangers were close to winning the fight, and several of them, supported by some of the braver settlers, were now hastily trying to patch up the hole in the wall. Kurren accelerated and slammed his palm onto the horn. The Rangers and settlers scattered out of the way and stared in astonishment as the transport drove past them, smashing through the last cluster of Roamers, some of them bouncing off the bodywork and falling into contorted heaps as the transport sped out of the settlement. Kurren checked his mirrors and saw that the Rangers were dealing with the last of them. The settlement would be safe. Contented, he turned the vehicle in the direction of the city and floored the accelerator.

"We did it, Sal!" Kurren said. "We're on our way."

Maria smiled at him, and then looked back through the partition glass into the compartment at the rear. Ethan was crouched over Summer, calmly tending to her wounds. He caught Maria looking at him and found himself smiling back at her. A warmth flooded through his veins, and despite everything that had just happened, he felt relaxed and at ease.

CHAPTER 17

The journey back to the space port went without incident, much to everyone's surprise and relief; they had done enough fighting for one day. Using the transport's systems and something Kurren had referred to as a 'transponder ID', they were able to enter the main hangar deck through a previously sealed – and therefore Roamer-free – slip road. The bodies of the Roamers they had fought previously were no longer there, and a chill ran down Ethan's spine as he considered the possibilities of what might have happened to them. This time, though, the platform was quiet. Eerily quiet.

Kurren stopped the transport just inside the main door to the launch pod that housed the UEC transport they had located on their first visit and got out, telling everyone else to remain in the back until he gave the all clear. The weapon he had used with such proficiency during the settlement attack was at his side. He slowly made his way over to a control console on the wall opposite, weapon raised and constantly sweeping from side to side, checking for any signs of movement. Maria now also got out and, armed with her pistol, which Kurren had also recovered from the stash in the barn, climbed into the rear compartment of the transport to provide cover, if needed.

Ethan had tended to Summer's injuries during the journey, and also given her a mild sedative that Maria had passed through to him in the back compartment, so she was still out cold. There was a bandage covering her temple and left eye, which was bruised from the impact of the transport's door slamming into her face. Ethan was still a little groggy, but had largely recovered. He also felt no pain, thanks to some remarkably potent painkiller tablets that Maria had given him at the same time as the sedative for Summer, which made him feel slightly lighter than usual, as if he was walking on a quilt made of wool. He moved over to sit alongside Maria in the rear compartment. She was quietly surveying the room, keeping watch for any unusual movements and signs of danger. Neither of them spoke; it was so quiet that Ethan could hear the inhalation and exhalation cycle of Maria's calm, rhythmic breathing. He watched her chest rise and fall in time with the sounds and, in his drugged state, became slightly mesmerised by it.

"Ahem, eyes front, Soldier," Maria said, noticing that Ethan appeared to be staring at her breasts.

Ethan blushed and sharply turned away, doing his best to look at nothing in particular. "I'm sorry, I wasn't..." he stammered. "I was just noticing your breasting... I mean breathing!"

Despite the tense situation, Maria couldn't help but laugh and smile. "You must have hit your head harder than I thought!" she teased.

Kurren's voice boomed out of the darkness. "Hey, you two, I'm glad you're having a nice time, but how about you save the chit-chat until I'm somewhere with less chance of being brutally murdered?"

Ethan snuck another look at Maria and saw that she had returned to surveying the room, but was still smiling. Perhaps it was the drugs she'd given him, but he actually felt good.

He looked around. The hangar was dark and cold and seemed as lifeless as the eyes of the Roamers that had assaulted the settlement. It was strangely calming and Ethan found his mind wandering. His thoughts strayed to Elijah and Katie, and his good mood ebbed away. He knew both were safely barricaded in the bakery during the attack and he knew that the Rangers had managed to kill the last of the Roamers, but still he worried. He felt bad for not thinking about them at the time and for making sure they knew where he had gone, and during the journey to the space port he had reflected on his choice to come with Maria and Kurren, and was having doubts. Only the knowledge that Maria would die without his help kept him from backing out. But still, he had chosen saving the life of a near-stranger over protecting the lives of his own family, and this troubled him deeply. He knew it was selfish, and he didn't consider himself to be a selfish person. After all, he'd chosen to be a Ranger, and to put his life in harm's way for the sake of others. *What could be more selfless than that?* he thought. But despite being uncomfortable with his choices, he did not regret them. The thought of abandoning Maria to her death made him feel physically sick. No matter what was the rational course of action, he knew he couldn't just walk away. But it was more than just noble sentiment that was driving his decision; he cared for her and, perhaps, it even ran deeper than that.

After what had happened between him and Summer, Ethan had learned to box away his personal feelings. It was easier that way, certainly when it came to Summer, because boxing his feelings also meant closing off his guilt and shame over their brief relationship. It was easier if she was just a friend, a colleague. But he did not want to box his feelings for Maria, despite the parallels with Summer. Maria made him feel good about himself, excited and free, yet at the same time also guilty because these feelings had turned his attention away from his sister and nephew. Was love so limited, he wondered? Could you not care deeply for a person without it stealing love away from someone else? And what of Summer, still lying unconscious in the back of the transport? In his concussed, confused condition at the time, it had made sense to bring her, to make sure she wasn't left to the Roamers. But now he wished he had left her behind in the settlement. Summer also mattered to Ethan, and as she lay prone and helpless in the mud, bleeding from the impact of the door, he had realised just how much she meant to him. Summer had always been stronger than him, and so she had never needed his protection, and he had never needed to worry about her, until that moment. In hindsight, she would have been better off on her own. Maybe him leaving was good for her, Ethan considered. Perhaps it would allow her to bond with someone else, and maybe even fall in love.

The more immediate question was what to do with her now. He couldn't leave her in the spaceport, days travel from the settlement, alone and without proper provisions, but she wouldn't come willingly to wherever it was he was going. *Into space?* he wondered. That seemed absurd to him now. But regardless of the destination, if it involved Ethan going with Maria and Kurren then Summer would fight and do everything in her power to prevent it, even if that meant killing Maria and Kurren, and perhaps even wounding Ethan. Or she'd get killed while trying. Neither option was good, neither choice acceptable.

A low hum followed by a deep, throbbing vibration through the floor, powerful enough to shake the transport, roused him from his daydreams. The lights above them flicked on and Ethan had to shield his eyes from the sudden, intense brightness. As his eyes adjusted, he saw Kurren running back towards them.

"Okay, power is back on, so let's get on the other side of the pod door, before any visitors arrive," said Kurren, slightly out of breath.

Maria jumped over the side of the transport and helped Kurren to lift Summer down. Then both together, an arm slung over a shoulder each, they dragged Summer across the floor and over the threshold of the hangar door. Ethan followed, still feeling a little woolly-headed. When they were all through, Kurren went back for the transport, drove it just across the threshold and then jumped out to close the door, all the time keeping a steady eye out for any movement outside. After what felt like an eternity, the door finally thudded into the metal decking with a force that could be felt through the air itself.

"Okay!" Kurren said, chirpily. "No crazy people are getting in here, that's for damn certain. Well, apart from the ones that are already in here, that is." He chuckled at his own joke, but neither Ethan nor Maria appeared amused.

"You're sure there's nothing else in here with us?" Maria asked, calmly, but with a seriousness that made Kurren's response equally earnest.

"Aside from maybe a few rats, there's nothing here but us, Sal," Kurren said, confidently. "Relax, we're on the home stretch."

"I'll relax when we've reached orbit," Maria replied.

"Where's this 'orbit'?" Ethan asked, unable to disguise his obvious concern.

Kurren laughed. "You'll see, kid," he said, and winked. This did not help to put Ethan's mind at ease.

They moved down a long corridor that lead to the hangar pod and laid Summer down on a dusty couch in a room off to the side that was filled with equipment, none of which appeared to be working. Ethan smoothed the hair away from Summer's face and looked at her. She looked peaceful.

"What happens to her now?" he asked without looking up from her face. "How do we get her home?"

Kurren and Maria looked at each other, unsure of whom Ethan was addressing, but Maria's look told Kurren that he should do the explaining. "We send her back in the transport," said Kurren, as if it was obvious.

Ethan looked over his shoulder at him, eyebrow cocked. "She can't control that thing," he said.

"She doesn't have to, it can drive itself," said Kurren. "I can just set it to go back to the settlement, back to where it started. Strap her in, and she'll be home in no time."

"What if Roamers try to stop it on route?" asked Ethan, sounding wary of this plan. "What if it meets some kind of... I don't know... obstacle?"

Maria stepped forward now. "Don't worry, Ethan," she said. "Kurren knows what he's doing. We can make sure it gets back without incident, I promise."

Maria's assurance helped, though Ethan was still distrustful of the contraption that had brought them here. It appeared to be the only way, though. "Can we set her off, before we leave?" he asked, standing back up and facing Maria. "So I know she's safe. I need to know she's safe, before I go with you."

Kurren looked over at Summer and rubbed his chin, thoughtfully. "We'll have to keep her sedated," he said, "because I doubt she'd go back willingly, at least not without you." Ethan agreed with that assessment. "I can track the transport's transponder from here, so we'll know when it's back," Kurren added.

Maria smiled. "It'll be okay, really."

"Okay," agreed Ethan. "So let's do it now; let's get her home."

Kurren dumped his gear and jacket in the side room and then they all left with Summer still unconscious on the couch. Kurren went back down the corridor to the transport to begin making the modifications needed to auto-control it back to the settlement, while Ethan went with Maria, at her request, to help prepare the ship, by loading supplies and generally just doing what she asked him to do. The UEC ship loomed large in the middle of the hangar, and as they approached it Ethan began to wonder how such an enormous object could possibly get airborne.

Maria and Kurren set to work, chatting to each other using some sort of voice relay that Maria called a 'comm', using words that Ethan did not understand. He tried to keep busy by packing the remaining provisions, and scouting the hangar for anything else potentially useful, although he had no idea what was useful and what was not when it came to space travel. Eventually, Maria got out of the ship and asked Ethan to stand back against the wall with her. She manipulated some controls on a panel nearby and then Ethan watched in quiet astonishment as huge metal arms swung down from above them and manoeuvred the UEC ship into the centre of the hangar, as if it weighed no more than a small child. Part of the decking then rose up and attached to the sides of the ship, before the entire floor opened beneath it, tilting the ship upwards. A hatch then hissed open, slowly, and Ethan guessed that was how they would get in. The noise that accompanied all this was near deafening and Ethan imagined that if the Roamers didn't know they were here before, they certainly would now. Hopefully the doors at the entry point to the launch pod were as solid as they looked.

"Don't worry, this is perfectly safe," said Maria, smiling at Ethan. She was amused by his look of boyish wonder. "It's going to be one hell of a ride, though."

"This whole experience so far has been one hell of a ride," Ethan replied, honestly. Kurren appeared from across the other side of the hangar and attached a couple of large tubes to the rear section of the vessel, and then proceeded to check a nearby console that was blinking and flashing, with lines of text scrolling along a brightly illuminated screen. "It all seems so unreal." Ethan mused, out loud.

"You ain't seen nothing yet, kid," Kurren said, grinning down at the console. He was then quiet for a few moments as he concentrated on the text as it floated past. "We're pretty much done here, Sal," he eventually added, more loudly and more seriously. "Everything checks out, and it has enough power to reach the base. Air might be a little stale, but it's breathable."

Maria nodded. "Okay then, let's go."

"You... are going... nowhere."

They all turned around to see Summer standing in the doorway of the side room. She was holding a weapon, one of the smaller guns that Kurren and Maria wore. Ethan looked at Maria and saw the glint of a pistol's metal grip inside her jacket pocket, but Maria was looking over at Kurren, who had his hand where his weapon should be. His face told the story.

"The jacket," Maria said quietly, so that only Ethan could hear. "He left his jacket in the room."

Ethan understood. The weapon was not a relic, but fully working, and loaded. Ethan looked back towards Summer. She was aiming the weapon at Maria, her finger clasped around the trigger. Ethan began to panic. "Summer, wait..." he began, but he was sharply cut off.

"No, Ethan!" she shouted back at him. "This has gone far enough. You're coming back with me, or I kill her, right here, right now!" Her voice became more intense as she completed the sentence, and her grip on the weapon tightened. Maria looked scared. Ethan tried to fight the fear swelling in his gut, and tried to think. He looked at Summer, helplessly. "I won't ask again, Ethan!" she said, fiercely. "Either you come with me, or she dies. The soldier can go back to where he came from in that... thing... for all I care. But if you want her to leave here still breathing then you stay."

Ethan started to walk towards her, but only managed two small steps before Summer fired the weapon. Ethan's heart stopped. He looked back at Maria, desperately hoping she wasn't hit. She was still standing, but her expression showed pure terror. Summer had aimed the weapon off to her side, but not by much, and not with any aptitude. She was too full of anger and adrenalin; missing was as much luck as judgement.

Summer stepped two paces forward, her arm outstretched and rigid with tension, pointing the weapon directly at Maria. Her eyes flashed with malice. "I saw enough of the soldier over there to know how to use this, Ethan," she warned. "It's just like shooting a bow, really, and you know how well I shoot a bow, don't you? So do as I say, or the next one goes in her pretty head."

Ethan stood, numb, not knowing what to do or what to say. Summer had killed Roamers before, so she was not squeamish. But murder? Would she kill Maria if she was pushed to it? Ordinarily, no, he reasoned, but Summer had gone past her tipping point, and exhaustion, anger and fear had taken over.

"What's it to be Ethan?" Summer started again, "your family and your home, or her?" and then she practically screamed at him, "WHAT'S IT GOING TO BE?"

Not knowing what else to do, Ethan instinctively stepped in front of Maria, his heart racing and head pounding, placing himself between her and the outstretched arm of Summer, still clasping the weapon with deadly intent. Summer did not adjust her aim, though her expression betrayed a wavering of her resolve. She did not want to shoot Ethan, but she had committed to this course of action and to back down would mean letting him leave with Maria and Kurren. She would not allow that.

"Summer, please put the weapon down," Ethan said as calmly as he could manage, but with strain breaking his voice. "Look, you win, I'll stay. I'll stay, Summer. But only if you put the weapon down and let them leave."

Summer was not so easily placated. "No, Ethan. I don't drop this weapon until they are in that thing, and you are well away from her. Only then."

Ethan again tried to take a pace forward, but Summer adjusted her aim to his right and squeezed the trigger. The shot rang out and again Ethan froze in terror as he heard the speeding projectile ricochet off the metal decking behind them. The sound was like a bell ringing, loud and clear, signalling danger.

Tears began to trickle down Summer's face, tracing a chaotic course over her cheeks to the corners of her mouth. She was fighting to remain composed, but the pressure was intensifying. She had backed them both into a corner and there was no return. Either Ethan would give in, or someone would die.

"I will do it, Ethan!" urged Summer, fighting back her emotion. The weapon in her hand quivered but remained pointed at him, the barrel oozing smoke like blood seeping from an open wound.

As this was occurring, Kurren, had, unnoticed by any of the others, quietly entered a sequence of new commands at his control console. All of Summer's attention had been focused on Ethan and Maria, and likewise their focus was purely on Summer and the outstretched, smoking weapon. Kurren hit a final sequence of keys, careful to keep his actions unseen by the others. The words, 'Fire Suppression Override' flashed up on the screen. Glancing up briefly to make sure he was still unobserved, he took a deep intake of breath, held it, and hit another button on the console. There was a sudden, violent rush of sound from vents in the decking below them, and the room rapidly filled with a cloudy gas. Summer coughed and gagged, lowering the weapon and instinctively covering her mouth with her free hand, and in that instant, he charged towards her.

Kurren had improvised this plan moments after Summer had arrived, weapon in hand, her intentions clear from the venomous way she had looked at them, and the rigidity of her posture, muscles taut and ready for a fight. He was perhaps seven or eight metres away from Summer and had banked on this distraction giving him sufficient time to close the gap and disarm her. As he advanced, legs and arms pumping with maximum effort, he saw Summer's head turn towards him and panic spilled into his gut. Still retching and struggling to breath, Summer fought to bring the weapon up, tilting her body and shifting her weight with a nimbleness honed from years of training. Now Summer was focused only on Kurren, her expression a blend of pain, surprise and fear, but her eyes still burning with deadly intent. With less than two metres between them, Kurren realised to his horror that he was not going to make it. A shot pierced the air, clearly audible even over the hiss of the gas. The console where Kurren had initiated his plan exploded, launching splinters of flame and electrical energy into the air and then, fractions of a second later, he piled into Summer with the full force of his momentum, knocking her backwards; the weapon flying from her hand and spiralling into the far corner of the room. Kurren collapsed into a heap, rolling uncontrollably into a stack of containers against the wall, sending some of them bouncing around the hangar. The fire suppression vents closed as quickly as they had opened and pumps began to whir, emptying the gas from the room. There was a momentary, deathly silence, punctuated only by the chaotic sparking of electricity from the console. Then a siren sounded and the lights dimmed. Red lanterns dropped from the overhangs, pulsing in time with the klaxon's wails, and huge slabs of metal slid down from inside the hangar doors, one of which closed off the corridor and another the side room where Summer had been lying on the couch moments earlier. On them were written three words in bright yellow: LAUNCH BLAST DOORS.

The gas had caused Ethan to collapse to the ground directly where he was standing, with Maria on her knees beside him, both coughing violently. As they began to recover they reached over and helped each other to stand. The pulsing red lights illuminated them for brief moments, casting a blood red sheen over their faces. Maria looked over to the console and saw the tell-tale scorched puncture wound in its metal panel, and the cause was immediately obvious to her.

"Oh no!" Maria said.

Ethan did not hear her. Instead he was looking at where Summer lay on the decking, motionless. "Summer!" he shouted, but there was no response. He struggled to run over, stumbling, falling and getting back to his feet multiple times before he reached her and dropped to his knees at her side. He rubbed his eyes with hands grazed and bloody from all the falls to try to clear his vision as he stared down at her face. She was breathing and semi-conscious, but the wound on her head had re-opened and was weeping blood. "Summer, can you hear me?" Ethan shouted. But his words were drowned out by a deep, mechanical growl, like the guttural noise the transport vehicle had made while bringing them here, but far more powerful and ominous. The sound was coming from the UEC ship.

Maria shouted over to him, "Ethan, something has gone wrong, the launch cycle has activated. We have to get in the ship now, all of us!"

"I'm not bringing her with us!" Ethan shouted back.

"We've got no choice!" Maria pleaded with him. "The launch has been activated, and without that control console, it cannot be aborted. The doors are sealed, there's no way out, and in a few minutes the ship's engines will ignite and this entire hangar will become a furnace. Nothing can survive!"

Ethan looked down at Summer and shook his head. "You proud, stubborn fool," he said, angrily. "You should have let me go. It's my life to risk, not yours. I didn't want this for you!"

"Ethan, please!" Maria shouted again. "We have to go!"

Ethan heard her plea, but ignored it and continued trying to rouse Summer.

An artificial-sounding voice filled the room. "Emergency launch in five minutes. All personnel clear the hangar deck. All personnel clear the hangar deck."

Ethan listened to the voice. *Five minutes* he thought, *five minutes to save her, but how?* He turned to protest to Maria, but another voice cut him off.

"I'll get her to safety." It was Kurren. He was propped up against the side of the hangar, one hand pressed to his side. Blood was seeping between his fingers. Maria saw this and her eyes widened. She surged toward him, but Kurren raised his other hand, indicating Maria to stop. "Sal, it's okay," he shouted over to her, wincing with pain. "It's a through-and-through. I'll live. But I won't survive the launch, not perforated like this. And you won't either if you don't get in that ship."

"The blast doors are sealed, there's no way out..." Maria argued back, barely containing her panic.

Kurren pointed and Maria's eyes followed. "The hangar has a safe storage area, for munitions or fuel, or other volatile substances, like our Ranger friend here," he said. "It's not big, but it's enough to shield us from the launch. But it can only fit two, just about. Me and Miss Crazy over there will have to become closer friends than either of us want."

"Kurren, I can't leave you, I need..." but Kurren cut short her protestations.

"It's okay, I've had my time," he said, trying to offer comfort. "There's nothing for me up there now. I know you understand what I mean. You have it all ahead of you, Sal. So get this done and go live your life. Go, now!"

Tears ran down Maria's face. She tried to speak, but no words escaped her trembling lips.

Still on his knees beside Summer, Ethan turned to Kurren. The artificial voice filled the room again. "Emergency launch in four minutes. All personnel clear the hangar deck. All personnel clear the hangar deck."

"You promise me you will keep Summer safe and take her back to the settlement?" Ethan said, locking eyes with Kurren. The old soldier looked back at him, solemn and serious. More serious than Ethan had ever seen him. A large drop of blood fell from his hand and splattered on his boot.

"I'll keep her alive, kid. I swear. Now go."

Ethan held his eyes for a moment, looking for any sign of deception, any hint of a lie. But he saw nothing to give him doubt. He looked back to Maria. She was fixated on Kurren with a look of desperate sadness that made Ethan feel even worse than he already did. More alien sounds began to emanate from the UEC ship. Throbbing, pulsing, artificial noises unlike anything Ethan had ever heard before. "Emergency launch in three minutes. All personnel clear the hangar deck. All personnel clear the hangar deck."

Maria looked now at Ethan, on his knees beside Summer, his friend and comrade. She understood his pain and his conflict. "Ethan, I won't leave you," she shouted to him. "Whatever we do, we do it together."

"Sal, don't be a fool!" Kurren said hoarsely, and for the first time, Ethan heard fear in his voice. "With or without him, you must get out of here, now!"

But Maria ignored him and continued to stare at Ethan. Her eyes burned into his soul. A jumble of different thoughts raced through Ethan's mind: Summer, and their childhood; his sister; Elijah; Dorman's death at the hands of Roamers; Administrator Talia's anger towards Maria and Kurren, and her warning of the danger they posed; the flashes in the night sky; Ethan's longing to learn more, and guilt at allowing his desires to overshadow all else. Then his mind turned to his feelings for this mysterious stranger. The woman who was looking at him now, in a way no woman had ever looked at him before, not even Summer. He knew then he would go with her. He would go with her anywhere, and do whatever was needed to keep her safe. He no longer cared about The Fall and the war that caused it; none of that mattered now. What mattered was saving Maria, to keep them together. Maybe he was selfish. He didn't know, and didn't care anymore. This was his decision, his way to move his life forward and stop obsessing about the past. With one last look down at Summer, he pushed himself unsteadily to his feet, staggered back to Maria and nodded.

Maria half-smiled, with what was more relief than happiness, and then raced over to the open door of the ship and stepped inside. Ethan looked back at Summer on the floor. Kurren was kneeling beside her, injecting her and then himself with a small device from a container placed on the floor beside him. He looked at Ethan and with a weak smile gave a thumbs-up signal. Ethan turned and followed Maria into the UEC vessel, stumbling over the lip around the door hatch, still groggy from the gas. Once he was inside, Maria slammed a button on the door frame, causing the hatch to hiss shut and seal. "Emergency launch in two minutes. All personnel clear the hangar deck. All personnel clear the hangar deck."

Maria pushed Ethan into a seat and hastily buckled an elaborate belt over his waist and chest. "There are about a hundred things I should do before taking off in this thing," she said, while working the mechanism, "but there's no time. So just sit back, and hold tight, it's going to be wild."

The realisation of what was about to happen hit Ethan like a club to the head. He thought about saying, 'you're telling me this now!?' but his brain was a muddle and he was unable to get the words out.

Maria climbed to a seat at the front of the ship and buckled herself in. Above them, huge panels swung apart, revealing the black, open sky. The ship began to vibrate and Ethan felt the pulse of the engine resonating throughout his whole body. "Emergency launch in one minute. All personnel clear the hangar deck. All personnel clear the hangar deck."

He looked out through the hatch window to where Kurren had pulled Summer into the small compartment that he'd opened in the side of the hangar. The soldier looked towards him, but not at him, and held up a hand. At the top of the ship Maria waved back. And again, another bludgeoning wave of realization hit Ethan; Kurren was giving up his ride home to save Summer and to make sure that Ethan could go with Maria, to make sure the mission continued. He was doing his duty, and so much more. He understood the sacrifice he was making, and in that instant felt a deep respect for the older man; but also for Maria. She was saying goodbye to her comrade, her friend; a man who was injured, and despite his casual dismissal of the wound, could still be in danger of dying. She would never see him again, never know what became of him, or even if he lived or died. The finality of the moment hit him. He would also never see Summer again, never be able to say how sorry he was for how he'd acted, and for what he'd blindly led her into, without a thought for anyone but himself. He continued to watch as a huge slab-like door closed over the compartment, giving him his last glimpses of his best friend, who from child to woman had stuck by him and protected him all his life, and who he had now abandoned to the care of a practical stranger. Emotions finally overwhelmed him, and he wept openly.

"I'm so sorry. Forgive me, Summer! Please forgive me..." But the words were lost in the maelstrom of noise generated by the ship.

Without warning he was thrust back into his seat with a force unlike anything he had ever experienced. The noise was deafening, the vibrations truly horrifying. He screamed, though no-one could have known, the feeble noises emanating from his mouth being completely overshadowed by the ferocious, violent thrust of the ship's engines. The tears on his face were squeezed dry by the sheer force of the acceleration. They were ascending and Ethan could see the insides of the hangar bay quickly slipping away. The pressure pushing him back into his chair intensified, and he gripped the seat arms with such power that his knuckles completely emptied of blood and went snow white. His vision began to darken, and he went to scream again, but there was no sound. His heart was racing and he felt like it was going to explode. Panic overwhelmed him. He tried to force his arms up to his chest to unbuckle the belts and get out. He desperately wanted to get out, but he could not move his arms. He could not move anything. His vision dimmed further and then, as the silvery light of the night sky gave way to infinite blackness, he too passed into darkness and unconsciousness.

***

Katie squeezed Elijah's hand as they both stood in the settlement grounds with the others, watching the object rise into the dark sky above the old, ruined city, a trail of dense, white smoke in its wake.

"What is that!?" Elijah wondered, excitedly, and when no answer came, he looked up and saw tears falling down his mother's face, and he wondered why she was sad.

"Goodbye, Ethan," he heard her murmur weakly, the words seeping softly into the night air.

Confused, Elijah turned back to the object. He watched in silence as it steadily rose higher and higher, until it was nothing more than a flash of light in the clear night sky.

CHAPTER 18

Deep, black smoke belched into the air, twisting one way and then another as if it were alive. The flames burned with ferocious intensity and the heat was unbearable. Ethan tried to get closer, but was forced to back away. Or was he being pulled away? He tried to scream, to shout her name, but no words came out. Instead, out of the inferno he heard his name, an anguished shriek cutting though the roar of the flames.

"Ethan, help me!"

The words bit him like burning splinters. He fought, but he could not get closer, and still the fire grew hotter and the clouds darker. He fell to his knees, his face red with the heat. Then above the enveloping darkness appeared two bright shards of light, brighter even than the fire, intense against the black smoke. They hovered over the house for a moment, and then shot away, upwards, leaving them behind.

"No!" Ethan tried to scream, but again no sound. "Don't leave them! Come back!" He felt his throat burn as he made the sounds, but he couldn't hear the words. It was as if the blackness had also swallowed his voice. "NO!"

The house collapsed in on itself, a mass of flame and heat, and then the voice came once again, his mother's voice, calling to him, begging him for help. "Ethan!"

Ethan opened his eyes and forced himself upright, arms flailing wildly around him. His heart pulsed violently in his chest and his face and body were soaked with sweat. His breathing was shallow and rapid, and his temples throbbed. He grabbed his face and drew sweat away from his eyes.

"Damn it, damn it, damn it!" he cursed, angry at his own mind for continuing to force these images on him. Through sheer force of will, he urged his breathing into a more natural rhythm. It was a routine that he'd become quite practised in over the years, when the nightmare came, as it did almost every week.

Soon he had regained control. He squinted against the intense white light of the room he was in, which was doing nothing to help his headache. He raised a hand to shield his eyes from it, but found his arm to be weak and heavy. With his eyes still barely half open, Ethan attempted to take in his surroundings. He was sitting on a bed and, as his eyes slowly adjusted to the light, he began to see more clearly where he had awoken so violently. The room had a clean, white design and from the materials used it looked not dissimilar to the type of rooms he had seen in the space port on the planet, just 'newer' and without the filth. Maybe he was still there, he thought. Perhaps Maria had been forced to abort the launch and had managed to find an area of the city that had been largely preserved, even after all this time.

He slid across and sat on the edge of the bed. Pain shot through his shoulders and arms. In fact, his whole upper body felt bruised and sore. In the room were various items of furniture and a host of objects he did not recognise. There was a single door with frosted glass in the top section, and a large single window on the opposite side. Outside this window he could see an interconnecting web of tunnels and curious dome-shaped buildings of various sizes, all starkly contrasted against the night sky. He got off the bed and was shocked by the coldness of the floor. He was not wearing any shoes, in fact he wasn't sure what he was wearing, only that they weren't his clothes. They had been replaced by some lightweight, loose-fitting garments which were very comfortable, but wholly unsuitable for life in the settlement. Feet aside, however, Ethan didn't feel cold; the air in the room was warm, almost too warm.

He walked closer to the large window and placed a hand on it to steady himself. He felt oddly lighter and less rooted to the ground. Through the window he observed that the stars were far brighter than he was used to. It was an entirely cloudless and absolutely crystal-clear night and Ethan was struck by the beauty and intensity of it. He waited by the window, looking out for several minutes, his mind a jumble of everything that had happened in the past few days. Despite the intensity of the images in his mind's eye, he felt oddly numb. He knew he should be wondering where he was, if he was in danger, and what had happened to Maria, and to Kurren and Summer, but he felt no urgency to deal with these questions.

He stood by the window, looking out, feeling the coolness of the floor on his bare feet. After his abrupt awakening, he found it soothing. In the sky beyond the last of the grey domes, he noticed that the moon appeared unusually large and bright, and also radiating a colour that he'd never seen before. And then the realisation struck him like a falling boulder, shaking him from his trance-like stupor. It was not the moon, but a planet, bright and blue against a backdrop of nothingness. His planet – he was looking at his planet from the moon base. He stood a little away from the window and looked on, awestruck, dumbstruck. They had made it.

"Pretty, isn't it?" The voice startled him and he physically recoiled. He was still feeling on edge. "I'm sorry, I didn't mean to scare you," said Maria. She had entered the room without Ethan noticing, and was standing a few paces behind him. Without thinking, he went over and wrapped his arms around her. This took Maria completely by surprise, but she returned the embrace warmly. "Hey, it's okay," she said softly into his ear, "we made it."

Ethan released Maria and stepped back a pace, returning his gaze to the window. Maria noticed the wetness of his clothes, and felt it on her cheek and neck from their hug. "Are you okay?" she asked, concerned. "Let me get the medics to check you out." She went to leave, but Ethan stopped her.

"I'm fine," he said. "Just, shock, you know. I maybe panicked a little. But I'm okay, really."

"Are you sure?" said Maria, looking him over.

"I'm sure, Sal," replied Ethan, smiling.

Maria liked it when he called her, 'Sal', and she smiled back. "Everything must seem a little unreal right now," she said, nodding over to the window, with the vibrant blue planet framed in the centre, "but give it time. You'll get used to it."

She was dressed in a uniform, which was sleeker and more fitted than the utilitarian outfit she had been wearing when they first met. She looked good, Ethan thought, certainly compared to himself. He looked down at what he was wearing – loose fitting beige trousers and a thin shirt that buttoned up at the front. It was very comfortable, but compared to Maria, he felt quite under-dressed.

Maria sensed his concern over his clothing. "Don't worry about what you're wearing; we'll get you something more appropriate soon."

"Can I have my old clothes back?" Ethan asked, hopefully.

Maria hadn't been expecting this. "Oh, I'm afraid we... er... got rid of them," she said, sheepishly.

"Got rid of them?" Ethan repeated, mildly offended. "How? Where?"

"We sort of incinerated them," said Maria.

"*Sort of* incinerated them?"

"It's okay, we'll get you some new clothes," Maria added, trying to sound positive.

Ethan took a deep breath and nodded. Katie had made the clothes for him, but now, like her, they were gone. The enormity of what he'd done was starting to hit.

Maria tried to change the subject. "You're in the hospital wing," she said. "You've been here for about half a day – a planetary day, we use the same measure of time up here."

Ethan looked surprised. "Why so long?"

"The medics needed to attend to your injuries," replied Maria. "They gave you a cocktail of medicines to help you get back on your feet, but it knocked you out for a bit too."

"I still feel a little... strange," Ethan said. "Like, I'm not quite on the ground. Does that sound crazy?"

Maria shook her head. "Not at all, gravity here is a little lower than you're used to on the planet, so you may feel a bit lighter, but you'll get used to it."

Ethan had to ask Maria to clarify what gravity was, and though he didn't fully understand the definition she gave him, he accepted the explanation. He turned around and looked out of the window again, trying to process everything, and trying to think of something to ask. He expected to have a million questions, but after a period of contemplation, all he could manage was a feeble, "So, we're on the moon?"

Maria smiled, warmly. "I think I need to get the medics to

check your head again, make sure nothing inside has turned to mush."

Ethan smiled back. "My head does feel like mush. If I'd have known the journey here would have been so..."

"Wild?" Maria suggested

Ethan laughed. "Yes, wild!" he agreed. "If I'd known then I'd probably have stuck to fighting Roamers on a desolate planet with scant food and the constant threat of death. It seems a lot safer."

Maria laughed. "Glad to see your sense of humour survived the trip," she said. "So, now that you're up, what do you say we get started? How about a quick tour?"

Ethan again looked at what he was wearing. "Do you think I can get some proper clothes first?"

Maria laughed again. "Sure, I'll have someone bring you in a few choices and sizes. Wear what you like."

She seemed at ease, comfortable and happy, and this made Ethan feel good too. But then he remembered what he'd left behind, and guilt stabbed at him again. His smiled faded and he looked down at the cold, white floor. "What about Summer and Kurren?" he asked solemnly. "Do you know what happened to them, if they're okay?"

Hearing their names also had a sobering effect on Maria. She also looked away momentarily, before forcing herself to look back at Ethan. Her right hand trembled slightly and she pressed it tightly against her leg to steady it. "I monitored for as long as I could," Maria answered. "I know the launch bay doors were released, which means Kurren and Summer would have been able to get out. But beyond that, no, I don't know anything more."

Ethan considered this in silence for a few seconds, and realised that of the two, it was Kurren that was most in danger. Summer would survive, he had to believe that; she was a born survivor. But Kurren was injured, and also Summer's enemy. He was less convinced about him, but for Maria's benefit he would play the optimist. He could see she was hurting.

"So long as they could get out, they'll get back to the settlement." he told her, convincingly. Maria nodded and managed a weak smile. "And I'm sure Kurren will be fine," he added. "Summer is skilled at treating injuries, so she'll be able to patch him up." He thought about adding, 'So long as she doesn't kill him first', in a joking way, but reconsidered, because he didn't want to tempt fate. Nevertheless, Ethan's comment seemed to make Maria feel more at ease again.

"I'm sure you're right," she replied, maintaining the weak smile a moment longer. "I'll have someone bring you some clothes and then we'll meet up again soon, okay?" Ethan nodded, and Maria touched him gently on the shoulder, tugging on the thin material a little. "Thank you, Ethan," she said tenderly, and then added, with a touch of melancholy, "and, I'm sorry."

The latter took Ethan by surprise and he was unable to process a reply before Maria had turned and left the room. Perhaps she meant about Summer and the mess they had all made in getting here. But, still, it was an odd thing to say, and it gnawed at him.

A few minutes later the doors slid open again. This time a young man entered, carrying some clothes and a couple of pairs of boots. He acknowledged Ethan with a nod, but walked past him and placed the items carefully on the bed. He was dressed in a uniform that more closely resembled Kurren's when they had first met, but with less elaborate adornments. Perhaps he was a lower status or rank. He turned to Ethan and said, very formally, "Please put these on, Sir. I will be waiting outside to escort you to the briefing room."

Ethan walked over and inspected the clothes. They were

functional and well made, and also clearly designed for utility, with multiple pockets in the trousers and reinforced shoulder and elbow areas. But they had no insignia or adornments, save for a UEC emblem on the breast pocket.

"I guess the tour has to wait?" Ethan asked, but the man did not react and simply excused himself, formally, and left.

Ethan changed into the clothes and walked towards the door, which he was surprised to discover opened for him automatically as he approached. The young uniformed man was standing outside, as promised, and he gestured for Ethan to follow him. They walked along clean, white passageways and past a series of similar-looking rooms, some bigger and some smaller like his own, but all with a similar, sterile look to them and all bustling with people getting on with whatever it was they were doing. This place was big, Ethan thought, as he passed the tenth or eleventh room; he had lost count. They then exited the hallway into a much larger room, at which point the uniformed man momentarily broke his silence to explain that this was the medical wing's main reception area. Again, people moved to and fro, not paying Ethan or the young man any attention, save the occasional polite 'hello' or nod. Then they continued outside, at which point the surroundings changed considerably. The sparse, white design of the medical building gave way to scenery much closer in look and feel to that of the city near the settlement on the planet, with angular buildings made from synthetic-looking materials. The big difference was that these buildings were intact and clean, unlike the weather-beaten, broken and battered streets and buildings of the city on the planet. Despite this, however, the similarity in design was unmistakable. The most impressive of all the architectural elements was the vast domed ceiling. Ethan looked up in amazement at the size and scale of the place they were in. They could fit perhaps a dozen or more settlements the size of Forest Gate in this single domed area alone.

"Is that all that's between us and... out there?" Ethan asked the man, feeling a little queasy at the prospect of what lay beyond the dome's oddly translucent boundary.

"I'm not authorised to answer any questions, Sir, but don't worry, it's quite safe," was the young man's polite reply.

Ethan was now aware that more people seemed to be noticing him. Couples and people in small groups would sometimes slow down or stop and whisper to each other as they passed by. He thought about asking the young man about this, but didn't as he guessed at what his answer would likely be. After a couple of minutes of this close observation Ethan was beginning to feel a little paranoid, but he saw with relief that ahead of him was large, grey building with an impressive looking UEC insignia above the main doors, and assumed this was their destination. Ethan noted that the insignia was the same one that was emblazoned on the uniforms that Maria and the young man wore, and it also matched the one on his shirt.

The man stopped as they reached the door, which opened for them automatically. "Please go inside Sir," he said, politely, "Captain Salus is waiting for you."

"Who?" said Ethan, before remembering and feeling a little stupid. "Oh, never mind." The man did not react.

"I'm instructed to inform you that venturing outside of this building, unescorted, is forbidden." The announcement took Ethan off guard. It sounded like the man was reciting from a script. "There are many restricted areas and areas that are off-limits to you..." the man stopped abruptly and hastily corrected himself, looking quite embarrassed, "... that are off-limits to non-UEC personnel. This is for your own safety, Sir," the man added, returning to his scripted delivery style, but the flush of his cheeks gave away that he'd made a mistake. The man then said his goodbyes and marched off.

Ethan frowned. "Off limits to me?" he wondered. "For my own safety?"

"Ethan!" The friendly shout was from Maria. She was walking towards the door, motioning for him to come inside. She looked happy to see him, the earlier trace of melancholy now gone.

"What did he mean when he said there are areas off limits to me?" Ethan said, as she got close enough to hear him without raising his voice.

Maria shot him a confused look, clearly surprised by the question. Ethan explained what the uniformed man had told him, including his slip-of-the-tongue. Ethan noticed that Maria's smile buckled slightly, and she stuttered a hesitant reply, though her voice remained cheerful.

"Oh, don't pay it any attention," said Maria, "there are areas that are off limits to lots of people, it's just a safety thing, you know?" The answer, though cheerfully delivered, was unconvincing and evasive. Ethan felt himself getting cross.

"I think I can manage not to kill myself," he said, tartly. "I've managed so far."

"I know," Maria replied. "But, for now, where you need to be is in here, with me. We can perhaps have that tour later, okay?" The intention was clear; Maria didn't want to talk about 'off limits' areas, and Ethan realised that the young man's slip was a bigger mistake than she was letting on. For the first time since he'd met her, Ethan felt suspicious of Maria, and this made him feel anxious and exposed in this alien environment. Up to this point, he had taken it in his stride, despite the strangeness and enormity of the situation, because of his unflinching belief in why he was doing it and, more importantly, for whom.

Maria noticed his unease. "Hey, it's okay Ethan, I'll look

after you," she said. "I know this is all really strange, but we're together, okay?" And again, the tender tug to the shirt sleeve. Despite his doubts, Ethan couldn't help but feel reassured.

"Okay, Sal," he said. "Better get to it then." She led him into the building and he followed her through a large and strangely empty hallway into a small room. The door closed behind them. "It's a bit small for a meeting, isn't it?" said Ethan, wondering why they had left the larger room to stand, cooped up, in this metal box.

"This isn't the meeting room, Ethan," Maria said, stifling a laugh. This made him feel both annoyed and embarrassed. Maria again picked up on Ethan's shift of mood, something she was getting adept at, and held back from teasing him further. "Just hold on to the rail there, and your lunch..." she added with a knowing smile. Ethan frowned as she took out a flat piece of plastic from her shirt pocket and pressed it to a panel on the wall. The room instantly shot upwards. Ethan was completely unprepared and buckled at the knees due to the sudden acceleration. Since he hadn't held onto the rail as Maria had suggested, he nearly crumpled into a heap on the floor, but was saved this further embarrassment thanks to his quick reflexes, which allowed him to catch the railing just in time. Almost as quickly as it had begun, the pressure eased, allowing Ethan to adjust and regain his balance. Through slits in the walls of the room, he could see that they were travelling upwards. Then the little box decelerated with the same alarming speed and Ethan felt like his feet would leave the floor. This time he was holding on to the rail, though, and so managed to keep his balance, and dignity. A note chimed in the room, like the sound of metal striking metal, and the doors opened into a grand room with an enormous black table at the centre, surrounded by twelve impressive-looking black chairs. At first, Ethan thought the room had no walls and simply existed in a void, but as he followed Maria out of the box he could see that the walls were of a transparent material, similar to the windows in the room where he had woken up. He chanced a look out and wished he hadn't; the room was a long way up. How high Ethan didn't really want to know, but it was high enough that the people on the surface looked like bugs, scurrying in and out of the various buildings below. Ethan had never experienced the sensation of being so high and he felt a little queasy.

"We call it 'The Teardrop'," said Maria as Ethan gingerly backed away from the transparent walls. "It's sort of a symbolic meeting space."

Ethan cocked an eyebrow. "If it's called 'The Teardrop', I'm almost afraid to ask what it symbolises."

"I could tell you, but Talia wouldn't be happy," said Maria, cheekily.

Ethan laughed. "I think we're past the point of worrying what Talia thinks," he said with a smile.

Maria walked over and stood beside him. Together they looked out over the vast area of the moon base. It was an incredible sight that made Ethan wonder just how majestic the cities on the planet must have been, before The Fall.

"A long time ago, this is where the planetary leaders met to sign the treaty, guaranteeing energy security on equal terms to all people," said Maria. There was pride in the way she spoke this, Ethan noticed. "This beautiful, transparent room, high above the surface, was meant to symbolise the openness with which all present entered into the treaty," she continued. "Just as the room hid nothing, so would all of the representatives. No hidden agendas."

"So why not call it, 'The Transparent Room' or 'Open Room', or something like that. Why 'Teardrop?'" asked Ethan.

Maria smiled. "Ah, well that's the best part," she said,

clearly glad that Ethan was paying attention, and was interested. "As the story goes when the final governor to sign the document finished her signature, she also shed a single tear, which fell on the paper and mixed with the ink, creating a tear-shaped stain. It was considered the final mark of acceptance and approval, and so they named the room after it."

Ethan had to stare solidly at his feet to stop himself from feeling sick, and barely heard Maria. "That's great, Sal," he said, uneasily, "but couldn't we have done this somewhere, you know, less high up?"

Unseen to Ethan, Maria smiled broadly. "It's a great honour, Ethan. This room doesn't get used much these days."

"No world leaders left, I guess, huh?" Ethan quipped, and Maria's smiled disappeared. Ethan hadn't intended to be so cutting, and the sharpness of his response surprised even himself. It reminded him of Summer. He fought that image back; he did not want to be reminded of her right now. He felt sick enough as it was.

"Well, the sooner we start, the sooner we can get back to ground level," said Maria, plainly.

Ethan looked from his feet and towards the centre of the room, which helped to steady his stomach. It was then he noticed that two of the large black chairs were occupied. The chair at the very top of the table was filled by an older man, perhaps similar to Talia's age, dressed in the same uniform as Maria, but with many more adornments to the collar and cuffs. The chair to his left side was occupied by a severe-looking man dressed in utilitarian clothing, similar to the sort Ethan was wearing, again with the addition of some designs and metal studs to the collar and cuff. He was younger, perhaps late middle-aged, and looked like he'd seen a fight or two in his life.

Ethan approached them, still a little gingerly, and the man at the top of the table at once stood up, followed swiftly by the man sat to his side, who then took a step back. The older man wore a warm, but carefully controlled smile, not unlike the one Maria had given Ethan earlier, when they were discussing his restricted movements. This made Ethan instantly distrustful of him.

"Welcome, welcome!" the older man said, gesturing for Ethan to come closer. "It's an honour to meet you, Ethan. Captain Salus has told me so much about you." Ethan glanced over at Maria, wondering what she had been saying about him, but Maria was standing rigidly, hands by her sides, a plain, serious expression on her face. "All good, of course," the man added, casually, still smiling, as if he thought this qualification was important. "I am Governor Archer, Thomas Archer," he continued. "I have the honour and privilege of running this base and presiding over the UEC governing council. Please excuse the formality of the uniform; it's merely protocol in these situations."

"What situations?" asked Ethan, abruptly. He was genuinely interested, but the way he blurted out the question seemed to visibly disconcert Maria, who he could still see in his peripheral vision.

Governor Archer's face retained its easy smile. "Defence protocol, Ethan," he answered, after a slight pause. "I am Governor, but also the commander of our security forces here – the defenders that protect us from GPS attacks and keep us safe and secure." Archer walked around the edge of the table so that he was standing more directly in front of them, and then added, "I understand that Captain Salus has already briefed you on our situation?"

"Yes," said Ethan. "Sal showed me some images on a holo, or whatever it's called."

"Already on first name terms, good!" said Archer, enthusiastically.

Ethan thought he saw Maria wince, and considered that his familiar tone perhaps wasn't appropriate in this situation, though he was merely responding in the same, casual manner in which he had been welcomed. His mind was then overtaken with memories of what the 'holo' had shown him, and what Maria had said. It seemed like such a long time ago, and so far away, and in the excitement and strangeness of recent events he'd almost forgotten. He remembered the meeting in the settlement hall, in far less grand circumstances than these. The thrill of learning the truth and the crushing disappointment and regret that followed. He recalled the suspicion, anger and resentment from Summer, and the ultimatum from Administrator Talia to Kurren and Maria, with its passive-aggressive undertone and its own sense of bitterness. In recollecting all this, he felt a sudden sense of uneasiness, as something didn't quite add up. And then he realised why.

"Maria, I mean Captain Salus, said that people up here were in danger?" said Ethan, conscious that he perhaps shouldn't sound too personally attached to Maria. While it was clear that Maria and this Governor Archer had talked before his arrival, he was pretty sure Maria would have left out any personal details. "She said that it was something related to the same sickness that causes The Maddening on the planet?" Ethan added, again phrasing the sentence more as a question.

"That is correct," said Archer, a little hesitantly, the reason for Ethan's question unclear to him.

"So where is the danger?" Ethan asked, annoyed that he was having to spell it out. "Forgive me for being blunt, but I don't see anything wrong up here. Everyone seems just fine." The more he spoke the more Ethan found himself becoming irritated. "In fact, Governor, it seems that you have it pretty good up here, compared to us Planetsiders, anyway."

The Governor listened patiently, impassively, wearing the

same, easy smile. For some reason he irked Ethan. He had felt uneasy ever since arriving; a feeling that something wasn't quite right. And now, standing in front of these men, dressed in their immaculate uniforms, in this pristine room poised almost magically above their peaceful kingdom in space, with its artificial lighting, comfortable temperature and total lack of any apparent threats or dangers, the realisation struck him. Life on this base was good. There was no suffering, no adversity, at least none that he had witnessed. Compared to the daily struggle and constant threat of danger that he had lived with his entire life, this base was a paradise. He questioned why he had risked so much – and sacrificed so much – to be here.

Maria comprehended the cause of Ethan's agitation and was now also visibly uneasy. "Ethan, if you'd just give the General, I mean Governor, some time to explain..." she began, nervously.

The slip of the tongue didn't go unnoticed to Ethan. 'General', she had said, not 'Governor'. This was not a domestic matter, but a military one. Before Maria could continue, Governor Archer interrupted.

"It's okay, Captain," Archer said to Maria, and instantly she stood down and assumed her previous, erect posture. "Ethan, I understand your frustration," Archer continued. "Compared to the life you're used to, this place must seem like a paradise." Archer's perceptiveness took Ethan by surprise.

"You're right that life on this base is incomparable to life on the planet. You know that our conflict with GPS is what caused the devastation on the planet, and for this reason, any anger or resentment towards us is completely understandable. The imbalance between our situation and yours is unfair and unjust."

Hearing Archer admit this so freely deflated the bubble of anger that was threatening to expand into a cloud of rage around Ethan. He felt his heart rate ease and rationality begin to assert itself again. He noticed Maria, who was carefully observing him, also relax slightly.

"There is no 'maddening', as you call it, here on the station," said Archer. "Our medical technology is able to counteract the effects of the exposure levels on the base, so that the worst that can be expected is a shortening of life expectancy by a number of years, not a degradation of life of the sort that you witness planetside. But things *have* changed, Ethan, and that is why you're here." Governor Archer gestured for Ethan to take a seat, still with that easy smile on his face. Ethan looked at the chair and hesitated slightly before deciding to take up the offer and sit down. Archer's words had gone some way to appeasing his doubts, but there was still more he needed to know.

Archer sat also, but Maria and the other man, as yet still to be introduced, remained standing. Ethan regarded the man momentarily from his new position in the chair. He had a hard look about his slightly craggy, rough-shaven face. There was a scar around and below his right ear, Ethan noticed. Not a cut, but more a mottling of the skin, which was also darker than the skin around it.

"I'm sorry" said Archer, noticing that Ethan was staring at the man. "I forgot to introduce you to Major Kurren, here."

"Kurren?"

"Yes, Major James Kurren. You knew his brother, of course, Commander Chris Kurren."

Ethan's heart sank. Kurren's brother. Kurren who had sacrificed his own ride home so that Ethan could be here. Kurren, Maria's friend and comrade who, in all likelihood, was now dead, either from his wound, The Maddening, or the journey back to the settlement. For all Ethan knew, Summer may have killed him herself. He stood up and met Major's

Kurren's eyes, which were a vivid blue; cold and severe.

"I'm... I'm sorry about your brother," said Ethan, with genuine warmth. "I didn't know Commander Kurren at all, really, but I saw how he acted, and he was an honourable man." Ethan noticed the Major's eyes waver momentarily as he said the word, 'honourable'.

"Thank you," Major Kurren replied stoically, not adjusting his stance.

Ethan sank back down into his chair, his mind again a muddle of thoughts and emotions.

Archer regarded him carefully, allowing him time with his thoughts, waiting patiently for the optimal moment to speak again, so as to have Ethan's full attention. When Ethan finally looked up, Archer continued.

"Ethan, what you see here on this base is the result of an uneasy stand-off with GPS, who are still out there on their orbital platform." Archer made a sweeping gesture upwards with his right hand as he said 'out there'. "But for two generations we have fought them. Skirmish after skirmish, each one repelled, but each one cutting us a little more, and a then little more. Yet we survived and built a life here." And then with more emphasis, he said, "We *created* life here. Families, Ethan, just like down on the planet. We are no different."

Ethan thought for a moment and then said, "So what changed. Why do you need me now?"

"What happened is that GPS changed tactics, and we did not see their intentions until it was too late," Archer said, plainly. Archer tapped at a screen built into the table in front of him and a three-dimensional display appeared in the centre of the table, similar to the image that Maria and Kurren had shown him and the councillors at the settlement. Ethan watched intently as the display showed a huge object, constructed of a large centre platform and a network of smaller platforms connected by conduits, which jutted out in all directions like an enormous spider's web, hanging in space above a planet.

"What is that?" asked Ethan, leaning in to get a better look.

"That is the primary orbital base of the Global Power Security corporation," said Archer. "Or, at least, it used to be. At first, it was simply the centre platform, but over time it grew. Before the conflict began, the governments of the world tried to curb its expansion, fearing it was becoming too big; too self-sufficient and powerful. They were correct, of course."

"And they've continued to expand it ever since?"

"Correct," said Archer. "Now it has become even larger than this base, or at least what remains of the habitable sections of this base," he added, casually. Archer started to tap at the console again. The images began to move. "One day GPS suddenly stopped their raids, which had been a regular feature of life here for decades, and started to direct their weapons onto an area of debris, located some distance from their platform, but well away from the moon base." The images moved as Archer spoke, following his words and keeping in time with the events as he recounted them. "At first, we couldn't understand it," he continued. "There appeared to be no threat to us and no tactical benefit for them. We thought that perhaps they were looking to extract some ore, and maybe they had run low on fuel. But since the destruction of the refinery, one thing we are not short of in space is ore to use as fuel." Archer let out a muted laugh as he said this, but no one reacted. "What we discovered too late was that this debris was the remains of a refinery node, still full of ore, and that the detonations had not only altered the orbit vector of this debris, but also atomised the ore," he continued. The terms were unfamiliar to Ethan and he frowned in concentration, trying to follow what Archer was saying, something that didn't go unnoticed by the General and Governor. "In simple terms, they had created a biological weapon of sufficient size and toxicity to kill everyone on this base. To wipe us out, once and for all."

The images moved along with Archer's description of the events, and Ethan watched as the image projected a line spiralling from the debris cloud around the planet towards the moon base.

"But you stopped it?" said Ethan. "I mean, you're all still here, so you must have found a way to stop it?"

"Yes, but not without significant consequences," Archer said. He tapped the panel and the display updated, showing ships taking off from the base and heading towards the debris cloud. "We evacuated the station as far as possible, and launched everything we had at the debris field, including ships laden with ore, to use as flying bombs. Our hope was that we could alter its orbit again, away from the station. Sadly, we were unable to fully succeed in this endeavour, and it cost us most of our ships and weapons."

The display showed ships exploding in space, pushing the debris cloud off its deadly course, but not quite far enough. While most of the debris field missed the moon, elements remained on a collision course. Ethan watched as these smashed into the moon base. It again reminded him of the images he had seen back on the planet. How similar their fates were, he thought.

"It's ironic, isn't it?" Ethan said, to no-one in particular.

Archer's face contorted into a curious frown. "What is, Ethan?"

"That you faced a fate so similar to that of the planet."

"Yes, I suppose so," Archer said, with some agitation, as if he were slightly annoyed by the comparison.

Archer tapped a button and a three dimensional plan view

of the moon base flicked into view. Suddenly, sections began to turn red – the first time the display had varied from its usual, pale white light.

"Fifty-eight percent of the base was immediately rendered uninhabitable. Over ten thousand died. Another 3500 followed within days of the impact from intense exposure. There was no time for The Maddening, as you call it, to take hold with these unfortunate souls, which is perhaps a mercy." Archer's tone had darkened once again, and his easy smile had gone. "We set our emergency protocols into action and started to intensify our production of anti-toxicity medications, while also funnelling resources into creating newer, more effective medicines. Still, another two thousand died within a year, either from the toxic radiation, or the newly reinvigorated GPS, who again started their regular attacks with the hope of finishing us off."

The more Archer talked the angrier he became. He paused, and after a deep sigh, his expression changed again, the easy smile returning. When he continued, the earlier, smooth delivery resumed.

"A democratic decision was made by the UEC council to place the base under military control, which is when I became Governor. We fought back against GPS and inflicted enough losses to keep them contained on their platform. But the damage was done. That was fifteen years ago." The display changed again, now displaying a roster of names, with huge swathes turning red. The display zoomed out, and out again, with more names appearing and turning red. "We have now lost nearly 90% of our original number, leaving only 2587 of us on this base," Archer said, his tone again carefully controlled. "Many are families; the descendants of engineers and ore industry workers from decades ago. Our medical knowledge has contained the effects of the radiation. So what you see here, while peaceful on the surface, is still a fragile existence."

Ethan thought back to his earlier comment about the irony of the situation, which he now realised was insensitive. While the loss suffered by the people on the moon was small compared to the billions who perished on the planet, they had still suffered and were still having to endure. It wasn't fair to make it a numbers game. Also, the total number on the station had shocked Ethan. For some reason, he had imagined a vast population in space, while the truth was that life up in this black and cold void was as precarious as that of life Planetside. The fragility of their existence was brought starkly into view.

"I am sorry if I came across as insensitive earlier," said Ethan. "When I said that it was ironic that your fate was similar to that of the planet, I didn't mean to make light of your situation, or suggest any sort of poetic justice."

"No apology necessary, Ethan." Again, the easy smile.

"I still don't understand why you need me, though," said Ethan. "Sorry to be blunt, but why am I here?"

Archer's smile dropped a little, and he tapped again on the table. The display changed back to the view of the planet and the debris cloud in orbit, a line extending from its centre and spiralling around the planet as before. "When we deflected the debris cloud, it remained in orbit around the planet, and we have monitored it ever since. It moves chaotically, changing direction from time to time as it collides with other debris, sometimes creating small detonations inside the centre, also resulting in unpredictable adjustments to its course." Ethan watched the display chart the erratic course of the debris field around the planet. "This has had the useful side-effect of significantly reducing the size and lethality of the cloud. It's mostly a dense cluster of dust and fragments now," Archer continued, "nothing that could cause damage to the base in itself, if it were not for the toxicity."

"So what you're saying is that this toxic radiation cloud is going to hit the base again?" Ethan speculated.

"Yes, Ethan, precisely," Archer confirmed. "Sadly, chance is no longer on our side and in less than thirty rotations, it will hit the base again, and we no longer have the means to alter its path. Our only hope is to synthesise a new serum, a more powerful serum that can protect us. As your immunity protects you, planetside."

Ethan thought for a moment, processing all this new information. It still didn't add up. "But why do you need me?" he said, the frustration evident in his voice. "You could have just brought back some of my blood. What use am I to you?"

"Because we don't have the medical tools needed to create the new serum..." Archer began, but Ethan cut him off.

"But how does that involve me?!" Ethan shouted, interrupting Archer and banging his fists on the table in frustration. The display in the centre hummed off, pitching the room into a soft darkness, illuminated only by a light running around the edge of the ceiling. It was dim enough that Ethan didn't notice Major Kurren instinctively reach for his weapon, or Maria unseen behind Ethan's back, hold up her hand to have him stand down. Ethan was too embroiled in his own emotions. He had given up his life and his family to be here, and all he was getting was a history lesson and no real answers.

He felt a hand on his shoulder. It was Maria. "Ethan, I know this is a lot to take in, but please stay calm," she said softly. "We're only trying to give you the full picture, to help you understand the seriousness of the situation and how we arrived at this point."

"Sal, I think I understood the seriousness of the situation when I had myself blasted into space with you," he said, sarcastically.

Maria looked at Archer, who nodded gently. She sat down

next to Ethan. "Remember, back on the planet, I told you that we needed your help to get something we needed?"

Ethan tried to think back that night in his house, when Maria said she would die if Ethan didn't help him. "Yes, vaguely, it seems like so long ago now," he said, recalling their conversation.

"Our only hope is to rescue a ship that was damaged during the original attack on the refinery," Maria said. "On that ship is the equipment we need to create the new serum, one that will protect everyone once the cloud impacts the base."

Ethan again thought back to the initial briefing on the planet, and remembered this large ship, and how it had spiralled away from the base, fire licking at its hull. "And this is what you need my help to recover?" he said, and then hearing his own words, he was painfully aware of how ridiculous this sounded. How could he help to recover a space ship?

"Yes," Maria said. "The ship was damaged. And it's also old; its power systems are long since depleted. But more importantly, it drifted onto the dark side of the moon, where the impacts from the debris cloud were most heavily concentrated. No-one on here can survive that level of toxicity, Ethan. None of us can get even close to the ship. But you can."

"You need me to rescue a space ship?" Ethan said, and the words sounded no less ridiculous a second time. "You do realise that I'm not a space ship pilot...?"

"That's where Captain Salus and Major Kurren come in," said Archer. Still the easy smile. "Captain Salus will pilot another vessel to take you as close as possible, using a high dose of our existing anti-con medications to ensure no critical exposure. And then you will get into an EV suit and Kurren will help you to pilot it onto the ship."

"An EV what?" said Ethan.

"Extra-Vehicular," said Maria. "A special suit that means

you can go out into space."

"Out into space?!" Ethan protested, but Maria smiled at him and said, "Don't worry, it's nothing compared to what you've already been through."

Ethan remained unconvinced, but before he could protest further, Archer cut back in. "Once inside the ship, Major Kurren will talk you through manually jump-starting the ship's systems with a portable power splice that we will give you, initiating the ship's emergency backups and installing a mobile transponder to allow him to remote pilot the ship back to the base, where we will decontaminate it and recover the equipment. It's very simple."

Ethan didn't understand any of what Archer and Maria had just said, but they certainly sounded confident that the task wasn't difficult. Nevertheless, Ethan had not anticipated that this would be the reason they had brought him here. He had assumed a simple medical procedure, not an 'extra-vehicular' journey into space. He sat in the huge, black chair, his drawn white face starkly contrasting against it.

Archer, seeing that Ethan was struggling to process the information, filled the awkward silence with more, smoothly delivered words. "With this equipment and your blood, we will be saved, Ethan," he said, in a mildly more upbeat tone. "The difficulty is not the task, but the fact that no-one on this station could survive even a minute inside that ship. In fact, even with our current medications we would be unconscious before even making it inside. Believe me, we've tried."

Quick to dispel the notion that anyone was sent on a suicide mission, Maria hastily added, "The Governor means that we've had people volunteer..."

"Quite..." said Archer, seemingly grateful for the clarification. "But you, Ethan, with the help of our anti-con medications, can be inside for at least an hour with no adverse effects whatsoever."

Maria jumped in again. "Only someone born on the planet, born with a genetic resistance to the toxic effects of the radiation, can survive," she said. "Within your own blood is the key to our survival. But we don't just need your blood, we need you too, Ethan."

Ethan looked at Maria for a moment and let the words 'we need you too, Ethan' repeat in his head. He couldn't help wonder whether, had he not volunteered willingly, they would have tried bringing him – or someone else – by force. He chose not to be blunt once more and question Archer about this, but it added another weight to the scale of doubts that were building inside him.

"Once the ship is back here, we can decontaminate it and recover the medical equipment we need to synthesise the new anti-cons," Maria added. "We'll have the time to synthesise what we need for everyone on the base, so that when the cloud hits, we'll all be protected. You'll have literally saved us all."

Ethan's mind was still a blur. Between the technical terms he didn't understand, and the simple facts he did understand, such as their suggestion that he would venture out into space itself, he was struggling to process the situation. Life had very rapidly become unreal. He considered for a moment if this could all be a dream, but if it was then he was sure that any one of the many terrifying events of the last few days would have shook him violently from his sleep.

Everyone in the room was silent, conscious that Ethan was processing a lot of information. Eventually, it was Archer who again broke the silence. "Well, Ethan, this is a lot to take in, on top of what was already a considerable amount to deal with," he said smoothly, but with genuine feeling. "You've gone from a local Ranger of a small settlement to confronting the descendants of your space-faring ancestors on a technologically-advanced station on the moon. And then to be told only you can save them. If I were you, I wouldn't believe it either!" The last sentence was rounded off with a sort of stuffy guffaw of laughter.

Ethan nodded his head. "This is pretty unbelievable," he agreed. "It feels like a dream."

"Perhaps some time to reflect is in order," said Archer. "Major Kurren will prepare the mission, and tomorrow, if you agree, we will guide you through what needs to be done. For the rest of today and tonight though, get some rest and give yourself some time to adjust."

"I'll take you to your quarters, Ethan," said Maria, looking at him, expectantly.

Another question surfaced in Ethan's head, but he decided not to ask it. He felt out of control, and this was making him anxious. He had no real idea what was going on, but was uncontrollably swept up in it now, like a twig sweeping down a fast-flowing river. He realised then how much his own feelings had changed, and how foolish he must have seemed to friends back in the settlement, who put up with his regular pining for 'the truth' and 'to know what really happened'. The truth was ugly and unsatisfactory. There was no great mystery to unravel, just the usual story of people fighting over one thing or another.

Ethan also did not believe Archer's claims that their two stories were similar. These people were nothing like the Planetsiders. The war between the UEC and GPS had cost almost everything, and it still threatened to destroy one or both of them. Neither side had evolved beyond what they were generations ago. But down on the planet, they had rebuilt, and through struggle and common purpose they had created a new civilisation, with the settlements living in peace with one another. Only The Maddening remained to threaten that peace, and yet even this was a by-product of these two warring factions. Ethan realised now that he didn't care who started it, or who was right or wrong. It didn't change what had happened on the planet, and what was still happening today. Though now distant and detached from the world below, their deadly influence lingered on.

He remembered how he had looked up at the flashes in the sky and seen guardians and protectors, and how the death of his family had driven him to question his beliefs and want to know more; to know the truth. Well, his wish had come true, and what a fool he had been! He had walked away from his sister and nephew, and from people who cared for him and loved him. Summer had warned him, but he would not listen. Administrator Talia was right, Ethan realised. It was better to forget these people, forget the past and move on without them. And if it wasn't for Maria, he would. Uncertainties now lingered around her, uncertainties that would have to be dealt with, but not now. Not yet. She was still the reason he was here. Strip away everything else and there was still Maria, and Ethan's need for her to live.

"Okay, Captain," he said, emphasising Captain a little too much, as if to tease her. He pushed himself out of the cavernous black chair and stood beside her. "I could do with some time to reflect I think."

Maria smiled at him, and then nodded in the direction of Archer. She put her hand to the small of his back, as if to usher him gently back to the elevator, and they moved together out of the room and away from the two men standing at the head of the table.

"You're doing us a great service, Ethan," the governor announced levelly to their backs as Ethan and Maria entered the lift. As the doors slid shut, Ethan turned around and saw on Archer's face the same, easy smile.

CHAPTER 19

They walked back out into the hustle and bustle of the base's neatly laid out, clean streets and Ethan followed Maria as she led them past blocks of buildings of varying sizes and configurations, all built from the same dark, glassy-looking material. Ethan paid no attention to where he was going, and neither of them spoke as they walked. Ethan observed the other people on the streets and noticed that most appeared to be dressed in uniforms similar to Maria's.

"Is everyone here part of the UEC military?" he asked the back of Maria's head.

Maria briefly turned her head towards him and smiled. "We're not the military," she said, and then looked ahead again and continued walking.

"You all certainly dress like you are," said Ethan.

Maria stopped opposite a door in the building they had been walking alongside, one of the larger and grander looking of those they had passed by. "We're here," she said.

"If you're not in the military then why is your governor

called a 'General', and why are you 'Captain' Maria Salus?" Ethan pressed. "Almost everyone I've seen dresses like you."

Maria's smile faded. "What are you getting at, Ethan?" she asked, agitated by the continual questions. "What's going on in that head of yours?"

Ethan looked at her wide-eyed, and almost laughed. "What's going on in my head?" he said, amazed at the question. "I feel like I'm in a dream, Maria. This place, the things you've told me, it's just so unreal. I came here to help you. I didn't expect... any of this."

Maria reflected for a moment. "I know it must be overwhelming," she said. "But you must have known things would be different here." She paused again and then added; "But that's not what's really bugging you, is it?"

Ethan's wide-eyed expression remained, but was modified now by a wry smile. "You are getting to know me, aren't you?" he said. Maria just winked in reply. "Or maybe it's your secret military training allowing you to read my emotions," Ethan added, teasing again.

"That's not funny," said Maria, seriously. "So, come on, out with it. What's really bothering you?"

Ethan bounced the question around his mind for a moment. The question he had wanted to ask Archer, but hadn't for fear of what he might say. And although Maria had been acting a little differently since returning, away from Archer or any other observer, he still felt he could trust her.

"What if I say no?" he said after a tense pause of a few seconds.

"No to going inside this building?" said Maria, jovially. "I guess you can sleep on the streets if you want."

"I'm serious, Sal," Ethan replied. "So far, everyone has assumed that because I'm here, I'm game for whatever you need me to do. I just want to know, what if I did say no? What if I say to Archer, I want to be sent back home?"

Maria's face fell, and suddenly she looked older, more serious. "Ethan, this isn't a game."

"I know that Sal, I just want to know what he'd do," Ethan said. "I came here because of you. You, Maria Salus, not the UEC. I didn't really think about what would happen when I got here."

"I know that," said Maria, looking and sounding concerned. "But you did come, so it's only natural to assume you will do what's needed. Am I wrong? I don't understand what you're telling me."

Ethan threw his arms out to his side. "I don't know how to explain it!" he said, frustrated by his own ability to clearly define the doubts and questions that were swimming around his head. "I don't trust him, Sal," Ethan then admitted. "I wish I'd never learned about the UEC and GPS. I just didn't want you to die, and that's all I was thinking about."

"Archer has been far nicer to you than your Administrator Talia was to us," said Maria, focusing in on Ethan's mistrust of Archer.

"He's nice while he thinks I'm helping," replied Ethan. "But if I say no, what will he do? Force me, coerce me somehow, threaten you to get to me? It's obvious he can tell we're..." he thought carefully about his next word, and chose caution over valour, "...close."

Maria raised an eyebrow at this and pressed her hands to her hips. "Close?" she said, sounding insulted.

Ethan's cheeks flushed and he looked away. "You know what I mean, Sal. I'm not good at this stuff."

Maria closed her eyes momentarily and when she opened them again, she was calmer. She moved closer and took hold of Ethan's hands, squeezing gently. Ethan looked back into her eyes. "I know what you mean," she said, and she held his hands for a second longer and then let go again. "Look, the truth is that no-one has even considered the possibility that you'd say no," she added, starting to worry that Ethan's doubt was real and not merely hypothetical. "Do you want to say no?"

Ethan shook his head gently. "No, I want to help," he said. "I just wish it was simpler. I just want to help *you*. Everything else makes me, I don't know, uneasy."

Maria grabbed him by the waist and pulled him closer. "Then forget about everything else, and just focus on me," she said, sounding like the old Maria; the Maria from the planet. "You came here for me, I know that, and I'm thankful of that. I know what it meant for you to leave. And so I'm here for you now."

"And what about after?" Ethan replied, nervously. It was another question that he was afraid to ask for fear of the reply.

"After what, Ethan?" asked Maria, looking at him quizzically.

"After you make this serum and everyone is safe, and you all go on living your lives up here. Then what happens?"

Maria shrugged. "If you still want to return to the planet, we'll find a way to..."

"I don't mean about me, Sal," Ethan interrupted. "I mean what happens about us?" He was almost physically shaking as he spoke the words.

Maria looked down and was silent for a moment. Ethan felt her grip on his waist tighten. "Do... you want there to be an 'us'?" she asked, softly, still looking down.

Ethan lifted her chin so that their eyes were level. "Yes," he said.

A pulse of energy swept through them, shaking the ground and causing the windows of the nearby building to shatter violently outwards, assaulting them with jagged fragments of the opaque material. They grabbed each other instinctively and ducked away from the blast, covering their heads, but the force of the pulse knocked them to the floor. The vibrations subsided and they helped each other to stand, shaking fragments from their hair and clothes. Save for a few grazes and minor cuts, they had escaped serious injury. Maria was first to look in the direction of the explosion. A fireball had erupted outside the base, beyond the protective dome, but still clearly visible from where they stood. Liquid fire poured into the blackness outside as reverberations from the unseen cause of the detonation throbbed throughout the base.

"It's an attack!" said Maria, urgently. "The raids have started again, I need to go and help!" She pushed off from Ethan and began to run down the street in the direction of the explosion.

"Sal, wait! Where are you going?" Ethan shouted after her, his ears still ringing from the blast.

Maria slowed and turned back towards him. "I've got to help, Ethan, I'm a pilot," she called back. "Go inside, they're expecting you. You have to stay safe!" And then she turned again and started running.

"Wait!" Ethan called after her, but it was no use, she was already too far ahead.

Another explosion rocked the base, this one a little farther off, and in the direction that Maria was running. Ethan saw her stumble and fall, tumbling down the street, before he too was knocked off his feet again. He got up, rubbing bruises on his elbows and shoulders, and looked for her. "Sal!" he shouted, but there was no answer. He could see her, climbing back to her feet. She looked back and motioned with her arms, pointing towards the building, and then she set off again, running away from him.

Ethan looked at the building to his side. There were people inside, shouting for him to come in, to shelter, but Ethan ignored their cries. Instead he ran, legs and arms pumping, desperately trying to catch up with Maria. If she got herself killed, this was all meaningless. It would all have been for nothing. The surroundings became a blur as Ethan accelerated, heart pounding in his chest. The floor shook again as another explosion erupted further ahead, and he had to fight to stay upright. Far beyond the perimeter of the dome he could see objects moving in the darkness. The shapes were similar to the crashed spacecraft that Ethan and the other Rangers had found, a world away below them. He saw that Maria had stopped at a gate to a large compound and he ran up beside her. His body was shaking from a combination of adrenalin and exertion.

"Ethan, what are you doing?!" Maria shouted over the roar of more ships leaving the dome and entering into the blackness above them. "You have to get to safety!"

"Not without you, Sal," said Ethan, the words a struggle as he gasped to regain his breath.

"I have to get out there, Ethan, I'm trained for this, they need me," said Maria.

"Others can do that, Sal. I need you with me, I can't do this without you."

Maria turned and started working on the panel again. "We don't have time for this," she said. "There might not be anything left to save if we don't stop this assault."

A searing shard of light blazed overhead and Ethan saw one of the spacecraft silently erupt into flame and spiral away from the base in a chaotic, almost hypnotic pattern. The gate opened and Maria stepped through. Ethan put a foot into the threshold and gave Maria a determined look. She knew he would not do as she asked.

She let out a cry of frustration and then said, "Okay, come on, I can find you shelter inside."

She ran through the door and Ethan followed her onto a large open strip, which seemed to jut out beyond the main domed habitat. The overall design looked similar to the hangar of the space port on the planet, but several times larger. On the strip were sitting six angular, aggressive looking spacecraft, the same shape as those that he'd seen moving rapidly in the darkness outside. In front of each a large metal door, beyond which was a short corridor that poked out into the blackness beyond, like silvery fingers.

Maria surveyed the surroundings as Ethan caught up with her. He was about to speak, but Maria knew what he was going to say and headed him off. "I'm still going out there, Ethan."

"Sal, if you get killed out there..."

"I won't," she said with conviction. "I've landed on a planet, and I've flown back to the base. No-one has ever done anything like that before. I think you can trust my piloting abilities. I think you can trust me."

Ethan was silent for a moment. "I do trust you, Sal," he said, "but, if I remember correctly, you crashed on the planet." Though not actually meant as a joke, Ethan couldn't help but choke back a laugh.

Maria scowled. "You're as bad as Kurren!"

A man dressed in thick coveralls ran up to Maria, holding a helmet and some kind of harness. "Captain, she's already fuelled and ready, Sir," he said urgently, pointing to the spacecraft closest to them. Maria took the items and nodded at the man, who promptly ran off. They were briefly illuminated by more streams of light flashing overhead. It reminded Ethan of the lights in the night sky back on the planet, only far more intense.

Maria pointed towards a building at the base of the open strip they were standing on. "Go into that building. It's the pilot's ready room. You'll be safe," she said. Ethan opened his mouth, but Maria again headed him off. "No buts, Ethan!" she said, forcefully. "Go, now. I'll be back soon."

"If you get killed, I'm going to be really annoyed," Ethan said, admitting defeat.

Maria smiled. "That will make two of us. Now go." Ethan nodded, and started to run towards the building. Then he heard Maria call his name, and he stopped suddenly and turned back to face her. Shouting over the commotion of ships taking off, she called out, "If anything does happen, Ethan, I want you to know one thing. That this... us... this is real. Okay?"

Ethan nodded reactively, but was confused. He was about to shout back, but Maria had already turned and was running at full speed to the spacecraft, poised ominously on the deck. He stood and watched. Flashes again illuminated them, reflecting off the smooth surface with an intense red hue. Two more explosions, more distant this time, reverberated through the base. Outside Ethan could see the spacecraft moving through the blackness, visible only through the glow of their engines and the bright shards of light that erupted from one towards another and then vanishing off into the distance.

Maria arrived beside her ship and hurriedly put on the harness and helmet. She was about to climb the ladder to the cockpit, but something made her stop and look back. Seeing Ethan still standing on the pad, watching, she lifted a hand and waved. Light danced around them and then the spacecraft on the deck next to Maria's exploded into flames.

The shock wave hit Ethan moments later, knocking him cleanly off his feet. He landed on the hard deck, stunned both from the blow and the blinding flash of light from the fireball that had utterly consumed the ship. Dazed and disorientated, he scrambled back to his feet and tried to find Maria, but there was just a white haze. He struggled to stay standing, an intense ringing in his ears causing his balance to falter. He pressed his eyes shut and clasped his hands to his temples, shaking his head, trying to clear the fog. "Sal!" he yelled, desperate to find her "Sal!"

A smog of black smoke covered the area where the six angular craft had stood. Ethan ran towards it, instinctively, but was unable to balance and stumbled and fell, grazing knees and elbows with each futile attempt. Voices were shouting behind him, but he forced himself up and on towards the black cloud. The smoke was thick and tasted bitter. It stung his eyes and made them stream with dirty, grey tears.

"Where are you?" he coughed into the darkness.

Covering his mouth with his sleeve he pushed on through the dense, smothering fog. Then he saw her, lying on the ground, blown clear of her own ship, which had shielded her from the worst of the explosion, but was itself now on fire. Terror gripped him, but he forced himself on, still stumbling every other step until he was at her side. With all the strength left in him he managed to pull her up and draped her arm over his shoulder. His legs burned, and his throat felt like he had swallowed thorns. He could see outlines of objects moving through the smoke and fought on towards them, forcing his eyes to stay open, despite the searing black smoke that burned like acid. He drove on until the fog cleared and then he collapsed to the smooth, hard deck, Maria falling as a dead weight on top of him. He again heard urgent voices shouting. Above him, a gaping hole in the dome had been sealed by a black web of fibres that had shot out from nearby cross-sections. He coughed violently and felt a bitter mucous in his mouth, which he tried to spit out. It oozed down the side of his face, and he wanted to wipe it away, but couldn't move his arms. The voices grew more distant in his ringing ears, and his vision darkened. He coughed violently, tasting the thick, bitter mucous again, and then passed out.

CHAPTER 20

Ethan opened his eyes and bright light flooded in, making his eyes sting and his head throb. As his vision adjusted, he realised that his eyes were still stinging, so the brightness could not be the cause. Everything was a blur of white and grey and his throat felt as dry as tree bark. And there was still a distant ringing in his ears, like the sound of the wind chimes hanging from his sister's porch, heard from outside the walls, from the old tree on the mound where he would gaze up at the lights and wonder. A blurry, white face stood above him.

"Elijah?" he rasped groggily.

"Ethan, can you hear me"? he heard a voice say, dimly. Then he felt a sharp pain in his arm. "Ethan, if you can hear me, say something," said the same voice, closer now.

"Sir, if you wait a few moments the stimulant should bring him around," said a different voice, also not recognisable.

He felt the fog in his head begin to lift and instead of a white blur he could now discern shapes in front of him. He blinked a few times and looked up again. Two faces were now clearly visible in front of him. One was Governor Archer and the other was a middle-aged woman, serious-looking, with piercing blue eyes and dark blonde hair.

"You're not Elijah," said Ethan, and instantly regretted it, realising how stupidly obvious that was. Then panic flooded into his gut. "Wait, Sal! Where is Sal?" He tried to sit up, but a stabbing pain in his chest fought him back down. He coughed roughly and his throat stung. He gagged with the taste of bitter mucus.

"Please, you must rest," said the serious woman. "We're still processing your blood. You are going to be fine, but you must let the medicines do their work."

"Where is Sal? Captain Salus, I mean, where is she?" pleaded Ethan again, ignoring the woman and again trying to sit up, with the same lack of success. He slumped back down, and exhaled a painful, exhausted breath. "Captain Maria Salus," he asked again, weakly. "Tell me, is she okay?"

"Ethan, this is Governor Archer, can you hear me?"

"I can hear you," said Ethan, frustrated that his one simple question had still not been answered. "Where is she? Please, I must know!"

Archer placed a hand on Ethan's chest, with just enough pressure to keep him from trying to sit up again. "Easy there," he said, in a comforting tone. Ethan wasn't able to see, but he was sure Archer was wearing his usual, easy smile as he said this. "You saved her life," Archer continued. "Your brave – some might say reckless – rescue attempt was a success. You pulled her out in time, but..."

"But... what?" interrupted Ethan, panicking again. He struggled against Archer's hold, feeling himself getting stronger. Seeing this, the woman also now joined in the effort of keeping him lying flat.

"You must lie still," the woman said, sternly. "Captain Salus is in a serious condition, but she is stable." Ethan relaxed a little. Stable at least meant she wasn't at immediate risk. As he relaxed he became more aware of his own body again, and that he was already feeling more able. He looked over to the table beside him and saw a syringe, presumably the source of the sharp pain he felt earlier. Whatever had been in it was doing a good job of reviving him.

"If you'll remain calm, Ethan, I will adjust the bed so you are sitting more upright," said the woman. "But you must agree to remain calm and restful. High stress will increase your blood pressure and inhibit the work of the medicine I gave you."

Ethan nodded. The woman ducked out of view and then the bed began to tilt upright accompanied by a mechanical-sounding whir. When he was at about forty-five degrees it stopped and the woman reappeared next to Archer, who was now wearing the same utilitarian style of uniform as Maria. The woman on the other hand was dressed in a white, short-sleeved shirt and trousers. She had an ID badge pinned to her left breast pocket, which read, 'Angela Salus, Consultant'.

Ethan's eyes widened. "Are you..."

"Yes, Maria is my sister," the woman said, anticipating the question. "So believe me when I tell you, her care is my first priority."

"Of course, yes, I'm sorry," Ethan said, feeling embarrassed.

"Nothing to apologise for, Ethan," said Archer smoothly. "I'm aware that you and Captain Salus have formed a bond, which is not surprising considering your shared ordeals."

Now it was the Doctor's eyes that widened slightly. Ethan felt suddenly exposed and tried his best not to look at her. This wasn't how he'd imagined meeting a relative of Maria's, not that he'd even considered that as a possibility. After Maria had told him about the death of her parents, Ethan had assumed that Maria had no surviving family members. He wondered what else he didn't know about her, and realised he knew barely anything at all. He tried to clear his mind and it was then he remembered interrupting Archer.

"You were about to say 'but'," Ethan said to Archer.

"Excuse me?" replied Archer, confused.

"Earlier, before I interrupted you, you said I pulled her out in time, 'but'. "What is the 'but'?"

Archer nodded, remembering, and took a deep, thoughtful breath. "Ah, yes," he said. "Well, perhaps Doctor Salus can explain." Ethan eyed Archer suspiciously, wondering why he had suddenly deferred responsibility to his companion, and shifted his gaze towards her.

"I shall put it plainly," said Angela Salus. "Maria's injuries I can treat, but her exposure to the fumes after the explosion was severe. Your apparently highly robust constitution protects you from more than just orrum exposure, it seems. Maria is not so lucky, and I am unable to purge the toxins fully from her blood."

"But I thought you said she was stable?" Ethan said, feeling the panic begin to surge again.

Angela was quick to clarify. "She is, for now, but in order for her to remain that way I need a far more potent anti-toxin. Fortunately, Governor Archer has just informed me that you are here to recover the very equipment I need to synthesise such a serum. A happy coincidence."

Ethan slumped back into his bed. "The device on the stranded ship?"

Angela Salus nodded. "Yes."

Ethan felt on the verge of losing his composure again. He hated how they danced around subjects, never speaking plainly. "How long does she have?" he asked, addressing Angela specifically.

"Seventy-two hours." The reply was clinical, matter-of-fact, almost cold. Ethan couldn't understand her lack of emotion. Ever since their arrival these people had talked about their impending doom with the sort of emotional detachment he had only seen in Roamers. Ethan had felt like a raw nerve for so long he couldn't remember feeling any other way, existing in a persistently heightened state, trying to process everything that had confronted him. Had it not been for Maria, he likely would have snapped.

Ethan squeezed his hands together, flexing and stretching his fingers. Then he wrapped his arms around himself, squeezing tightly, trying to measure the level of his own strength. He continued to feel stronger and more clear-headed. He brought his hands again back into a clasp and looked resolutely at Archer. "When can we be ready to go?"

Archer smiled, but this time it was not the practised, easy smile that Ethan was wearily tired of seeing, but something more natural, as if Archer respected Ethan's boldness and willingness to jump into action. "Kurren will have everything prepared in just less than six hours," he said. "We will need to give you some basic instruction too, but we can fit that into the time. I suggest we go as soon as everything is ready!" he added, enthusiastically, but the Doctor's reaction was less so.

"That is too soon," said Angela. "He needs more rest and more treatments to fully recover."

"There is no time, Doctor," Archer shot back, just as firm. "They are already re-grouping for another attack."

"How do you know that?" said Ethan. "Why are they being so aggressive now?" Archer considered the question, and exchanged tense looks with the Doctor, as if they knew something and were weighing up whether or not to tell Ethan. "If you know something, tell me!" snapped Ethan, unable to hide his agitation any longer.

"They know we have a Planetsider," Archer replied without further hesitation.

"What?"

"They know we recovered a Planetsider. They know why. And they intend to prevent us from succeeding with our plan."

There was a chilling silence in the room. And then Ethan understood. The realisation sent a shiver down his spine and turned his stomach into knots. "They intend to destroy the ship?" he said.

"Yes," replied Archer, calmly.

"But, how do they know?" said Ethan.

"We're not entirely sure," Archer admitted. "They may have intercepted some communications. Or they could have hacked into our systems. We're checking every possibility. But the assault was not random, it was also for reconnaissance, and we believe they have now detected the location of the ship, and will be coming for it, at any cost."

Ethan swung his legs out of the bed and placed his feet on the floor, which was hard and cold, but he didn't flinch. He fought himself upright, pushing back the pain that shot through his body like a thousand nettle stings. Angela Salus instinctively went to grab him, expecting him to fall, but Archer understood better, and remained still. Angela's hands caught Ethan's arms, but instead of weakness, she felt strength. And when she looked into his eyes, she saw his resolve, and gingerly let go.

"Take me where I need to go," Ethan said to Archer, staring intensely into the General's clever eyes.

"Of course..." Archer began, but Ethan had not finished.

"But first, please let me see Sal," he said. "Let me see Maria, I need to see her." Angela looked over at Archer, and he nodded.

"I will have someone bring you clothes and then, when you

are ready, we will get started," Archer said, and then turned to leave. After a few steps, he paused, and half-turned back. "You are a very brave man, young Planetsider," he said. "She is lucky to have..." and then he hesitated for a moment, glancing across to Angela, before adding, "... a friend like you." Ethan was grateful for Archer's discretion, but also encouraged by it. Archer's subtle acknowledgement that he understood Ethan and Maria to be more than just friends almost felt like it made them 'official'.

"What you are is a reckless, headstrong, impulsive fool," Angela said sharply, once Archer was out of earshot. Ethan was quite taken aback, and despite himself, almost laughed. But then Angela smiled warmly and added, "Which is probably why my block-headed sister likes you."

Ethan smiled back, relieved that Angela's anger was not genuine. She then led him through a door and into an adjoining room, similar in overall size and design to the one they had left. On the bed, laid flat, fed with tubes from a number of strange looking machines, each with differing patterns of flickering displays, blinking lights and mechanical noises, was Maria. Ethan felt his heart sink.

"Don't worry," said Angela, sensing his disquiet, "she is fine. Sedated, but fine."

Ethan stood in the room and looked at her. The blinking lights and rhythmic noises were quite soothing, almost hypnotic, and he felt his anxiety and worry slowly ebb away. He noticed that Angela was standing beside the bed, gently holding Maria's hand. He thought of his own sister and family, and realised how they must also be feeling now, not knowing whether Ethan was alive or dead, and was again racked with guilt. But there was no time for that now.

A man walked into the room holding a bundle of clothes and a pair of boots. "For you sir," he said, politely, as he placed the items on a chair at the back of the room, "I'll be waiting outside for you when you're ready, sir," he added and then left the room again.

"I'll get you what you need to save her," Ethan said calmly a few seconds later.

"I don't know why, but I believe you will," Angela replied. But then she said something that surprised him. "And then what will you do?"

Ethan leant over, closer to the unconscious face of Captain Maria Salus. She looked peaceful, he thought. Peaceful and beautiful. "I don't know," he replied, honestly.

Ethan didn't see Angela smile, he only heard her words. "When you come back, you should ask her."

"I'm afraid of what she'll say," said Ethan without thinking. And there it was, unveiled as much to himself as to Angela. He was afraid that after this was over, there would be no Ethan and Maria. That he had imagined her affection towards him, or read too much into it. And that he would be alone.

"We're all just living one day to the next, Planetsider," said Angela. "Whether it's up here, or down on the planet, makes no difference. You just need to decide where it is you belong."

Ethan straightened and turned to face Maria's sister. He could see the similarities now, in the shape of the mouth and the eyes, and the way their hair fell over their faces. "I've never really felt like I belonged anywhere," he said, openly, "But I'm wondering now if, maybe, I belong with her." And then his face betrayed a sense of concern, "I just don't know if she thinks the same."

Angela smiled again, and this time Ethan saw it. He was glad to see that it offered genuine warmth, perhaps even affection. The doctor shrugged and said, "Well, why don't we start with you coming back here in one piece, and then let's all of us find out together."

CHAPTER 21

Angela had wished Ethan luck and left the room to allow him to change into the clothes provided. This proved more of an effort than he anticipated, as he struggled to fasten the various straps and buckles. Satisfied that he had finally done everything correctly he went out to meet the man who was to take him back to Archer to start his preparations. His steps were awkward at first, but he soon felt his joints and muscles loosen, and the aches and pains ease. He was far from fully fit, but he was much stronger than he had been only an hour or so previously, and much stronger than he had expected to feel in such a short time. If they can do this for him then with the right equipment he was sure they could save Maria. And then he was truly in uncharted territory, probably for the first time in his life.

His sense of wonder, and what Summer called his 'obsessive curiosity', always meant that Ethan had something to chase after. Whether it was his desire to learn about the past, to uncover the mysteries of the lights in the night sky, or to charge blindly into the unknown to investigate an alien object without a moment's hesitation, Ethan had always been driven. It was what had kept him motivated and made him effective as a Ranger. But it was also what prevented him from living in the moment, like he could never do with Summer. Perhaps that's why she was always so competitive with him, Ethan wondered, because by challenging him, she retained his interest, and he kept her in his sights, instead of dreaming of something always just out of reach. Now Maria was the ultimate mystery, the ultimate obsession. She was the very embodiment of the unknown, and so naturally Ethan would be drawn to her.

On top of his anxiety about Maria, Ethan was still tormented by conflicting emotions. There was his guilt for leaving his sister and Elijah, which had swelled from a small acorn in his belly and sprouted roots that tugged harder on his insides each passing day. And then the worry about Summer, and if she had survived, or if she had killed Kurren – Maria's comrade and friend. His uneasiness about the moon base and the people on it, whose comfortable lives were an insult to the suffering and struggle of the Planetsiders. The injustice made him feel almost physically sick. And then there was Maria, the tempestuous, alluring stranger who had exploded into his life like a volcanic eruption and changed everything. She had revealed to him the truths he had desired since he was a boy, and at the same time shattered his fantasies about the past and his hopes for the future. It had been a rude awakening that had left him searching for purpose for the first time in his life. And so he had latched on to Maria, because of what she represented, and because it gave him a cause. Perhaps that was all there was to it. Perhaps once this was over, Ethan would again be left as barren and empty as the world below them.

He mulled these thoughts over and over in his mind as he walked, silently, alongside the man who was escorting him.

Ultimately, such considerations were pointless, he realised, because he had no answers. All he could do was the same thing that had led him to this place – follow his gut. And his gut told him that he loved her. And it was enough for now, Ethan realised.

They arrived at a large, slab-fronted black building with a UEC logo high on the side, and as he entered his escort peeled off, saluting and saying 'good luck' in a way that made Ethan feel that it was said simply because his training had told him to be polite. Major Kurren was standing by a large arched doorway. His eyes projected a certain menace, very unlike his brother, who had eyes that were welcoming and friendly.

"This way," said Kurren, gruffly. "We're ready. I'll take you through what you need to do, and we can begin." Ethan nodded and followed Kurren through the doorway; the doors swinging open automatically with a powerful, mechanical-sounding growl. They entered a large room with one side made almost entirely from glass, beyond which the base gave way to the open surface of the moon. Hanging above a dusty courtyard of white rocks, attached to a tubular passageway built into the glass wall, was a long, sleek-looking vessel, pulsing with lights. There was a windowed section at the front, illuminated brightly from the inside. "That's our ship. She's the best we have left," said Kurren, proudly.

"Good to know," said Ethan, absent-mindedly, his thoughts still a jumble of a dozen different things.

"Do your part and I'll make sure you get back, safely," Kurren said. It sounded more like an order than an attempt to reassure.

"I'm sure you will," said Ethan, unsure of what else to say.

"I will," said Kurren with determination. "I only wish my brother had received the same treatment."

The reason for Kurren's menace was finally laid bare. It

wasn't just a military gruffness, it was anger over his brother. And Ethan was the target of this blame.

"I meant it when I said I was sorry about your brother," replied Ethan, matching Kurren's resolute tone. "He saved Maria. He's the reason I'm here, and that Maria is too. I didn't mean for him to get stranded on the planet."

Kurren's eyes narrowed. Perhaps he hadn't expected such steel from the Planetsider. "It was his choice to volunteer," he said, matter-of-factly. "I don't blame you, Planetsider. I just hope you're worth it, that's all."

"So do I," said Ethan, honestly. Kurren seemed to appreciate Ethan's candour, as his eyes lost some of their piercing sharpness. "Show me what I need to do."

Kurren nodded and led Ethan over to the console, where they were joined by two other men in plain blue overalls. Neither spoke to Ethan, nor did Kurren reveal their names, simply referring to them as 'mission specialists'. For the next hour, Kurren and the specialists covered the details of the mission and the part Ethan needed to play. He was given a replica of the EV suit that Kurren would remotely pilot close to the stranded ship, and for another hour he trained in this suit, learning the core functions, the vast majority of which he wouldn't need, since Kurren and the mission controllers would handle almost everything remotely. However, once he was within ten to fifteen metres of the ship it would be down to him to pilot inside, navigate to the cockpit and insert the 'override control spike' in to the pilot's console. This was a metal shard about thirty centimetres long and roughly the same thickness as his thumb, which slotted into a section on the pilot's console, clearly marked by a two red circles, one surrounding the other. He was shown a replica of the pilot's console and made to practise this procedure more times than he felt necessary, given the clear simplicity of the task. Once the shard was inserted, Kurren explained, it would activate the ship's backup power generator, and boost the signal so that Kurren could remotely access the ship's systems and pilot the vessel back to the decontamination area, safely away from the moon base's habitable zones, with Ethan still inside. The way it was described to Ethan made it all sound perfectly simple, though something told Ethan that the real mission would be somewhat more challenging than these simulations.

After three hours of continuous training, Ethan was both exhausted and thoroughly sick of the continual repetition of tasks. The latest simulation came to an end and Kurren looked pensively over the simulation results with the same intense concentration as the previous twenty-one times. Then he looked up at Ethan and said, "Okay. We go in thirty."

The words had a sobering effect on Ethan, and he suddenly had a burning desire to do another twenty simulations, rather than face the prospect of venturing out into space for real. But he was too tired to argue and instead just slumped back into the training seat and grunted his acknowledgement.

Kurren smiled – the masochist in him seemed to have enjoyed beasting Ethan around for the last few hours – and reached into his top shirt pocket, removing a small round container. He popped it open and shook out a small, red pill, which he handed to Ethan. "Take this," he said. "It's a stim, we use them all the time. It will make you feel incredible for a few hours, which is all the time we need to get this done."

Ethan took it and placed it on his tongue, where it almost immediately dissolved; leaving him with tingling sensation that began to spread throughout his body, washing away the fatigue. "Wow..." said Ethan feeling an intense rush of energy. "What happens after this wears off?"

Kurren snorted, which Ethan supposed was as close as this man came to laughing. "Then you'll have one hell of a hangover."

Ethan stood up. He felt amazing. "What's a hangover?" he asked.

And this time Kurren did laugh.

CHAPTER 22

"Ethan, your heart rate is rising, try to take some regular, deep breaths."

The comlink crackled off, silencing the voice of the nameless 'mission specialist', who was Ethan's ethereal companion. Ethan could feel his heart pounding, and tried to do as instructed, but the breaths were still coming rapidly, a combination of the stimulant that Kurren had given him, and the fact he was flying through open space inside a shell made of fabric and metal. In front of him, hanging ominously in the blackness, set against the bright blue backdrop of the planet itself, was a large, black, spacecraft. It looked like a giant arrowhead with three blades sweeping back from the head section, like huge shark fins, with powerful-looking engines positioned between each V. It was both considerably larger and more elegant-looking than the boxier craft that had brought him from the surface to the moon base, and looked like it could swallow up three or four of the sleeker combat aircraft he'd seen on the deck, before Maria was injured. It was nestled among a flotsam of shimmering, twisted metal debris shrouded by opaque clouds of dust that almost looked like they were guarding it.

"Two minutes to contact. Adjust 1.7 right, Z+ 0.2. Initiate remote hatch unlocking."

He adjusted the controls, as he'd practised so many times before, making another minor correction to his trajectory. Ethan liked the comlink chatter. It had been almost constant throughout the thirty-four minutes it had taken him to reach this point, since he had jettisoned from the craft that Kurren and the two mission specialists had piloted to a position the minimum safe distance from the ship. And despite not understanding most of the content, he had welcomed the company. With the comlink silent, he was painfully aware of his rapid, shallow breathing, and the pumping of blood in his ears.

"Ethan, concentrate on your breathing. You're doing great, nearly there," the crackly voice announced.

Ethan took consciously deeper breaths and felt his heart pump more slowly and evenly. In front of him the black object was looming large in his visor. A ring of lights illuminated between two of the huge fins, near the rear of the craft. "Remote hatch unlocking successful. Commander, over to you."

"Affirmative, I have control." The second voice was Kurren's. It was the first time Ethan had heard it since boarding the vessel that had brought them closer to their target, and then spat him unceremoniously out into space. "Okay, Ethan," said Kurren's voice, solid and steady on the comlink. "This is the docking manoeuvre, you've practised this, you can do it. Initiate on my mark."

Ethan nodded instinctively inside his helmet and then flipped the sequence of switches that he had committed to memory. "Ready," he said, his voice far less steady than Kurren's. There was silence for a few moments as Ethan considered his glide towards the flashing lights, which outlined the port docking hatch. "Come on, come on," Ethan said out loud, the comlink disabled, urging Kurren to give the order.

"Three...two...one...initiate!" came Kurren's voice out of the silence. Ethan fired the jets on their pre-programmed sequence. The sudden and rapid change of direction and orientation was briefly confusing and made Ethan feel queasy, but the sensation was momentary as he halted directly in front of the hatch opening. "Well done Ethan," said Kurren, sounding almost nice. "It gets easier from now on." Presumably one of the many probes that had been attached to Ethan could detect 'queasiness', in addition to seemingly every other physical condition that a person could experience.

"Good to know..." said Ethan, sarcastically. He manually pulsed the rear jets and felt himself move forward towards the hatch opening. The blackness of space was now replaced by blinding white lights, some of which emanated from the suit itself and reflected back off the metal shell of the ancient vessel. The object now looked far less forbidding, and Ethan again began to feel calmer, as if the end was close.

Come on, you can do this... he said to himself as he passed through the opening and into the guts of the ship. Then following his training to the letter, he pulsed the thrusters one last time and felt his feet hit the decking. They stuck to it firmly, a phenomenon that one of the mission specialists had called 'magnetism'.

"Package on site, initiating ambulatory mode," The comlink crackled, and Ethan felt heavy, as if he was falling. His natural instinct was to steady himself, adjusting his footing and balance, and to his surprise, the suit reacted in the same way as his muscles, stopping his fall. He stood tall and moved his arms and legs. It felt natural, just as in the simulations.

"You've done the hard part," said Kurren over the comlink, his voice sounding thinner and more distant. "About fifty metres ahead is the cockpit. You know what to do."

Ethan reached down with his right hand and grabbed the spike, which was attached magnetically to the thigh section of the EV suit. Holding it in front of him, he paced, deliberately, carefully, down the hallway of the ship. It was almost exactly like in the simulation, and he knew precisely what to do. His heart rate was climbing again, but he felt in control, knowing he was through the most challenging section. He reached the cockpit door and held out his left hand in front of the panel to the door's side, and just as in the simulations, it flashed into life, scanning his hand with a line of intense green light, before shutting off. The door hissed and slid open, but only half way. In the simulations, it had slid open entirely. Ethan started to feel panicky.

"Kurren," said Ethan, stress evident in his voice. "The door... it hasn't opened. What do I..."

"Stay calm, Ethan, it's not a problem," the comlink crackled, cutting Ethan off. "Just grab the edge of the door and force it, just as you would normally. The suit has the strength to open it."

Ethan took several deep breaths and grabbed the edge of the door with his gloved left hand. Then with all his physical strength, he pulled back, and the door slowly slid open, grinding against the frame and causing it to buckle slightly. Kurren was right about the suit augmenting his strength. Words and symbols flashed up in his visor as he continue to push the door back, accompanied by a pulsing low tone.

"Easy, Ethan, easy!" said Kurren urgently. "We want you to open the door, not tear the ship in two!"

Ethan let go of the door, and the symbols slowly started to

disappear, followed shortly after by the pulsing tone. "Is everything okay?" asked Ethan, worried that he'd caused some serious damage. There was a momentary silence, which felt like an eternity.

"Yes, integrity checks out okay. Just, take it easy, huh?" said the voice of the anonymous mission specialist.

"Ethan, head into the cockpit and insert the spike. Then we can get you out of there." This time it was Kurren again. His steady and assured delivery, in contrast to the other man, actually made Ethan feel better. He walked through the doorway and into the cockpit. It looked identical to the simulations. He moved over to the left seat, the pilot's seat, and found to his horror the corpse of the pilot still strapped to the seat. His pulse and breathing spiked, causing a concerned mission specialist to check if he was okay.

"You could have warned me there would be bodies in here!" Ethan shouted angrily into the comlink.

"We didn't want to warn you in case it played on your mind and affected the mission." It was Kurren speaking, sounding wholly unsympathetic and almost annoyed.

"Well, it's playing on my mind now!" Ethan replied, irritated by Kurren's casual dismissal.

"Just focus on the mission," Kurren replied a moment later. "You're almost there, just insert the spike."

Ethan studied the console, looking for the port where the spike needed to be inserted. It was exactly where it was supposed to be, surrounded by two red circles. He moved closer, trying his best not to look at the corpse beside him, and positioned the spike over the port.

"I'm going to insert the spike in three...two...one... inserting," he said into the com, and then without waiting for a reply, he pushed the spike in, and turned it ninety degrees left, just as in the simulator. Then he waited. The comlink crackled in the background, but no-one spoke. After a tense few seconds the console lit up, and a few more seconds later there was a deep throbbing sound that resonated through the floor, vibrating through every inch of his suit. Lights came on in the cockpit, and then as Ethan turned to look down the length of the vessel, more lights pulsed on. The relic was coming back to life.

"It's working," said Kurren over the comlink, and Ethan detected some uncharacteristic excitement in his voice.

"I am receiving telemetry. I should have control in three minutes," said the other man, more calmly this time.

Ethan could feel his body loosen. It was at this point that the simulation started coming to an end, and Kurren would tell Ethan that all he needed to do now was sit back and wait for them to bring him and the ship back to the base. In the simulation this gave him no comfort, as it wasn't real, but this time they would have whatever equipment they needed to create their medicines to heal Maria, and everyone else. This time it mattered. Ethan moved back into the main body of the ship and looked around as he waited. He observed that various items of detritus that had been floating weightlessly in the cabin were now resting on the deck. He lifted his feet, one then the other, like some strange dance, and noticed that the sudden, tell-tale pull of magnetism as his boot approached the decking had gone. Gravity was being restored, and soon he would be on his way. This was also part of the simulation, because Ethan had to learn to adjust to the changes in forces on the suit, and how this affected his movements.

The comlink crackled in the background. He could hear voices and the strange artificial sounds that emanated from the many devices the UEC relied on. The voice grew louder and faster, but still not clear enough to hear. Ethan thought nothing of it, and just looked out of a nearby window at the planet, spinning silently in front of him, trying to keep his mind off the dead body in the cockpit. Would he go back, he wondered? With or without Maria, would he go back to the planet? Would they let him? The sounds and voices grew louder and more urgent, and reclaimed Ethan's attention.

"Is everything okay?" Ethan said into the comlink, but there was no answer. He tried again; "Hey, Kurren, what's going on?" but there was still no reply. The lack of response was starting to worry him. He looked around the ship for any dangers, such as a fire, but there was nothing obvious. So he looked out again at the spinning ball of blue and the darkness surrounding it, and this time there was something else there. Advancing directly towards the ship was a shape, now cleanly silhouetted against the vibrant backdrop of the planet, and it was growing larger.

"Ethan, get out of the ship, get out now!" It was Kurren, and for the first time since Ethan has met the man, his voice lacked composure.

"What? How? Why?" Ethan said, startled and confused.

"No questions. Go back to the hatch and jump out. Do it now!" Kurren shouted, his voice distorting uncomfortably through the comlink.

"Jump out? Are you mad?!" exclaimed Ethan, now feeling terror start to grip him.

"Just do it, I'll get you back. Go now, now, now!"

Ethan manoeuvred his suit towards the door of the cockpit as fast as he could. Glancing back, he saw the object pass over the top of the cockpit, so close that he could feel it. It was another spacecraft, much smaller than any of the vessels he'd seen so far, perhaps only big enough for one person.

He ran – as close to running as was possible in the suit – back down the centre section of the ship and towards the hatchway through which he had entered. He was almost there when the starlight outside the hatch vanished. The entire vessel shook and jolted to one side, knocking Ethan to the floor. He tried to recover, but fell again. He had trained for the possibility of falling prone and having to recover, but faced with this unknown threat, Ethan was panicking and struggled to recall what to do. Instead, he simply flailed around on his back, unable to right himself, like an overturned cockroach. Two more jolts pulsed through the structure of the ship, and then the training finally kicked in. He managed to turn over and bring the legs of the suit up underneath him. He stood up, breathing heavily from the exertion; he was facing back towards the cockpit, his heart was beating fast and his chest burned. He span around towards the hatch, but standing directly in front of him outlined by an array of lights that dazzled him, even through his visor, was another suit.

"Who... who are you?" Ethan spluttered. He felt a shock run though his body, from head to toe. He tried to scream, but was paralysed. As the pulsing stopped, he felt the weight of the suit drag him down as it lost power, and he hit the deck hard. The suited figure stepped over him and looked down. He could not see a face behind the glass, only a rim of lights surrounding the visor, leaving a dark, empty centre. The suited figure looked up again, stepped over Ethan and moved swiftly down the centre section of the ship, towards the cockpit. Red lights and symbols began to flash up in Ethan's visor. He felt dizzy and weak. He waited, unable to move, occasionally calling out to Kurren, but the comlink was inactive. Powerful vibrations again surged through the framework of the ship, shaking Ethan's bones, and the lights inside the vessel grew brighter. He heard a mechanical whirr and then felt a solid thud reverberate through the decking nearby. The hatch door had closed, with him still inside.

The comlink crackled and fizzed back into life, but the

voices and artificial sounds were gone. The words 'Power Levels Critical. Emergency Life Preservation Initialised' were spoken by a robotic-sounding voice, the same voice that had announced the launch warnings in the hanger pod on the planet. He felt a stabbing pain in his neck from a needle and the tell-tale hiss of something being injected into his blood stream. His vision started to darken and his mind fogged over. He felt movement, not from his suit, but from the inertia of the great vessel surging forward. He tried again to move his neck and arms, but could not. The red lights continued to flash in front of him as his eyes closed involuntarily and he slipped into darkness.

The arrow-shaped craft cut a path through the debris that had surrounded it for generations, breaking free from its orbital graveyard and on through the darkness of space towards an object that was a mere dot of light in the distance. An object as old as the ship itself – the orbiting space station belonging to Global Power Security.

CHAPTER 23

Ethan opened his eyes. His temples pulsed and his head felt woolly and sore. He was still wearing the UEC flight suit he'd been given before embarking on the mission, and was sitting, slightly reclined, in a large, black chair with a padded headrest, in a small, grey room, with just a strip light above. The room felt unfamiliar and Ethan felt fear start to overwhelm him as he realised he was not on the UEC moon base. This was somewhere else.

His heart began to race and adrenalin surged through his body. He remembered the mission, the intruder, and being attacked. He jolted himself upright and then froze. In front of him was a tall, thin woman with dark red hair that fell arrow-straight to shoulder level. Her thin red lips were pressed into a patient smile. She was middle-aged and dressed in a formal-looking, plain grey suit that neither flattered nor obscured her figure. She stood with her hands held together in front of her, displaying a calm serenity that was the exact opposite of Ethan's near overwhelming anxiousness.

"Hello," she said. Her tone was warm and casual.

Ethan could hear the blood pounding in his ears. "Hello," he replied nervously, after a short pause.

"You must be tired of waking up in strange places and being confronted by strange new people," she said, and her smile widened. Her delivery was sociable, as if she was talking to someone she already knew.

"I suppose I'm getting used to it," replied Ethan, honestly, heart still racing, but no longer gripped with panic. The woman did not seem a threat. He looked around again; there was no-one else in the room. He wasn't restrained, and other than the throbbing headache, he didn't appear to be injured. There was a door to his left, closer to him than it was to the woman, and Ethan considered making a run for it.

"There is nothing to stop you leaving, if that's what you're thinking," said the woman openly.

This caught Ethan off guard. "Erm, I wasn't, I was just..."

"It's okay," said the woman. "In such a situation, my first reaction would be fight or flight too. I'm just glad you're tending more towards the 'flight' option."

Ethan almost laughed at the joke, but despite the woman's attempts to make him feel at ease, he was still far from it. "Running would be pretty pointless," he said. "I don't even know where I am."

"You're on a habitat orbiting the planet," the woman replied without hesitation. "Long ago, it was the headquarters of Global Power Security, which you have no doubt heard of." Curiously, it wasn't phrased as a question, and so Ethan chose not to answer. "You are in no danger here, young Planetsider, so please, relax and regain your strength."

Ethan looked at her intently. She had remained entirely still, in the same position, smiling warmly at him. He was reminded of Archer, but there was something different about this woman's smile, something more earnest. He began to feel more in control, and as the instinctive fear response subsided, it was replaced with a confidence, and anger. "Who are you? And why am I here? How am I here?" demanded Ethan. As he heard the words in his own ears, he was surprised at how forceful and composed he sounded. Despite the woman's reassurances, he still felt under threat.

"My name is Diana," the woman said. "You are here because circumstances unfortunately compelled us to act, in order to prevent you from retrieving the stranded vessel for the UEC. You got here on that same ship, which was recovered by one of our pilots. A regrettable last resort, I'm very sorry to say."

"A last resort, what does that mean?" wondered Ethan.

"Ah..." said Diana, sombrely. "To answer that question will require a little more explanation. But please, this is not an interrogation; let's leave. We can walk and talk, okay?"

Ethan studied her face. The thin smile and high cheeks, framed by the straight red hair were certainly striking. And then he noticed her green eyes. Piercing, intelligent, sincere eyes. For some reason, this woman engendered trust, more so than anyone he had ever met, even Maria. Then he suddenly remembered Maria. He tensed up, like a coiled snake.

"I need to get back!" he said, urgently. "A friend... she's in danger!"

He sprang to his feet and advanced quickly at the woman. Diana uncoupled her hands and stepped back a pace or two as he approached, but she remained composed and did not attempt to fend him off, or even appear frightened, even when Ethan grabbed her by the shoulders.

"They need something from that ship to cure her!" Ethan blurted out. He held her tightly. "That's all I wanted. Keep the ship, I don't care, but please send me back with the equipment they need. She will die!"

"It's okay," said Diana in a soft, hushing tone. She took Ethan's hands, removed them from her shoulders and then held them firmly together with hers. She looked calmly and reassuringly into Ethan's eyes. "Don't worry about your friend, she will be fine," she said, sounding sincere. Ethan still looked desperately at her, and tried to plead, but she did not let him interrupt. "I know you have no reason to trust me," continued Diana. "But, in time, hopefully I will earn that trust. For now, I promise you, on my honour – on my own life – that your friend is not going to die."

"But, how can you know..." urged Ethan, frustrated by the cryptic response.

"I promise I will explain everything," Diana interrupted again. "But, please, understand this... You are not a prisoner here, and I wish no harm to you, or anyone else, including your friend."

Ethan let go of her hands and stepped back. He looked over at the door again. "I don't think you're lying to me," he said, "but I can't risk that you might be. I need to get back." He looked over at the door again.

"If you want to leave, I won't stop you," said Diana. "I will even make sure you get back to the UEC base, if you so wish. But at least give me a chance to explain why we brought you here."

"I don't have time!" said Ethan. "She has only a few days, at most."

Diana thought for a moment. "How long exactly, do you remember?"

Ethan threw up his hands. "I don't know!" he said, exasperated. "They told me seventy-two hours, but I don't know how long ago that was."

Diana turned around walked over to a worn metal cabinet

that had been obscured from Ethan's view up until now. On it was a device on a strap, which he recognised. Kurren had put it on him before he got into his EV suit. "This is your PVSM," said Diana. "A Personal Vital Signs Monitor." She threw it over to Ethan and he caught it. On the display was a screen, with a number that was steadily increasing. It read 21:03:02. "Twenty-one hours," said Diana. "That's how long since your 'mission' started."

Ethan thought back to the medical area and his conversation with Maria's sister. "Seventy-two hours" he said. "She had seventy-two hours. But I spent some time training too, I don't know how long. It felt like days, I know it wasn't that long really, but it was certainly hours."

Diana nodded. "Then give me just twenty-four hours," she said. "twenty-four hours here, as my guest, and if you still want to leave, I will personally make sure you get back long before your seventy-two hours is up."

Ethan considered this. "With the equipment?" he asked. "The medical device they need?"

"There is no need for any equipment," said Diana, but before Ethan could question why, she added, "But yes, you can take anything you want from the ship."

Diana had piqued Ethan's curiosity. She was not threatening, and had given him no reason to distrust her, besides having someone violently abduct him. Yet, there was something about her that felt real. Something that made him want to find out more. "Okay," he said, "twenty-four hours, and no more."

"Thank you," said Diana, sincerely. There was relief, also. "I say again, you are not a prisoner," continued Diana, "so I want you to know that during your time here, there is *nowhere* that is off limits." There was heavy emphasis on 'nowhere'. Ethan remembered back to what Archer had told him about off limits areas on the moon base, and Ethan knew this was not a random statement. But if it was deliberate then why?

"I don't trust you," said Ethan, plainly.

"You have no reason to, yet," Diana replied, still calm and composed.

"No, not because we've just met," said Ethan, pressing the point. "Or because you abducted me and brought me here against my will..." he added pointedly, which caused Diana to raise an eyebrow. "But because you know more than you're letting on. The mention of 'off-limits' areas, for example." It was a gamble to press Diana so soon, but Ethan was fed up with playing cloak-and-dagger games. He wanted to see if he could find any chink in her intellectual armour.

She smiled broadly and laughed, which was not the reaction Ethan had expected. But again it was a warm and genuine laugh; he sensed no hint of malice. "This is just my attempt at subtlety," Diana said. "I don't want to overwhelm you. But, if you prefer, I will talk plainly – I would actually prefer that. But you may not like, or believe, what I have to say. Nevertheless, it will be the truth."

Ethan took a deep breath and rubbed his temples, which still throbbed. He thought about Maria, lying unconscious back at the moon base. "Okay," he said, "I'll go along with this, for now."

"Thank you, Ethan," said Diana, using his name for the first time.

"So, you do already know my name," said Ethan. "And you clearly know something about my time on the moon base. Who are you?"

"Who I am is not important right now, Ethan," she replied coolly. "But what I am not, is a General." Then she gestured, open palmed, towards the door. "Shall we?"

Diana's obvious reference to Archer was again not lost on

Ethan. The militaristic nature of the UEC had always concerned him, most especially because their leader was both civil overseer and military commander. Diana wanted it made clear that she was not a military leader, and more than that, she knew that highlighting this fact would engender his trust. He admired Diana's subtle tactics, and understanding that her careful choice of words was clearly intended to manipulate him into trusting her, Ethan felt himself starting to trust her all the same. But he was also deeply suspicious of her, and her motives. And always at the back of his mind was Maria. He would play this game and see where it led, and hopefully along the way there would be an opportunity to escape – although how, he couldn't begin to fathom – or at the least find a way to contact the UEC.

He walked over to the door, turned the handle, and stepped out.

CHAPTER 24

Diana and Ethan walked through a series of corridors and rooms, some of which were populated with people working at desks. Diana had commented that they were in the main administrative wing of the station, which dealt with mainly service matters, such as power, water, food and reclamation. Ethan was only vaguely paying attention though, because his senses were focused on gathering as much information as he could about his new surroundings. The most obvious difference was how much more basic the station was compared to the moon base. It was bright and clean, but functional in design, with none of the grand, sweeping domes of the moon base, and it seemed somehow much older, as if most things could do with being refurbished or replaced. In fact, it wasn't until they reached the 'central concourse', as Diana had called it, that Ethan saw any windows out into the starlight. The central concourse was, however, quite impressive, in an industrial sort of way. They were standing on a balcony at the eighth level, and below and above them were additional levels, reaching perhaps fifty metres above him and perhaps another twenty to thirty below. At the bottom was a plaza with a number of stalls and seating areas and a healthy bustle of people. The plaza itself was perhaps a hundred metres from one side to the other, although as it disappeared under the first level balcony, it could have extended further.

"There are twenty-five floors in total," Diana said, as if reading Ethan's mind. "The lower level is a recreation area, where people can go to eat and relax. It is about the only part of this station where the original use has been preserved after the cataclysm that stranded us here."

"You mean the war *you* started that killed billions?" said Ethan, candidly, leaning on the railings and still looking down over the plaza. It was a deliberate attempt to provoke, to see if he could test her composure.

Diana turned and also rested against the balcony railings. She folded her arms across her chest and looked at Ethan. For a moment they were silent, but Ethan was determined to play this out, and let her move next.

"Okay..." said Diana, breaking the impasse. "I'm just going to lay it out for you, and then we'll see. All I ask is that you hear me out, and then I promise I will answer any questions you have. Deal?"

Ethan remained pressed against the railing, but turned his head slightly to look at her. Her face was more serious now. The lips pursed tighter, with no hint of a smile. She looked almost sad. He looked away and stared aimlessly at the hubbub below. "Just tell me why I'm here."

"Very well," said Diana. Ethan heard her clear her throat, and could tell she was anxious, nervous even. "I know that you were recovered from the planet's surface by a UEC expeditionary unit," she said. "We tried to destroy the UEC ship before it reached atmosphere, but failed, obviously, since you are here."

"Sorry to disappoint," said Ethan, sarcastically. Diana did not react.

"We know from our own intelligence-gathering and surveillance that you have been shown holos depicting the circumstances that led to the destruction of the Refinery, and the near total annihilation of the planet's surface population. In fact, for decades, we thought life on the planet was extinct," and then she added more casually, "all human life, anyway." Diana turned around slowly and rested on the balcony, mirroring Ethan, staring down at the people below. "We know that you have been told the ship you recovered, the one we captured with you on-board, contains specialist equipment needed to synthesise a medicine to combat the toxic effects of orrum radiation poisoning. We know that you were told that we – or to be more precise, Global Power Security – instigated a plot to eradicate the UEC, thus ending the generations-long war that GPS started. And we know that you believe this equipment will also save your friend, Captain Maria Rose Salus."

Ethan felt shivers run throughout his body and he fought hard to remain calm and composed, but he was deeply shaken by how Diana had described everything with chilling accuracy. What did that mean, he wondered? He kept his gaze focused below.

Diana waited for a reaction, and when none came she stood up from the railings and faced Ethan. "Am I right so far?" she asked, with genuine interest, rather than presumption.

Ethan looked at her nervously out of the corner of his eye. Diana's hands were clasped in front of her in the same position as when he had first seen her. Adrenaline was surging through Ethan's body, making him feel sick. He just wanted to run, to get away, but to where?

Diana waited a few moments longer and when it was clear Ethan wasn't going to answer, she sighed heavily. "All of that is a lie."

The words hit like a hammer, but Ethan's first reaction was denial and anger. He shook his head and laughed. "Why would I believe a word you say?" he demanded. "Of course you'll try to turn me against them. You captured that ship so that they would die. So that you can finally win this war, admit it!"

"Don't be a fool!" Diana replied, her voice suddenly powerfully assertive. She looked strong, resolute, and just as angry as Ethan felt. "If all we needed was the ship, why am I talking with you?" she added. Ethan tried to hit back, but Diana had a point, and instead he hesitated. "Look around you," Diana continued with voice lowered, but no less forthright. "This is not a military base. We are not soldiers. You have been with the UEC for days. You've seen how they live. Do they look like the victims?"

Again, Ethan tried to think of a counter, but could not.

"You have been fed lies in order to coerce you into getting the one thing they need, but for years have never been able to secure."

"Stop talking in riddles!" shouted Ethan, pushing away from the railing. He was desperate to fight back, but in his gut he felt that Diana was speaking the truth. "Just tell me what is going on here!" he said, desperation creeping into his voice.

Diana saw the chink in his resolve and continued to chip away. "The ship you recovered is a warship, Ethan," she said. "They want it for only one purpose, which is to destroy this station, and everyone on it, once and for all. To end the war *they* started."

"What are you talking about?" said Ethan, his head in a spin. "You started the war, not them!"

"They are the aggressors, Ethan. They always were," said

Diana, coolly. "The story you have been told is a twisted fiction. And deep down, I think you know it."

Ethan shook his head again. "But I saw the images; they showed me what you did."

"A fabrication," said Diana. "We can make the holos show whatever we want, just as they can."

Ethan paced up and down the walkway. "This is crazy," he said, despondent. "You're telling me that they lied, but how do I know you're not lying too?"

"I understand your predicament," said Diana, the softness returning to her voice. "It's why I have chosen not to show you holos, or give you the alternative, real, history. Ultimately, it doesn't matter what happened all those years ago. What matters is what happens next, and what you do."

"But why am I so important?" said Ethan. "They needed me to get this ship, but what do you want from me? You already have the ship." Mention of the warship, if that was what it was, reminded Ethan of the suited figure he had encountered inside. "Wait, you sent your own man to the ship," he said. "You didn't need me at all?"

Diana's eyes dropped to the floor. "Ah yes, we did sent a pilot," she said. "But like our friends on the moon base, we also can't tolerate the levels of radiation out where the vessel became stranded. However, once you inserted the spike and re-enabled the ship's systems, we only needed a short time to hijack the controls."

"But then why not kill me, or throw me out?" Ethan challenged her. "He had the opportunity…"

"She, actually," interrupted Diana. "And she died. She was dead before the ship even reached this station."

Ethan was dumbstruck. "She's dead? You sent her knowing she would die?"

"No!" said Diana, firmly. "She volunteered, knowing it was

the only way."

"And what about the attacks on the base, were they also the only way?" said Ethan, pushing.

"If we had succeeded in disabling the UEC's remaining fleet and launch bays, there would have been no need for Kayla's sacrifice," said Diana, angrily. "That was her name, by the way, in case you care at all?"

The last remark was deliberately spiteful, and Ethan could see by the tightening of her expression that Diana immediately regretted it. Ethan had finally pushed her into an emotional reaction, but it had only reinforced his feeling that she was sincere, and made him doubt the UEC even more.

Sensing her emotions starting to take over, Diana tried to compose herself. She took several deep breaths and gripped her hands even more tightly in front of her, and when she spoke again, she was more restrained. "I am sorry, you did not deserve that," she said. She stared down at her hands. "I am not an unfeeling woman, Ethan," she continued. "Perhaps now you see how serious this is."

Ethan gripped the railings tightly and again stared down at the people below. His mind was a mess of conflicted emotions and conflicting information. Was it true that he had been lied to and manipulated? Had Maria been complicit in that? Or was he being lied to and manipulated now? It was impossible to know one way or the other. But his instincts told him there was at least some truth in what Diana was saying. He sensed a sincerity he had never felt from Archer.

"So, if you're not the aggressors, what is it that you actually want?" he asked levelly, still looking out across the chasm occupying the centre of the station.

"We want to return to the planet," said Diana, confidently and without hesitation.

Ethan was stunned. He turned to face her. "Return to the

planet? Why?"

"The warship," said Diana. "We can convert it from an instrument of destruction into a vessel of salvation, literally. We can use it to transport our people off this station, and take them home."

"But why?" said Ethan, incredulously. "The planet is a wasteland. You have more here than we could ever dream of down there."

"Ethan, I am the third generation to be born on this station," said Diana. "We are all children born after the event you call The Fall. And like you, we bear no responsibility for it. Or blame. The planet is still our home, just as it is yours."

Ethan shook his head. He was trying to process Diana's words, but it went against everything he thought he knew to this point. "This is hard for me, Diana, I just don't know what to believe anymore."

Diana moved closer to Ethan and rested on the railings next to him, so that they were almost touching. If she had offered to hold his hand, or even hug him, Ethan would have probably accepted. She didn't, but still he appreciated the closeness of another person.

"Much of what you were shown in the holos is actually true," said Diana, "at least in terms of how things happened. What is different is who played which part, and the parts we play now."

"I used to believe that knowing the truth about The Fall was the most important thing in the world to me," said Ethan, sadly. "But when I was finally told what had happened, or at least the UEC's version of it, I wished I didn't know. The truth is, I really don't care anymore. I came here only to save Maria. I left my family and friends behind for her, because she told me she would die if I didn't help her. But if what you say is true, she is the biggest lie of all."

Diana shrugged. "For generations, people on both sides have grown up hating each other, and believing the other to be at fault. She perhaps believed the deception to be necessary; that it was the right thing to do, from her perspective."

Ethan hadn't expected Diana's response to be so diplomatic or balanced, and he admired her for not using his doubt over Maria to press her advantage. But, the realisation that Maria may well have been deceiving him was hitting Ethan hard.

"As to the question of why," Diana continued, "that's the simple part, Ethan. It's simply one side wanting to defeat the other. Two old enemies, unable – or unwilling – to reconcile their differences. The finer details are unimportant now."

"Talia warned me, but I wouldn't listen," said Ethan, solemnly.

"Talia, is that your mother?" asked Diana with interest; encouraged that Ethan seemed to be opening up to her more.

Ethan laughed. "No, I suppose she's a bit like you;" he said, "a leader. She warned me that we're better off not knowing about The Fall. She told me that we needed to create a future free of the past."

"She sounds like a smart woman," said Diana with obvious admiration.

"Could you even survive?" said Ethan, returning to the subject Diana had raised earlier. "Down on the planet, I mean."

"Yes, for a time," Diana said nodding, the thin smile returning to her lips. "Your natural resilience is down to being born on the planet, as a descendant of a survivor who also possessed an innate resistance," she continued. "It is woven into the very fabric of your body, in a way that no medicine can replicate fully. But there are treatments that can counteract the toxicity, and extend life-expectancy, hopefully by long enough."

Ethan gave her a puzzled frown. "Long enough for what?"

"We hope..." and then Diana paused for a moment and corrected herself, "...my hope, Ethan, is that we too can build settlements and have children. And that our children who are born Planetside will possess a powerful natural resistance to the radiation, just like you."

"Your children would have a better life here," said Ethan, looking around the vast structure of the space station.

"More comfortable, perhaps," said Diana, "but not better. Either due to the UEC, or simply the advance of time, eventually this station will decay. Many sections already have, and many others have been adapted and repaired so many times that it's a miracle it's still functioning at all."

"Is it worth the risk, though?" wondered Ethan. "Maybe you could defeat the UEC, or destroy their ships. Then you would be safe."

Diana thought for a moment before answering. "Do you ever have nightmares, Ethan?"

Ethan swallowed hard and a knot tightened in his gut. "What?" he asked, shaken.

"Nightmares, bad dreams," Diana clarified, unaware of his discomfort. Ethan didn't reply. He fought back the images in his mind. "I often dream about the station being attacked," Diana went on. "Sometimes, I wake and it's actually real," she added, wistfully. "But, sometimes I have the same terrible dream. The station is burning, people are dying. There are UEC soldiers everywhere, killing men, women and children, indiscriminately. I try to get to my office to broadcast a warning and to tell people to escape, but instead of my office, I step onto a ship, dead in space, and I'm looking out of the cockpit at the station. It's no longer burning, but it's broken, crippled. And inside are bodies, pressed against the windows, with tormented looks on their faces. Hundreds of tormented dead bodies, and all I can do is stare. I can't look away." Diana swallowed hard, paused for a moment and then stared blankly at the plaza below. "Then I'm standing in the middle of the plaza," she continued, eyes fixed on the circular GPS motif in the centre of the floor. "Everything is smashed, the lights are out, and dead bodies are floating all around. And they are all staring at me. Judging me with their dead, unblinking eyes..." She paused again, and closed her eyes tightly.

"That sounds horrible," said Ethan, his mind filled with images of his own nightmare.

"Yes," replied Diana, weakly. "Yes, it is. And it's what I fear will happen if we stay. I fear this place will become a graveyard, and that nothing of who we are – the people we are now – will survive. I couldn't bear that, Ethan. Can you understand that?"

Ethan shook his head. "I don't know," he admitted, as much to himself as to Diana. "If you'd have asked me before all this had happened, I would have said no, because I didn't see a future for me, or for anyone Planetside, if I couldn't understand what had brought us to this point."

"And now that you do understand?" Diana asked.

Ethan exhaled deeply. "Now I see how precious what we have on the planet really is," he said. "A new beginning, free of the past, and not condemned to repeat the same mistakes. We came together in our bleakest moment, and we survived and still look out for each other today."

Diana nodded. "Yes!" she said with renewed vigour. "That is what I want for the people living here; a new beginning. Even if it means we have to struggle and endure, even if many of us die to get there, or die on the planet. It would be worth it so that we can begin again, don't you see? So that our future generations will survive and thrive, free of the past, just as you are."

Ethan thought of Elijah and felt deeply ashamed. "I can't help you," he said. "I already had what you want, and I turned my back on it."

"There's still time," said Diana. "There's still time for us both."

Ethan looked at Diana leaning over the railings, her head turned towards him, her straight, red hair hanging down over her cheeks, hiding her ears and drawing even more attention to her powerful, green eyes. Recent events had made him question his ability to judge character, but Diana was heartfelt and seemed deeply sincere. He wished he had paid more attention to his doubts when on the moon base. Compared to Diana, Archer now seemed so obviously fake, and there had always been something nagging at the back of his mind, telling him that all was not as it seemed.

But then there was Maria. She had been a little more guarded and formal perhaps, which was understandable once she was back amongst her superiors, but she was undeniably the same Maria, the same headstrong woman who had woken up in his bed, and made him feel furious and terrified, but also wonderful and alive. More alive than he had felt in a long time, not since that one stolen kiss with Summer years ago. But if what Diana said was true, Maria had played him for a fool. He didn't want to believe that he could be so easily manipulated, and despite his gut feeling that she was telling the truth, he didn't want to rule out that it could still be Diana herself that was the master manipulator. But then, if she was manipulating him, to what end? She already had the ship. If she was the aggressor, she would have already used that ship to destroy the UEC base, and would have no need or reason to talk to him. No reason to keep him alive. Or at least, no reason that Ethan could think of. And this was still the missing piece. What did Diana want with him?

"Assuming, for a moment, I believe you..." Ethan said, before hastily adding, "and I'm not saying I do. But, if I did, you still haven't explained what you need from me."

"We want you to be our emissary," said Diana, again confidently and without hesitation.

"Emissary?"

"We want you to be our representative," Diana clarified. "To introduce us to your people, to show them we are no threat, and to help us become a part of your world."

Ethan remembered back to the meeting hall in the settlement, and to what Administrator Talia had said about the other off-worlders that had come before. He knew how deep their resentment was for these people, because they represented a dangerous link to the past. At the time, Ethan had found this view narrow-minded and xenophobic, but after seeing what he'd seen, he was beginning to understand Talia's concerns. These people, whether UEC or GPS, or whatever they were calling themselves now, did represent the 'old' world. And despite Diana's claim that they were separate from GPS and their generations-long war with the UEC, they were still a part of a world that the Planetsiders had chosen to leave behind, and forget. Ethan knew that they would not be welcomed. They would be seen as dangerous relics, who could use their knowledge and technology to rebuild the cities and begin again on the dark road that had originally led to The Fall. But this was not something he wanted to bring up with Diana now. Besides, he still wasn't sure how much he could trust this woman, or even if she was genuinely telling the truth. The only thing he knew for sure was that someone was lying. Whether it was Maria and the UEC, or Diana, he didn't yet know. And that meant Ethan could only truly trust himself, and his own instincts. Those instincts told him to keep this hidden from Diana, until he knew for sure that she was telling the truth.

"You've given me a lot to think about," he said finally.

"I understand," said Diana. "I will leave you to think. Take your time, and go anywhere you wish. Down to the plaza for some food, or simply wander and explore the station. When you are ready, come back here and then..." she paused, trying to find the right words, "...and then we'll see what happens next, together, okay?"

She reached into her right trouser pocket, pulled out a small, rectangular card and handed it to him. Ethan took it and looked at it. It was similar to the one Maria had used to open doors on the moon base.

"This is an access pass," said Diana. "It is a copy of *my* access pass, in fact. I told you that there would be nowhere on this station that is off limits, and I am true to my word."

"So with this I can go... anywhere?" said Ethan.

"Yes," said Diana, "although I'd advise against the air-locks leading into space." It was obviously intended as a joke and she smiled. Ethan did not – he was reminded too much of his earlier visit to deep space, and did not want to think about it again.

"Simply touch it to the silver pad beside the door you want to open and when the panel surround turns green you can enter," Diana explained. "Or leave, depending on which side of the door you are, of course." Then she gestured down towards the Plaza. "You can also use it to get food, if you wish."

"And I meet you back here?" said Ethan

"Yes," said Diana. "My offices are back through that door." She indicated back towards the door they had gone through earlier in order to reach the balcony. "Till we meet again, young Planetsider!" she said, enthusiastically. And then smiled and walked back towards the door she had just pointed out to Ethan.

***

With Diana gone, Ethan was surprised to find himself feeling anxious and even afraid. He was used to spending time alone on the planet; it was actually something he needed and actively sought out. But here, in this alien environment he felt exposed and vulnerable. Before, he could think of Maria and draw comfort from knowing that she was with him, and that he was doing something to help her, and to help them be together. But if what Diana had told him was true, he was being used to help kill hundreds, maybe thousands. Who knows how many people lived on this vast floating city, but whatever the number was, he did not want to be responsible for their deaths. He craved the hill and the old tree outside the settlement on the planet, where he would go to seek solace. He missed Forest Gate far more than he had ever expected.

Eventually, he summoned up the courage to push off from the railings and began to wander around the balcony, not really paying any attention to the doors, corridors and rooms that he passed. This circular, central area was huge, he observed, perhaps two-hundred metres across, and each level seemed to have its own network of adjoining areas, like a huge three-dimensional spider web. Strangely, while he could see people walking around on the levels above and below him, there was almost nobody on the same level as he was. He'd seen perhaps only two or three others, far on the opposite side of the balcony.

This thought was rudely interrupted by a loud gurgle from his stomach, and he realised that he was actually quite hungry. He fiddled with the square slab in his trouser pocket, remembering what Diana had told him about it also allowing him to get food, and decided to make his way down to the plaza. He looked around for an elevator, or at least something that resembled one, surmising that they must look pretty much the same here as they did on the moon base. He spotted a likely candidate about twenty metres away and started walking towards it, but then something caught his eye. It was a huge door, set back from the balcony edge. It reminded him of the doors in the city space port back on the planet, where he had first met Maria, and where he'd later made the fateful decision to have himself blasted into space with her. Ethan approached it more closely and noticed a sign, surrounded in a red and white striped border that read, 'Restricted Area – Level C9. DO NOT ENTER'. To the side of the large door was a smaller door, and next to this was a square, silver pad. Ethan reached into his pocket and pulled out the square card that Diana had given him. Written on it was, 'Diana Neviah – C9' and a picture of Diana's face, framed by her red hair. He looked at the picture. The green eyes stared back. The thin, red lips were pressed together, not smiling. She looked younger in the photo and, despite not smiling, somehow happier. He read the name again, 'Diana Neviah – C9', then looked again at the sign on the door: 'Restricted Area – Level C9'.

He stood for a time with the square card in his hand, looking at the door. Diana had made it clear that nowhere was off limits; she had made of point of it more than once. But she hadn't mentioned any restricted areas. Did she secretly want him to go in here? Or was she just trying to show that she trusted him, by giving him access to all areas, but trusting also that he wasn't stupid enough to enter a restricted area? He flipped the pass over and over in his hand, tossing the different possibilities around in his mind. Maybe behind this door there was something to help confirm Diana's story, or throw it into question. The temptation proved overwhelming. Ethan walked up to the door and pressed the pass against the silver square to its side. Moments later, a green border lit up around the square and he heard a solid, mechanical thud from within the door. He pulled the handle, and it opened.

CHAPTER 25

Ethan walked through the door and let it close behind him. As the latch clicked into place he heard the same mechanical thud as the door locked shut again. He was in an empty room, colder than the balcony area and with only one dim lamp for light. The air smelled stale. At the other end of the room, about ten metres away, was another door, the same size and shape as the one he'd just entered through. He walked over to it and saw another sign. It was covered in a layer of black dust, which was slightly damp and as a result had turned into a sort of oily grime. He touched the door and it felt colder than the first. Using the sleeve of his flight suit, he wiped away the grime on the sign, leaving black smears on the coarse fabric and on the smooth material of the sign itself, but it was still clear enough to read. There was a word he did not recognise followed again by, 'DO NOT ENTER'. He looked for the silver square, and found it, masked by grime, in the same location as on the other door. He wiped away the grime as best he could and stood looking at it.

The first door had been a simpler choice. There didn't seem much danger, and curiosity, fuelled by a resolve to this time not be coerced or hand-held had made it a relatively easy decision. But this room was different. From the taste of the air, and the dirt and darkness, it was clear that no-one had been inside for a long time, and that this second door had stayed shut for at least as long. Ethan's senses were heightened, on edge. He knew this was dangerous, reckless even. But it was recklessness that had led him here, alone, the only Planetsider to have left the planet behind and step back in time, into the middle of an ancient war in which he had become a key player. The risks he had taken to be here had been because of someone else. This he would do for himself; his choice for his own sake. Perhaps behind this door there was something to help make sense of everything, or perhaps it was part of another trick, another lie.

Ethan pressed the card against the grimy, silver square and waited. Nothing happened. He removed it and scrubbed again at the panel, clearing more of the black sludge away. Then he took a deep breath, exhaled, and pressed the card to the panel again. A few seconds later, a dim greenish border appeared around the panel, followed by three dull, mechanical thuds, heavier-sounding than with the first door. Thud... Thud... Thud. A hiss of air escaped through the cracks and the door crept open, creaking at the hinges, and scraping away a layer of dirt to reveal a clean wedge of grey flooring. Ethan nervously looked through the crack that had opened. Beyond was a corridor, again dimly lit, but the air smelled fresher. He pushed at the door to widen the crack far enough to squeeze through and stepped into the corridor beyond, leaving the door open behind him.

Ethan walked cautiously forward, wincing at each thump of his boots on the hard floor, which seemed abnormally loud in the total silence of this environment. The corridor widened into an open area, which looked like a smaller version of the central plaza, with glass-fronted rooms lining the walls, and benches and stalls in the centre. Some of the windows were smashed and Ethan could see, further ahead as the space opened wider, that there were metal beams hanging down, with bundles of cables tangled up with them, and debris littering the floor. There was some artificial lighting, at a high level, above the glass-fronted rooms, and some at floor level, like illuminated paths, but the main light source seemed to be ahead, filtering down from above. Ethan walked further into the space, tip-toeing around the larger chunks of debris and trying, unsuccessfully, to avoid stepping on glass. The sound of it shattering underfoot was excruciating. He reached what looked like the central point of the wider space and looked up at series of balconies layered above him. It was exactly like a smaller version of the plaza area he had just left. Some of the glass-fronted rooms on the lower level had displays of items. In one, dusty clothes hung from life-sized models of people, arranged into strange poses. Other rooms had different objects inside, and some rooms appeared empty. He looked for an elevator, but then thought better of it. This place was old and broken and the last thing he wanted was to get stuck here. Instead, he dusted off a bench and sat down to think.

It would have been an impressive place once, Ethan considered. His gaze landed on a part of the dome at the very top of the central area, through which the starlight was shining and casting a silvery glow over everything beneath. A large section of the dome was covered, as if a huge hole had been gouged out and then hastily patched up. It reminded him of how the dome on the moon base had 'healed' itself after the attack. Then Ethan noticed other similar sections of patchwork in the walls, like old scars that had never fully healed. The damage suggested the reason this place had been evacuated and now lay abandoned. But it was clearly intact and habitable, and would merely need some cosmetic improvements, so why had it been left to rot, Ethan wondered?

Then there was a sound, like a shard of glass scraping along the hard floor. Ethan froze, trying to place it, trying to confirm if it was real or his imagination. The air was completely still again. His pulse began to climb. He held his breath to remove even the sound of his own breathing, and listened hard. The sound came again, and then movement. There was the unmistakeable sound of footsteps, but these were not clean steps; it sounded as if the boots were stepping and then dragging along the floor. But where was it coming from? And how many feet? Ethan could not tell. He stood up, very slowly, trying to remain silent and calm. He closed his eyes, trying to pinpoint the location of the sound. The slow, drawn out steps were coming from inside one of the glass-fronted rooms. He couldn't tell exactly which, but he could place the direction, and it was from behind him, between him and the doorway to the main part of the station. He backed away, trying to manoeuvre himself to the opposite side of the corridor to the footsteps, and started to slowly retrace his path. He looked around and saw a section of metal pipe about a metre long on the floor. He picked it up, and it felt reassuringly weighty in his hand. It would suffice as an improvised weapon, should one be needed. He hoped he wouldn't need it. Ethan tried to quicken his progress without making too much additional noise. He stepped sideways, facing where he thought the sound was coming from, but as his pace quickened, so did the frequency and volume of the noise from the darkness ahead of him. He was being stalked, or hunted.

"Show yourself!" shouted Ethan into the blackness, and then immediately regretted it, as his voice sounded weak and unconvincing. *Come on Ethan, pull yourself together...* he chastised himself. He looked towards his destination. He was perhaps a hundred metres from the corridor leading back to the second door, but in less than twenty metres the space between him and the other side of the corridor would narrow, and whatever was lurking in the shadows would be forced to show itself. He continued on, stepping side-to-side, metal bar raised, gripping it so tightly that his fingers were beginning to numb. Then he stumbled over some loose rubble that was littering the floor and fell. The bar slipped from his hands and rolled down the corridor away from him. The noise was agonising, like a bell being rung, inviting whatever hunted him to attack. Ethan scrambled to his feet, but remained crouched low, ready to spring in any direction and sprint to safety. The bar finally came to rest and there was again silence, for a short time, before the scraping resumed. Ethan stayed low, motionless, watching. Slowly, out of the darkness a figure emerged. As the silvery light caught its features, Ethan recognised it immediately and his stomach twisted into knots. Panic threatened to overwhelm him. It had the same long, grey face, the same sucked in cheeks and straw-like grey hair, lifeless like dried weeds. And the same cold, black eyes, which were fixed on his. It was one of the Maddened, there was no doubt in his mind, and Ethan knew that he had to run.

He pushed off and accelerated as fast as he could, using all his effort. The harrowing sound of scraping glass and debris behind him told Ethan that the creature was chasing him. The detritus littering the hallway made it difficult to accelerate, and Ethan found himself struggling to get a good footing and run at the speed he knew he could, and that he knew he needed to in order to evade this thing. He approached a broken wooden bench and pushed it as he passed, scattering fragments of wood along the hallway in the hope of creating an obstacle to his pursuer's progress. He chanced a look back and wished he hadn't, as the maddened creature ploughed through it, undeterred.

Ahead he could see the second door, still ajar, and he pushed on harder, gasping stale air into his lungs. The distance was narrowing, but then his foot landed on a shard of glass and slid out from under him. He fell, hard, and tumbled across the floor, the scattered mix of broken wood, metal and glass bruising and cutting at his skin, and came to a painful stop against the door, his momentum pushing it shut with a heavy thud. He heard the familiar sound of the bolts inside locking, and knew he was trapped. There was no option now but to fight it. Without a weapon, he knew his chances were slim, even with his abilities. The Maddened were strong, resilient, belligerent and – ironically for something already so close to being dead – very hard to kill.

He pushed himself to his feet. His head was bleeding and dripping blood onto his cheek, and he could feel glass and shards of metal sticking into his legs and arms and back. He was panting heavily, exhausted from the anaerobic sprint, and he felt dizzy, but there was no time to recoup his strength. Ahead of him, the creature had slowed and was advancing towards him patiently, like a wild animal that knew it had a sure kill. Ethan raised his fists. In his head were thoughts of Elijah, Katie, Summer and the great tree under which he had found such solace, but that had also fuelled his curiosity and led him to this end in such a dark and unfamiliar place, led him to abandon his family, led him to be deceived and used as a weapon, led him to an early death, alone and far from home. Maybe it was what he deserved, he thought.

The creature was now just a few metres away, black eyes fixed on him. Ethan knew that it would charge at any moment. But he would not go down without a fight, not to this thing. If he was to die, he'd die a Ranger, doing what he was trained to do, what he was meant to do. Perhaps there was a sliver of honour to be regained in that. It was all he had now. With all the strength he had left, he thrust himself towards the creature, screaming as loud as he could, arms outstretched and aimed towards its throat. He surged forward, but was then slammed backwards. He landed hard again against the door, and looked up, expecting to see black eyes staring down at him, but it was not there. Instead, there was a series of bright flashes and deep, unnatural, pulsing sounds. Hovering about two metres off the floor in front of him was a dark metallic object, about twice the size of a human head. Pulses of light emanated from it, striking the creature in the chest, and pushing it back and away from Ethan. It wailed horribly as the flashes of light struck, but as much in frustration or anger as in pain. Three more beams hit it in rapid succession and this was enough to turn it away. It fled down the corridor and back into the silvery shadows where it had been lurking.

The object span around slowly and emitted another beam of light, this time towards Ethan. He raised a hand to shield his face, expecting to be pushed backwards, as the creature had been. Instead, a thin strip of light panned up and down Ethan's body, accompanied by more of the unnatural squawks and beeps that characterised the technological devices used by both the UEC and GPS. The beam shut off abruptly and the round object shot rapidly upwards and out of sight. Then there was silence again.

When it was clear that both the maddened creature and the object had gone for good, Ethan got up and carefully dusted himself off, cautiously removing some of the larger pieces of glass and metal that had stuck into him during his fall. He ached all over, and his chest burned from exhaustion. Reaching into his pocket, he searched for the small, square card, and to his despair found it missing. The last thing he wanted to do was go back and search for it, but he had no choice. It seemed likely that there would be more of these things lurking in the shadows, but he tried not to think of how many there could be. Perhaps his spherical metal friend would come to his aid again, he wondered, but it was not much comfort. He sighed heavily and, gingerly, started to walk back out into the narrow corridor ahead.

He hadn't gone far before a sound from behind startled him and caused him to swing around. It was the unmistakable sound of the bolts in the door, sliding open. The grime-covered panel beside the door lit up green and the door swung open slowly, its old, worn hinges groaning as it widened. Two figures in black outfits and black face masks rushed though, holding weapons. Ethan instinctively held up his hands in submission, but the figures moved swiftly past him, and Ethan watched in confusion as they took up kneeling positions, covering the corridor with their weapons.

"You do enjoy an adventure, don't you Ethan?" He swung around again this time to see Diana, standing in the middle of the room beyond the door. "If you'd please come this way," she said in her usual, affable way, red lips pressed into a gentle smile. "I can't go any further into the quarantined area, you see. I'm afraid I don't possess your natural resilience."

Ethan said nothing, and simply did as requested, stopping in front of Diana feeling hazy and dazed. The two black figures returned swiftly behind him, and one pulled the door shut. The three bolts fell into place. Thud... Thud... Thud.

"Thank you, you may leave," Diana said to the black figures, who nodded and left promptly, without a word. Ethan was still very out of breath, and he was suddenly aware of feeling extremely weary; the effects of the vast surges of adrenalin were wearing off. "Shall we?" said Diana, motioning towards the door leading back to the main concourse. Ethan looked at the door and walked through it, without looking at Diana or acknowledging her. He went to the balcony, and leaned heavily on it with both forearms, his hands clasped together in front of him. He felt strangely calm and at ease. He wasn't thinking about what had just happened, and the fact he had been moments away from a gruesome death. He was thinking about the settlement. He was thinking about home.

He heard the thud of the bolt securing the door behind him, and the delicate tap, tap, tap of Diana's footsteps approaching from behind. A few moments later, she appeared at his side. She faced in the opposite direction and rested with her back on the railings. She casually crossed one ankle over the other and waited, head angled towards Ethan, green eyes fixed quizzically on him.

"You knew I'd go in there, didn't you?" said Ethan, calmly.

"I suspected you probably would, yes," Diana replied.

"Why didn't you tell me what was in there?"

"Because I knew you had to see for yourself," said Diana without hesitation, obviously expecting this question. "You've been lied to continuously for days, Ethan. I didn't expect you to just take my word for it. It was a gamble."

"A gamble with my life," said Ethan, candidly.

"You were never in any real danger," said Diana. "Our Sentry – the metal ball you encountered – was always watching you."

"It would have been nice to have encountered it sooner," said Ethan with a hint of annoyance.

Diana laughed. "Yes, well I did say it was a gamble," she said. "And I understand that you're angry, but hopefully you can appreciate why it was necessary."

"I'm not angry," said Ethan. "I'm tired, tired of tricks and lies. No more games."

Diana nodded. "Agreed. Here, swallow this." She handed him two small capsules. "They will help with the pain."

Ethan was only vaguely aware of the soreness in his body now, but he took the capsules and placed them in his mouth. They liquefied on contact with his tongue and, as with the medication that Angela Salus had given him on the base, he began to immediately feel more invigorated. He wondered what role Angela had played in the UEC deception. *Was she even Maria's sister?* he asked himself.

Ethan turned around and faced the door to the quarantined zone. "What happened in there?"

Diana stood away from the railings, and her expression changed again, showing the sadness that Ethan had seen before when she talked about difficult events. "There was an attack," she said. "One of a kind that has, thankfully, never been repeated." She walked back towards the door to the quarantined zone and stopped about half way. Ethan followed and stood next to her, looking at her in anticipation. "We have always been closely matched in terms of combative and defensive capabilities," Diana continued, "which is why this war has gone on for so long. But then they tried something new. They loaded a small fighter craft with semi-refined orrum, reclaimed at great risk from a section of the destroyed Refinery, orbiting behind the planet, so we couldn't see what they were doing. And then they flew it into the station."

Ethan was astonished. He tried to think of something to say, but could find no words.

"It wasn't spotted until it was too late," Diana continued. "The ship was too small to cause any significant structural damage, but the orrum was atomised inside, and, well, you saw the result."

"How long ago did this happen?" said Ethan, still incredulous.

"Oh, a long time ago," murmured Diana, lost in her own thoughts.

"The thing in there, the creatures we call The Maddened... it was once one of your people?" said Ethan, now beginning to understand. "How many more are in there?"

"We don't know exactly," said Diana. "Probably fewer than a hundred now."

Ethan knew that even half that number would be a threat to everyone on the station. "Why have you not..."

"Killed them?" interrupted Diana, turning to look at him with her sharp green eyes.

Ethan was taken aback. "Well, yes! Surely they are a constant danger?"

Diana sighed heavily. "After the attack, we knew that the people in this section would be exposed beyond our skill to heal," she said, looking back towards the doorway. "The area was sealed quickly, and contained. But there were hundreds trapped inside. And they were still people then, Ethan."

Ethan could see melancholy starting to sweep over Diana. It had started to colour her speech, and even affect the way she stood. It was also written on her face, in the lines around her eyes that only appeared when her guard started to fall. He could see now that Diana had been just as distrustful of him as he had been of her. But now she was letting him in.

"They were given a choice," Diana continued, folding her arms tightly around her chest. "They would be helped to die, peacefully, before the change took hold and stole what remained of their minds and bodies, or they could live here, in the quarantined zone. And be allowed to become..." she paused, "...well, you know the rest."

"Maddened," said Ethan, shaking his head.

"We call it The Degradation," said Diana. "But 'maddened' works just as well."

Ethan took a deep breath and let it out slowly. "This is unbelievable."

And then he had a thought. "But why did they not try it again? You said this was the only time they attacked in this way?"

"They did try," said Diana. "But there was an accident while they were loading the ship, or at least that's what we believe happened, and a significant section of their own base was heavily damaged, and contaminated. We estimate that hundreds of lives were lost, if not many more. After that, it seems likely that they considered it too dangerous to attempt again; too much of a risk to themselves."

Ethan remembered the talk about off-limits areas on the UEC base and another piece of the puzzle clicked into place in his mind.

"That's why you made a point of telling me there was nowhere off limits, isn't it?" said Ethan. Diana smiled weakly and nodded. "They told me you had attacked them in this way," said Ethan, remembering, "by using this toxic ore as a weapon. It's why they said they needed the ship and medical equipment."

"Yes," said Diana. "Ironic, isn't it?"

Ethan walked back to the balcony and looked down at the plaza, and the people going about their everyday lives. Just as the people of his settlement were probably doing, he imagined. He wished he could stand on a balcony and watch them instead, to see if they were talking about him. Did they miss him, he wondered? Were they safe? He felt a longing that he had not experienced before, a longing to be among the people who cared about him. Or, at least, used to. "I think I want to go home now," he said, mournfully.

Diana appeared beside him. Her mouth was more relaxed, not pressed into the thin, red smile he was used to, and her eyes appeared fuller, rounder. She put a hand on his shoulder and said, "Come with me."

CHAPTER 26

Diana led Ethan to an elevator on the other side of the balcony to where they had been standing. They passed several other elevators along the way, but the one they finally stopped at looked different.

"Where are we going?" asked Ethan, genuinely curious.

"To see your ride home," Diana replied, with a half smile. She touched her security pass to the elevator door panel, causing the doors to hiss open. Ethan stepped inside, followed by Diana. She pressed a button on another panel inside and the doors closed. Shortly afterwards they began to descend rapidly. Ethan looked at Diana, standing calmly with her hands together in front of her. She was unlike anyone he'd ever met.

"What makes you different?" said Ethan, almost thinking out loud. Diana cocked her head towards him and shot him a quizzical look. "Both sides have been fighting for so long that you've grown up knowing nothing else," said Ethan, taking the cue to elaborate. "So why are you different? What makes you want something other than war?"

Diana considered this for a moment. "It's a good question, Ethan," she said. "The answer is that I have to believe there's something better; that we don't just have to accept what we're given. Does that make sense to you?"

Ethan nodded. "More than you know," he said, softly. "But maybe sometimes, it's better to hold on to what you have."

"Perhaps," said Diana, thoughtfully. "We're alike, you and I."

"Oh?" said Ethan, now tilting his head quizzically back at her.

"We both dare to dream," said Diana. "And we're willing to chase our dreams, even when it leads us to places that others fear to go."

Ethan stared back ahead at the blur of motion behind the glass. "Yes," he said, "sometimes foolishly."

"What you consider foolish, others would consider brave, even noble."

"I don't think Talia would see it that way."

"Well, perhaps I can help her to see things differently when you introduce us," Diana replied, smiling.

Ethan did not respond. He admired Diana's conviction, and she was right that they were alike in many ways. But he still did not believe that Diana and her people returning to the planet was a good idea. He would need to find the right moment to tell her, to explain. But he didn't want to. He didn't want to be the one to crush her dreams, as his had been crushed.

The elevator came to an abrupt halt and the doors hissed open.

"After you," said Diana.

Ethan stepped out into a large circular room that seemed to be the same diameter as the plaza. It rose five storeys, with the upper sections configured as what looked like offices or storage areas. The lower deck occupied around two-thirds of the total area and was divided into quadrants, each with an array of consoles and machinery that Ethan was now used to seeing. At the outer edge of each quadrant was an enormous viewing window, staring out into open space. Three of the windows gave an unobstructed view into the darkness beyond, but the fourth was almost entirely obscured by a massive object, attached to the station via a long umbilical. Ethan recognised it instantly as the ship he had been sent to recover for the UEC.

"There's your ride home," said Diana, who was standing slightly behind Ethan.

Ethan looked at the hulking ship through the window and shuddered as he remembered what had occurred inside. He approached the window to get a closer look and then noticed the unmistakable blue glow of the planet hanging in space, far beyond them, but so clear and vibrant that he felt he could reach out and touch it. The first time he had seen the planet from space he was too awestruck to appreciate it, but now, looking out at the shining blue orb, he realised how truly beautiful it was. And how, despite the dangers it still contained, and the hardships it required its inhabitants to endure, its preservation was vital. Whether it was the UEC or GPS, or what they had evolved to become in the generations after the start of the war, it didn't matter. The Planetsiders' new civilisation had to be protected. Over several generations, the survivors of The Fall had, by necessity and choice, struggled and worked together to build a new society that was entirely separated from the civilisation that preceded it. A unified society. A better society. In contrast the survivors cut off in space had continued to feud with each other, passing on their hatred to the next generation.

Ethan knew the price that Diana would ask in order for him to return home. She would want to return with him with a delegation of her people, and with Ethan as her envoy. But

Ethan understood now that it was too high a price to pay. He would not risk everything that the Planetsiders had achieved in order to fulfil his own selfish desires. It was his selfishness that had led him to this point. And it was Ethan alone that must suffer the consequences, even if that meant staying on the base for the rest of his life. Even if it meant dying here, a casualty of their perpetual war.

"You still mean to return with me, to the planet?" said Ethan, not turning to face her.

"I do," said Diana. "I was hoping we could return together."

Ethan turned and saw Diana standing as she usually did, hands clasped in front of her, red lips pressed into a thin smile. "Diana, I want you to know that I believe you and admire what you're trying..." he began, but Diana interrupted, quick to head off any suggestion of refusal.

"Ethan, you don't have to decide now, take..."

"Diana, please, hear me out," implored Ethan cutting across her. He looked pleadingly into her intense green eyes. Ethan could see that she was desperate to speak her mind, but she fought back her impulses and allowed him to talk.

"I understand what you want, Diana," said Ethan, "and I want it too. But the Planetsiders are not ready to accept you back. Not yet."

"Ethan, I mean no harm to your people..." said Diana, unable to contain herself any longer.

Ethan held up a hand to stop her again. "I know," he said, believing her. "But they are not ready. And, while this war continues, neither are you."

Diana opened her mouth to speak again, but her words were drowned out by the sudden blaring of a siren. Diana's face hardened like stone. She ran over to the nearest docking quadrant and spoke to a uniformed man, who was staring intently at a screen. Ethan followed, but hung back a little so as not to get in the way.

"How many?" Diana asked the man.

"Three fighter craft, four kilometres away, heading straight for us and closing fast," the man replied promptly. "Command has launched a full response from the upper ring."

Diana raised a clenched fist to her chin and stood there in deep thought. "What are they doing?" she said, addressing no-one specifically.

"Are we in danger?" said Ethan, concerned.

"No," said Diana, but Ethan was far from convinced by the response.

"Then why do you look worried?" he asked, beginning to feel more anxious.

Diana moved over to the console nearest the uniformed man and started tapping at the screen. "Three light fighters pose no threat," she said, while still watching the screen. "Even if our fighter response doesn't intercept them, they would be destroyed by the main batteries before they even got within a kilometre."

"Perhaps they just want to test our response times?" suggested the uniformed man.

"Perhaps," said Diana still looking at the screen. "It's unusual though. It's as if they..." She stopped abruptly, mid-sentence. The panel in front of her started to beep frantically. Diana hit the screen and the display switched to an external camera. Diana squinted at the screen and then she saw it, the outline of a fourth vessel, cutting silently through space directly towards the lower docking ring where they were situated. It was completely powered down, with no engine glow, no lights and no electronic emissions, so it was practically invisible against the starscape. Ethan could see that Diana knew their plan. She looked up at Ethan, her eyes wide. "It's as if they want to distract us from something else."

Ethan opened his mouth to respond and then it felt like an earthquake hit the station. He was knocked from his feet, and thrown awkwardly onto the hard metal floor. He saw Diana lying prone next to him, and pulled her towards him. An explosion erupted from the quadrant opposite, and Ethan shielded Diana from the blast. The lights went out. For a moment there was total darkness and then the emergency lights kicked in, bathing the area in a harsh, red hue.

Ethan got up, and helped Diana to her feet. "Thanks," she said, dusting off her grey suit, which was now ripped and blackened in places. Before Ethan could respond, she had rushed back over to the console. The other man lay on the floor, bleeding out badly from a wound to his head. Ethan went to help him, but Diana called out. "No, there's no time!" her voice was urgent. "They've breached the dock. They will be coming!"

"Who?" shouted Ethan.

"The UEC," said Diana. "They've come for the ship. We have to get to the auxiliary control room. We've got to destroy that ship, or they will take it and use it to destroy this station!"

Ethan nodded. Diana was right; the ship had to be destroyed.

"Follow me!" shouted Diana, and she ran towards a metal stairwell that snaked up to the balcony level, overlooking the four docking quadrants. Ethan followed closely behind. As they reached the first junction, Ethan felt another explosion rock the lower ring. He turned and saw that a hole had been blasted through the docking bay door in the quadrant opposite, close to where the initial explosion had occurred. Soldiers dressed in blue body armour and helmets charged through the opening and immediately began shooting. Each wore a full face shield with a dark visor; all expect one. As the soldiers charged in, filing to the left and right, shooting at anyone that moved, the unmasked man walked down the centre line, almost casually, carrying a rifle at the low-ready position. It was Major Kurren.

"Quickly, we don't have much time!" shouted Diana, who was surprisingly agile, and already several seconds ahead of him. Ethan set off back up the stairs to a background of weapons firing below, and the sickening screams and shouts of people being killed. They reached the balcony and Ethan followed Diana across the front of a long room, with darkened glass windows. She swiftly unlocked the door with her pass, pressed it open and motioned for Ethan to go inside first. Bullets ricocheted off the railing and walls nearby.

"Hurry!" shouted Diana, as Ethan practically fell into the room. Diana followed close behind, closed the door and then held her pass to the silver panel until the rim around the panel turned red.

"The lock will hold them for a while, but not for long," Diana explained, through laboured breaths.

"What are we doing here?" Ethan asked, looking around the room. "What is this place?"

"It used to be a command centre used by GPS, but we've not had need of it for years," Diana replied. "We can still remotely access the warship's systems from here."

"To do what?"

"To destroy it," said Diana. "I can set it loose and overload its engines remotely. I just need to access the program and run it."

"What can I do?" asked Ethan, feeling helpless.

Diana went to a metal storage cabinet next to a nearby console and, holding her pass to the silver square on the front, unlocked it. She opened the door, reached inside and pulled out a pistol. "Do you know how to use one of these?" she asked.

"No, but I'm a fast learner," said Ethan.

Diana slid a magazine into the weapon, pulled back on the top section and handed it to Ethan. "It's loaded and armed," she said. "Just point, and squeeze the trigger."

"I thought you said you weren't a General," said Ethan, surprised at how deftly Diana handled the weapon.

"Long story, no time," she replied. Ethan held the weapon in his hand. It was cold and heavy, but comfortable. He practised aiming at the door while Diana worked at the console. "Come on, come on!" she said to the screen, urging the text and numbers that were flashing across it to move faster. A second screen lit up nearer to Ethan. On it was a video image of the warship, still attached to the station by the umbilical. He could see lights switching on across its hull, and its three giant engines begin to glow.

The sound of heavy boots thudding on the metal decking outside drew Ethan's attention back to the door. He waved at Diana to get her attention, and then pressed a finger to his lips. Diana understood the signal, and slipped down low behind the console, making deliberately slower and more careful inputs in order to stay as quiet as possible. Ethan moved to the other side of the room, and hid behind a cluster of desks, weapon aimed at the door. Outside, he could see the shadows of two figures behind the dark glass. They were outside the door, trying the handle. Then he heard muted voices and they moved away. Ethan waited, his grip on the weapon's handle so tight his knuckles were white.

Moments later there was a sharp detonation and the door flew inward. The blast startled Ethan, but he quickly steadied himself and regained his focus. The two soldiers rushed in, scanning the room with lights fixed to the ends of their weapons. The first soldier saw Diana and tensed. Ethan stood tall, aimed and squeezed the trigger three times in rapid succession. The soldier fell. The second figure fired at Ethan and debris erupted from the wall beside him, showering him with dust and fragments of a stone-like material. He ducked lower and threw himself behind an adjacent desk. The soldier fired again and Ethan stayed low as more fragments showered him from above. He reached over the desk and fired blindly in the direction of the noise, before crawling behind a second desk further into the room. He chanced a look, and saw the soldier shifting away, looking, he presumed, for Diana. He took a deep breath, held it, and stood, raising the weapon towards the masked figure. The soldier reacted quickly, shifted again and turned the barrel of its weapon back towards him. Ethan squeezed the trigger twice and the figure flinched instinctively, but did not fall. Ethan expected to be shot, but instead Diana appeared from behind the console and struck the soldier in the back of the head with what looked like a metal table leg. The soldier grunted and fell heavily to the floor. Ethan ran over and checked the body. It was either dead or unconscious.

"There will be more coming," Diana said, handing Ethan the metal bar. "Here, perhaps you'll be more useful with this."

Ethan took it and handed her back the pistol. "How long until you're done?" he asked.

"I don't know, perhaps another ten minutes," she said. "Our response force won't get here in time, not with the docking ring on emergency lock-down. The doors are automatically sealed in case of a hull breach and it will take them perhaps twenty minutes to override. You will have to buy me more time, Ethan!"

Ethan gripped the bar. It felt familiar and comforting, like he was fighting on his terms, finally. He moved over to the door, and glanced outside. Two more soldiers were approaching. "Be ready," he said to Diana. She nodded and tried to take as much cover as possible, while still working on the console.

Ethan closed his eyes and listened to the footsteps approaching, gauging their speed and distance. They would not be expecting a melee, and would not be expecting someone to be standing so close behind the door. That would give him the early advantage, or at least that's what he hoped. When they were almost on him, he took a deep breath, opened his eyes and swung hard, striking the first soldier cleanly in the throat, crushing the windpipe instantly. The second reacted more quickly and skilfully dodged Ethan's follow-up. It raised its weapon but Ethan smashed it from the soldier's grip, sending it to the floor in shattered pieces. Ethan stepped to the side and lunged, but the soldier deftly evaded the move and delivered a hard kick to Ethan's ribs, knocking him backward. A second kick from the soldier forced Ethan to drop the bar. Pressing the advantage the soldier attacked again, but Ethan blocked it, and landed a hard punch to the side. The soldier groaned and stumbled backwards, rebounding off the dark glass wall. Ethan landed a swift follow-up to the head sending the soldier down, its face mask falling off as its helmeted head hit the floor with a sharp clunk. Dazed, the soldier scrambled forward and pulled a pistol from the belt of its fallen companion. Ethan froze as the barrel was raised towards his head. The soldier moved forward, weapon outstretched. A sliver of light from the open doorway illuminated its face and Ethan's heart almost stopped beating.

"Sal?" Maria Salus said nothing, but kept the weapon aimed at Ethan's head.

"Ethan?" said Maria, astonished to see Ethan standing in front of her. "Is it really you?"

Ethan dropped his guard and stood looking at her, overwhelmed by a cocktail of emotions: a nauseating pain at the confirmation of Maria's lies; furious anger at the crimes she was now committing; all mixed with an instinctive, bittersweet joy at seeing her again, alive and well. He shook his head. "It was all a lie," he said despairingly, still struggling to believe it could be true. "Everything you told me... us... it was all lies."

Maria's mouth hung slightly open, as if trying to speak. Her face appeared pale, drained of blood. The weapon in her hand trembled uncontrollably.

"Ethan, what are you doing? Stop her!" shouted Diana from across the room. She was aiming the pistol towards Maria, but Ethan was standing between them, preventing a clean shot.

Maria instinctively shifted her aim in the direction of Diana's voice, but her hand was still shaking, and she could not take her eyes of Ethan.

Ethan did not hear Diana's cries. He could no longer hear the gunfire, the screams, or the sirens; everything but Maria had been blocked out. "You lied to me," he said, the words still sounding alien and unbelievable.

Maria stared back at him, an almost stupefied look on her face. She lowered the weapon to her side, but still no words came. Ethan had thought a lot about what he might say to Maria, if they ever met again, but in truth, he had never expected to. Now that she was here, these rational thoughts and questions were simply overshadowed by the anger that was swelling inside him. "You lied to me!" He was shouting now, willing Maria to respond, to offer a defence or at least an explanation. Even another lie would be better than silence. Maria looked deeply uncomfortable and confused. The weapon remained at her side, but her other hand was now clasped over her mouth, while her eyes stared blankly back at him. "Say something!" Ethan continued, now closing the gap between them. "Another lie, I don't care, but say *something!*"

Ethan's advance jolted Maria into action. She stepped back,

raising the weapon again. "Keep back, Ethan, please!" she urged, her voice shaky and unsure.

But Ethan was not afraid and would not be pushed away. "I gave up everything for you," he said, continuing to advance towards Maria. "You told me you would die!"

"Ethan, please..." said Maria, on the verge of tears.

"You used me," he said ignoring her pleas. "I love you, Sal. And you just used me."

"Ethan stop, please!" implored Maria again. She dropped the weapon to the floor and clasped both hands to her face, trying to force back tears that were now freely flowing down her cheeks.

"You made me fall in love with you, and then you used me," said Ethan again, now almost face to face with Maria. Saying the words out loud suddenly made them more real, and more terrible. He fought back tears of his own. "And for what, Sal?" he continued, voice shaking. "So you can murder these people. Is that it? Is that all this was for? Is that all I was to you?" He fell to his knees and begged her. "Tell me I'm wrong, please!"

Diana rushed out from behind the console and aimed the pistol at Maria, but neither Maria nor Ethan reacted to her, remaining fixed on each other.

"It wasn't all lies, Ethan," Maria sobbed. "I tried to tell you. Before the attack, before I got hurt. I tried to tell you that this was real, that *we* were real, don't you remember?"

Ethan laughed. "What, that you love me too?" he said. "You expect me to believe that, after all you've done?"

Maria wiped her face with the backs of her hands, and used all of her military discipline to compose herself. "Yes, I lied," she said, more calmly. "Our mission was to retrieve a Planetsider, and convince him or her to believe in our cause, so we could retrieve the ship and put an end to this war."

"I told you, Ethan," said Diana, bitterly. "They are all the same, and they will never change! We don't have time for this; we have to destroy that ship, before they take it and kill us all!"

Maria glanced at Diana contemptuously, but then returned her attention to Ethan. "So yes, I used you. I used you because that was my mission," she said, her emotions now more under control. "But I swear to you now that not everything was a lie," Ethan laughed again and shook his head, refusing to hear her. "Ethan, it's the truth!" said Maria, almost shouting. "My feelings for you are real. That wasn't part of the plan. And my parents *were* killed, just as I described to you, by a GPS attack," And then she looked again at Diana and added with venom, "Killed by these people who claim to be so innocent!"

"Ethan, that was a long time ago," Diana cut in. "I want to end this stupid war, they only want to kill us!"

Maria continued to glare at Diana, anger swelling in her gut, "You are not blameless!" she shouted. "It doesn't matter that it wasn't your order, or even that it was your ignorant, idiot father's order that killed them, we've both done terrible things."

"My father was as stupid as your pompous idiot, Archer," said Diana, savagely.

"That doesn't excuse what he did," said Maria, with matching venom.

"I don't make excuses for him!" Diana hit back. "It's because of what he did - *who he was* - that I'm trying to change things, for the better. I am not my father, but you people, you just want to continue down the same path, making the same foolish mistakes, again and again."

"Both sides are to blame for continuing this war," countered Maria.

"In the past, yes. But this is now, and I want to end it, without any more killing," asserted Diana, "and we still can.

The question is, what do you want, Captain Salus?"

"I want an end to this too!" said Maria, desperately. "But we've no reason to trust you, just as you have no reason to trust us. For all I know, you want that ship to blow up the moon base!"

"That's Archer talking!" Diana replied, scornfully. "His paranoia, ignorance and hatred pollutes and blinds you. I have tried to reason with him, tried to make him see that we can end this peacefully, but he will not listen. He does not want to!"

Maria appeared to be taken aback at this last statement. "You two are in contact?"

"Yes," said Diana firmly, lowering her weapon. "Clearly, there is much he doesn't trust you to know. He has twisted your mind, made you believe there is no other option but war, no choice but to destroy your enemy. Well here I stand, Captain Salus. What do you see?"

Maria's eyes remained locked on Diana's, probing for any hint of a lie, any suggestion of deceit, but there was none. From Diana she felt a purity of purpose that she had once felt too, but the Planetsider mission, and the web of lies it had required her to weave, had eroded her conviction. And now, with Ethan again standing before her, alongside the woman who was supposed to be her enemy, she felt the last of this conviction crumble to nothing. Everything she had believed was now called into question.

"Say I believe you," Maria said, cautiously, "say I want to help you end this... what happens next?"

Diana's eyes lit up and she was about to respond, but Ethan spoke first, catching both of them by surprise.

"Send me back to the planet," he said, calmly. Diana and Maria both looked at him, confused.

"Send me back, alone," he continued, "then you will have to settle your differences without resorting to mass murder.

Without that ship, you'll have no choice."

Diana raced across to Ethan. "No, let me come with you, please!" she begged.

Ethan, reached out and held her shoulders. "You will only bring the war down to the planet," he said. "Your people need you here. They need your compassion, and your foolish dreams."

"It's true," said Maria. "Archer will never stop pursuing you. Even on the planet. He'll follow you down there if he has to."

Diana backed away from Ethan shaking her head. "No, please, I have had enough of fighting."

"They need your strength, Diana," said Ethan. "You can find a way to end this war, peacefully. And then perhaps one day you can come home." He looked over to Maria. "You can all come home."

Maria stared into Ethan's soft brown eyes and smiled, and in that moment he recognised once again the Maria Salus that he had fallen in love with.

The sound of gunfire from the lower level sharply focused all their attention. As it died away they stood, silently, listening for an indication of approaching soldiers.

"I will help you," said Maria, breaking the silence.

"How?" asked Ethan.

"I will help you take the ship back to the planet. I will help send you home." Diana looked at Ethan, and then at Maria, and there was silent agreement.

"We have very little time," said Diana. "Can you get him onto the ship?"

"Yes," said Maria, resolutely.

"Then go," said Diana. "I will upload the program from here and try to get you as close as I can."

Ethan didn't understand. "As close as you can to what?" he

asked.

"To your settlement, of course," said Diana. "To your home." Diana turned to Maria and handed her the weapon. Maria looked surprised to be offered it so freely, but took it from her, checked it and reloaded it with a magazine from her webbing. "Good luck," Diana said.

"To both of us," replied Maria. She turned to Ethan. "Are you ready?"

Ethan reached down and picked up the metal bar from the floor. "I'm ready."

Maria looked again at Diana. "Perhaps one day, we'll meet on better terms."

Diana smiled. "I did not expect such foolish dreams from the UEC."

Maria glanced at Ethan. "I've had some help in that regard."

Diana then turned to Ethan and said, "Till we meet again, Planetsider."

"Till we meet again," he repeated, warmly, and they shook hands.

Maria made her way to the doorway and crept outside, checking the walkway. "Clear," she said, and Ethan closed in behind. "The ship is docked in quadrant two," said Maria. "We have to get down those stairs, and across to the umbilical airlock, there." She pointed to a circular, dark red doorway on the lower level. "There's a second airlock at the other end of the tunnel," she continued. "I get you inside, close the hatch, and your friend up there does the rest. Understood?"

Ethan nodded, "Let's go."

Maria stepped outside, staying as low as possible, and Ethan followed. There was still fighting on the lower level, and Ethan could see that some soldiers were also working room-to-room on the opposite side of the upper level. They reached the stairs and descended carefully. At the bottom, Maria held up her arm, hand clenched into a fist. Ethan stopped.

"There are two at the dock controls," she whispered to him. "Their mission is to bypass the launch controls."

"What do we do?" asked Ethan.

"I'll walk you over to them at gunpoint and tell them you're my prisoner," Maria said, confidently.

"I wish I hadn't asked," Ethan replied.

Maria smiled again, and looked into his eyes. "I missed you," she said, softly.

"Sal, let's not do this now," said Ethan, looking away.

"We won't have another chance," said Maria. "I didn't know you were still alive. They told me you were killed."

"Your friends are skilful liars," said Ethan, "as are you."

Maria turned away. She thought about saying more, but Ethan was right, now was not the time. "When I tell you, step out in front of me," she said. "And look scared, look like you've been roughed up or something."

"I'll do my part," said Ethan.

Maria waited for a few seconds and then said, "Go!"

Ethan stood up and stepped in front of Maria, holding the metal bar behind his back. He felt the barrel of the pistol between his shoulders, pressing him forward, and started walking towards the soldiers. His heart started to race as they noticed their approach, and raised their weapons at him. Then they noticed Maria.

"Captain, sorry, I didn't see you," said the lead soldier.

"Prisoner," she said. "It's the Planetsider. Take him back there and bind him, ready for transport to the base".

"Yes sir," the soldier replied, smartly. He took something from his belt and advanced towards Ethan. Ethan waited until the soldier was in range and then swung the bar solidly into his ribcage. He fell heavily to his knees, and Ethan struck him again in the head, knocking him out. At the same time Maria raised her weapon and shot the second soldier in the chest twice. It was over in seconds.

Maria looked around to see if their actions had drawn any attention. And then, from across the other side of the deck, she saw Major Kurren looking directly at them, weapon still held at the low-ready position. There was a pause of only a fraction of a second, though to Maria it felt like hours, before she saw him raise the weapon and charge towards them. "Let's move!" she said, pushing Ethan roughly towards the doorway. The panel turned green almost as soon as they reached it, and the door slid open. "Your friend is still alive, it seems," said Maria. "Come on!" They ran through the door, which closed automatically behind them, just as bullets ricocheted off it with piercing, metallic chimes. Moments later, Kurren reached the door and hammered on it with his fist. "Cutting team, on me, now!" he shouted, enraged, and soldiers responded instantly, rallying on his position. One unloaded and ignited a cutting torch and started immediately to slice through the metal hinges that held the door in place. Kurren impatiently watched on, his eyes burning hotter than the flame of the torch.

Ethan and Maria ran down the curved, umbilical tunnel that led to the warship. At the end of the tunnel was the hatch into the ship, which was closed. "Come on, *come on!*" said Maria, impatiently. Then she heard the thunderous hiss of the cutting torch, reverberating through the tunnel, and she knew time was short. Maria aimed her weapon down the tunnel and took a few steps towards the door that led back into the docking quadrant. She could see metal melting and dripping onto the deck. "They're cutting through!" said Maria, alarmed.

At that moment, the second umbilical hatch hissed and opened outwards, followed by the ship's docking hatch, which swung inward. "Quickly, inside!" shouted Maria. Ethan almost fell through the opening. He recognised the huge central cavity of the vessel, and knew where to go. He ran up ahead, to the control area at the front of the vessel, with Maria close behind.

A light was flashing on one of the panels. Maria walked over and flipped a switch nearby. A distant-sounding voice filled the cabin.

"This is Diana. Is Ethan on board?"

Maria responded. "Confirmed. Is the nav package loaded?"

"Yes. Select 'Nav Package, Planetside One'. The ship will do the rest."

"Understood, selecting 'Nav Package, Planetside One' now," Maria handled the controls swiftly and expertly. The ship began to vibrate as the engine power started to increase. "It's done," said Maria. "The ship is ready to launch."

The comlink crackled back on. There was shouting in the background. "Good luck, Planetside One," said Diana, and then the sound of gunfire crackled sharply through the cabin speakers, and the comlink went dead.

Ethan looked at Maria, his face white, a sudden coldness creeping across his skin.

"They are coming, I have to stop them!" said Maria, and she started running back down the central aisle of the ship.

"Sal, wait!" Ethan shouted after her, but she did not stop. Ethan ran down the aisle after her, catching her at the docking hatch.

"What are you doing?" she said, crossly. "You have to strap yourself in, now!"

"Come with me!" said Ethan, holding out his hand to her.

"What?" Maria said. "No, Ethan, you know I can't..."

"We can work it out, Sal!" Ethan pleaded. "We can start again, on the planet!"

A violent mechanical buzz resonated down the umbilical, and an alarm sounded. Maria knew that the UEC soldiers would soon have cut through the first hatch, but she did not tell Ethan. She realised this would be her last chance to speak to him, before he left her, forever.

"Ethan, I'm sorry I lied to you!" Maria said, tears welling in her eyes. "When I met you, it was just a mission, I was just doing what I thought was right. I didn't want to lie to you, but everything moved so fast, and soon there was no way back!" Maria choked back tears, and Ethan instinctively moved closer to offer comfort, but Maria held her arm outstretched to hold him away. "I wish I could change what I did, but I can't. I wish we could be together, but we can't. All I can do now is get you home, to where you belong."

Ethan shook his head. "I belong with you, Sal. We can start again. Come with me!" he begged, his eyes wet. He reached for her, and this time caught her by the waist and pulled her against him. Their lips met and they kissed, deeply and passionately. When their lips eventually parted, they rested against each other, foreheads touching.

"I love you," said Maria, tenderly, "which is why I have to do this." She put her hands on Ethan's chest and pushed with all her strength. He fell backwards into the ship, and landed heavily. Winded, it took him several seconds to get back to his feet, and by that time, Maria was on the other side of the hatch, and the hatch door was swinging shut.

"Sal, NO!" Ethan yelled. He ran to the hatch and tried to pull it open, but it was impossible. It slid shut with a heavy thud and he heard the bolts hammer into place – thud, thud, thud. The outer hatch closed next. He could see Maria through the glass porthole, looking at him from the other side. She reached across to something out of view and Ethan heard a comlink crackle open.

"I wish I could come with you," said Maria. "I wish we could start over, I truly do. But, I got you into this, and I have to make it right. Forgive me, Ethan."

"Maria, open the door, there's still time!" begged Ethan, hammering on the hatch with his fists.

Maria stood calmly, eyes locked on Ethan's. "Tell Elijah I said hello," she said softly. Then the comlink crackled off. Ethan screamed at Maria through the porthole, but she could not hear him.

She moved over to the glass panel next to the comlink and smashed it with the butt of her pistol. Inside was a red lever, marked 'Emergency Docking Detach'. She pulled hard on it and a succession of tiny explosions severed the connection between the warship and the umbilical. She moved back to the window and looked out as the hulk of metal slowly pulled away under its own power. Behind her, she heard, and felt, the heavy crash of the docking ring door smashing into the deck, and knew she had only a few seconds. She pressed a hand to the window. "Goodbye, Ethan."

The giant warship's engines burned brightly, accelerating the arrow-shaped craft through space, aimed directly towards the planet, with one passenger on board.

CHAPTER 27

For a long time after the warship had detached from the dock and started its automatic course back to the planet, Ethan had sat, slumped against the hatchway. The throb of the engines resonating through his bones was the only sensation he felt; every other sense was numb and cold. Time had stopped for him, and in his mind, all he could see was the hatch closing with Maria on the other side, and himself unable to reach her in time, as if some invisible force was holding him back. It was like a nightmare, only he wasn't asleep.

Eventually, he forced himself to stand, but he felt unsteady and weak. A deep sadness overwhelmed him. Not only sorrow at the loss of Maria, though this pre-occupied his mind the most, but also a sadness at leaving, knowing that nothing had changed between GPS and the UEC. His naive hopes of a benevolent and wise pre-Fall civilisation that had simply met with some unfortunate, but ultimately non-malicious end had been crushed by Maria back on the planet. But there was still the hope that by helping Maria, he could also do some good;

that he could make a difference. But it had all been lies.

He had seen a glimmer of hope in Diana and Maria's choice to throw aside their differences and work with common purpose. It was as a sign that perhaps these two old enemies could move beyond the hate of the past; that deliverance was possible. But Diana too may also now have been lost, and perhaps all hope of redemption faded with her. As for himself, he was saved, and for this he felt guilt and shame. The Planetsider who, through his arrogance and selfish pursuit of his own desires, had been moulded into a tool that almost brought forth the destruction of an entire civilisation. He knew he wasn't to blame, but his part in it was undeniable, and something he would have to live with, if he ever made it back alive.

More time passed and the blue orb grew larger and brighter through the cockpit glass. Ethan could feel the increasing pressures on his body and the growing strain on the massive hulk that contained him, as it creaked and shuddered onward. Fear and the instinct for self-preservation overrode his grief, shaking him from his near catatonic state. He fought against the intensifying forces to reach the front of the ship and sat in one of the chairs, pulling the straps down and across his chest, buckling them just above his navel. In front of him was an array of dials, numbers and flashing lights. The control column moved by itself, as if controlled by an invisible pilot. Above the array of dials, the window was filled with the planet, and Ethan could now clearly make out huge continents and smaller islands. It was almost incomprehensibly vast, and Ethan appreciated for the first time just how small and precious their tiny pocket of civilisation was, and how little of this world he actually knew. Were there other settlements in other parts of this planet, like his, he wondered? Or was their settlement, and the small network of settlements nearby, really all that remained of the Planetside population?

His thoughts were interrupted by a buzzing sound coming from one of the large screens on the console. It showed a flashing red dot to the lower left, slowly getting closer to the centre of the screen. Streaks of light flashed by on his left and then disappeared into the bright haze of the planet. He looked back, trying to identify a source. At first he could only see the tiny outline of the space station, but then he saw movement, and more flashes sped past, this time closer. He tried to loosen his seat buckles to get a better view and then he saw it, snaking in and out of view. It was another ship, the same configuration as the one he saw explode next to Maria on the moon base. It was the UEC. Ethan felt helpless. He could do nothing. He sat back and looked out ahead. Flames now obscured his view of the planet, and were expanding along the side windows too. The cabin was filled with a deafening roar. Another streak of light flashed past and then he felt a hard jolt. Alarms sounded in the cabin. He looked to the rear and saw a smouldering black circle next to the docking hatch. The ship had been hit. The flames continued to grow, and two more streaks of light flashed past, barely visible through the inferno. More alarms sounded. He gripped the arms of the chair tightly and stared ahead into the wall of fire.

There was nothing he could do now but wait. Perhaps, he had never really been in control of this journey. But it no longer mattered whether it was his own irrational desires, or the manipulations of those around him that had brought him to this point; he was here now, and whatever will be, will be.

He felt strangely calm. He closed his eyes and shut out the noise, the vibrations, and the fear. Outside, the ship was plunging through the planet's atmosphere, but inside, Ethan was peacefully oblivious. He pictured Maria standing on the other side of the docking hatch, hand held up at the glass, becoming smaller and smaller until he could no longer make out her face or even her outline. He pictured Katie in the bakery, making her amber biscuits, and Elijah lurking nearby, waiting to steal one. He pictured Summer, laughing and joking with him out in the fields and valleys around the settlement, beautiful, confident and free. And he pictured his favourite place under the old tree, on the mound outside the settlements walls. And then he was there, lying on the dirt and staring up into the night sky as a solitary streak of light flashed overhead.

CHAPTER 28

Ethan awoke still strapped into the chair at the front of the ship. The glass around the cockpit was smashed, and the consoles were fizzing and sparking, emitting crackles of blue energy. There was a smell of burning all around him.

He unbuckled the harness, pushed himself upright and checked himself quickly all over. He felt some pain around where the harness had been fastened, and his neck was a little stiff, but otherwise he was remarkably unharmed. He fanned some of the smoke away from his face, stepped closer to the smashed cockpit screen, and then managed a weak smile. Instead of space or the cold, metallic surroundings of a space station, there were rolling, green hills, and above them, a hazy blue sky. It was either dusk, or approaching dawn, Ethan had no idea which. He climbed onto the console and pushed himself out, through the now empty window frames, and breathed in deeply. The air smelled fresh and vibrant and alive.

From his vantage point, Ethan looked back and saw that the ship had gouged a deep ravine through the valley and had eventually come to rest by partially burying itself in the side of a steep hill, the soft earth cushioning the impact. Ethan could also see a jagged hole in the rear section of the ship, presumably where it had been hit by the UEC's attacks. It was burnt black and still smouldering dangerously.

He walked across the nose of the ship and jumped off onto the hill. The soft ground felt strange and was a stark contrast to the solid metal flooring that he had become used to. He manoeuvred himself down the side of the hill, stumbling several times, so that he had to steady himself with his hands. The feel of the cold dirt beneath his fingers was reassuring. It felt real.

At the foot of the hill, he took stock of his surroundings. Certainly, none of the features of the landscape were familiar to him; the ship had crashed somewhere he'd never been before. But then, there were many directions in which he'd never ventured that far from the settlement, and so he could still be quite close. Or he could be on the other side of the planet; he had no way of knowing.

In a clearing down in the valley a few hundred metres ahead he spotted what looked like fabric, billowing in the gentle wind. He walked over, feeling the breeze in his hair, and discovered a cluster of metal containers, attached to the fabric by thin white wires. Written on the containers were the words 'Disaster Pod' and above this was the UEC logo. Ethan assumed they had been automatically jettisoned by the ship during the crash, as part of some sort of automated emergency procedure, or had simply fallen from one of the many breaches in the warship's arrow-like body. One of the containers was split open. Ethan looked inside and found that it contained supplies – a mixture of clothing, bags, food and tools. One of the packs contained bandages and a wallet housing seven of the small medical injectors that Ethan had become all too familiar with, plus a collection of blue and yellow capsules. He shuddered at the memory of these injections, placed the wallet back in the container, and instead searched for some sort of outer-wear. The space station had been as artificially warm as the moon base, but now he was back on the planet, exposed to the wind and the elements, he was feeling cold. He found a jacket that looked sturdy and well made. On the right shoulder was a patch with an embroidered UEC emblem on it. He tore off the patch, discarded it in the dirt and stood on it, pushing it down into the black soil with the heel of his boot. For some reason, this felt good. Slipping on the jacket he then packed as much food and water as he could into one of the large backpacks, and slung it over his shoulder.

The ship continued to crackle and spark behind him, and a giant plume of black smoke was rising from the crash site. He climbed part-way up a nearby hill overlooking it and saw that the vessel was now on fire, flames enveloping the rear, steadily creeping forward. He remembered how violently the ship on the deck of the moon base exploded, and realised that he should start to put some distance between himself and the wreckage. But, despite this, he remained for several minutes more, watching the ship burn. It was comforting to him to know that this instrument of destruction was now safely out of the hands of the UEC. It was now just another burnt and destroyed relic of the war. It seemed fitting that it would finally come to rest on the planet; just one more to add to the collection of charred remains from a failed civilisation. Soon the flames grew fiercer, and Ethan's sense of danger compelled him to leave for fear of being caught in the blast, should the ship explode. Looking around he picked a direction at random and started walking.

It felt good to be outside again; to feel the cool breeze on his face and the soft earth under his feet, but the additional pull of gravity compared to the base and space station, plus general weariness, made walking a struggle. And on top of the added physical weight, he also walked with a heavy heart. Away from the stresses and dangers he had faced on the moon base and space station, his mind was free to wander and Ethan found himself focusing again on Maria. He knew that she only meant to save him, to try to make amends for what she had done, but without her he felt empty. The planet, despite its comforting familiarity, no longer felt like his home. He had meant what he said to Maria about them starting a new life together, but Ethan understood now that he needed this as much for himself as for Maria. He couldn't go back to the life he had; he had learned and experienced too much to simply go back to how things were. Without Maria he was stuck in a limbo. He quickened his pace, trying to drum her out of his mind, but he could not do it. He didn't even know if she was alive or dead, not that it mattered; he would never see her again, and the realisation of this was now striking him hard. He felt the wetness of tears on his cheeks, but pushed on harder, trying to drive the images out of his head, trying to stamp them out with each faster and more laboured step. But it was no use, and eventually he collapsed to his knees, consumed with grief and fatigue, and buried his head in his hands, sobbing freely.

Soon the sun started to edge over the horizon, and Ethan was bathed in a warm, golden light that made him look up, and shield his eyes. The beauty of the sunrise was a welcome tonic that worked to relax and invigorate him, as if the sun's rays contained the power to cleanse the soul. Ethan knew it wouldn't last, but for now it felt good, and so he remained on his knees and let the glow wash over him like an ocean wave.

"Good morning," he said out loud to the rising sun.

"Good morning to you, too," a cheery voice replied.

Startled, Ethan span around, and moved to a low crouch,

ready to push off and run. But then he saw an old man sitting beside a rock about ten metres away, and he dropped back down to his knees with a relieved sigh.

"Sorry!" the man shouted. "Didn't mean to scare you, young man!"

The hermit was almost as dirty and weather-beaten as the rock itself, which had the effect of creating a natural camouflage. On his back was a giant pack that jutted out above head height and looked to be almost half his size. He was also wearing a huge coat, with more pockets than Ethan could count, and he wondered idly what could possibly be in them all. Even more of a wonder was how this man managed to move at all, given how much he was carrying.

With an elaborate groan, the hermit inelegantly pushed himself to his feet, and then almost fell backwards against the rock, letting it take the weight of his enormous backpack. Ethan stood up, and brushed the dirt off his knees. "It's okay," he said. "I just didn't know you were here."

"Aha, well that's a skill I've developed over a long period of time, young lad," the old man replied. "When you're an old hermit like me, it helps to know how to stay out of sight."

"I'm sure," said Ethan, managing to crack a feeble smile. Then, feeling a little self-conscious, he added, "How long have you been there?"

"If you mean, did I see you sobbing into your hands like a man who's just found out his wife has run off with the blacksmith, then yes, I'm afraid to admit I've been here for long enough," the hermit said, with a bubbly mischievousness that made it impossible for Ethan to feel embarrassed.

"Oh," said Ethan. "I'm sorry you had to see that."

"No apology necessary, lad. Happens to the best of us," the hermit replied. "So, was it the blacksmith or the baker?"

Despite everything, this made Ethan laugh. "It's... a little more complicated than that," he said, as he walked over to where the hermit was resting against the rock.

"It always is, lad," replied the Hermit, sagely. "So, what weighs so heavy on your mind that you would find yourself out here at such a low ebb?"

Ethan smiled. "You wouldn't believe me, even if I told you."

The hermit's eyes widened, "Ah, don't be so sure, my young friend," he said, knowingly, "But I don't think what troubles you is quite so hard to understand. I have seen that look before. You lost something, and now you're lost too." Now it was Ethan's eyes that widened, betraying his surprise at the hermit's intuition. "You don't survive to be as old as me without losing a few things along the way," the hermit added with a warm smile, but also a sombre tone.

"Losing something means there's a chance of finding it again," said Ethan, lowering his gaze. "What I've lost, I can never get back. And now I don't think I belong here anymore."

The old hermit mulled this over for a moment as he studied the young man in front of him. Then he sighed and said, "I may not be the cleverest, lad, but I know this much... belonging isn't a place, it's a state of mind. Loss is something that follows you, wherever you are, wherever you go. You have to make your peace with it or it will eat you up inside, and you'll be no better than a Roamer." Then he paused, and looked around him, at the rolling hills and grassy valleys that surrounded them. "Me, I belong out here. You... well, you will figure it out eventually. But, no matter what you've lost, never lose hope. That is the most valuable thing of all. With hope, you'll find where you belong." And then he added in a more jolly tone, "Take from it from someone who has been everywhere and seen everything!"

Ethan looked up at the hermit and smiled, "Thank you for

your advice, I'll try to bear it in mind."

"Ah, don't thank me, young man," he said with a dismissive wave of his hand. "You're young; you've got time on your side. I'm not worried for you. Besides, you have the look of a Ranger about you, and they are tough cookies."

"I *am* a Ranger," said Ethan more brightly. "Or, at least I was. Maybe I can be again."

"See, that's the spirit; there's hope inside you still!" and both of them laughed and smiled.

"When I first saw you, I actually thought you were a Ranger out looking for the meteor."

"I'm sorry, the what?" said Ethan.

"Surely you saw it?" the hermit asked, surprised. "The fireball was probably visible for miles and miles around."

Ethan understood. The sight of the ship crashing through the sky would have been spectacular. He'd seen something similar himself, he remembered. "Yes, it was quite something. But, no, I'm not out looking for it. I was just..." and then Ethan hesitated, trying to find the right words.

"Lost?" suggested the hermit. Ethan smiled and nodded. "Then we should probably find you a home. You must come from somewhere?"

"Yes, but I've been gone for a long time, and I don't know my way back," Ethan replied, rubbing his hand through his hair. "We call it Forest Gate. I guess that doesn't help though."

"Not really, lad, they're all the same to me," the old man said with a toothless grin. "Here," he added, removing a wooden box from one of his many pockets and holding it out to Ethan. "Are you hungry? Have one of these; it will make you feel better."

Ethan did feel hungry and so gladly accepted the invitation. He looked into the box and couldn't believe what he saw. Inside were eight amber-coloured biscuits. He took one out and held it up to the light, studying it in disbelief.

"It can't be..." he said out loud, causing the hermit to adopt a confused frown. Ethan took a bite, and closed his eyes. The taste was unmistakable; they were Katie's biscuits. They were made by his sister.

"Wow," said the old man. "I know they're good, but I've never seen anyone enjoy a biscuit that much before!"

"Where did you get these?" Ethan asked, excited, his heart pumping. "My sister makes them. They are from my settlement!"

"See!" said the hermit with a triumphant shake of his fist. "Hope!" Then he held out a hand to Ethan. "Help me up, will you?"

Ethan pulled the man away from the wall and watched as he climbed to the top of a small hill, using an ancient-looking wooden pole to help him up. Ethan scrambled up beside him and watched as the old man aimed the end of his pole towards the rising sun.

"There's a bakery in a walled settlement a few days hike that way. I traded some herbs for these biscuits," and then in a more hushed tone, as if revealing a secret, he added, "I think I got the better deal..." This made Ethan smile again. He liked this old hermit very much. "Just follow the sun and you'll find it. It's way up in the hills, near a large woodland. There's a hulking great city far away down the valley from it. You can't miss it."

"Thank you, my friend!" said Ethan, and the words were said with such heartfelt sincerity that the man was quite taken aback.

"It's my pleasure, lad," said the hermit. "I'm always happy to meet a fellow traveller; usually all I see out here are filthy Roamer types, so you're a welcome change."

Ethan too appreciated the company of a simple and honest man, with no hidden motive or agenda. It had been some time since Ethan had experienced such openness and honesty.

"Now, I must be getting on my way too." The hermit said, adjusting his backpack and doing a funny little dance on the spot to limber up his joints. Despite the bulk of his clothing and backpack, he looked remarkably sure-footed. "Good journey, my friend," said the old man, warmly, and he held out his hand. "I hope you find what you're looking for."

Ethan took the hermit's hand and shook it heartily. "I hope so too. And thank you again."

The old man nodded and smiled. The dawn was now fully breaking over the horizon, and both of them stopped to admire it. Ethan felt the warmth of the light penetrate and invigorate his entire body.

"Ah, lovely," the old hermit said. "The weather's finally turning good. I think Summer is waiting just around the corner."

Ethan smiled. "I hope so," he said. "I really hope so."

They shook hands again and parted ways. Ethan stood for a moment and watched the old hermit go. Then he turned back towards the light, closed his eyes, and breathed deeply. When he opened his eyes again he began his journey towards the rising sun. Towards home.

THE END

THANK YOU

Many thanks for reading this book. If you enjoyed it, please help by leaving a review on Amazon to let other potential readers know what you think.

If you'd like updates on future novels by G.J. Ogden, please consider subscribing to the mailing list. Your details will only be used to notify subscribers about upcoming books from this author.

http://subscribe.ogdenmedia.net

ABOUT THE AUTHOR

At school I was asked to write down the jobs I wanted to do as a 'grown up'. Number one was astronaut and number two was a PC games journalist. I only managed to achieve one of those goals (I'll let you guess which), but these two very different career options still neatly sum up my lifelong interests in science, space and the unknown, and computer technology.

School also steered me in the direction of a science-focused education over literature and writing, which strongly influenced my decision to study Physics at The University of Manchester Institute of Science and Technology (UMIST, now part of Manchester University). What this degree taught me is that I didn't like studying Physics and instead enjoyed writing much more, which led me to become editor of the University magazine, GRIP. This was the stepping stone into the first of my careers in IT journalism. The lesson? School can't tell you who you are, or what you want to be!

During my professional career, I spent seven years as a technology journalist, including creating and launching Custom PC magazine for Dennis Publishing, the most successful enthusiast PC magazine in the UK. I then moved into PR and marketing for world-leading technology brands. But, my passion for science fiction and writing only grew stronger and more than twenty years after choosing to study Physics instead of writing, I came full circle and now write and independently publish science fiction novels.

When not writing, I enjoy spending time with my family, walking in the British countryside, and indulging in as much Science-Fiction as possible. And I still enjoy building and tinkering with PCs.

90230352R00197

Made in the USA
San Bernardino, CA
08 October 2018